the Two Trees

Book 3 of the Simulacrum Saga

Julia J Gibbs

WARD

Julia J. Gibbs
www.theoaksremain.com

Publisher's Note: This is a work of fiction. Names, characters, places, and incidents are a product of the author's imagination. Locales and public names are sometimes used for atmospheric purposes. Any resemblance to actual people, living or dead, or to businesses, companies, events, institutions, or locales is completely coincidental.

The Two Trees/ Julia J Gibbs -- 1st ed.

Dedication:

To the great cloud of witnesses who have gone before us to the Alabaster City.

To Herman, who sat at my feet as I wrote most of the story and was a constant companion. You are missed, my friend.

To Lisa who read all of my books. Now that you are with the One Tree, you understand more than ever the words of the Hidden Books. I look forward to the day when we can discuss the end...and the final beginning of the life to come.

Artwork by Jerry Ward

www.theartisticward.com

Thank you Jerry for sharing your amazing talent! You have made the world of the Harper family come alive!

N
W
E
S
SIMULACRUM
Tomb of the Forgotten
Red Oaks

The TREE OF LIFE was in the midst of the garden,
with the TREE OF KNOWLEDGE…
And a river flowed out of the garden, and there it divided...
Genesis 2: 9-10

WARD

Prologue

Avshalom: In the Time of the Primogenes

Darkness covers the face of the earth.

" Sapru ..."

From the north side of the wind, the voice whispers the name from somewhere beyond the shadow of the mountain. This is not the first time I have heard it. The voice has followed me for many nights.

"Sapru," it murmurs on the breeze.

With my newly healed hand, I hold the bow steady. The dark hides many things.

"What is it?" Mara crawls silently toward me, considering every place her hands will touch as she moves.

I keep my nose against the wood of the bow while the arrow leads my eyes around our camp.

"Go back to Olam," I whisper.

She does not answer, and I am pleased she shows no eagerness to return to him. Her round, silver eyes shine like the moon that hangs in the dark sky above. The tilt of her head and the angle of her smooth chin tell me that she is lost in thought.

"Sapru," the voice rushes forth in a gust of wind. My shoulders stiffen. I shift the direction of my arrow right and left while my eyes strain to search the endless dark. Mara touches my shoulder. I feel her calm. It warms me to my bones. She raises her hand and points out into the darkness. I point my arrow in the direction of her gesture. In the murky darkness, I can barely make out the shape of a bush or maybe a large animal not twenty feet before us. A spark ignites and floats into the sky.

"Is it the Archaon?" I whisper, feeling the heat of my tseeyen burn up my arm. The newness of this blood still burns as it moves through my body, concentrated on the newly formed tseeyen imprinted on my arm. The comforting mark had first begun to form after we drank of the blood at the One Tree. Soon, on the inside of my right wrist, twelve stars appeared, encircling a single object that looked much like a crown.

"What is it, Mara? Can you see?"

We watch together as small slivers of light begin to multiply and grow. Blue-hot flames erupt from the bush, setting it ablaze.

"Mara!" I breathe out her name. "Mara, don't!"

But she is already moving ahead, cautious yet unafraid.

I should go with her. I want to follow, but my feet refuse to obey my mind. So, I stand rooted to the ground, sweat dripping down my brow.

"Mara," I say, just above a whisper, but she has reached the blue light. Finally, fear overcomes my caution and I shout," No, Marȧ! You will burn!"

She doesn't seem to hear, enthralled by the glowing flames before her.

"You called my name at the Tree of Blood," I hear her say in a low tone. " It is you, The One who gave us the blood of the Eiani."

The flames form the shape of a man, with skin of copper and fire, he stands as a shadow in the midst of the burning bush.

"Will you carry the door, Mara?" the fiery figure asks.

Mara drops her head and falls to her knees. "I am willing. Let it be."

"Hear the words, Daughter of the Blood. This one is appointed for the rising and fall of many. They will set their teeth against him, and your own soul will be pierced, but take heart, for by his words, the end will begin it all."

The sand lifts around her, and swirls as though a sand storm has suddenly come upon her, like the many sandstorms we have already endured in the desert.

"Mara,"I cry. I want to go to her, to protect her, but I cannot make myself move. I try to steady my hands, but they begin to shake violently.

The blue light from the tree reaches out toward Mara. Fingers of light create a braided pattern of light around her, twisting and spinning round and round her until she is enveloped and hidden from my sight.

More light, brilliant light, falls from the skies as stars plummet to earth, creating a sheet of rain that is not rain but a deluge of blue brightness. The ground beneath my feet trembles, and I fall onto my face.

The overwhelming light disappears abruptly. The night surrounds my eyes, and all is dark.

"Wake!" The voice of the one I love calls me to the surface, "Wake, you must not sleep. It is your hour to watch."

"Mara?"

She smiles at me. "Can you not stay awake for even an hour?"

"I brought you what is left of the water," she adds, handing me a small pouch.

Water is precious here in the desert. It has become like gold. I look out into the deep darkness of the night as I drink. The wilderness is vast, and we still have so far to go. The weight of this journey is pulling us all down beneath it. Can we survive long enough to reach Aria?

I sit up, feeling for the bow that rests beside my thigh.

Mara fingers the leather pouch connected to her belt.

"You have had that since the One Tree," I say. "What is inside?"

Mara looks down, lifting one corner of her mouth in a half smile.

"Seeds."

"Seeds?"

"From the fields," she answers.

"Were you supposed to take them from that place?"

"Why not? We were called there to drink of the Eiani, so why not take seeds from the fields? We can plant them at Aria."

"I must tell you— "

"What do you make of it?" she points to the great stone statue carved into the mountain before us, "It feels alive."

I laugh and scoot nearer to see her face, "The stone statue? You think it feels alive?"

"Do you not?" She keeps her eyes on the statue. "It must be the work of the Archaon, for who else could create such work?"

The great statue looks ancient, as though it was carved before time began. Covered in vines, dirt, and elements of age, it still glints like a pulsing star when hit by a sliver of moonlight or starlight. On closer observation, it appears to be carved from flawless obsidian, black and smooth, shining like polished glass. The warrior stands with empty hands frozen before his face, his lips puckered, and his eyes closed as though he was in the midst of blowing a great horn for battle. His stoic face is half shielded by a massive helmet that matches the grandeur of his uniform. We have seen many wondrous things on our journey back from the One Tree, where we drank of the Eiani, but I could not help but agree with Mara. This statue feels different. It feels as though he is waiting to wake from a long-forgotten spell.

"He is asleep," Mara whispered. I look at her, and even in the dark I can see her silver eyes are full of tears.

"Mara?" I want to touch her but keep my hands in my lap. "Everything is different now, Mara. The Eiani, it has changed me, it has changed us all!"

"Yes," she whispers, nodding her head slightly, but still I know she doesn't understand.

"Who I was before," I begin, trying to remember the speech I have rehearsed so many times in my head. I clear my throat and try again. "Who I was before the Eiani..."

The memories of the treacherous journey, the years of following a path we did not plan nor really even understood, flood in unbidden and unrestrained. None of it had been easy. In the end, before we reached the One Tree, the journey brought out the worst in every man and was unforgiving on the women. Shame colored my cheeks.

"Mara, someone had to lead during those years, and I ..." Forgetting everything I had planned to say, in exasperation I blurt out, "I am trying to say that I am sorry. I am sorry for the way I did it."

"I know," Mara answers without hesitation. "I hold nothing against you from before the Eiani. The pain and difficulties we experienced were like the travail of childbirth. So it is with us; the pain is forgotten in the joy of the baby's arrival. We have the Eiani, and everything is changed! All that matters now is this new life, this new way forward. We must do as we were instructed. We must follow the path home, return to Aria, and build. That is our way now."

I hear the joy in her voice, and I want to match it, but I am still struggling with the reality that remains before us.

"Return," I reply, and the word is heavy. "We've only just finished the work of harvesting the trees, and now we have months of traveling ahead of us."

"Do not complain," Mara laughs. "I think the way back is just as important as the way here. Maybe it's even more important."

I rub my beard, perplexed and disturbed, "How can you say that? Why would the journey back be important? We have the Eiani now, surely things will be easier. Isn't the important thing that we get back as quickly as possible and start building? The task is the important thing." Sometimes I do not understand Mara at all.

She leans into me a little. "I am not saying I understand it all, but this is what the Eiani in my veins is telling me. The journey back is just as important as the journey we've just completed."

"Why?"

"I told you. I do not know. But, I think, the way back will somehow show each of us the way forward. Look at the way you arrange your arrows. You prop them with the head up, not head down as others do."

"What does that prove?" I counter. "I've found that I can pull them into the bow and shoot faster that way."

"Did someone teach you this?" she asks.

"No, I learned it the hard way, through experience."

"Ah," she nods, "through experience."

We are silent. She knows I do not agree with her, but I do not wish to argue. Somehow, she can get under my skin quicker than anyone I have ever known, and I have wasted years arguing with Mara. But with the Eiani in my veins, I have vowed to myself never again to argue with this woman.

"Still," she says, "I do not think it will come with ease, even with the Eiani in our veins."

"Yes, the doors," I agree with her on that point. "Yes. It will be no easy feat to get the wood back, but..."

"Olam has a plan," Mara says, straightening the edge of her tunic, "He has everything ready to go."

Olam.

"What has the blood shown you?" Mara asks, and I see the expectation in her eyes. She smiles and encourages me softly.

"Tell me."

"Tell what?" I look at the dirt between my feet. Mara is so sure of everything, and I long for my words to matter to her.

"Tell me what you see." She turns her head and smiles.

I want to touch her face but catch my hand before I do anything to break this fragile newness between us. I will be different now. I will protect and give instead of taking and requiring. On the outside, I know she sees the change the blood has brought, but I have a plan to slowly show her the change that the blood has brought on the inside as well. I long to show her the depths in me that no one but the blood could see. I want, for the first time in my entire life, to not only be known, but to truly know someone else as well. And Mara is the one I want to know.

She is still looking at me, and I want so much to please her.

"What do I see," I repeat and pause. "We will make it, Mara. We will arrive at the city, and Achiel will be there waiting for us. But ..."

"But?" she leans close, her eyebrows knitted into a question.

"We must watch our right flank. We will come against a group of angry Friguscor men who will want the food we have. We must be prepared for them when we pass the second mountain range."

She breathes out, wonder spreading across her face.

"You can see!"

Her joy is infectious, and I cannot help but smile. The sun is beginning to rise behind her back and frame her bronzed face.

"I have been learning."

"From the Eiani?" her face was full of excitement, and I want to keep her looking at me forever so I add, "Yes, well, the Eiani has been sending one of the Archaon to me at night when I am on watch. He has taught me so many things about the gift."

"The Archaon have been coming to you?" she asks. "But I thought we would not see them until we reached the city? You must have a very special gift for the Archaon to come to you now!"

"No," I am suddenly reminded that my nighttime tutor had warned me not to tell anyone of his visits, so I try to cover my slip. "It's just because I am a Seer. I need special training because of what I can see through the Eiani, the blood; I need knowledge now that will help during our journey back."

"Oh?"

I hear skepticism in her voice and stumble on, trying to explain.

"So I don't misinterpret what I see or misuse the gift in ignorance. I mean, it could be dangerous to us."

I can tell she does not understand, but in truth, neither do I. The blood of the Eiani and the One Tree, and the beauty of my skin and eyes are all new. We are all learning new things every day. How can I explain what I've learned from the shining Archaeon who visits me at night when not even I understand it? The beautiful being had warned me not to tell anyone, and now I understand why.

"Mara," I ask, wanting to change the subject and bring back the joy to her face. "What has the Eiani given you? What is your role for the Simulacrum?"

Mara does not answer immediately but studies my face for a moment. "Remember what the Archaon told us? They warned us that there are others out there," she points out into the wilderness, "wanting the blood of the Eiani."

"I know, Mara," I answer, hiding nothing from her. "Trust me. I will heed every warning. I will never turn from the words that the Eiani spoke into my blood. That is why I must learn from the One Tree what I am to do with this gift. If I do not, then what use am I to our people?"

Mara considers my words and then slowly agrees with a nod. "That is true," she sighs before adding, "and wise. To tell you the truth, I am not like you or Olam; I was given a completely different kind of gift for the Simulacrum." Her voice is full of deep satisfaction as she says, "I am called to bear the weight of the first woman."

"The first woman?" I shake my head in confusion, "Why would you carry the weight of Chauvah? We have been given a new beginning! She is of the old!" I hold out my tseeyan which grows clearer with every passing day, "Why would Chauvah have anything to do with us now that we have partaken of the blood?"

Mara looks down at her feet. "Because Chauvah's actions happened and though the blood has started a new line in us, her actions still have to be resolved."

"How?"

"I do not know," she leans down and adjusts her sandal, "but I know it is true."

Dread sinks into my heart. "But you said it yourself, Mara, that what happened before the Eiani is the past, and all that matters now is the way forward." I feel despair creeping up my back and tightening around my chest. The pull of my past was dragging me slowly back. "All that matters now is who we are with the blood of the Eiani. Everything we once were is gone!"

"Yes, I believe that. At least, for us, for the Simulacrum, I believe that it is true. But for the world, for creation and the others ..."

Her voice trails off as she is lost in thought for a moment, her eyebrows pulling together in concentration. "I know the trees remember everything. And if the trees remember, then creation remembers as well. For us, we have found the Blood of the Eiani, but what about the rest of the world? It has to be reconciled somehow! The Blood of the Eiani cannot simply forget what happened to the Original Men. Remember what we saw when we drank the blood?"

"The brothers in the field," I answer slowly, "Yes, I remember it all."

"And if that memory, which is not even our own, but belongs to the blood itself is within us, that means it has not been erased from the memory of the Eiani," she insists.

"So what have you been called to do? What can you do about something that happened before you were even born?" I respond, fear pulsing through my veins. I know it should not, but it slowly spreads through my body like the effect of the tea I used to drink. It would start by dulling my mind and then spread until it blurred my vision and made it hard to hear. Fear crawls into the recesses of my mind and refuses to leave.

Mara looks up at the sky and speaks softly, "I will do what I have been asked to do, just as you will do what you have been asked to do."

She stands carefully. The rising sun outlines her perfect silhouette, and my breath catches in my throat. I see something I have never seen before, and my heart constricts.

"Mara?" I say her name slowly, giving the blood time to calm me. She puts a protective arm around her waist, pulling her tunic to her as though it is a shield. Our eyes meet, and I know I have seen correctly.

"Olam?" I breathe out his name. "Was it Olam?"

"No!" she says forcefully, obviously protecting him. "It was the Eiani!"

"The Eiani?" I stand. My head is spinning.

"It was that night," she said. "The night we saw the blue flames on the bush that did not burn."

"That was not real," I spit out the words, pain coursing through my tseeyen. "That was a dream!"

She shakes her head, "It was no dream; we both saw it! It was true. See?" She runs her hand down her waist, revealing the roundness of her belly, as though that is proof. "We have had four cycles of the moon since that night. You saw the blue light; you saw what happened!"

"No," I try to shake the old familiar feelings of anger and despair, "I ... I saw nothing, Mara! I fell down in the dirt. The light. It was too bright. I ..." My memory is a blur, altogether overwhelming. "It was just a dream," I repeat. "It was not real."

Mara looks straight at me.

"This is what I have been asked to carry," she says. "This is the weight I must bear."

"You know our laws, " I respond angrily. Tears of outrage begin to touch my eyes. "How could you allow this, Mara? You know what our laws say!"

"I have broken no law," she replies steadily. Her voice is filled with a plea for me to understand her, to hear her. "You know me. I have broken no law."

"It was Olam," I spit out, rising up from the ground. "You know what they will have to do, Mara! We have only just become a people; how could you cause such division?"

"They will do nothing to me!" she steps back from me. Her hands wrap protectively around her stomach. "I will explain."

"No one will believe you," I reply. My hands drop helplessly to my sides. "I do not even believe you."

Mara looks as though I have slapped her. She nods and swallows before speaking. "I am to be bonded today."

My eyes flash. "To Olam?"

"Yes," she says, raising her eyes to mine. "Olam will protect me. He will protect us both."

"Because it is his child," I accuse.

"You know that is not true," she answers calmly. "If you would just listen to the blood in your veins, instead of the pain in your heart, you would see the truth. You know what you saw that night. You know that I carry the gift of the Eiani within my womb.

Her unwavering eyes meet mine. She reaches out and touches my tseeyan with her hand.

"Hear me, please."

There is nothing I want more than to hear my name on her lips, but she does not say it.

"Mara," I step closer to her, "I wanted ..."

"I know," she looks down at the ground, breaking the contact between us, "but that was not the plan."

"Not the plan?" I feel the betrayal of her words. "Or do you mean, not his plan."

"Olam is a good man. He is a kind and gentle, and he will protect us."

I hate how she defends him. She loves him, that much I can see. But I loved her, and I had always loved her. She should be mine!

"Mara?" a familiar voice calls.

Her back stiffens and she turns from me to answer, "I was just telling of our good news." She adds, "He is very excited for us, Olam."

I do not look at Olam who has now come to stand with Mara. Instead I look down at her face, memorizing the shine of her silver eyes and the cleft in her chin. A quiet awkwardness rises between the three of us. Olam does not look at me, or at Mara, but out at the vast wilderness as though he is giving us this moment alone.

Mara has made her choice. I step away from her and feel the pain of longing grip my chest.

"You know what they will do to her, Olam," I spit, forcing the words between my clenched teeth. "How could you? We are called to protect, not to harm! Look what you have done to her!"

Olam considers me. He has a way of making me feel at once both uncomfortable and yet fully accepted. Olam does not answer directly but instead says, "I am sorry if I have caused you any pain. If it is possible, let there be peace between us."

The old man in me who demands his way and must be in control of all things awakes and begins to rage, screaming from the cage beneath my ribs. I have wrestled with him many times since we drank of the blood. Because of him, the good that I want to do, I often do not do, and the things I do not want to do, I do in spite of myself. For a time I can silence him, but he will not stay dead.

"The way is in the blood," I whisper to remind myself.

The way is in the blood.

This is our motto, our marching song as we travel through the wilderness. When the old man beneath the new blood wants to overtake us, we begin chanting these words. Olam heard me and added his support by saying, "And the tree is life."

He steps closer to me and leans in, his voice soft and calm, "The Tree is life and the blood is now our essence."

I understand his words, and I understand his struggle. We are the same, Olam and I; we had both been men of great darkness before the blood, but now, we are struggling to fully live the life the blood has given us.

Olam put a hand on my shoulder, a gesture of brotherhood and said, "Lignum Vitae."

I drop my head and feel for the blood in my veins. We all need a new beginning. We must make it to Aria and start afresh like the Archaon has directed us to do. But as Mara had said, it has not and will not be easy.

"Et sanguis et essential," I finally force the words from my mouth. They burn my throat like bile.

Mara gives me a goodbye smile and turns to leave with Olam. But Olam stops and turns back.

"A man arrived an hour ago," he says. "He has brought something for all of us."

My heart is pounding so loudly that I can barely answer him.

"What did he bring?"

"Books." Olam replies, "books that he wrote for our people. I believe they are history books."

Mara looks at Olam. Her face brightens with excitement, and it is like a knife in my heart.

"Books!" she repeats eagerly.

"I need to finish my watch. I will be there shortly," I stall.

"But," Mara says, "your watch is finished! The sun has arrived; there is nothing to fear in the day!"

Before I can answer, Olam catches my eye, and I know he understands. "Leave the man to his work, Mara. He will join us as soon as he is able."

Olam places his hand at the small of Mara's back, and they leave together. The image of his hand on her back robs the last of my strength.

I collapse to my knees in defeat and then fall hard on my side in the dirt.

"Ahh!" I groan as I realize my mistake. I have fallen on my own arrow. I roll over and pull it from between my ribs. Blood drips into the sand, and I struggle to breathe.

"I brought you a gift," his voice calls out, startling me. I have never heard it in the daylight.

"You're here," I say, wincing. I know the pain will resolve in a moment. On the journey, we have discovered how quickly the Eiani heals our wounds.

"You ... did not come ... last night," I say between gasps of pain.

My tutor is approaching me from the direction of the mountain. I look at him for a moment but pull my leg back quickly in response to a black beetle scrambling across my foot. Without thinking, I smash it beneath my foot.

I steal another glance at him. He is the most magnificent and beautiful being I have ever encountered. His face is chiseled in aquiline perfection. Gleaming white, almost iridescent, hair falls past his waist and blows in the morning breeze, creating streaks of light against the green and brown landscape of trees and sand. He is as the first morning star in the eastern sky, just before the rising sun eclipses its brilliance.

As he approaches, I see something like wings fold behind his back, but I can't be sure. I don't dare ask this creature too many questions, though he has been secretly teaching me and revealing many secrets of the Archaon in the past few months. It is information for the good of mankind, and I am honored that he has chosen me as a pupil, awed that I alone have benefitted from his superior knowledge and abilities. Yet, as I look up at this towering creature, I am also aware that I am nothing more than an insect when compared to his glory and power. He could easily crush me beneath his foot just like the beetle, one of the horrid desert insects I have come to hate.

"You have been injured," he remarks smoothly. "Your blood is being wasted upon the ground."

I feel the constant throb of the injury but also the wholeness beginning to pulse through my veins. "The Eiani can heal it. It will take only a short time. I just have to wait."

"Why wait? I can heal it now," my tutor steps forward and leans over me. "The pain will be gone in an instant."

His eyes flash a crystal blue. He is the color of a full moon and is so beautiful that it scares me to look at him for very long. He smiles knowingly.

"I can heal all the pain," he says.

I groan, trying to get a deep breath. Why does the Eiani take so long?

"But, it will cost you," he continues, tilting his head so that I could see directly into his blazing blue eyes. "In return, I will never leave you. I will stay with you and protect you."

"Cost me?" An alarm strikes somewhere deep within, but then I feel his mind stretching out to comfort me. It offers a calm and peace that I yearn to possess.

"I have taught you many things," he says, his voice like cool water running through my fevered mind, "and there is much to teach you still. You will lead them," he motions toward the others in camp. "You are called to be a leader to the Simulacrum, but you will need help. That is why I have come."

"I have the Eiani in my blood, is that not enough?" I ask, trying to understand, "The One Tree said ..."

"How do you feel now? Struck with your own arrow." Looking down at my blood on the ground, then toward the camp, he adds, "and betrayed by the one you love."

The image of Mara's swollen belly flashes across my eyes. My mind feels broken into pieces I cannot put back together, "Maybe it was the flaming bush of light like she said, maybe it was not a dream."

"She is bonding herself to Olam, is she not?" the being interrupts.

"Yes," I wince.

"And she is with child?" he continues to probe.

"Yes," I say louder, anger rising up as heat in my body.

"Do you need more proof of what you are seeing?"

Self-condemnation falls over me like a heavy blanket. How could I not see it? Memories of Olam and Mara come back to me. The touch of their hands at dinner. The way they walk together and speak of the One Tree. How Olam always seems to find Mara in the midst of the crowd. Of course, that is the answer. How could I be so blind when I have been gifted by the One Tree to be a Seer?

"You are not blind," my tutor offers kindly, "But you do need help to become what you are intended to be. I can teach you. I can train you. I will not leave you to wander alone through the wilderness, but I will guide you all the way to the end."

"We have not been left to wander through the wilderness— " I begin.

"Have Achiel and the others joined you?" he asks, looking around expectantly.

The throb of my wound coupled with the difficulty of taking a breath makes me wince, and I adjust my side to relieve the pain. "No," I answer with effort, "after the wilderness, they will meet us ..." I struggle again, "at the city."

"Why?" he challenges.

"Why?" I shrug. "That is the plan."

"Whose plan?" my tutor asks. "Why make you trudge through the wilderness by yourselves? Why not simply bring you back to Aria? The Archaon have the ability to take you. Did you know this? And so, why would the One Tree have them abandon you to this desolation?" He motions to the sparse landscape with the few trees.

"I do not know," I say, feeling the frustration of the old man rising beneath my ribs, "We are supposed to make the trip back together. That is what we were instructed to do. To follow the way provided."

"I can help you," he offers again.

"How?"

In his eyes I find compassion.

"You do not have to make this arduous journey through this unforgiving land," he says. "I can show you how to arrive at Aria today. It is a city beyond compare, flowing with clear waters and tables of delectable foods. And I can heal your wounds, so that you do not have to feel this pain."

"But, are we not supposed to make this journey? Aren't we supposed to learn as we travel together through the wilderness?" His words are beginning to make sense, and I am becoming more confused.

Why haven't the Archaon offered us this help if they have the ability? Why would the One Tree require this misery of us if it is not truly necessary?

As if the being has read my mind, he says, "Is there truly a reason for this trial? Is it a kindness to send you into the heat of the sun with scarce food and water? How can suffering be of any good? Did the One Tree really tell you to trek through the wilderness, or was that just the plan of the Archaon?"

My heart drops. "I...I, do not know. I do not remember."

"Behold, Son of the Blood." The great giant opens a pouch on the side of his breastplate and removes a small bag. He opens it and beckons to me.

"Feel what is inside."

Curiosity leads me to obey immediately, but I cry out in pain when I lift my arm and put my hand to the pouch.

"Water?" I shake my head. "How can you keep water inside of a bag?"

"It is not water as you know it. This is of the first waters, the waters of creation, the waters at the beginning of time. It is the only thing left of that first world. I have kept it because it holds the secrets of time and space within it."

A vague fear creeps up my spine.

"I do not understand."

He opens the bag and pours the liquid onto the ground. It does not splash nor creep but creates a perfect oval upon the sand.

"What is this?" I ask in fascination, momentarily forgetting the pain of the arrow.

"A tera," he explains as he runs his hand over the top and then dips his hand into the water. His hand seems to disappear beneath the surface. "It is the swiftest way to Aria, or wherever you wish to go."

"How?" I begin but find I have no words.

"There is so much more to this world than the One Tree has disclosed to you. There are mysteries you cannot even begin to imagine. And I can show them all to you," he promises.

The thrill of his words filled the emptiness in my chest.

"But first, you must let me heal you."

Day 1 Boker

Before

"It begins at the end, for it is the end that begins it all."

"Long ago, when the darkness had almost overtaken the sun, a warrior whispered silent words into the night," Mother read.

"She's still doing it," Adair turned an angry eye at me. "You're still not listening to Mother."

Pressing my lips together, I blew onto the glass windowpane, creating the perfect canvas for my drawings. I looped the tale onto the dragon and peered at him in wonder.

"Adair," Mother corrected. I turned back to see them as she added, "You must try to remember that everyone has a different way of learning. Veelee is listening and you must also remember that I am the teacher at Red Oaks University, not you!"

"I could teach a few classes here," Adair sulked back into the winged back chair.

"We can't have a twelve-year-old for a teacher!" Ausley added, lifting a paper doll with blonde hair and a pinstriped dress in her hand, "Right, Caraway?"

"Ausley," Mother put the book in her lap, "What is her name?"

"Caraway," Ausley smiled, showing the beauty of her paper doll, "See!"

"That is an interesting name," Mother said, "Where did you hear it?"

Ausley looked down at her dolls and began to organize the shirts into one pile and the pants into another, "I don't know."

Mother watched her with silent lips for a moment that seemed too long.

"Mother," I motioned toward the book still lying in her lap. "Keep reading! I want to finish this one before bed."

Her eyes smiled as she said, "Veelee, the library is filled with the Histories. You have years to read them. Don't rush the stories, or you won't remember them."

"To be honest, the stories are boring," Adair said, turning to flip her legs over the right arm of the large winged-back chair. "Just a bunch of stories about a bunch of fallen people that we won't ever know."

"Thank you for your honesty, Adair," Mother cocked her left eyebrow. "But I don't remember asking for your honesty, just your listening ears."

"Can I please go help Daddy? You know he will not put everything back where it should go..."

Right then, we heard a crash from the kitchen. Daddy's calm voice rang out.

"Nothing broken! Don't worry about it; keep reading to the girls. I've got this covered."

"Of course, Edwin," said Mother.

She looked at Adair and nodded. Adair jumped from the chair and ran to help in the kitchen, full of joy at the task that lay ahead.

"Keep going," I said, as soon as she was gone. "Please?"

I wanted to hear the rest of the story. It was in a time that I could not yet fully imagine. It scared and yet thrilled me to think of what it could have been like to be the great warrior, Hizkiah, fighting back against the sea of Friguscor. The last standing Original Man, leading the few remaining of his soldier against the onslaught of the Friguscor horde. It was an impossible battle. That many Friguscor against so few of the Original Men would only end in bloodshed and death, but still, Hezkiah fought on.

History told me the end of the story. He would fall and be defeated by the Friguscor. They would take over the earth, as the death in their veins would spread across the land and the sea, leaving not one drop of the blood of the Eiani in the veins of man.

"No," Ausley shook her head. "Don't wead anymore Mama. Is too sad. I don't like it."

Mother bent down, tucking the book of our History beneath her elbows as she caressed Ausley's blonde curls.

"Why don't you head on to bed, Ausley. You may take your dolls, and I will be up soon to tuck you in."

Eager to leave the uncomfortable tale behind her, she gathered her paper dolls quickly.

"Maybe if you knew the end it would not be so bad?" Mother asked.

Ausley shook her head. "No," she insisted. "Veelee already said he would fall, that's how it ends."

Mother shook her head, "No, Ausley, that is just where this story ends. But look at all of these books," she said, gesturing to the shelf that held the Histories. "Hizkiah might have fallen in this book, but the story of the One Tree goes on and on, through the lives of all of those who would come after Hizkiah. It even goes on through you."

Ausley's eyes filled with tears.

"I don't want it! Not me!" she cried.

Mother rose and quickly pulled Ausley into her arms. Ausley melted into her, forming her arms and legs around Mother's waist and neck. Mother spoke loud enough for me to hear from the window sill where I sat watching them. "Remember girls, we are Simualcrum, so we will not fear, for we know the true end of the story."

"The true end?" I said, fearing upsetting Ausley again, yet wanting an answer more. "Hizkiah will fall during the battle. He will fight against the Friguscor horde who seek his blood and he will lose. All of the Original Men will fall, and they will be no more. The Simulacrum people will not exist for 400 more years, and the world will be full of darkness and death. That is how that story ends."

Mother kissed Ausley's head.

"Ends?" she asked. "You mustn't confuse the middle of a book with the ending. If you see your life, or any man's life as a book, then you only see half of the story. A man's life is not a great novel, but only a chapter in a book that runs from the beginning of this age to the end of all time. We are but chapters in this book. We are not the whole story."

Ausley peeked out with one beautiful blue eye.

"So he doesn't fall, and the Friguscorky don't eat him?"

"Oh, they eat him," I said quickly.

Mother shot a sharp glance at me that clearly said "Hush," and began again to tell the story, laying words down like paint on a canvas.

"Let me tell you how the story ends for Hizkiah. As the days rolled on, and the battle turned into a siege within the City of Light, Hizkiah grew sick over the dread of his end. Sennach, the prince of the Friguscor, would no doubt defeat his people, and fear began to grow within Hizkiah. On his death bed ..."

"He didn't fall in battle?" I interrupted.

"Listen Veelee," Mother said, sitting in the rocking chair and placing Ausley in her lap. "Come and flip the book open, so you can see as I tell you what happened."

Greedily, I ran to the book and flipped the pages open to see the scene come alive in the paint: Hizkiah laying in a great bed, with curtains of purple, gold, and blue making a canopy over the bed.

Mother continued, and her voice came with me into the room of Hizkiah where I stood watching him.

"A Wakeful One, a messenger from the One Tree, came into his room one night. Hizkiah was almost gone. His body was losing connection to this world, as the Wakeful One walked from the window toward the bed.

"'Hear the words spoken across the waters of the One Tree,' the Wakeful One said. 'You grope for the wall like one born blind; you stumble at noon as in twilight. Your strength is poured out as wax. You moan and cry out for help, though you have closed the door with your own hands. But, the Eiani has heard your cry.'

"The Wakeful One rose and hovered over Hizkiah's body. He blew into the king's nostrils, giving him life from the One Tree. 'Your house shall not be forgotten, for memory never ends,' said the Wakeful One. 'Your city shall be rescued, and you shall not sleep with the Forgotten. Years shall be added to you, for on the third day, a deliverer shall come.'"

"Did he get up?" Ausley asked.

"Yes," Mother said, "and he went to battle with the promise that on the third day a deliverer would come."

Flipping the page, I saw a set of stairs and read the words.

"But he didn't believe the Wakeful One, not really. He asked for a sign."

"Correct," Mother said, "and the sign was that the One Tree would move time back ten steps on the sundial," she pointed to the book. "Those large steps there. And that would turn back time three days, to give Hizkiah time to prepare for the battle with Sennach."

"Which is what he was supposed to be doing while he was in the bed crying," I added without taking my eyes of the book. "Right?"

"Right," said Mother. "And now you girls are off to bed. I will finish the story tomorrow night. Go on now."

Ausley kissed Mother and left the room as I stood staring at her.

"I can't go to bed now," I said, beginning to leaf quickly through the pages. "What did it mean to get three more days? Why move back time? What did more time give him, and why would the One Tree do that? It was his fault. Hizkiah laid around in bed and wanted to die, wasting his time, instead of getting ready for the battle. He knew the enemy was coming all along, and he did nothing to prepare. Why give him more time?"

"The same reason I would give you more time if I could," Mother answered. "Because I love you, and I don't want you to be defeated by our enemies—even if you don't listen to me the first time. Now, go to bed, Veelee."

My feet did not move, though I knew they should. Instead I asked one more question.

"But what about this? This picture here?" I lifted the book in her direction, hoping she would answer this last question. "Who are they and why are they important to the story?"

I saw the familiar flash of interest in her eyes, and I knew I had bought more time.

"He was the first GateKeeper, or what would come to be known as the GateKeepers when the Simulacrum were born."

"And why is the Wakeful One him?" I pointed to the mysterious man in the picture, shrouded in shadow.

Mother gently touched the face of one of the men with such affection that I wondered, irrationally, if she knew him.

"The book does not tell us the full story. Just snapshots. But my grandmother, Vera, would look at this one picture all the time. She would take her hand, just like this and touch his face. One day, when I asked, she told me that this man had survived the wars and that he alone had carried the promise of Hizkiah's Stairs to the Simulacrum people, by giving the GateKeepers keys that would somehow protect the people, or something like that."

"The keys?" I shook my head. "What keys? Only Daddy has a key, because he's the Guardian of the Gate."

"GateKeepers also have keys Veelee. Their keys protect the land above from the land below, just as the Guardian's keys protect the Gates above."

"But we don't have a GateKeeper here."

"Mr. Westbrooke is kinda like a GateKeeper around here, wouldn't you say?"

"I guess," I shrugged.

"I just wish we knew the full story," she sighed, closing the book.

"Does it continue in another one of the Histories?" I asked looking up at the tall bookcases.

"No," she answered, "My grandmother knew things. She told me things I have never found in these books."

"How?" I asked, "How would she know if she didn't read it in the Histories?"

"I'm not sure," she said.

I looked up at the books, "Maybe we are missing one."

Mother followed my eyes to the shelf.

"Maybe. But if I had to guess, I would say we are missing more than one."

Adair 1:1

The air is thick and humid, like the dog days of August, but somehow there is movement here. Before my eyes even open, I hear the trickling of water and feel sandy soil beneath my cheek. Instinctively, I reach out, palms down, to steady myself against the ground. I open my eyes. Instead of lying beneath the quilt my grandmother made in my own bed, under the light of a silver moon at my home, Red Oaks, I now lie beneath the shade of a single great oak tree, on the edge of what appears to be a dried-up riverbed. The sun in the sky tells me it is midday.

"Adair?" A voice calls to me.

My body shifts quickly, but not my vision. It drags, transforming the world around me into a record skipping on the turntable. "Nathan?" I ask. Shielding my eyes from the blaze of the sun, I see the form of a person, but I can't quite make out who it is.

"Adair," he says again, as though my name is an explanation.

It is Nathan; I recognize the voice of my sister's son. I look around and ask, "Where are we? How did we ... I was in my bed asleep, but now...?"

"You still sleep in your bed," the boy answers simply.

"What?" I counter, trying to make sense of what I am seeing and hearing.

"You still sleep in your bed, Adair," he offers. He comes closer and squats low, rocking back on his heels to speak eye to eye to me and smiles confidently. "This is a dream."

"A dream?" I look at him, anxious for his smile to reveal jest in his words, but his eyes are serious. "Nathan, that is impossible," I answer, "I do not dream."

"No," he agrees, nodding. "But I do."

He holds out his hand and I take it. He pulls me to rise, but I remain sitting, trying to understand.

"Nathan, how is this happening? I can't be inside your dream," I protest.

"And yet, you are," he says and turns to walk away. Without knowing how or when I stood up, I realize I'm walking beside him in the dusty riverbed. A small stream, if you can even call it such, trickles lazily down the center, dribbling alongside us as we walk.

"Watch and see what you hear."

"Hear?" I ask, but he moves away from me, jumping back and forth across the stream.

"I don't understand," I say.

I stoop to touch the ground again, checking its solidity. Movement catches my eye. Beside my right foot, a pebble begins to shake. The rocks around me begin to tremble, and the ground quivers. I raise my head toward Nathan.

"Something is coming," I shout in alarm. "It sounds like a stampede of horses!"

Nathan is still jumping back and forth over the stream and if he hears, he does not respond.

"Nathan!" I call, but my words are lost as a wall of water bursts around the bend and rushes toward us.

The river bed fills, and suddenly I am in waist-deep water.

Nathan is unalarmed by the rapid progression of the river and swims happily in the rising waters.

Before I can ask another question, the thunder of stampeding horses fills the air again. "Nathan!" I scream in panic, "The water is coming again! Swim to the bank!"

Once again, my words are lost to the tumult of rushing water. The water continues to fill the riverbed, until we are in a river too deep and wide to cross.

I swim furiously against the current and distance, but no matter how I try, I cannot reach the bank. It seems the closer I get, the farther away the bank moves.

"Nathan!" I yell. "Stay afloat! Swim for the bank!"

"You can't reach the bank," Nathan says nonchalantly. Now, he is swimming beside me, not struggling, but treading water with the ease of duck. "Stop fighting against the current. Just let it take you down the River."

"But we will drown!" I scream, starting to feel the weight of my drenched nightgown pulling at me. "If we don't get out of the River we will drown!"

Nathan swims effortlessly to face me.

"What if the true evil is not the drowning," he says evenly. His boyish face and voice morph into that of an old man. "What if the true evil is getting out of the River?"

"But that is the only thing that will save us!" I scream and reach, in vain, for him.

Surprising even myself, I cry out, "We needed the Law, Nathan! The Law was our only way of saving our people! Veralee broke the Law when she changed you, and now, the Law is being swept away and all we have left is the rising waters of chaos!"

The current is too strong, and we are quickly separated by a great distance. As he drifts farther and farther away, he calls back to me.

"The Law could never save you, Adair! Listen and hear me. Those who save themselves will lose it all, and those who lose it all, will save themselves. Now let go of what is finished, and let the River take you—even if you drown."

His head disappears beneath the surface of the waters.

" Nathan!" I scream, "Nathan, no!" I try to swim to where he went under, but I cannot.

The current is too strong.

He is gone, and I am left to the will of the River. I scream his name again and again, but there is no response.

I hear his words echo on the wind ...

"What if the true evil is not the drowning?"

I gasped for air as I jerked awake. Sweat was pouring down my body. Closing my eyes, I took three breaths, relieved to be able to breathe again.

"Adair," I jumped as he said my name. Nathan was standing by my bed, his hand shaking my leg to wake me.

"Did you see?" he demanded.

"What?" I tried to focus. It was still dark. What time was it?

"Did you see?" he asked again.

"What time is it? Are you okay? Why are you out of bed, Nane?" I replied, using his nickname to reassure myself more than him.

He took two steps closer and put his hand on my cheek.

"You did see. I know you did."

"It was a dream," I muttered as I rolled back over, "Just a dream."

"Adair!" Hearing my mother's weak voice, I jumped up. Nathan ran out the door and ahead of me to Mother's room. Though my mother is Simulacrum and had the immortal blood of the Eiani within our veins, her health had been steadily declining in the last few weeks. No one knew why. It should not be; the Simulacrum did not decline like the Friguscor, and yet, she was. Now, every faint breath she took made my heart pound with fear.

I sat on the edge of Mother's bed. My little daughter, Mattox, was snuggled up under the covers with her grandmother. Hadley, the family dog, lay obediently at Mother's feet with watchful eyes.

"Mattie," I reached over and stroked my daughter's cheek. "Why don't you go back to your bed, baby girl, and let Grandma sleep a little. It's not even morning yet."

Nathan stood beside the bed, his hand on Mattie's arm. Since Nathan had first come to Red Oaks after being changed from Friguscor to Simulacrum by Veralee's blood, the two cousins had become inseparable, though Nathan was several years older than Mattie.

"No," Mother breathed, her skin glistening with sweat, "No, I need her."

Mother's hand reached out and took hold of Mattie's other arm. I flinched, thinking Mother's desperation might scare Mattie. Mattie touched her grandmother's cheek with her chubby hand as she promised, "I'll stay wif you."

Mattie was so brave.

"Mother, I'm going to get you—" I stood, but Mother grabbed my wrist. Out of habit, I brought my right arm over to her and let the tseeyen imprinted on my skin brush the one on her own arm. The connection was more than any words could communicate. It was the voice of the Eiani in our veins, the immortal life within us, that spoke through the mark on our wrist. It claimed us as mother and daughter, as family, and as Simulacrum.

"Adair," Mother gasped. She was wheezing with almost every breath, and her eyes were wide. "Listen to me. I have already told this to Mattie ..." She grimaced as though in pain.

"Mama?" I leaned over her. "What's wrong, Mama?" I touched her forehead and found she was burning up. We had never had fever in our lives. This was not our way. Sickness was the way of the Friguscor, the Coldhearted ones, the rest of the world that did not have the Eiani in their veins. This was not the way of the Simulacrum, the Image-Bearers to the One Tree.

"Mama, what's happening?"

"I ... am failing, Adair."

It was too much, I had already lost my father and my sisters; even Jackson, our childhood friend, seemed lost to us.

After the Council meeting in the Oaks of Mamre, I had been the only one of my sisters to return to Red Oaks, finding our home on fire. Though Phineas, Mother, and all of the others at Red Oaks had worked hard to put out the fire and set the house to rights, the smell of the smoke lingered.

Ausley, my youngest sister, had left us, fooled by Absalom, who was once the Seer of the Council but now was the Traitor. Veralee was—well, the truth was, I had no idea where my middle sister had gone after she was banished by the Council for breaking our Sacred Law. Wherever she was, I was sure of one thing. Atticus, the Ayindalet, the Watcher for the Door, was by her side. That much, I had learned from Tessa when she arrived with the others. The massive group of misplaced Boged had arrived at Red Oaks seeking a haven from the storm of the failing Friguscor world beyond the protection of our land.

"Adair ..." Mother said.

"No!" I cried out. "No, Mama; please, no! We need you, Mama! I need you here! Daddy's gone; Veralee's gone; Ausley's gone; Jackson's gone! Our people are going missing all over! And now I've got all these others here to care for! I don't know what to do! You can't leave us! You can't! I can't do this without you!"

I dissolved into tears I could not control.

"Adair!"

I recognized the stern voice I had heard all my life when my mother meant business. The momentary strength in it shocked me into quiet focus.

She continued in a softer voice.

"Listen to me," she reached for my hand, and I clung to hers for comfort. Despite the fever, her hand was cool and clammy.

"All those years, your father acted as the Guardian in my place, he had to use my blood. It was all that we could do after ..." her deep cough could not clear the rattle in her chest, but she continued. "After my mother was banished for my crime. I do not understand it, but it connected your father and me as no others are connected."

Tears began to roll slowly down her cheeks, then she said, "Mattie has taken the key."

"What?" I looked over at Mattox who was uncharacteristically peaceful, as though she was not lying in the bed with a woman about to leave this life. Just beneath the collar of her nightgown, I saw an unmistakable golden glow where the key had not completely settled into her being. She had the key now. It was even now being knitted into her blood.

"She is the Guardian of the Gate of Red Oaks now," Nathan explained.

"But she is only a child," I began to tremble. "Mother, she is only a child."

"You cannot take the key, Adair," Mother said. "You have the mantle of the LawGiver, and you must stand for the Law in the days to come. Let no man take the mantle from your shoulders."

"Mother," I touched her face as tears filled my eyes. "Mama..."

"You must stand as LawGiver against the Lawless One who is to come..." She took a deep breath.

"I don't understand," I cried. "Mother, tell me how to help you."

"Truth will overcome the love of the Harlot, and the chains are readied for the end."

She exhaled, and her eyes closed.

"Mama?" I touched her face and then shook her shoulders, "Mother!?" I grabbed her hand and felt her wrist, "Mama! Mama!" Her tseeyen was unresponsive to me, and she had no pulse.

Mattie sat up, and I saw tears streaming down her face. Nathan was also crying.

Lightning cut through the sky illuminating the room. I thought it must have been a storm, because the lightning seemed to go on forever. For a moment, I was blinded by the brilliant light, but when I opened my eyes, Mattie was sitting quietly beside my Mother's still form. Nathan was gone.

"Nathan?" I turned to see if he had gone around the door. "Nathan?"

I looked at Mattie. "Where did Nathan go?"

"He's gone," she said, her lower lip beginning to quiver. "He's gone from here."

A coldness crawled up my back and covered my chest. "What do you mean?"

"He's gone, Mama. Just like Grandma."

I stood up and stepped back from the bed.

"Nathan?"

I turned around and called down the hall, tears flowing down my cheeks. My knees trembled, my heart was frozen, and I could barely make my feet move as I stumbled out of the room.

"Nathan?!" I began to scream. "Answer me! Where are you? Nathan! Answer me, please!"

I tore through every room upstairs, and then downstairs. I pushed to the kitchen and out the back door, "NATHAN!" I screamed, panic pulsing through every fiber of my being.

"NATHANNNNN!!!!!"

Hadley ran behind me, barking in response to my distress. She ran past my legs and bounded purposely toward the Boged camp.

I looked up to see Phineas running toward me from the direction of the Boged camp. Seeing my bondmate gave me a measure of comfort and relief, but I knew even he couldn't make things right.

"Nathan's gone!" I screamed as I ran toward him, "Mother, she's ....

she's ..."

I couldn't finish. I couldn't say it. I fell, sobbing into his chest, throwing my arms around him in a desperate embrace.

"Adair! Adair!" He pushed me back to look into my face. The alarm from his tseeyen washed over me, and I realized he had news of his own.

"They're gone, Adair. Gone, they are all gone! They've vanished!" His words rushed out as if he was trying to understand them, even as they escaped his lips.

I stopped sobbing and looked at him in disbelief.

"What do you mean, they're gone?"

He tried again, his voice distant.

"I went to the camp to find Tessa."

"Tessa?" I asked, "Why?"

"I wanted to know what she meant. Why she said someone was looking for me...why she spoke of the luminaries." He shook his head and continued, "The sun had not yet risen, but still I heard the sounds of people waking, or softly talking in their tents. Tessa came out of her tent."

She said, "I have to go to the Terebinths. To the Alabaster City."

"There is no way to get there," I began to tell her, "Not while the Gate is closed. It will not open again for many years."

"You're wrong," Tessa said, "Even now, the key is in the door..."

"Without warning, the entire sky burned like it had been set ablaze. Lightning came down in great heavy sheets like I've never seen. Not just one or two, but hundreds of strikes, all at one time."

"I saw the lightning," I began.

"After the lightning, Tessa was gone. She had just been standing in front of me, but suddenly, she vanished and all the tents...everything was quiet."

"Quiet?" I was trying to understand what he was telling me.

"Yes," Phineas continued. "Everything in the camp went silent. After lightning like that, everyone should have been awake. But nothing moved in the camp. Not one child crying or a single flap open. I called Tessa's name but as I stood there, in the midst of the camp, I realized that something was terribly wrong. I should have run to the first tent, but I could barely make my feet move. There was nothing there. No sound, no movement, nothing. There was just nothing."

"PH, what are you saying?"

"They're gone, Adair. Every last one of them has vanished," he repeated.

My heart began to constrict tightly in my chest.

"No," I cried out. "No!"

"I went from tent to tent. They're gone," he repeated. "I looked everywhere!" He was shaking his head, "All of the Boged, Adair. They are all gone."

The Boged, who only weeks ago were the stuff of myth from the legends of the Simulacrum, had arrived in real flesh and blood at Red Oaks only days ago. Each one of them had been changed from Friguscor into Simulacrum through the blood of the Eiani. Giving our blood to the Friguscor was forbidden. It was against our Sacred Law, and in defiance or maybe compassion, each one of them had been given the blood by my own sister, Veralee.

Now they were gone. And Nathan?

I put my hand up to silence Phineas.

"No!" I shouted, turning back toward the kitchen door and slamming it open. I ran down the hallway toward the stairs, taking them two at a time. As I ran, I saw the dream play before my eyes. Nathan in the River. Nathan going under the water.

"No," I cried out. "No, Please!"

Now let the River take you, even if you drown.

The memory of his voice floated across me as I flung the heavy oak door to his room open with a thud. I wanted to collapse when I saw his bed. Sheets ruffled, pillow laid toward the window so that he could feel the first warmth of the morning sun on his face.

"No ..." my voice was a mere whisper as I turned and ran back through the house. "Nathan?" I called again, my hope fading. No, I would not give in to fear. He was here somewhere. I had just missed him, or maybe he was hiding. He was here; he had to be.

"Nathan, answer me now, young man! Where are you?"

Mattie came out of Mother's room, rubbing her eyes. Phineas had come up the stairs just behind me and went to her, scooping her into his arms. I paused before taking one step inside Mother's room. "Nathan, are you in here with Grandma?"

Silence answered me.

Denial was draining out of me, and despair was replacing it. I continued toward the bathroom. Finding it empty, I ran first to Ausley's empty room and then toward Veralee's. Phineas was there before me and stood in the hallway, Veralee's door wide open behind him.

"Is he in there?" I asked, nodding toward Veralee's room, unable to control the trembling in my voice.

"Mama?" Mattie's voice called me into the room. Sweat ran down my back, though I was cold as a winter day. All these rooms, once filled with laughter and warmth, now felt like cold, vacant tombs to me. A place to bury everything I had lost.

I pushed past Phineas, looking first into Veralee's bathroom and continuing into her bedroom. "Is Nathan in here with you? Mattie ..."

I stopped short when I saw my daughter standing in front of Veralee's bed, staring at the mural on the wall. "Mattie?" I whispered her name as I fell to my knees beside her. Phineas came to stand beside us.

The mural on the wall was stirring. The colors were slowly drifting, seeping into one another. The two trees were still visible, but everything was blurring together. Wind was blowing through the room, but it didn't come from the open windows. It was coming from the mural, ripping from the wall. It blew open the balcony doors, but none of us moved to close them.

We all stood, mesmerized by the painting, shifting and changing as we looked, moving outward to transform the room. The golds, yellows, and reds melted from the One Tree in the painting and stretched out as though paint were being poured from a bucket out of the wall onto the floor. The paint formed a river around the three of us, leaving us on a small island of dry ground as the rest of the floor was covered. The air filled with the pungent odor of pigments blending together. I gathered Mattie closer to me. She turned and looked at me, and I saw no fear in her eyes. That made it a little easier to breathe.

Then, directly in front of the three of us, a figure of a man rose up out of the painting though not rendered in paint. He was brilliant gold like the light of the sun compressed into the form of a man.

He raised his arm and motioned toward us, "Talithi Cumi. Little girl, arise."

Mattie wiggled free from my arms and stepped forward. I meant to let her go, but my arms would not obey, so I held onto her right hand. With her left she reached out toward the gilded figure.

"Talithi," the figure continued, "you are the last Guardian of the Gate of Red Oaks, for the time of the Boged is complete, and the days of night are upon this world. The hands of the clock are now moving, and in its hands are seven days. Do not fear the darkness. As you were formed in your mother's womb, I was with you, and I will come for you again. I will not leave you as orphans. I have sent Achiel, the great prince who watches over your people, to you, for now is the time of great distress, a time that has never been and never shall be again. But in the fullness of time, your people shall be delivered, indeed all whose names are found written within the pages of the book. Those who sleep now, in the dust of the earth, shall awaken. Go your way until the end, and you shall have rest and shall stand in your allotted place at the final beginning."

"Why is this happening?" Mattie's voice sounded so very small against the voice of the golden man.

He cupped her chin with his hand and bent low. His words were gentle, as a father to a beloved daughter. "If you would have been but willing, I would have gathered the Simulacrum as I did the Boged, but you were not willing. Instead your people have left your house desolate. And I tell you now, I go to my place, and you will not see me again until your people hammer upon the Door begging for it to open unto you."

Mattie raised her eyes to the man. "But the Door, it has already opened."

"And many who were not called have passed through. They are hidden now, for a time and a time. But you must remember what is, you ask for what has come and you watch for what will be. Listen, Talithi, for the day is coming swiftly when all will be revealed through fire. What survives the flame will be forever and what is lost has never been."

Mattie nodded her head and then reached out to touch the golden man as she asked, "Where is Nane?"

But her hand fell into paint as the image did not answer, but melted, and reformed into a gold ribbon before our eyes. It wrapped around her. The rushing wind grew stronger. The key inside of her chest beamed brightly through her nightgown, revealing what was hidden within her blood. I watched helplessly as her feet rose inches from the floor.

Phineas stretched out his hands to her in an instinctive gesture of protection. But, against all of our desires, we did not stop her. She was no longer simply our child. She was the Guardian of the Gate at Red Oaks, and we both understood what that meant.

The golden ribbon wrapped around Mattie and began to swirl faster and faster around her. Though she stayed still, the ribbon spun at greater and greater speed until it burst into colorful flames, engulfing my child. The gold reflected a million colors of light, and we felt the heat rolling from her. Flames of light burst from her hair, and then the light exploded through the room.

The force threw me back against Phineas, and we fell to the ground, crumpled together. For a moment, I felt like there was no oxygen in the room, but then air rushed through my lungs. I gasped as I sat up.

"Mattie?" I called her name.

A smoky mist covered the room, but I could still see the painting on the wall. It had changed again.

"Mattie?" Phineas called. "Mattie, where are you?"

As though answering his question, the mist cleared, revealing the silhouette of a young woman lying on the hardwood floor of Veralee's bedroom.

Phineas approached the woman, rolling her gently over to reveal her face. Her eyes were closed as the golden pigment drained from her body ran up back into the wall.

"Where's Mattie?" I asked, somewhat in shock. I pushed myself off the floor and looked around the room. "Mattie?"

"Adair," Phineas was hovering over the woman.

Who is that woman?

"Where is Mattie?" I began walking out of the room, in search of my baby.

"Adair, Wait!" Phineas said. The tone in his voice stopped me. I turned back to look at him. He was cradling the sleeping woman in his lap. He motioned me to come. Feeling every step, I crossed the distance between us. Silently we both looked at the woman. With trembling fingers, I reached down to move the hair. It looked more like some form of bronzed copper than hair, but it was soft to the touch. I had never felt any substance like this before.

Bending down to my knees, I leaned over the young woman, examining her closely. Her nose, her cheeks, the small birthmark on the hollow of her neck.

I carefully examined her tseeyan. It was well-defined. A palm branch resting on a pair of scales.

"It can't be," I said out loud.

Her eyes opened. She lay there, looking out from large, familiar blue eyes. Eyes just like Daddy's, eyes just like mine.

"Mattie?" I said in wonder.

She nodded.

"Mom?"

Immediately I heard the difference. She had not called me the familiar, "Mama."

"Mattie," Phineas came close to her and looked at her face, "What has happened to you, baby? How is this possible?"

"Papa?" she reached up and touched his face, and I saw tears coming down Phineas's face. "It's me," the young woman said, "It's Mattox."

Mattox. We hardly ever used her given name. She was always Mattie.

"Mattox? I don't ... " I tried to speak but found I could not.

Phineas hugged her to him, this woman who was no longer a little girl.

"It is you," he said. He kissed her head and tightened his arms around her as if doing so would keep her near him forever. "I would know you anywhere."

Mattie laughed slightly, her face beamed. "The paint from the picture covered me, and The Man of Words took me on a journey. I lived all of those years in a moment."

"The Man of Words?" I trembled beside her. "You saw the Man of Words?!"

"Inside the picture," she thought for a moment, "but I wasn't in the picture really, I was really there. In the horizon between the two trees."

"Yes," she said, her blue eyes strikingly bright. "That seems right. From a space between. It was not there, and it was not here." She struggled, her words coming slowly as she said, "I was caught up, taken into the picture, and I don't know if I was there in body, or just in a dream, or maybe it was a dream that came through to my body. And I heard things that I cannot tell you, things that I don't have words to explain. I was beneath the Trees somehow. And there was a sea that lies beneath the trunk of the One Tree. It's crystal clear and emerald green like a giant emerald or something; I really can't describe how beautiful it is! At one end the sea turns to something like molten silver and becomes the River that runs through the earth. The River is time itself. It moves all of us along the days that become our lives until it ends at the final beginning. The River, is the power of Paraclete himself. And Paraclete was there. He gave me a cup and told me to dip it in where the sea meets the River and drink. As I bent low to dip the cup deep into the River, another was suddenly beside me. He spoke to me, and his words filled the cup so that both words and the River mixed within the one cup that he offered me.

In a voice I had never heard before Mattie quoted, "Your life is merely a breath. Take, drink the years offered to you. You will arrive at the appointed time, and we will lengthen your days for you are the last Guardian of Red Oaks. A shadow of the things to come. Drink and know that you have the words within you."

Time ticked on the grandfather clock in the foyer, but we were frozen in the moment.

"Mattie," I said carefully, forcing my emotions down beneath my thumb. "Grandma said she gave you the key?"

Mattie raised her eyes to me.

"Yes, just before she closed her eyes. Last night, after you had put me to bed and went to help the Boged. I fell asleep for a short amount of time. But then I felt her calling me through my tseeyen. I got up and went to her room. She asked me to crawl into bed with her. She was so warm, and the house felt cool from the night. Her body felt like it was on fire against my skin."

Phineas looked at me, his face stricken.

"Gail? Your mother ... she's...."

I nodded and began to shake, unable to stop the emotions running through me. I turned back to Mattox.

"Did she say anything else?" I asked. I was suddenly filled with deep relief; Mother had not been alone last night. Mattie had been right beside her.

"Yes," Mattie confirmed, "She told me that the Seventh GateKeeper was falling. She said she could feel it in her blood. That the blood of the Seventh had been spilled, and so she was going with him. She told me it was a gift she had asked for many years before. She asked for her lifeline to be tied to his."

"To his?" If words could choke you, these would be the ones that would end me. "Daddy is ...?" Again, I could not say it.

Phineas met my eyes, and though he did not say it aloud, I heard him in my heart.

They are gone, Adair. They have all vanished.

Veralee 1:2

Atticus grabs my hand, "Come with me, Veralee."

I follow him willingly, as he works his way through the darkness. The small candle he holds aloft flickers dimly against stone walls.

As we walk, I know I have been before.

"We are inside the cave," I cry. "Atticus, I don't want to go back through this cave!"

"I know. Follow me, I am Ayindalet, The Watcher for the Door," he responds with a firm grip on my hand, propelling me steadily forward. "It is time for you to remember, Veralee."

"Remember what?"

"You must remember what will be."

Atticus stops when the cave opens into a larger room. Several white-washed stalagmites jut from the cave floor.

"I remember these," I whisper as I rub my hand across the face of one of the stones. "They show stories from my past."

"No," he corrects, "They showed you the lineage of the Eiani within you."

The dark cave suddenly floods with light. I squint until my eyes adjust to the brightness. When I am able to see clearly, I realize the stone before me has come to life once again.

A woman, with beautiful black hair flowing freely to her waist, sits against a tree, caressing a man whose head lies in her lap. A small campfire burns dimly in front of her, casting shadows on her deerskin dress and tear-stained face, creating an island of light in the forest surrounding her. The eyes of the man are open, but unseeing; his mouth sags lifelessly. As the woman cries, she chants in a language I do not know. But I can tell it is a song of lament, as she touches her forehead to his, shedding tears over his body.

Suddenly, she jerks her head up, straining to hear some faint noise over the crackling of the flames. Cautiously, she eases the man's head onto the ground.

"Forgive me, my love," she whispers over him as she stands up. She peers warily into the darkness, and her face pales with recognition and stark terror. She breaks into a hard run through the trees. A shadow passes over the campfire and disappears into the darkness in the direction of the fleeing woman. The stone goes blank, and the cave is enveloped in total darkness.

When my eyes adjust again to the darkness, I see Nathan, instead of Atticus standing before me. We are in the ruins of what looks like an old ballroom, its grandeur long gone. The floor is patterned elaborately with the design of a wheel within a wheel. The walls are half demolished as though a bomb has ripped the once-glorious room to pieces.

"Nathan!" I sob, "Oh, Nathan! I can't believe you're really here!"

"I'm not," he answers kindly. "You are. I have gone through the Door, and we abide here for a time, times, and half a time. We are preparing."

"What?" I answer, thoroughly confused. "Preparing for what?" I reach to gather my little boy into my arms, but suddenly he is no boy at all. Instead, he is a man, a man outfitted in warrior's attire.

He smiles knowingly and responds in a voice no longer that of a child.

"We prepare for the coming battle." He stretches out his arm, "Now see what was, what is, and what is to come."

With that, the ground trembles, gently at first, but quickly convulses into a violent earthquake. I struggle to keep my balance and stumble back against one wall of the room, my palms pressed against the stone. The middle of the floor cleaves in two and water roars through the fissure, breaking the south wall and escaping into a sea beyond. Ripping and carving the fissure into a canyon, colossal waves lift massive warships, rigged for battle, onto the sea. The sky boils with threatening black clouds. Thunder and lightning crack and peel, as an icy rain begins to fall.

"Nathan!" I shout, trying to be heard above the din, but there is no answer.

Lightning strikes the remaining wall near where I am standing. Bricks tumble down, and I fall to the floor.

When I recover, I find myself on the deck of a giant wooden ship, its bulging, black sails straining with the wind. The emblem on the mainsail is a seven-headed, serpentine dragon coiling around Poseidon's trident. Each head has glowing blood-red eyes, and flames of fire spurt from each ferocious mouth. The bottom of the trident divides an infinity circle. I do not recognize the dragon emblem, but I shudder nonetheless.

A vast armada of ships flying the same black sails follow in battle formation. A whipping wind carries the ships swiftly through the rolling, gray water. I hear something carried on the wind: the screams of men. I am sure of it. I can taste agony mixed with the salty drops that touch my tongue. The screeching of metal crashing against metal joins the cacophony of wind, wave, thunder, and screams. Above my head, the sky churns with darkness that has nothing to do with color.

My blood curdles with recognition. I have seen this before. I am on the Leviathan, the ship that carries the caged birds.

An icy voice calls from below.

"We see you."

The voice begins to chant, to call to me, louder and louder over the storm brewing in the sea. I look frantically to the left and to the right. There is nowhere to hide, nowhere to run. In panic, I bolt for the side of the ship, go over the gunwale and fall far, far down into the waters below.

"The Seventh Gate of Bariyach has fallen."

"Her name shall be Veralee, for she shall be a shelter for the truth hidden within her veins..."

The churning water dragged me down into the depths, beneath the heart of the sea. I clawed for the surface, for air, to no avail. The weight of the water dragged me down, down. My lungs burned. Darkness surrounded me, closing in to rob me of life. Weeds wrapped about my head, holding me prisoner to the depths below.

I was drowning, and I could not save myself. I let go and floated with the rocking waves. It was peaceful now.

Something wrapped around my chest and pulled at me, disturbing my peace. I felt myself thrust upward and opened my eyes to see light shining above the surface. The surface! Instantly, I regained my fight, my will. I wanted to reach the surface; I wanted to live!

The strong arm around me forged a path upward, gripping the sea with the other hand, forcing it to yield. Together, we broke through the surface.

"Atticus!" I gasped his name in short, ragged breaths, "Atticus!"

Desperate to touch him, to feel his skin and the breath of life on his lips, I gave myself over to the chaos in my head. All I needed was Atticus, and all would be right again. Heat ran through my cold veins. Life coursed through me. A moment ago, I was dead. But here, with him, my heart beat again.

"Atticus," I sucked in more air, "Atticus, they're all gone..."

I couldn't finish. My mind froze. The world went silent. Spinning round and round in the water, I searched for him. My heart began to constrict.

"Atticus?!" I screamed his name three, four, five times.

But he did not answer.

"No!" the word came out as a broken cry, banging against the wall of pain just behind my chest.

"No!" I thrashed around in the small pool of water. "Atticus!?" A hollow nothingness answered back. My body began to tremble.

"Don't go; please, please don't leave me!" The last words came as a desperate whisper.

"Atticus!"

Only emptiness answered.

The River had taken him from me.

Then I remembered. The city beneath the earth flashed like lightning through my mind. Atticus, Rhen, and I had just been in the City of Bariyach, in the land of the dead ones, where the Rephaim dwelled in darkness. I had seen the Giant and heard his voice.

Then the memories came faster and faster: Daddy's sacrifice; Rahab the murderer plunging a knife into Ausley's stomach; her lifeless eyes. The shadowy figures of the Giants of Old breaking into the dimension of men just before Achiel arrived to save Atticus and me. Achiel showing me the room of my lineage, the room where the trees grew, and the branches were interlaced with names of my family tree. Then, he had brought me back to Red Oaks, to the night of the great battle during the Civil War. Vera was not my great-grandmother has I had always believed, but she was ... my mother! Atticus had been there, helping Vera, and Achiel had given me the ....

The book!

I turned around and around in the water again and realized that not only was Atticus gone, but I had once again, lost the book that Sarah had given me in the forest. The lost Histories.

I screamed his name again, and the cry came from the sorrow deep within me.

Atticus!

The weight of it all began pulling me back under. My body began to shake. Tears rolled down my face; my chest heaved.

No, no, no, it can't be...

Atticus was not here, and neither was the book. We had entered the river of time together, but it had deposited us in different places. He could be a thousand years away, lost to me forever in this life. Nauseating sorrow washed over me.

"No! I can't do this without him. I can't." I whimpered in defeat. "I just can't."

The pain was suffocating; it was too much to bear. For a moment I stopped treading water and started to sink again. This time I welcomed it, and the water seemed to murmur soothingly.

Yes, just let go. Come, let the depths wash away the pain. It will be so easy.

My mind wanted to acquiesce.

The pain will be more bearable. Drowning will be so mercifully short.

But I heard my father's words sternly reminding me, as I drifted down.

The sun will turn back ten steps the moment my blood falls to the ground. You cannot save me, Little Bird, for this is part of the plan. But you can save the others. You can save them...

His voice was so real, so present that I turned in the water to look for him. I didn't see him, but even so, Daddy reached for me across the folds of time and pulled me toward the surface. I knew then it had not been Atticus lifting me from the bottom, but the words of my father.

"Save them?"

With those words on my lips I broke through the surface of the water once more. This time I swam, trembling, still feeling the new reality cutting into my chest.

"But Daddy, I've lost him. I've lost you all."

Daddy and Ausley had fallen, Atticus was gone, the book was gone, and I was alone. I bit the inside of my lips, tasting blood on my tongue, and I began to be aware of my surroundings. I was in water over my head, but I was in a small pool inside a cave. I swam to the side of the pool where I found stone steps leading up from the water. I collapsed as though dead over the worn stone.

Finally, I sat up. Still wearing the hoodie Atticus had given me in Montgomery, I pulled up the hood to hide my hair. Once dark, now it was a shimmering white, a sign that I had met Paraclete, the spirit of the One Tree.

I remembered the message I had received at that meeting, my calling.

Gather what had been scattered.

What good was the message and the calling to me now? I wanted to forget everything and to hide even the evidence of my meeting with Paraclete.

I retreated to the war raging within me. I fought against the despair, the closing darkness, that threatened to take the very breath from my lungs.

My mind screamed silently. Why had the Eiani allowed this? Was I being punished?

"Atticus!" I screamed aloud and pounded the rocks with my bare hands until my anger burned out, and everything had poured from me. The heel of my hand was bleeding, but I felt nothing. I was empty.

I wanted to whisper his name, but I found I could no longer bring myself to say it out loud. Something inside began to detach from the world around me. Cold anger froze every fiber of my being.

I would save his name, locked away as a piece of him that no one could take from me. When he had existed only in my dreams, I had known only his face, but never his name. In that name was the essence of the man I loved. Atticus. Shakespeare was a fool. A rose called by any other name would not have been a rose at all. For in his name lies the truth of the man himself.

I made a silent vow.

I will not speak his name again, until what is mine returns to me.

Suddenly, the hot warning of danger surged through my tseeyen, the mark that claimed me as Simulacrum.

"Stand up and come out of the water," demanded a cracked adolescent voice. "Slowly!"

I heard multiple footsteps approaching, but it was the smell that immediately surrounded me and revealed who or what they were.

Death, decay. Friguscor.

This time I turned my body to see them. I raised my eyes to the face of the one holding a large gun on me. Beyond him, I saw more boys, not quite men but all of them emboldened by their weapons.

"Who are you?" I asked, alarm forcing my senses back to the here and now.

I stood up and began to take stock of my situation. I was beside a pool in a great cave of stone. I glanced back at the water where I had surfaced. It was crystal clear, probably fed by an underground river or spring. Barrels of fire placed around the room were the main source of light and meager heat. Large torches flickered and threw shadows against the stone walls. Wet and cold, I shivered.

"I'm back," I whispered to myself. Back in the great hall of the Boged, no longer beneath the earth in the City of Baryiach. But how? How did I get here?

Atticus and I had been here before. Was it only months ago? It seemed like years since I had been banished from my people by the Simulacrum Council, for breaking the Law. But I didn't regret it. I could never be sorry for giving Nathan my blood, for giving him life and making him my son.

After I was banished, and after the meeting with the Archaon, Atticus and I had traveled to Montgomery to find Agatha. On our journey to Agatha, I began to find more and more of the Boged, those people who were Friguscor but had the ability to change through the power of the Eiani in my blood into Simulacurm.

When we finally made it to Agatha's shop in Montgomery, we found the decomposing bodies of Sonith, the LawGiver, and Mr. Dupree, Agatha's bondmate. Agatha was gone.

On the back of a page from the Histories, she had left a cryptic letter for me.

Quickly, I dug into my wet pocket for the paper and sighed with relief for this one thing I had not lost. It was written on paper from The Histories themselves. Paper from the land of the Archaon. Water could not hurt it.

Veralee, it began. I read the now familiar the lines quickly.

If you are reading this, then you have arrived too late ...

Too late. I was too late. The only thing I managed to save was just a reminder that I had failed.

Atticus and I barely escaped from the Rapha, after receiving this message at Agatha's bookstore. I was sure our time would end there, in each other's arms, but a tera was opened by Albert at the last second, a rift in time and space that brought us to the Boged. Here in this cave under the earth.

And here I was again.

"I said, who are you?" The boy asked again, impatience coloring his cheeks bright red.

These boys were Friguscor, that was certain. Where were the Boged now? Why would the Friguscor be here with the Boged? The answer surfaced in my mind.

The Elektos.

When Atticus and I had been here before, I had been amazed at the difference between the Simulacrum way of life and the Boged we found living below the earth. Simulacrum were born into the Eiani; it was part of our identity, but it was not so for the Boged.

Though born Friguscor, the lingering lineage of Simulacrum blood lay in their genetic code gave the Boged the ability to change. At the Elektos ceremony, each person had the choice, to drink of their parents' blood and gain the life-giving Eiani or to choose to remain Friguscor.

Had these boys chosen to remain as Friguscor? The smell of death in their veins stood as a witness. They were undeniably Friguscor. I swallowed hard, trying to steady my stomach against their stench and its implications.

"I'm here to help," I began, as I climbed out of the pool. Before I could finish, one of the boys grabbed my wrist with a bony hand and twisted my arm behind me, wrapping the other skinny arm around my neck to pin my back to his chest.

The sun will turn back ten steps the moment my blood falls to the ground ...

Daddy's voice floated through the cave. I felt uneasy, as though I was walking between two worlds.

"Daddy?" I began but pain flooded my mind, "It's me," I cried out, trying to get loose to see the boy's face. "It's me, Veralee!"

The boy, who could not be much older than eleven or twelve, let me go. I wondered if he recognized me or simply realized his strength could only hold me for so long.

"How did you get here? Who sent you?" one of the other boys demanded.

Like the rest, he was thin, much too thin. He had the look of someone who was wasting away. Pain radiated from him. Compassion rose in me, in spite of my own suffering.

"Where is your mother?"

I had touched a nerve. A look of surprise and pain was quickly replaced by rage.

"Answer the question!" he barked.

"I'm Veralee. I've been here before, remember? I've..."

I looked from face to face but saw no recognition in them. Mistrust and cynicism stared back at me.

"You've never been here before," said one. Not quite old enough to shave, his skin was already showing the dry, scaly patches that plagued the Friguscor. "We know everyone who comes here. Or at least Napoleon does. Well, anyway, his brother did, and his brother never mentioned anyone named Veralee."

"Napoleon and his brother?"

"Yeah," shouted another boy, gesturing with his gun to emphasize his power. "Rhen. He was the team leader for the guard."

"Rhen!" I said with relief at the familiar name. Rhen had helped us escape the caves of the Boged and brought me safely to the forest to meet my grandmother, Sarah. The thought of seeing the man who had fought so bravely beside me in the City of Bariyach gave me a sliver of hope.

That memory also pricked my heart. My mother had been accused and found guilty of changing me from Friguscor to Simulacrum, which was against Simulacrum law. Sarah had invoked Padha, a provision which allowed her to bear the punishment for my mother, and thus, had been banished from the Simulacrum lands and life. She had left Red Oaks when I was very little, and I had never known what happened to her until Atticus and I came here to the Boged. She had been living here among them. She had sacrificed her life with the Simulacrum for my mother, and then she had given her life to save me from the creature of the night that was hunting Atticus and me. But, that was in the past. I forced my mind to return to the present.

"Take me to Rhen. He will tell you that I've been here before. We've both been here. Last time we came through the tera with the help of Albert. You know, your council leader, umm... his grandson helped us through a tera, but this time ..."

"Us?" the third guy interrupted as he came into view. He was taller and older than all the others, and big, though I imagined he was still in his teens. He had broader shoulders than most workhorses. Dark and clean-shaven in the style of the Friguscor men, his whole manner was menacing. Like most of the boys, he carried a gun and looked ready to use it.

""Yes, I..." I looked back to the emptiness of the pool that testified against what I had just said. It was empty, and I hated it for its emptiness.

"No," I answered, "It's just me. Only I made it through this time."

I made myself say the words, "I am alone."

For a moment, silence echoed through the dark hall. I pushed up and over the emotion, forcing myself ride the wave of sorrow that threatened to drown me even now that I was on dry land.

"Where is everyone?" I asked suddenly aware of the stillness in the room. "I must speak with Rhen."

I felt an odd urgency. The room seemed to grow colder as I spoke.

I plowed on, desperate to make them understand, "I have to speak with him now. I have been to the Gates of Bariyach. The Seventh Gate has fallen. Everything has changed."

The hall was too quiet, too still, too empty. Even though my tseeyen had stopped burning, I knew that something was terribly wrong.

"You're not going anywhere," said the boy who first spoke to me.

"You don't understand," I said feeling more and more frustrated. I turned to appeal to the tall, skinny boy, hoping to find a more reasonable soul, "I need to speak with Rhen."

"You can't" the skinny guy began, "Rhen's g—"

"Napoleon," interrupted the small boy with the large weapon interrupted, spitting out the bigger boy's name, as though ordering a guard dog into action.

In response, Napoleon leaned toward the thin boy, and leered, "We warned you." Without another word he raised his weapon and shot the skinny boy in the chest.

"No!" I screamed and dove at the boy's body as it crashed against the stone floor. Before time could click off another second I put my wrist against the boy's mouth and squeezed the spot where I had scraped it just minutes ago. One, two, three drops fell into his mouth before I was ripped away by violent hands.

"Leave him!" Napoleon cried out as he flung me back, wrenching my arm painfully. The dead boy did not stir.

"What have you done?"

I swallowed, realizing the danger I was facing.

When I had first come in contact with the Boged, I had thought many of their ways barbaric. But this, this was complete anarchy.

The sun will turn back ten steps the moment my blood falls to the ground... Daddy's voice echoed again but this time I realized it was inside my mind. Achiel's voice followed, "The sun has turned back ten steps on the Stairs of Ahaz. Ten steps on the Stairs of Ahaz are three days in the linear lives of men. You have stepped three days back in time."

The words caught in my mind like a record skipping, Three days back in time, time, time...

"Where are Rhen and Gunner and..." I searched for the name as desperation began to build in my voice, "And Apex?" Apex was their Council Leader. It was his grandson Albert who had saved my life and Atticus's by sending us through the tera.

Three days back in time...

"Apex?" A new voice spoke. A woman's voice floated down from an upper part of the cave. "He is gone. They have all gone."

"Gone?" I asked, scrambling to get back on my feet, "Where have they gone?"

"Gone? Yes, where have they gone." The last was a statement, not a question. The voice continued, "They were, but now they are not. They have—," the voice paused, chewing on the word before spitting it out, "vanished."

I stepped forward into the thin torchlight, "What do you mean, 'vanished'?"

"Who are you?" the voice demanded.

I looked up searching for the person speaking. Now I could see the row of twelve thrones I remembered from before, lifted above the rest of the room on a dais. Five large, limestone steps led to the platform where the stone chairs stood. All but one was empty.

I addressed the lone figure, shrouded in shadow above me.

"I am Veralee Harper of Red Oaks." I said forcing my chin up, straightening my back. My mother had raised no coward.

The figure stood, illuminated by the pale light of the flames from below, decidedly female.

"What did you say?" she demanded.

I didn't answer.

"You are from Red Oaks? From the land of the Guardians and the Keepers? Are you a Guardian, Veralee of Red Oaks?"

"No," I answered truthfully.

The shadowy figure continued her interrogation.

"Then who are you to come here now?"

"I have come for the Boged, for Rhen and Apex and—" I faltered.

"They are gone," As she said this, she began descending the stairs. "They have all vanished. You see, Veralee of Red Oaks, we too, are alone."

"Zulika!" I cried out as I recognized her.

As I said her name, Zulika the Oracle stopped walking and turned to look at me. She was the sister of Decimus, the man who had gambled everything to change Atticus from Friguscor to Simulacrum. She was also the woman who betrayed Atticus, though she once—and something told me still—

loved Atticus.

Without taking her eyes off of me, she came down, gliding more like a water moccasin crossing the surface of a lake than a woman traversing stone steps.

"Remove your hood so that I may see your face. I have not seen you in my dreams."

I raised my face to her, noting more than distrust in her voice as I pulled away my soaking hood, revealing my wet hair—once dark but now solid white.

She gasped audibly.

Zulika's eyes never left my face as she held a hand out to touch my hair.

"I have seen you in my dreams," she murmured more to herself than anyone else.

I flinched as she grabbed a section of my hair and examined it closely. I took an unwilling step toward her to keep the hair connected to my scalp.

"Remarkable!" she whispered, leaning in to smell the tresses she held tightly in her fingers. "You are the Nikud."

She released my hair suddenly, and I stepped back again.

Zulika was much changed. She was not the woman she had been the last time I had been here.

"They have been looking for you," she smiled with a raised eyebrow. "And with everyone gone..."

"Where are Apex and Callie?" I asked again, trying to get the answers I needed, "What has happened here?"

"They have gone." She answered plainly.

"Gone where?"

Her mouth opened, and I thought saw a forked tongue slip between her red lips, "Vanished, along with all the rest. I alone am left among our leaders."

I steadied myself, feeling panic rise through my body.

"Left? You mean the Boged have gone? Where did they go?"

"Yes, the Boged are gone. They were, and then, in the blink of an eye, they were no more. Only a handful of wanderers remain, and of the Council, I alone sit on the throne."

As she spoke, the train of her dress twitched behind her, "We must not stand amazed. The time for wonder is over; 'They who began in a night have vanished in a night.' Or so the old words read."

Her words triggered my memory and suddenly, I heard my father speaking again,

"The sun will turn back for ten steps the moment my blood falls to the ground. It was the safety net for our people, placed there by Paraclete for the time when the Seventh Gate finally opened. Do not try to save me, for the gate has already opened. But you can save the others."

"I can help. I am here to save the others."

"Others?" she laughed, her ample chest heaving beneath a transparent bodice. "How can you save what has been lost? They are gone, child. Hear me when I tell you: the Boged are no longer."

"It's not true," I said defiantly, "I have been sent to gather them. They are not gone."

Suddenly Zulika rose up and looked down on me. I saw the unmistakable tail of a snake, flick from beneath her train, and I knew what was coiled beneath the voluminous folds of her gown.

I gasped and started backing up. I wanted to turn and run from the horror of the creature before me, but I was more afraid to turn my back to her. Zulika smiled and slid along with me as if we were in some macabre dance.

A stone wall abruptly stopped my backward progress, and Zulika quickly pinned me against it with the tail she no longer bothered to keep hidden. Her forked tongue flicked in and out of her mouth as she smelled the air around her.

"You smell of the sweetest honey."

I remembered the picture of the beastly monster from a book of the ancient creatures., and before I could stop them, Hesiod's ancient Greek words escaped my lips: "Born in a hollow cave, Echidna was the mother of monsters."

"What did you say?" Zulika asked, her words sibilant, as she pushed the upper part of her body toward me, the half that was shaped like a woman. She narrowed her eyes, staring at me intently for a moment and then whispered, "So you, too, can see what the blind cannot. Who has opened your eyes?"

Her tail came up and began twisting around my neck.

"And what hides within the honey that smells so delectable? What secrets lie beneath your flesh?" Her tongue flicked against my cheek, and I struggled in vain to free myself.

Secrets.

Zulika held my gaze, seeing something that interested her there.

"Seer," I heard Napoleon say, "it is time."

Suddenly a loud bell sounded, interrupting Zulika's deadly taunting.

"It is time," she announced, releasing the hold on my neck, "for the Elektos."

It was just as it was last time ... Maybe I was not too late after all. Maybe I had come in time!

Zulika grabbed me by the arm and held my gaze.

"It is time for the Elektos," she said, "and afterward you will show us all how brightly you can truly shine."

They led me through a familiar door into the great cave. I recognized the vast room immediately. Carved by rainwater dripping through the limestone over thousands of years, its white walls swirled and undulated like a giant Van Gogh painting. Mineral impurities spattered ruby reds, tourmaline blues, and jasmine yellows across the canvas. Silver moonlight poured through a natural opening in the roof illuminating thousands of quartz crystals embedded in the stone, making them twinkle like constellations in the dim light.

A wide stream ran through the middle of the cave with water so clear that it had to be disturbed to be seen; otherwise it just appeared to be a sandy floor. Around a great tree, large natural columns of limestone rose majestically from the cave floor and hugged the ceiling. Around the tree was a stone platform, surrounded by the waters of the crystal river, creating an island out of the tree and the platform. At the edge was an elaborately carved limestone bridge, the only way on and off the stone center. It was so beautiful, but the beauty did not erase the feeling of disgust I had experienced the last time I was witnessed this ceremony.

It wasn't the scenery; it was the choosing that had made my stomach churn. The Boged way was completely alien to the Simulacrum ways of my childhood. They were born Friguscor but lying in wait within their veins was the lingering memory of the One Tree. Though they did not recognize just what they craved, their bodies inherently yearned to be reunited with the blood that granted life. Yet, until they tasted of the Eiani, the Friguscor death destroyed them a little more with each passing day.

That was what the Elektos, the Day of Choosing, was all about. On that day, the children of the Boged would stand facing their parents on the wooden platform, in the midst of the great underground cavern. The only light in the room came from the large, round hole in the ceiling, where a full moon bathed everything in silver.

I had watched at that other Elektos, as Cephas had handed the same ceremonial dagger to each parent. The parent had cut his or her wrist, exposing the blood of life for their child. Then, as if it was the most natural thing in the world to do, as a mother would offer milk to a new babe, the blood was held out before the waiting child. Eagerly, most had chosen life, and drank deeply of the blood, but there had been one. One boy who denied the blood, had chosen death that day.

Rough hands pushing me forward focused my attention again. Napoleon ushered me onto the same balcony where I had last stood with Apex, Callie and Zulika. However, the pressure of the gun behind my right kidney told me that we were not at our final destination. Down the spiral stairs we continued until at last we stopped directly behind Zulika on the stone platform of the Elektos. Before Zulika stood ten children of varying sizes ranging in age from ten to maybe seventeen.

Immediately I noticed the tree in the center of the stone platform. Last time I had seen it, it was full and shapely, with low-hanging fruit, ready for harvest. This time, it was barren. Though still alive, it had not one leaf to cover its nakedness. Fallen leaves of yellow and red made a carpet of color across the stones.

The cave was full of older children. Scared, tear-stained faces with swollen eyes looked up at us. These were the children of the Boged.

The air was heavy with fear. The children clung to each other with desperate fingers, as though that alone might save them. I searched the massive assembly for any adults but saw no one who looked older than eighteen or so.

The sound of a trumpet, clear and bright, announced the beginning of the ceremony. Zulika raised her voice, and with an obvious attempt to calm the underlying panic she began.

"Children, children. Do not look so afraid." As she spoke she walked among the choir of ten children, touching each one of their faces with a motherly hand, "It was a shock for us all to wake and find our loved ones missing. But take heart, dear ones, your parents have not left you, but have merely gone before you."

Her words floated across the tear-stained cheeks and offered a hope that was as tangible as the setting of a broken bone, "They did not intend to frighten you, my little doves; they simply went ahead to prepare a place for you. Do not be angry. Sometimes we adults forget to include you in our plans. Can you forgive us? We ask that you stay together and follow directions until we can reunite you with your parents and siblings."

"Where are they? I want my daddy! Where is my mama?" A hundred voices broke out in question at the same time.

Zulika held her hands out to silence them; when they didn't respond, she began clapping loudly, impatience showing on her face. When these efforts failed to quiet the crowd, her façade of gentleness broke.

"Silence!" she screamed, and the room obeyed. Children, unlike adults, often know that something is wrong, not because they have great knowledge, but simply because they still trust their instincts.

Zulika cleared her throat and regained her composure. She continued, "Your parents have gone on to the Terebinths of Mamre to prepare a place for all of you. When they arrive, for it is a far journey, they will send word and we will join them. As your Oracle, I have volunteered to stay with you until we see you reunited with your parents. Napoleon and the others will help us, too"

"But today was the Elektos..." a young girl with dull red hair and determined eyes stepped forward, "Today, I was supposed to drink the blood."

Almost in unison, the myriad of eyes turned to Zulika, expectant and hopeful for her answer.

Zulika smiled, "Of course you were," she smiled, and I saw her eyes narrow with her words, "but that is no longer the plan. A new day is dawning, and the old ways are no more."

The brave, uncertain girl shook her head, "But, we have waited all our lives for this day. My mother would never have left me without first giving me the blood. She wouldn't..."

"What is your name?" Zulika leaned forward, eyeing the child with the coldness of a rattlesnake.

The girl backed up as she answered in a whisper, "Henley."

"Henley," Zulika said the name as though she owned even the letters that formed it, "Do you doubt me, Henley?" Zulika's tone was smooth, but stony.

"No," Henley tried to correct herself quickly, "It's just that my mother said that this was the most important day of my life, and—"

Zulika cut the child off, "Is that what she truly said? Are you sure? Or do you think she meant more?"

"More?"

"Yes, could it be that she knew she was leaving to go to the Terebinths of Mamre, and that she was actually referring to the day you join her there, and not to this day, not to the Elektos?"

The girl flushed suddenly and looked very unsure. She frowned and looked down at her shoes, tears dropping one by one to the ground.

"No." The sound of my voice against the mood of the room, surprised me. It sounded weaker than I had intended.

I made it stronger as I said, "No! The girl is right. Her parents would not have left her like this..." I motioned to her skin, "For how will she enter the Terebinths if she has no Eiani in her veins? It makes no sense."

Zulika cut her eyes toward me with such rage that I was sure she would kill me had she the chance. "They will change them in a ceremony right outside the gate!"

She kept the smile on her face, breathing through her nose, "Until then ..."

"No!" I said again, my voice becoming steadier.

I knew what we needed to do, "We will change them now!"

Napoleon eyed me curiously but did not make any move to stop me.

"I offer my blood," I stepped forward to the ten standing already on the platform, "The blood of the Eiani to any and all who wish to come and drink! I do not know where your parents have gone, but I know that Boged or not, they would not have left you as Friguscor."

"These ten are not for you!" Zulika demanded, "They serve a greater purpose!"

"What greater purpose is there than the blood?" I countered.

The room sat silent with fear as the tension between Zulika and me grew until not one in the assembly was left untouched. Suddenly, a gust of wind blew down from the hole in the ceiling above and rushed through the cool room, leaving most shivering. It blew steadily like the harbinger of a great storm.

Zulika had her head down, buried into her chest. She began chanting words, slowly and rhythmically beneath her breath. I could not hear all that she was saying, but I knew the language well enough, for I had heard it before. It was the language spoken by the winged beast in the bookstore that tried to kill Atticus and me when we hid inside the shrunk just before we came through the tera. It was the language of the Rephaim, the language of the dead.

"Ati Me Peta Babka," she began. I heard the words translated in my thoughts.

GateKeeper, Sapru, open your Gate before me.

Zulika turned to face me; her eyes were rolled back and covered in a bright blue haze. I saw the shadow of one I had seen before cover her face, so that Zulika's visage became a combination of both. She opened her arms wide and continued chanting.

A shadow emerged on her breath and slithered across the room. It glided over the assembly, and I saw the eyes of every child go black as though tar had been thrown across them. Screams of terror erupted, and the room degenerated into chaos.

I crouched down and pulled the Atticus's dagger from my boot, but my hand became weak as I heard Zulika's next words, "Usella Mituti Ikkalu Baltuti."

I will raise up the dead; here they will come to consume the living.

Zulika came a step closer, her hair and the dead leaves of the tree beginning to swirl in the twisting wind, "Ati Me Peta Babka," she said again.

GateKeeper, open your Gate before me.

My hand began to bend to the voice of the stranger speaking through Zulika, I felt the dagger's point drawing up to my throat, stopping just above my heart.

The wind intensified, and with it, the sirens I remembered from my last time in this place. The half female, half bird creatures descended in a hoard of talons and teeth upon the children, flying low enough for the beat of their wings to thrust the smaller ones to the ground. Advancing to the stone dais in the middle of the pond, they surrounded the ten children who still stood on the stone stage.

Scrambling toward the nearest child I threw myself forward, trying to keep them from the claws of the sirens. Instead, I felt wings wrap around my arms and begin to lift me from the ground. I fought to free one arm and twisted the dagger I still held in my hand. When I could manage, I thrust it into the siren's ribcage.

The creature screamed, and wrapped in wings, arms, and legs, we came down together, hard and fast. She landed on top of me with the full force of her weight. Above us the sound of thrust, screams, and screeches assaulted my senses, and I tried to shake off the jolt and free myself, but the bird was too heavy for me to push off. I kicked and pulled myself forward with my elbows, but just as I was nearly free, her clawed wing came down on my neck. She dragged it down my back, ripping flesh from bone. I screamed with pain but saw only red as anger fueled my struggle.

I managed to turn over, kicking the beast full-force in the face. She extended clawed fingers toward my legs this time, tearing ribbons from my skin. Through the blood and pain, I saw the dagger still protruding from her side. Summoning all my strength, I threw my weight on the creature, flipping her onto her back. I grabbed the dagger and pulled it down to cut deeper into her torso. The creature's scream was like an explosion in my ear, but I held on. I pulled the dagger from her body and plunged it again and again into her neck until the beast was dead.

"Girl!" I heard a voice, "Veralee!"

With blood dripping from my body and hands, I looked up to see Napoleon coming toward me. He lifted me easily enough, placing me on my feet. Without looking at the siren beneath me he ordered, "This way!" motioning toward a door.

Another siren came toward us, wings opened for war. Without hesitation, Napoleon lifted his gun and shot the thing three or four times. It folded into a ball of feathers and gilded skin as it fell to the stone floor.

I turned to look for Zulika and saw her crumpled body laying lifeless on the ground.

"I won't leave these children!" I screamed at him.

Several more birds had escaped with children in their claws. Napoleon shot another blast or two into the cave as the last bird, holding a smaller child in her talons, made its way through the opening into the freedom of the night.

After the maelstrom, the silence suddenly filled every available space in the room, broken only by the muffled sobs and whimpering of the children.

Napoleon dropped the gun to his side, his voice almost a whisper, "You won't have to," he said pointing out to the assembly of blind children, "You're now the leader here," Then he added, "I just hope you know how to save them."

Ausley 1:3

Lantern made of iron and chains hang from the walls of the great hallway. Burgundy, purple, and gold tapestries of battle scenes long forgotten cover every other wall between the large, iron, and beveled glass windows. A breeze blows cold through the hall, causing the light of the candles to flicker.

"Ausley," I hear a voice calling my name. I step forward. Alarm and fear burn from my tseeyen. I am not safe here. This place is evil.

"Ausley," the voice calls again. The voice is coming from behind a set of double doors at the end of the hall. The double doors hang slightly open. The doors themselves are covered with stars. Bright, brilliant stars.

"If they were together," I hear Veralee speaking in my ear. She stands directly behind me, "They would form the dekeract."

She raises her arm from behind me and points, "See?"

I do, and I nod in agreement.

"If they were together," Veralee's voice echoes through the hall, "If only they were together ..."

"I can close them, I can pull them together," I say.

"I will get one side, Ausley," she whispers, "You find the other."

Just as I start toward the door, it moves farther away. The distance down the hall has doubled. I start to run toward the doors, but suddenly I am no longer in the hall, but in a great museum like the ones in the city. I am looking at a Gothic painting of the hallway where I just stood.

I lift my fingers and though I know I should not, I touch the painting. The paint is fresh and wet. One finger is red, the other is a smear of blue, and I rub them together. Suddenly Issachar is standing beside me. The Caterpillar pulls a pipe from his mouth, and in the old language says, "What was divided for a time, for the purposes of creation, must be united. Two must become one."

"What must be united, Issachar?" I ask.

He points to the picture, "Unite the Dekeract."

Water begins to fill the ground of the museum. Before I can react it is up to my knees. Benches began to float. Trashcans are turned upside down. Issachar smiles and winks at me, "Do not fear, child." He leans closer and whispers, "You will drown, but it is just the River. Nothing to fear."

"Essie," Uncle Austin called my name sharply. "Essie, get inside."

Why did he keep calling me Essie? He knows I'm Ausley.

He stood directly in front of me, his small frame draped in a tailored black suit, his gaunt eyes watching me expectantly under the false lights hanging from above. Behind him, a solid brick wall stood in sharp contrast to his frailness. A simple headline ran across the augmented reality screen hanging above his head. It read, "The Vanishing Felt Across the World." Just then the pixels broke apart, creating a chaotic mosaic of black, white, and color across the screen before it shut off entirely.

"Essie!" Austin seethed, his patience wearing thin.

"What?" I answered, vaguely recognizing the name as part of my identity. But why? My mind felt numb. I blinked several times and looked down at my hands. I had the undeniable feeling that I had just been holding something very important, but my hands were now completely empty. I stared at my fingers as I stretched them out and then drew them into a fist a couple of times as if to confirm that these were indeed my hands. Why did they feel so odd?

How did I get here? I could not remember. I was just somewhere very important. The taste of blood lingered for a moment in my mouth but was gone as soon as it came. I felt a piercing pain in my abdomen, but just as the taste of blood, it too vanished before it fully materialized.

What was happening? Where was I? My mind searched for answers that did not come. As though I had not yet awakened from a terrible nightmare, I heard distant screams and saw flashes of dark, shadowy figures standing atop a large stone platform. I shook my head to clear it. I felt just moments away from a distant place of incredible evil and darkness.

"Am I dreaming?" I asked breathlessly, stretching my hand out to touch Austin. "Am I awake or asleep?" I asked honestly, wanting him to tether my senses to some kind of certainty.

Austin stepped in front of me, his dark eyes screaming, though his words were oddly controlled. "You are going with us to the Machine, whether you like it or not, so cut the crap and get on the transport before I have them drag your bloody body into your seat."

"The Machine?" I stammered. "The Machine?"

The foreign words pulled up a deep terror from my bones that shook me to my core. I was suddenly unstable on my feet and started to tilt. The picture of a woman in a facility beneath the ground ... Liza? Was her name Liza? Her eyes were inhumanly blue like the poison dart frogs of Brazil and she had six fingers on each hand. Then, I remembered.

"We want to see the Machine, and then the success stories." Austin said.

"You think that's for the best?" Liza answered, straightening her lab coat.

"What's the Machine?" I asked, staring at the woman's eyes. The doctor didn't acknowledge me but instead pulled a card from her pocket and sighed, "Okay, but you're responsible for the results."

Austin grabbed me roughly by the arm, righting me. I looked at him, my favorite uncle from childhood, and then at the scene around me. Suddenly everything came into focus. The walls of augmented reality screens, the fresh concrete floors, dim green and white fluorescent lights, clear, glass entrance and exit gates, and the unmistakable smell of trash, filth and death, poorly covered by a coat of fresh paint. We were standing in the Friguscor hyperloop station, the transportation system that wrapped around the city. And I was Essie, a name that was supposed to protect my identity and me. It didn't seem to be working.

"How did we get here?" I asked. "Where's the Machine we were going to see?" I continued, afraid of his answer, but somehow unable to control my need to hear it. I just couldn't shake the feeling that I had just been somewhere else, and whatever it was, it was still terrifying me. What was happening to me? My fingers trembled and then ached with emptiness as though my body knew something my mind was hiding. Then I had a feeling that was as real as my fingers before me: I had just been with Daddy. I had just held him in my arms. I looked around, sure that he was here. He was not.

"Daddy? Austin, is Daddy here?" I began, but Austin's look of pure disdain stopped me.

He snarled, "Get on the hyperloop," he snarled. His self-control was diminishing, revealing the rage beneath as he buried his fingernails into my arm. "Or I will drag you myself."

"Hyperloop?" I whispered. Instinctively, I pulled back, away from him, and his wretched breath which smelled of fermented honey. "Austin, how did we get here? Where are we going?"

Behind me, one of the guards who worked for BaVil, the medical research company, cleared his throat indicating his lack of patience with the situation. I glanced back to see who had spoken and saw several guards standing at attention, scanning the small horizon with their guns. Reality hit me like a cannon, and I wanted to vomit.

"Enough," I heard a man say.

"Ellington?" I asked, just as he thrust his foot into my back, sending me violently forward, sprawling onto the floor inside the hyperloop transport. The guards laughed at me and entered in haste while Ellington barked commands.

"Secure the area and then buckle down."

"Clear," they began calling out. "All clear."

"Can I help you?" A familiar voice asked.

"Hegai?" He knelt down before me. My mind searched for something, but I didn't know what. "Hegai," I reached for his masked face. "I ..."

"Your hand is bleeding," he answered as he snatched it down from his face. He worked quickly, producing a knife from his pant leg and cutting at the bottom of my shirt before wrapping my injured hand.

"Keep it covered," he said, "We don't need the smell of your blood in the air."

"Get her up, and put her in a seat!" Ellington commanded.

Obeying orders, Hegai lifted me easily from the ground and deposited me into one of the empty seats. He fumbled awkwardly with the safety belt, struggling to make the clips meet. With my uninjured hand, I touched his gloved palm. He went still.

"I'm scared, Hegai," my voice trembled.

He put his other hand on top of mine. Part of his wrist, where his sleeve had pulled ever so slightly up, touched my skin. Electricity pulsed between us.

"You have no smell," I said without thinking, "The other guards, they have the smell of death, but you ..."

Hegai remained focused on the task at hand as he warned in a hushed tone, "The suit covers all smells, and the other guards may not smell so great, but they do have ears."

I pulled Hegai's arm toward me and put my hand inside of his. Electricity shot through me when his skin touched mine. Familiar feelings of home, warmth, comfort and security, rushed unexplainably through my body.

Suddenly I saw him—inside a far-off memory, standing in a closet, so very close to me as he removed his black mask. It was him.

I gasped and whispered his name as a plea, as a statement, as a sudden truth.

"Jackson." My chest constricted, and my lips trembled. "It's you ..."

When he had finished bandaging my hand he pulled back his glove, and in a moment that I had hoped for all of my life, he pressed his tseeyen fully against mine. A million words were said inside a second of time. A million thoughts passed from his heart to mine as the tseeyen bonded us together in one unbreakable chain of love. It was him. It was Jackson.

You were never alone, Ausley.

I felt the words though his lips where silent.

Do not be afraid; I will not leave you ever again. I will see you all the way home.

I saw us standing together on the bridge that fateful day so many months before, in the Terebinths of Mamre. Jackson, little Nathan, and me. We had been together within the sacred lands of the Simulacrum people just after Absalom, the Seer, had left us and had betrayed his people.

I saw the scene through Jackson's eyes.

"Jackson," I heard my own voice, "We were just leaving. Mother told me to get Nathan home to Red Oaks. I have to check on Mattie." Through Jackson's eyes I look much more nervous and much younger than I have ever seen myself.

"Ausley," Jackson said, "I'm going with you." I can feel his concern, his desperation to go with me, to take care of me.

"You can't" I say just as Nathan said, "Yes!"

"Can't?" Jackson laughed, "Someone needs to lead you home. Whoever left you to go by yourself was crazy. I'm going with you."

Then I had kissed him for the first and the last time. After that kiss, I had grabbed Nathan and ran all the way back to Red Oaks. There I had met Austin and packed to leave with him to come to the city. Daddy had been shot trying to stop me from leaving, and then the blackness that lasted longer than I could count had kept me beneath the waters of sleep.

In the seconds between one breath and the next, I had watched it all play out. It was that fast, and yet, I felt I had just been there and come all the way back again. Hegai stayed poised before me, not moving from his post, wanting me to see it all.

"You came for me," I whispered in disbelief, newly aware of the closeness of him, "You came."

The remembered the taste of his lips lingered on mine still. But no matter how sweet, it couldn't cover the regret and shame. That was the day I had left Red Oaks, the day I had trusted my uncle Austin more than my mother, father, and sisters, the day I had trusted the passions of my heart more than truth. And it had led me to disaster.

Daddy had admonished me so many times.

The heart is deceitful above everything else; do not trust it, dear Ausley. Though you have a good heart, a pure heart, and a strong one, it can lead you astray. Follow instead the Eiani in your veins; let it be your true North. The Eiani never disappoints, and its truth never fails.

But, I hadn't listened. That was the day I had betrayed them all, and it had led to this.

"Come on, man! Hurry up!" Ellington's clipped voice snapped me back to the here and now.

"Two hundred miles per hour will make your ass be the last thing that goes through your mind," another guard laughed.

"What are you doing?" Austin snapped. "Buckle her down, or she'll be dead when we get there."

He pulled his tseeyen away, but the connection was not lost.

"The girl is secure," Hegai announced. I looked up at him.

A rumbling sound echoed through the tunnel. Everyone froze. I saw the unmistakable look of terror stretch wide across Austin's face.

"Is she bleeding?" asked one of the guards.

A distant sound of movement, like a herd of locust moving across the fields at home grew louder.

"I fell," I held up my hand, "when I was pushed."

Guns flew up to a ready position. Ellington yelled, "Go! Go! Go!"

"What's happening?" I asked.

"They are in the tunnels beneath the city!" Austin began to shake as he tightened down his seatbelt. He dropped his head hard against his seat in defeat, "They can smell your blood."

I did not have to ask who. It was the Esurio, the hunger for Simulacrum blood that my people had feared and tried to avoid for centuries.

The sound of the hyperloop starting up could not cover the screams of the horde coming toward us. A single man jumped on the outer tube, plastering himself against the glass just as the train lifted off the tracks. He began beating his face against the glass over and over again, blood smearing across the window until ...

The train shot forward into the tube.

Tears ran down my face, and everything blurred around me as the sound of speed filled the air. Though I was sure the desperate horde was still screaming behind us, all I could hear was the promise of Jackson's words on that bridge so many months ago.

Someone needs to lead you home. Whoever left you to go by yourself was crazy. I'm going with you.

The lights flickered off and then on again. The speed of the hyperloop did not slow but kept constant. I looked over at Ellington. He was watching the blur of movement out the windows, fear evident by the arch of his shoulders. The lights faltered again.

"Warning," said an automated female voice, "We are experiencing difficulty." Almost as soon as she spoke the hyperloop began decelerating quickly. After moving so fast, it felt as though my body weighed eight hundred pounds.

"Warning; we are experiencing technical difficulties. A break in the power surge has been detected," the automated voice announced.

"Delfroe, check the control panels!" Ellington screamed. "The power surges in the city must have taken out the navigation system. It still can power up if you punch in the coordinates manually." Pulling his safety belt off as soon as the train slowed enough, he barked, "We are still a mile out from the Machine. If we don't get this thing going, they will consume us all."

Delfroe, motivated by fear, ran toward the controls at the front of the train. We were stuck inside the train which was inside the hyperloop tube. The sound of gravel and earth moving at a furious pace grew behind us. One by one, we all turned backwards, twisting our heads to see what was coming.

The lights in the train went black. The walls immediately lit up with red emergency lights.

"If we can't get it fixed," said another guard, "We can throw her out."

"How?" Ellington asked, "You can't get outside the train once inside the tube. And besides, I don't think they can break it, they're too diseased to do something like that." He added decisively, "But I don't want to find out."

Austin, sweat pouring down his face, demanded, "Get the train moving now, Ellington!"

A different sound began beneath our feet. I stretched to see beneath me, through the clear polycarbonate glass that comprised the bottom of our train.

"Oh no!" I gasped as I saw what Hegai clearly had already seen. Below us the diseased men and women were climbing on top of each other, using bodies like a ladder, scaling the support beams of the hyper loop.

"I've never seen anything like this," said one of the guards, "They are piling on top of each other, climbing each other like rats trying to get out of water."

"That's impossible," answered another, but as he looked outside, he stopped speaking abruptly.

The lights in the train flickered back on, and several of the guards cheered with excitement. Just then, I saw a woman pull herself up to the tube. She was gaunt and sickly, looking like a four-legged spider skimming across the glass. Several others followed behind her.

"The Esurio." I said as I closed my eyes to the sight of her slamming her face against the glass.

Within seconds, a hundred more people were on top of the tube, banging their flesh over and over again. The tube was quickly covered in smeared blood and flesh.

"How long do you think it will hold?" said a guard.

"Not how long," said Hegai as he looked at the masses covering the tube. "How much?" He meant how much weight could it bear.

The train powered up. And we were once again hovering above the tracks.

"Get buckled!" screamed Delfroe as he ran toward the nearest seat.

Two guards who did not buckle in time went flying past me. I heard the thud of their bodies plastering somewhere behind our seats. I held my breath. Bodies of people flew off the train car as we shot forward at twice the speed of the first time. Behind me I heard the screeches of the horde from the dark, screaming for blood.

Day 1 Erev

Veralee 1:4

The rope hurts. It digs into my wrists.

" O king, live forever!" Someone yells. Others echo the call.

It is hard to walk. Difficult to move with any freedom without pulling too tight, without yanking the rope that binds us tightly together. The simplest of movements causes the rope to jerk violently at Adair in front of me, causing her to trip and stumble. But if I pull to catch up to Adair, I jerk on the rope behind me, pulling Ausley painfully forward. Every step that we take affects the steps of the others. I want to ask why we are tied so tightly together, but the question dies on my lips.

Adair jerks the rope forward when her foot catches a rock, a domino effect occurs, and Ausley lands hard against my bare back. She leaves her head on the nape of my back as we fall into the dirt. She rests her tired head on me for a moment. Her breath is warm on my neck, reminding me of nights long ago. Ausley would come into my room in the darkest part of the night. Her small hand on my cheek, a plea for closeness, for safety from the fear. Pulling back the cover, I would make a place for her. Her tseeyen entwined with mine. Together we would fall asleep, arms locked together, holding on to the sisterly love between us.

"Are you ever scared, Veelee?" she would ask.

"Never," I would lie.

She would look at my face even in the dark of the night, searching for the truth. Maybe she found it, maybe she never did. Maybe she just wanted to believe. To believe that there was a place or a person that fear could not touch.

"I'm scared, Veelee. I'm scared at night."

I never wanted to admit the truth, though I knew that she had to know. She had heard me screaming in the night from the nightmares that tortured me. I just never wanted to tell her that my dreams were a warning of a coming darkness that had nothing to do with color. That Mother was so accustomed to hearing my cries that she never hesitated to come, to comfort me, to bring me back from the edge of the cliff where the fear had left me dangling. I had never wanted to tell Ausley that I was terrified of what my dreams showed me. I wanted more for Ausley. I wanted a world where fear didn't exist, where darkness never covered the land and where she could live in the light. Always in the light. So on those nights, I lied.

"Don't be afraid, Ausley." I would say, " Remember what Mother says. Remember our words. We are never alone. Never alone. We know how this all ends, remember?"

Her small lips would quiver and then finally relax as she trusted the words.

And then she would assert, " We will always be together, Veelee. Right, Veelee?"

No. The thought hurt as the truth spoke into my heart. But again, for Ausley, I lied.

"Of course." I hugged her to me, "I will always take care of you."

I remember the smell of her from those nights long ago lost in our childhood, of honey, oak, and lavender.

Music begins playing from a brass and wind ensemble ahead. When the horns play, the people fall to the ground, from the greatest to the least, shouting "Oh king, live forever!"

The man with a dark black beard screams something to us in a language I have never heard; then he yanks the rope upward, pulling us from the dirt. He forces us forward to the sound of the beating drum. We have no choice but to march. I think of us as girls, of the nights and the nightmares. How long have we all been afraid? How long has fear been the constant shadow in our periphery, the edge of a pencil that shaded our entire lives? I turn my head back toward Ausley. She kisses my shoulder, and I know it is goodbye.

"Remember our words," I say. The words are heavy, truer that I have ever known. How could I have not understood? How could I have been so naive? How could words spoken to me a hundred times in my life meant so little before, but now, as we march toward the end, how are they suddenly the most perfect words I have ever heard?

Adair turns her head to look back at us, "We are never alone."

I close my eyes. I hear everything she is saying. I hear the deep murmurings of the love we share, the memories floating between us, the moments that made us sisters, wrapped into the hours and days that came to complete the years of our childhood. Interwoven within them are the words of our people. Words that have been spoken a million times. Words that finally have found their place in my heart.

"For we know the rest of the story," I finish. We all finally understand.

And for the first time I realize we are marching toward a massive statue made of gold, silver, iron and clay. A sea of people eagerly watch our ascent up the stairs. Their eyes all shine a pale blue.

The trumpeters began blaring their call.

I know where we are going.

Ausley mumbles the words, "They are going to burn us."

I woke with a start, my cheek hot against my aching arm where I had fallen asleep. I lifted my head from the open book and looked again at the picture I had found in an old book in the library of the Boged. For a moment I let my head drop down against the desk again. My arm ached from giving blood throughout the night. To every willing child, which was all, I gave my blood until I could barely keep myself upright. When the last of the children drank of my blood, Napoleon brought me into the library and laid me down in the early hours of the morning.

I thought of the dream. My sisters had just been with me. I had heard their voices and smelled the sweet honey of their blood.

I heard Ausley's haunting words again.

They are going to burn us.

What did she mean? In my dream, just before I had awakened, I had known where we were going, but now, here in the early morning hours, I had no idea where I was going to go. My heart resumed the painful ache that had begun the moment I had realized Atticus was gone. I longed to say his name out loud, to start the replay that ran in my head. The chant where I said his name over and again while I recalled every line of his face, every way his hair fell over his dark lashes, every part of his body that my fingers could still remember, but I refused. I held it in as though I was fighting against my stomach not to vomit. I would not start down that path of misery; for if I did, I knew I would never come back.

Something hard and cold touched my shoulder. A hand gripped me. I turned but found no one there. A few steps away from me, several books fell from a shelf. For a moment, I thought I saw the silhouette of a woman wearing a long black dress. A shiver ran up my spine and fear clouded my thoughts. "Zulika?" I whispered. A long paused ensued, but the temperature in the room returned to normal. I found myself speaking comforting words out loud to myself, "No Veralee. She has fallen."

I'm beginning to crack.

I had to keep moving. I had to stay focused.

Hoping it was the one I needed, I picked up yet another, tightly rolled scroll from the desk. Though statistics and the size of the library set the odds of finding just the right scroll against me, I reached for another. My head felt slightly dizzy. The children would be waking in two days, and I had not made a scratch on even half of the books and scrolls here. While the children slept, I could at least search for the book I lost, the book my grandmother Sarah had given me in the woods the night the beast from BaVil fell her in the woods. That night had begun with a train ride with Rhen. He had helped Atticus and I run from the Boged caves after they accused Atticus of being a traitor to their people. Rhen had brought us to Sarah, my grand—I stopped breathing. I let the thought fall from the tip of my mind onto my tongue as I whispered aloud, "She is not my grandmother. She is my...sister."

"Hello," she stepped out from behind a tree. "I am Sarah," she said, but seeing my face, she stopped suddenly. She looked at me as though I were the ghost and not she. She clutched the tree next to her for support as her face transformed into a small child's with a simple word.

"Mama?" she said.

"Grandmother?" I countered.

My voice brought recognition to her blurry eyes.

"Veralee?" she asked, clearly confused. "Is that you, child?" She closed the years of separation between us, enfolding me into her arms. Her hair smelled of the lemony-sweet fragrance of my childhood that flooded my mind with pictures of saucer-sized magnolias and star jasmine. She wrapped her tseeyen around and touched it to mine. The embrace of family, of lineage, of thick blood and ingrained memory flowed into me. But, it was the knowledge of home that burned through my skin and into my bones.

Home, let me go home, my heart cried.

She turned to Rhen. "Where is the woman you were supposed to bring?"

Rhen pointed to me, "She's the one. She's the one Albert found."

"Veralee?" Grandmother stepped back and looked at me again. "You are the one?"

"Grandmother, why didn't you go to the Alabaster City?" I asked.

"I couldn't. I had to protect the past." She answered.

She produced a leather book. I recognized it immediately. It had a painting of gold and silver stars, point of light, connected through a spider web of lines and arches on the cover creating a dekeract. And it opened from the left side, as though you would read it from the end to the beginning.

"You have them? Agatha gave them to you?" I remembered the words of the note from Agatha, buried in my back pocket. It read: 'She hides what you seek. She searches for you even now. Do not fear to go when she calls.'

Sarah answered, "I have one, Sonith has the other. We divided them up. It was safer that way, my grandmother had said. "Not all in the Council are as faithful as they appear to be. There is a wolf in the fold."

"Absalom," I nodded.

"Yes," she had answered, "or shall we call him Avshalom."

Then Rhen had told me that Absalom was the traitor who had made a deal with the Lawless ones to destroy the Door and keep the Boged from entering. Grandmother and Rhen then told us how Avshalom was living on the blood of the Simulacrum, and that he was no longer Simulacrum. It made sense and explained a lot of things.

But before I could process that information and all the rest that she had told me, the hybrid beasts who had been tracking us attacked. Sarah had given her life to protect me and the book. Rhen had given me the book just before we escaped through the tera and ended up in the City of Baryiach.

"Grandmother Sarah," I said her name out loud, making it feel more real.

And then I saw them again. Jeremiah, leaning over Vera in my childhood home of Red Oaks Plantation, 175 years before my birth. I was the daughter of Gail Harper, the granddaughter of Vera, or so I had always believed. Before Achiel had brought me back down the River and shown me the truth of my beginnings.

Gail was not my birth mother; I was actually the daughter of Vera and Jeremiah! Achiel had moved me down the River just after my birth, and Gail had discovered me, saved me, and raised me as her own. Sarah had accepted me as her own granddaughter, even though I was not biologically Gail's daughter. Then she had accepted banishment from her family, from the Simulacrum, from all she knew, to protect Mother and me. I owed her so much; I owed her my life, actually!

And now I had lost the book she suffered so much to protect. I had lost it not once, but twice. In fact, I had lost it the first time in the blackness of the City of Bariyach, and Achiel had rescued it for me. I could not believe it was gone...again.

The painting from the book open on the desk caught my eye. It showed two leather bound books. Two books, each with half of the Dekeract seal. Two books. Sarah had given me only one. If I had gone back in time three days, then the books might still be here. But where?

Maybe they are here, or at least maybe one is here, I thought foolishly, knowing that I was probably wrong but willing to give everything I had to the search. Looking up, I saw the next level of books, just beyond the wood and metal balcony that lined the entire perimeter of the room. This was the library of the Boged.

Sarah had given me one of the Hidden Books from the Histories. Growing up I had read every one of the Histories that were stored carefully in Daddy's library, but I had never known of the Hidden Books.

I had lost it in the River, and Atticus, too.

His name bubbled up from deep within my chest and threatened to boil over again in screams of agony. I packed my anguish down beneath the drive of conquest. I would find the book. If only Apex were here...Where was he? What had happened? Why would all the Boged leave their children? I thought of Cephas, Apex and Callie and the others I had met. I may not have agreed with everything they said, and I certainly did not understand their ways, but I knew they had been devoted to their people. They would not have abandoned these children, especially before the Elektos. Something catastrophic must have happened, but what?

I thought of the skinny kid with the guns. Had they done something horrific? Mass murder? Could they have pulled that off? No, there was no way they could have done that, I decided. From what Atticus had told me, Cephas was a seasoned warrior. This group didn't have the brains or the muscle to overwhelm him and all the adults in the complex.

There had to be something here in these old scrolls and books to explain this. Lifting the book which showed the picture of the two Hidden books, I flipped to the next page. It was like looking for a certain penny in the ocean, but I didn't have many options.

Zulika probably knew more than she had let on. She had been old, ancient, really. Seers could live forever, it seemed. I thought of her body lying cold on the floor of the cave after the battle. She had fallen with blood dripping from her teeth.

Atticus had told me of Zulika. She was the wife of Cephas, the leader of the Boged, and the sister of Decimus, the Roman soldier who had changed Atticus from Boged to Simulacrum. She had witnessed the death of Beged himself and had been changed from Boged to Simulacrum by his very blood.

Decimus had been sent to the Roman Army to find Atticus. Ultimately, Decimus had given his life to change Atticus on the streets of Jerusalem. That debt had made Atticus susceptible to the scheming ways of Zulika.

At the thought of Zulika, my anger flared, even though she had fallen. Zulika may have started out well, but she did not end well. After Atticus was changed from Friguscor to Simulacrum through the Eiani in Decimus's blood, he had been given his mission from the Man of Words and entered the River of Time for the first time. When he emerged, he had found himself outside the wall of Zulika's city with soldiers ready to release their arrows on him.

He had arrived during the Dividing Wars between the Boged and Simulacrum. That day, Zulika had saved his life. When Atticus learned she was Decimus's sister, he knew the River had sent him there for a purpose. He felt obligated to protect Zulika in her husband's absence.

However, Zulika had wanted more, and when Atticus resisted her advance, she had allowed everyone to think Atticus had tried to violate her. He was brought to trial with Cephas as the judge. Jeremiah, the Original Man, had arrived during the trail. But just as they were to sentence Atticus, the Simulacrum Army had arrived, and a fierce battle had begun before they could sentence him. The Boged Council demanded Atticus fight with them, and during the battle Avshalom had attacked Jeremiah. Atticus fought to help Jeremiah, but in the fray, he had slashed Jeremiah while trying to stab Absalom. Jeremiah and Atticus fell into a tera and disappeared. From then on, the Boged had branded Atticus as a coward and a traitor, thinking he had killed Jeremiah and abandoned them in the battle. Through the centuries, the lie became truth, and all was lost.

"Zulika, you were the coward! You were the traitor!" I exclaimed out loud.

The candle flickered beside me. I looked up and saw the air shimmer. My breath came quicker, there in the musky darkness of the old library. I dropped the scroll from my hand. Zulika?

I looked behind me but saw only the tall tree which grew in the center of the library. I looked right and then left. Nothing but books, the thoughts and truths of my people, surrounded me. I was alone. I went back to the heavy book in front of me and started leafing through its many pages.

My people? A thought hit me. Vera had been Simulacrum. If Vera was my true mother, had I ever been Boged or was I always Simulacrum? Confusion had become my norm, and so I welcomed it's comforting cadence that numbed my mind as I asked unanswerable questions.

But what about my true father? What about Jeremiah? Who was he? Suddenly I realized I knew less than I had yesterday.

"What are you reading?" a voice asked.

"Ah!" I screamed and shut the book from the desk. "Don't do that!"

"What?" His gruff voice held no sign of true curiosity. "I'm not going to hurt you."

"What do you want, Napoleon?" I said, a little sharper than I meant to do.

He ran a hand across his clean-shaven face, looked around the room and then back at me as though I should answer my own question.

I raised an eyebrow at him. "What?" I demanded.

"Please," I said through my gritted teeth, "have a seat. You walk like a cat. I didn't hear you coming, Napoleon."

"Don't call me that," he said in short staccato words, as he slumped down in the chair next to mine.

"Call you what?" I asked, confused.

"Napoleon," he shot back.

"Oh. Ok. Isn't that your name?"

"No!" he grumbled. "My name is," his jaw tensed like he was not going to speak but then forcibly he said, "Eustace."

I raised my eyebrow, "Eustace?"

His hands twitched, and I saw fury in his eyes. I said, "I think I'll just call you Napoleon."

It was ironic to call such a large man Napoleon. But from the little I knew of Napoleon, I could understand the irony of the nickname was true. Instead of being a small man who thought himself too big, he was a big man who was in character, too small. But, he was the brother of Rhen, who had helped Atticus and me escape and had brought me to my grandmother Sarah. Rhen had stayed with us until the end, fighting the Giants in the City of Bariyach.

I looked at Napoleon. "I will call you Eustace if that is what you want."

"No," he shook his head, "Might as well call me Napoleon. My own brother called me Napoleon."

"You don't look much like Rhen."

"He looked like Pa, I took after Mom," he answered.

"And you were younger, "I continued to probe a bit.

"By ten minutes," he allowed.

"I didn't realize you were twins," I leaned and shifted some of my weigh in the chair, "Napoleon, what happened here? Where did everyone go?"

Silence.

His went blank as though he were trying to make his mind forget, but memory is not always obedient.

"It was lightning," he said.

"Lightning?" I shook my head, "Outside?"

"We are in caves, Veralee," he answered, "It was lightning inside the caves."

"Inside?" I questioned, "Lightning can't happen inside..."

"No," he agreed, "But it did and then, they were gone."

"I'm not sure I understand..."

"Neither do I, neither do any of those children. But it appears to be in that book you're holding. I found it yesterday...that's why it was left out."

"In here?" I began to flip the pages again.

"Yeah," he stood and came beside me and the book. The smell of death rolled off of him as he spoke, "I think this must be it."

The picture was drawn from the ground looking up into a great bolt of light. Small birds flew in circular patterns up toward the sky.

"Birds flying toward the sky...." I began, but suddenly I stopped. I had seen this before, in the garden of the One Tree, after I left the cave of death. Paraclete had brought me before the One Tree. I watched as its branches had trembled under a mighty wind, which had taken all the leaves and twisted them into the air.

'Look, what do you see?' Paraclete asked.

'The wind,' I answered.

'Look once more.'

'The birds,' I said, 'They are powerless.'

"See through what is in front of you. See the truth behind the shadows,' he said with authority.

The birds had grouped together, into a purposeful, synchronized pattern across the sky. The wind had been a force of nature, but it had been for them, not against them. They had flown in a pattern just like the picture in the midst of the wind, and then returned to the One Tree.

Napoleon shrugged, "I don't know. Maybe I'm wrong. It was just something about this picture. I think it's what happened to them. I think they are with the One Tree."

"I think you're right. I think the lightning was Paraclete...he came back to gather what had been scattered from the One Tree."

"But he didn't take your kind." Napoleon smiled with smug satisfaction, "Now, that is an interesting turn of events. We were always second-class citizens to your kind. You could not even bring yourself to say our name. You didn't even believe we existed, and now we have been taken back to the One Tree, and your kind...have been left, abandoned to the Friguscor."

We glared at each other. He was right, but still, it was hard to take from his arrogant face.

"Look, as fun as this is," I began, but suddenly Napoleon grabbed my thigh, pinning me where I sat as he leaned over me. Heat ran up my tseeyen and down my spine. I sensed that Napoleon's heartbeat was accelerating, and I could feel the sweat on his palm.

With my right hand I reached beneath me, down toward my boot and took hold of the dagger I had hidden there.

"I came here," Napoleon began, "because of what you did for those kids." His grip on my thigh remained a constant presence between us.

"I didn't reject Mom's offer of blood, but I..." he started and then abruptly stopped. He released my leg, "I thought I had time. I didn't want to choose yet. So, I stayed away. I left before they could make me choose. And then, Patrick was gone. I came back, but they were all gone."

I tried to follow his story.

"Patrick?"

"Yeah, my boss." He turned toward me, "I need your blood."

"Why?"

"You can change me. You changed those kids."

I shook my head. "No, I can't change you. Only the Eiani can do that. All I can do is give you my blood. The rest is up to the Eiani."

"That doesn't change the bottom line: I need your blood."

I looked at him. He had shot a young boy right in front of me. There was nothing in him that I understood.

"Why?" I asked, smoothly.

"Why what?" he answered.

Without moving, I tightened my grip on the blade.

"Why do you want to change? Why now?"

I felt the temperature of our conversation shift with my question.

"What the hell does it matter to you?" he shouted. "Just give me the damn blood."

His hand clamped down on my thigh once more, and he put his face close to mine. "I'll take it, don't think I won't. I am nothing like Rhen."

"No," I moved closer to him quickly, catching him off guard. Immediately I could tell he was a man who was used to women being afraid of him. I was not afraid. I knew what the blood could do, and I was willing to die to give him a chance.

"But soon you will be," I raised the blade slightly.

He grabbed my hand mid-air. "You bitch," he growled.

"I have to cut my wrist to give you the blood."

His eyes widened, "You lie."

"No," I said quickly, "I never lie."

He laughed and let go of my wrist. He was nervous—and dangerous. But I didn't care. I refused to be afraid. Men like Napoleon wanted to dominate women to make themselves feel better, and they were always dangerous when they felt out of control, But I would not be dominated. I knew what the Eiani could do. I would not be afraid. I will not fear a man who could kill this body. The blood within me was eternal.

"Of course not," he gestured for me to continue with a flick of his wrist. "Your kind never do."

His next words took me off guard, "Those kids need to get out of here. Zulika is not safe."

My hand faltered, and I dropped the blade down by my side.

"Veralee," he barked.

"Yes?"

"Can you do it?" He demanded.

"Do what?"

"Do you have somewhere for them to go? For the kids I mean." He added in an unmistakably accusing tone, "The ones you changed."

"Are you angry with me for changing them? You helped me!" After several hours of giving out blood, I had become weak and could barely stand. Napoleon had been by my side helping me continue until the children had all drank of the Eiani.

Hot anger was boiling just beneath the surface of his skin, "You changed them, and now what? Now what are you doing to do about them? It takes three days, lady!" He pushed himself off of the wall, "Three days for them to wake up! Are you staying around until they wake up or are you here," he motioned dramatically around the library, "just to pick up whatever the hell it is you are searching so frantically to find?"

"I'm not frantic," I began but realized that was not entirely true.

"You insisted that I bring you to the library!" He groused.

"I like books."

"Whatever! Are you going to take care of those kids or are you going to abandon them just like the rest of their parents did?" he yelled.

"Their parents didn't abandon them. They wouldn't do that. Maybe it was something Zulika did," I tried to reason with him.

"Like what?" he jerked his chin and widened his eyes, "Like she's got them all hidden somewhere? Just had them vanish into thin air and stashed away?"

"You are Boged," I said throwing it back at him. "Don't you know? Don't your people have any writings on this? Were you taught anything that would tell us what happened?"

"No!" he swiped several books off the desk. "We were taught, or should I say, fed a bunch of crap about the unity of our people, about the fellowship of our kind, about Paraclete and how he walked amongst those who had chosen the blood. Now—now look at this place!"

He threw down the chair that stood in front of him and then pushed a stack of ten or fifteen books onto the ground.

"Now we have been left, abandoned by all that we were taught! Did you see those children? Who leaves their own kid like that? Who walks away and leaves them to die all alone? What kind of people would do that to their own?"

He was almost panting, his anger spent.

I chose caution and truth.

"I don't know," I said. Picking up a book from the desk I held it up as a peace offering, "That's why I was looking through your writings, in hopes that I would find out what has happened here."

Jerking away, he shook his head silently and fervently.

"So, are you going to take care of those kids or are you going to leave them as well?"

"They need to go to Red Oaks; they need to be with the Simulacrum," I said realizing what that would mean, "and you will have to take them there."

"Me?" he looked as though I had slapped him. "Why the hell would it be me?"

I stood up, "Because I have to find my sister. She's missing."

He shot back at me quicker than I expected and grabbed my arm roughly, "I don't care about your sister. You just changed a hundred damn kids, and now you are going to have to deal with it!"

Pulling my free arm back, I landed a punch across his cheek and nose with all my strength.

"Don't ever touch me again!" I shouted.

He recoiled, more surprised than hurt, and growled, "You're going to have to take those kids, and you know it."

Did I know it?

Since I had left Red Oaks, I had been changing as many Boged as I could wherever I had found them. Atticus and I were constantly being pursued, so I'd had to leave all of them before their transformations were complete, telling them to find their way to Red Oaks. I didn't know if any had survived or what had happened to them. It was like leaving my children alone and defenseless. Like these children. At least I knew Nathan was safe with Adair and Phineas.

Before the catastrophe under the City of Bariyuch, Atticus and I had discovered that Ausley and Jackson were being held by an organization called BaVil in Atlanta and that BaVil was rounding up the Boged and taking them to Atlanta, too. We had hoped to get to BaVil and free them, but that hadn't worked out the first time. If Daddy's words truly meant that time went back three days, I hoped I had another chance, and I had to try. If Ausley and Jackson were still alive, they were at the mercy of BaVil. How could I not help my own sister and best friend?

But how could I find them?

A tear welled up and rolled down my cheek. Atticus would know what to do! Where was he?

I heard his voice, and what he had said when I first started changing the Boged in the city:

"Veralee, you do realize you can't stay with each one. It takes three days. You won't be able to stay once they've taken the blood."

Then, it was as if Paraclete himself had spoken it into my mind, "I know." I had said to Atticus, "I'm not responsible for what the blood does or where it takes them. I just have to give it to them."

Atticus had nodded his head and then with no argument in his voice had said, "So that is what you mean by gathering the Boged?"

It had been a hard moment then just as it was now.

Gather the Boged. Gather the...

The choice seemed impossible, but Napoleon was right. I knew he was right, and I hated him for it. Everything in me said to leave those kids, to go get Ausley. But Ausley and Jackson had three days, and these children had no one. Ausley would have to wait, and I would have to find the fastest way to get the children to Red Oaks.

Home.

The word made me feel weak and yet somehow strong all at the same time. I would take them home to Red Oaks. Mother would be there, and Adair. They would know how to help Ausley.

But I would need help moving that many children across Friguscor lands. Yet, below my deepest consciousness I vowed to Ausley that I would come for her.

Defiantly, I held up my wrist to Napoleon, "You are going to help me. You have to drink the blood."

He glared at my wrist, suddenly repulsed by the very thought. I saw his hunger rising as his breathing grew quick and shallow.

"No," he said quickly, "I'll help you get those kids out, but I don't want a drop of your blood."

"Then you're a danger to me, to the kids, to us all."

He nodded in agreement.

"You'll just have to decide if I'm worth the risk."

"You're not." I said quickly.

He looked shocked, and I added, "If you refuse the blood, and choose to stay as you are—as a Friguscor, then I'll take them on my own."

He tightened his jaw. "What's happened to you that made you so prideful that you would choose to do this alone rather than accept help just because I'm the wrong type of person?"

Without hesitation I answered, "Until you take the blood you are a danger to us. If I had another Boged or Simulacrum over the age of 11 offering to help, I would gladly take it, but you?" I shook my head. "I think a better question would be, what happened to you that made you so prideful that you would reject life and choose the death in your veins?"

Anger flooded my mind as I began to stack up the books that I pulled from random shelves.

"There is someone else," he said plainly. He was obviously diverting attention from my question.

I stopped and looked at him.

"Who?"

"Zulika had us searching for her when they all went missing. She was still here. She didn't leave with the rest."

"I thought all of the Boged were gone."

"No," he said shortly, "She's not Boged. She's Simulacrum."

"Who is it?" I asked.

He shrugged, "Her name's Sarah, or at least that's what I heard Zulika screaming before you got here. She was down in rooms below, in the Hall of Teras."

"Hall of Teras?"

"Yeah, where they keep the teras open. Anyhow, she was screaming for a woman named Sarah."

"That's impossible, Sarah has fall--" but before I could finish I heard, turned back three days in my mind. Three days from the City of Bariyach. I had gone back three days, and Sarah would still be awake!

"Take me to her!" I demanded.

"I'm telling you, I don't know exactly how to get you there, but I can get you pretty far. We have to use a tera."

After we had checked once more on the sleeping children, Napoleon led me deeper into the maze of tunnels cut out of the ground by the Boged.

"A tera?" the word made me feel uneasy, "Why a tera? You said Sarah was here."

"She is," he said smartly. "Or she was." He put both hands out, "I followed her down this hallway. Zulika had us searching everywhere for her. I was down near the Hall of Teras and—"

"The Hall of Teras? What's that?" I asked.

"It's a long hallway of doors. Behind each one is a certain or specific tera. Teras are so uncontrollable that I guess it makes them easier to navigate or something."

I nodded, "If they are so uncontrollable, why do you use them?"

Napoleon shook his head. "Don't ask me. I've never used one. Our people don't have the ability to open new teras so they keep the old ones going. But, as I said, I've never used one. My father claimed he did, but," he stopped talking and tightened his lips.

"So Sarah went to the Hall of Teras?"

"I followed her to the Hall, but at the end, she disappeared."

"Into a tera?"

He shrugged.

Where would you have gone, Sarah?

I felt a cold breath of air run down my back, but when I turned nothing was there.

"Wait a minute," an idea came to me. Maybe there was an easier way to get to Red Oaks with the children, "Do you know how to open one?" I asked, examining the long hallway of many wooden doors. He didn't answer. "Napoleon, did you hear me? Do you know how to open a tera?"

"I know their stories."

This man was driving me crazy. "The Boged stories? You know the stories of your people on how to open a tera? What are you are saying?"

"Yep."

"I really can't stand you," I said just before I began walking down the hallway adding, "But right now, you are necessary means to an end. So, hurry up, I don't have long before the children wake up, and I have to be there when they do."

"Why?" he sneered at me, "You don't even know them. Why do you give a--"

I turned on my heels and put my full anger into my voice, "I don't have to know them!" I was clenching my teeth, feeling the anger rising in my stomach, "They are of my blood now!"

I stopped. Suddenly I realized that I could no longer sense any of the other Boged that I had changed. Not Nathan or Tessa, or any of the others. It was as though they were gone completely. I realized the truth of it.

"All of the Boged are gone," I said. "But not the Simulacrum. I can still feel my sisters somewhere out there."

"Sarah, are you here?" I called into the hallway. Nothing but silence answered.

The Hall of Teras sloped downward descending into the earth as we walked forward. The air grew colder and thinner. I trailed my fingers on the wet, cold rock walls. Huge roots grew down along the walls to the floor. After my anger burned down into a low fire, questions began to build.

"Each of these doors opens into a tera?" I asked.

"I guess. That's what the old people said," Napoleon shrugged.

"Do you know where they go? I mean, is there a map or anything about where each one of them goes? Is there one for Red Oaks?" I continued.

"I told you, I don't know!" He was clearly frustrated.

I made a mental note to look for a map of the Teras. Surely there was one somewhere! If I could get the children to Red Oaks through one, I could leave them in Mother's care, get help, and get back to BaVil in time for Ausley and Jackson! I didn't really like the thought of using a tera, but it was a plan. Desperate times called for desperate measures.

I changed the subject, "How long have the Boged lived like this?"

"You mean, here?" he answered.

"Yes, how long have they been hiding underground?" I tried not to sound demeaning as I asked.

Napoleon wiped his nose and scratched at a patch of skin on his neck, "I'm not sure. If you believe their stories, the ones they slam down your throat as a child, then I guess you could say a thousand years or so. If you mean how long have the Boged been living in secret from your people, then they would say more like two thousand years."

My shoes were wet from the steady stream of water at our feet.

"You're killing me. How can you not believe your own stories when you know the truth?"

"The truth?" he looked at me, eyes full of mocking annoyance. "What truth?"

"You know the Friguscor world and you know the Simul—," I stopped and corrected myself. "And you know the Boged world is real. How can you see all of this, see the change happen in those children and yet still not believe your own history?"

The irony of the conversation was suddenly very close to me.

"Why are you smiling like that?" Napoleon looked at me as though I was both insane and contagious.

I shook my head, "I just realized that everything I am saying to you, is what I have been living for the past months. I grew up Simulacrum. I read the Histories, and I knew that the Friguscor were real people. But I still didn't believe it all, not really. Something in me fought against the rules, their excessive rules, and I allowed my disdain for their rules to blind me to everything else."

"They've got a lot of rules over at the Simulacrum? I thought they just had one. The Law, or whatever you call it," he commented.

"Yes. And the Law controls everything. It dictates all that we do," I agreed.

Napoleon nodded as he walked.

"But the thing is, even though I knew deep down it was all true, I allowed the brokenness created by humans, the law, and everything it was supposed to do—I almost let it blind me to everything."

"Got it, 'cause you now believe it all." He was being flippant. "Because what they told you really was true."

I grabbed his shirt sleeve and pulled him to a stop.

"No." I said, wanting to make him understand. "That's what I'm telling you. The Law, the rules, those things had somehow taken precedent over everything else. It became the center of our entire way of life. But it was the only way I had ever known... until I broke the Law and gave my blood, blood that I didn't create or do anything to deserve. I gave it to a little boy who was dying. And then, when the Archaon came, when I met Achiel. Then when I bonded myself to--" I stopped and swallowed down his name, keeping it hidden in my heart, "I realized that everything I had been taught was true. And the truth was so much more than our way of life or our traditions. Somewhere along the line, we had made the Simulacrum life about safety and preservation, but it was never supposed to be about that."

Napoleon shook his head with doubt, "And exactly what was it supposed to be?"

I thought for a moment, about the Council, my family, Nathan, the cave, Paraclete, Achiel, the City of Bariyach, those I had met on the streets of the city, and Atticus. I saw the memory of the One Tree and something in my mind found peace. "It's all true, Napoleon. My Mother used to say, 'Whether or not you believe does not matter. Truth is true with or without you.' She was right. It was never about the Law because all the Law did was show us how it couldn't save us," I said it freely, "They thought the Law would keep us safe forever if we just shut our doors and locked away the blood from the outside world, but it didn't; it couldn't. The Eiani within our veins—"

"Within your veins," he said sharply. His voice was dark and cold. "And I don't believe in the truth of your stories."

"But you see it. The truth is on your skin right now. Death is all over you; I can smell it." I picked up my pace to match his. "You smell like the death in your veins. And you see me. If it is not all true, then why do we look so different?"

He pushed me against the rock wall with his left arm and leaned over me. He was trying to intimidate me as he stared down at me with his dull brown eyes; his cheeks were ashy with dead skin, and his breathe smelled foul as he spoke.

"I don't see anything, except a girl who's accepted the silver spoon that's been shoved down her throat all of her life."

Several rocks crumbled beneath the strength of his hands as he pushed back away from me. And with his movement I felt a deepening in the canyon between us.

"What you believe doesn't matter, Napoleon. Death is in your veins, and regardless of what you believe, death will ultimately win if you do not choose the Eiani. Whether you believe it or not." I refused to be intimidated and defiantly held his gaze.

My tseeyen began to burn. Then I noticed that all of the loose rocks on the dirt-covered floor were trembling as if a great rush of something was coming. I held my arm up; it was glowing, white, sharp, light.

Napoleon released me and looked back, realizing something was wrong.

"What is happening?" I asked.

"I don't know," he said quietly and stepped to the other side of the walkway, putting distance between us.

The temperature dropped drastically, and my breath was transformed into white puffs of air. My wet feet now felt frozen.

Who are you?

Voices that sounded like a multitude of women spoke at once. They seemed to be very agitated, almost horrified.

Who are you?

Napoleon turned to the right and then the left in search of the unseen foe. Jerking his gun from its holster, he tripped forward a bit as though he had been pushed. The voices began to circle the rocks walls.

Are you the Eighth?

The voices fell, floated, swirled all around.

Who are you? Why can't we see you? Who hides you?

Round and round the voices of the women spun and bounced off the walls, echoing into a cacophony of strident sound.

"Stop!" I screamed. And all became quiet.

Before me, a dark blur materialized and black, flowing fabric began to swirl in the air. I could see no face, but the form of a woman's body became evident. Long black tentacles curled toward the ceiling, spread out across the walls and slid heavily across the ground. As the woman-esque form became more and more visible, I recognized the face. She had no eyes, just black orbs that leaked inky streaks onto her cheeks and brows. Where a nose had once been, the outline of ruined cartilage wheezed air in and out. Her once beautiful hair was a tangle of rope knotted around her balding head; it fell in clumps down her back and against her exposed breasts. Teeth marks covered her nipples all the way up her neck.

I closed my eyes and placed my mind behind a shield of disbelief.

"Veralee," a familiar voice called.

My eyes jerked open.

"Mother?"

"Yes, Veralee, it's me. "

When I opened my eyes, she stood before me with skin like fresh-poured milk, hair dark and rich, eyes as silver as the moon.

"Mother, how are you here?" I grasped her shoulders and pulled her into me, sobbing with relief. "Mother, I missed you so much! I'm so sorry! I'm so sorry, Mother, about everything! I love you so much!"

But something was not right; I should have known it immediately. She was not warm. She was not soft, and my tseeyen could not feel her. Instead it was raging with alarm.

This was not my Mother. The shock of feeling her again and then losing her just as quickly swept over me. Slowly I pulled back, shaking my head.

"Who are you?" I asked with disdain as I pushed back against the wall of rock.

She stepped closer, pleading.

"Veralee, it's me. It's Mommy. Don't you know me?"

"Mommy?" I let the foreign name slip from my mouth, feeling the distance it put between us. I had never called her Mommy.

With a cold, unfamiliar hand she attempted a comforting touch to my head, but I flinched away. "What are you?" I hissed.

Napoleon was standing behind her, eyes wide with terror. It was so cold in the hall that my hands were trembling.

"You don't know me?" She said, hurt filling her eyes. "But Veralee, it's me. Please, sweetheart."

Hearing Mother's voice, in such broken despair was like a jagged knife through my heart. I bit down on my tongue, forcing myself to feel the pain.

"No," I repeated again and again before deciding. "No! You are not my mother. Get away from me."

"Veralee, you speak true," the voice derided as it changed tenor. "I am not your mother." As she spoke, she turned, and I saw that the left side of her face was missing flesh. A shallow hole revealed a grisly sight of teeth, bone and flesh.

The horrific form taunted, "Who is your mother? Do you even know? You are a child without roots, a wandering star. Lost between two worlds." As she spoke, she turned again. Her head jerked to the right and then forcibly back to the left. Finally, the flesh that held any semblance to my mother was gone, and the woman from before returned. Black holes for eyes, knotted bands of hair, bare breasts stained black and blue by a hundred teeth marks. Though ghastly, she was once again familiar in a way I could never have explained.

"Zulika," I whispered.

"The Oracle is no more, her flesh has fallen," the woman said with the echo of a myriad of female voices all at once, "but we are still here."

"I saw you," I said quickly watching the tentacles stretch out from underneath the flowing black gown. "Zulika had a snake's tail."

A long tentacle slithered from behind her back and touched my face as the thing spoke.

"Who has opened your eyes, girl? Who has allowed you to see beyond the veil?"

The tentacle slipped behind my neck, cold, slimy and sharp. She cocked her head to the right and asked, "Who are you?" She opened her large mouth, and a long, bifurcated tongue slithered out. I struggled against her grip which was now tightening around my neck. Her hands ran beneath my shirt, and up my torso, her long claws scraping at the skin.

"Stop!" I yelled. "Napoleon, do something!"

The woman's hand stopped just over my left breast where she flattened her palm. "What?" she asked, her face coming closer to me.

"Napoleon!" I begged for help.

Cutting my eyes toward Napoleon I found him standing in an uneasy slouch a few steps away from me. He was turning the gun in his hand.

"What are you going to do, Zulika?" he asked in a low, tired tone. "You said all you wanted was a drop of her blood."

Zulika turned her head. With a hiss that churned my stomach, she said, "And you brought me nothing. Rhen was always better than you at these things, but then, Rhen was always better than you at many things."

Napoleon kicked the wall.

"She wouldn't do it, Zulika. She wouldn't cut her wrist. I went to the library and asked her, but she wouldn't give me her blood. What was I supposed to do? Cut her myself?"

I remembered Napoleon backing away from me, rejecting my outstretched wrist.

I had offered him my blood, but he had refused.

"It matters no longer," said the ghoul who was at one time Zulika. She began to breathe heavily and the black eye sockets glistened as she held her hand against my chest. "What is inside of you? Is there room for more?"

Her teeth began to show, and she rolled her head back. In her excitement she moved one tentacle away from my right foot. Without any thought I brought my knee up into her torso. It did nothing. It was if I was hitting air. She could touch me, but she was not physical. Panic rushed over me. What was this thing?

"We are from the City of Bariyach, where the Gates of Old hold back the darkness, a place of chaos and ruin." Her voice, a legion of voices, sounded loud, bold, and deep, rumbling the rocks beneath my feet. It filled me with terror.

"Once we walked this earth. Our fathers, the ancient ones, the mighty ones of renown, gave us life. But we were not immortal as they, and in time our flesh failed and blew into dust, but we did not. We live on, in the darkest places of the earth.

"Without flesh, we are only half alive. We cannot touch or taste, so we search, from one to the next for a place to exist, for a body of flesh and blood to inhabit."

Without warning, she sank her teeth in my skin. I felt them hard and cold on my neck. I felt her draw my blood and with it, I sensed her trying to thrust her spirit into me. It was as if a thief was ramming the doors of my body and psyche, trying to invade and possess all that was mine.

Napoleon moved toward me, but before he could even reach his hand out to grab me, the woman pulled her head back and sucked in air with a loud strangling sound. She quickly withdrew her tentacles and backed away from me as she uttered the words I had heard so many times in my dreams.

We see you.

The sound of those words sent my heart racing.

We see you, Sapruuu ...

The voices hissed gleefully. Dark mist filled the hall as she repeated the words over and over.

She backed away as she shouted, "You are the Eighth!"

She backed into one of the doors, and it turned into a watery film that I had seen before. It was a tera. The force of it began drawing her in, and with her clawed tentacles wrapped around my arms, me, too.

Napoleon sprang into action and grabbed me from behind, attempting to pull me back. But the pull was too great, and we all three began sliding forward. Light flashed from the swirling water.

Napoleon behind me. The creature before me. Together we fell into the watery unknown.

Darkness. Water. Spinning. Shadows. Rolling. Weightless abandonment.

And finally, solid ground beneath my feet. A horse neighing in the distance. Hooves riding hard against the ground.

My eyes opened. Instinctively, I turned my face up toward the sun, to feel the warmth of it against my skin.

Sand coiled around me, stinging sharply as it blew roughly through the wind.

The air tasted of dust and soil, reminding me of the dog days of August in Alabama when your clothes stick to your skin, the air barely moves and cotton is king.

My head jerked back. Zulika had materialized into a physical form and stood over me. She arched her back and screamed. An arrow was stuck in her back. In rage she clawed at it, and then, she turned from a physical being into black sand which swirled around me, scratching and biting until the wind carried it away.

In a haze, I looked around. A large figure stood hidden in the shadow of the trees, but I could tell who it was at this distance.

"Achiel?" I called out in hope, but a groan made me look down to see a single black boot, lying haphazardly on the ground. Four or five feet away was a body in great pain.

"Napoleon!" I crawled toward him where he lay sprawled on his right side. Sandy soil had blown in drifts around his arms and legs. "Napoleon," I called again, rolling him over to see his face. His eyes were closed, his lips silent. Sweat beaded around his forehead, and his hair was wet from perspiration.

Frantic, I felt his skin with my tseeyen. His heart was beating. He still had life within him.

"I will not let you go until you taste of the blood," I whispered into his ear. I pulled the blade from my boot and set it against my skin. He inhaled deeply and his eyes fluttered, stopping me in my tracks. His lips were slightly parted as he lay half asleep before me.

I could do this right now. I could let the blood drain through his lips, and he would wake in three days a changed man. A new man. A safe man.

I fell back onto my knees. It would be easier to do it this way, good even, but would it be right? I dug my hands into the hot sandy soil beside his arm. It was true that I had changed others without their express consent, but they had not objected either. Napoleon had made his choice clear. He had refused his parents' and my offer of blood more than once. I could not override his freedom of choice, so his life was not mine to save. At least not yet. Holding my clinched fist over his chest, I let the sand fall, slip into the wind to be carried away to places I would never know and never understand.

"Am I dead?"

His voice felt like water in the desert. Having someone with me right now meant having hope, even if it was Napoleon.

"No," I answered drily, "not yet."

Slowly, he raised himself up to his elbows, and then to a sitting position. He looked around, "Where are we?"

We sat under a blue sky that stretched as far as I could see. Something like pain or electricity or both cut through me as I looked out over the vast fields of cotton. Without another word I rose to my feet and smelled the dirt and soil in the air.

"It can't be," I began, but before I could finish, I was running as fast as I could through the field. Napoleon was calling my name, but I could not stop, I could not wait. My arm began to burn with unmistakable warmth that covered my entire body and seeped down through my soul. My heart was trying to fly out of my chest. My lungs tried to keep up with each rotation of thigh, knee, foot, as I ran faster and faster toward the dream I had waited so long to embrace. As we crossed through the woods, I knew it was here. As I burst through the final trees, I knew where I was.

"Home!" I cried, but the dream died in an instant.

"Where is it?" I turned back to see if I had come the right way. "Where is the house? I can't see the house!"

Napoleon came huffing behind me. "What house?"

"The Big House should be right there," I pointed across the vast empty field of trees as I turned in circles trying to understand where I was. I knew where I was with everything that was in me. Where was the house?

The sound of horses registered somewhere in the back of my mind. Confused, I turned again.

"Veralee, where—where do you think you are?" Napoleon wheezed. He bent forward and put his hands on his knees to catch his breath.

"We are at Red Oaks. I know this land, I know it!" I put my hand to my mouth and covered the desire to scream. "This is my home. But, my house is gone. It's like it was never there. The Oaks ..." then I realized how much was missing, "The large oaks that lead up to the house; they aren't even there! What's going on? Where are we?"

"We came through a tera," Napoleon said shaking his head and offering a shrug of his shoulders as his only help. "This could be the tera that Sarah used, or it could be ..." he threw a rock across the ground, "It could be a tera that thing opened. I don't know."

"Sarah?" Her name brought me back to momentary reason. "You think Sarah is here?"

"We didn't open the tera. And we were in the Tera Hallway that Sarah went down before she disappeared. So either Sarah left the tera open, or she re-opened it, or that thing opened it. Either way it seems dangerous to me."

"You sure know an awful lot about teras for a guy who doesn't even believe in them."

The war raging within him was so evident in his face that I blushed for him.

"Yeah, I guess so," he finally said. "My father was always talking." As he spoke his face took on a childlike innocence. "He always wanted to talk to me, to try to convince me. My mom would beg me to believe them, beg me to take the blood. I thought about it, I don't know, I—I actually planned to do it, but in my own time, you know?"

He stopped talking and looked off into the distance, and I didn't interrupt him. I realized this was something he needed to get off his chest.

"But they just wouldn't let it rest," he continued. "It started to irritate me, and then it just made me mad. We argued a lot about it." He dropped his head," Ok, so I yelled at them a lot." He looked at me again, "eventually they stopped talking to me about it altogether. I knew I was just being stubborn, and I guess by the end, they didn't know what else to say."

"Napoleon, I—" My apology was cut short by the sound of approaching hoofbeats. A band of four men were riding toward us on horseback. Immediately I thought of Atticus. He had had to survive situations just like this over and over again in travels along the River of time. What had he told me?

Ask very little questions at the beginning. It is better to be silent and let them talk when I first arrive.

"Napoleon," I whispered, "we don't know where we are or who they are. If they are Simulacrum or Boged, you have the curse of the Friguscor on your skin, so let me talk. If they are Friguscor, then you take the lead."

Napoleon agreed with a silent nod of his head.

The horses came to a stop before us.

"Who are you?" His accent sounded foreign to my ears. A plaid shirt and rough pants covered his medium-sized build. He had long jet-black hair that flowed almost to the middle of his back, chestnut skin, and eyes the color of coal. He lifted his gun slightly in our direction and used it to ask again, "Who are you?" The movement of his arm sent the sweet scent of honey and hickory smoke through the air.

"You are Simulacrum," I said smiling, as I offered the words of greeting, "Lignum Vitae."

But instead of answering, he nodded to the man beside him.

The second man, whose clothing and coloring were similar to the first, threw his leg over the back of his horse, hitting the ground with the grace of a gymnast. He took two light, but confident steps toward Napoleon, inspecting his skin in disgust.

Once his assessment was complete, he looked back at his comrades, passing on a silent but visible warning. With cautious eyes he turned to me.

"Do you seek the woman who came before you?"

Woman? I looked at the two men who stood only an inch or two taller than me.

"Sarah?" I asked, feeling the excitement. "Is Sarah here?"

"You have followed her," asked the man, "from what is to come?"

"From what is to come?" I repeated and looked at the two men uncomprehendingly.

"Have you come from the day after the sun has set?"

Feeling at a loss, I said, "You mean after the sun has set today? You mean have I come from the future?"

They nodded.

I looked at them, at their clothing, at the empty spot where my home should have been, and suddenly I had no idea how to answer them.

"I don't know. We came through a tera. We didn't open it. It was already opened, and we kinda fell through it. But I am looking for my grand—"

I stopped myself, the vision of Vera holding me as a baby on her back surfaced before my eyes and then slowly vanished. They noticed the catch in my voice as I said, "I am looking for a woman named Sarah. She is my—sister."

My sister. Sarah is not my grandmother; she is my sister.

The two men eyed each other and then made yet another silent decision.

"You are not welcome here," said the first man. "You have opened what should not have been opened. These gateways are to remain closed."

"Not welcome?" I almost laughed, "This is my home."

"This is our home," said one of the men still on horseback. He had eyes as wide as an owl, and a square head that practically sat on top of his shoulders without benefit of a neck. In seconds he and the fourth man dismounted and grabbed Napoleon's arms. He was calm as they tied his hands together.

"We are just here for Sarah. You heard the girl; it's her sister." Napoleon tried in vain to explain, "Then we will leave. We just need to get Sarah, and we'll be out of your way."

I noticed that Napoleon seemed drained, like he was having trouble even standing.

"No," said the man. He moved toward me as he said, "You come with us."

"Wait," I said trying to remain calm as he tied my hands behind my back, "Wait! Can you tell me where we are? Do you know the year? Why did you ask if I came from what is to come? Where is Sarah?"

I felt suddenly heavy, as though I was carrying a stone on my back. The muscles in my neck and shoulders began to cramp and spasm. I had no idea what was happening, but the unseen weight felt heavier by the moment, making it hard to breathe.

"I," they began pulling me through the trees, "I can't breathe," I stammered.

Still they pulled me forward. My knees sunk into the sandy soil as I fell onto the ground. Sound began to stretch out, blur into distorted voices.

"Lift her," said someone.

"It is the same as it was with the woman," said another voice.

Then another horse approached. Someone walked up swiftly behind me, his footsteps barely audible.

"She just arrived," said a voice. "Both came through the tera."

My eyes fluttered.

Someone knelt beside me, "They wear the same clothing as Sarah," a new voice spoke in the midst. I opened my eyes, desperate to see him, but the weight crashed down on my chest and I fell backward into his waiting arms.

"Can you hear me?" I would have known this voice anywhere.

I inhaled a hard, wheezing breath and for the first time since I had lost him, I spoke his name, "Atticus."

Ausley 1:5

"Welcome to BaVil's main research facility. Its formal name is MSHN, after a bunch of geneticists, but everyone just calls it the Machine," Austin smiled like a proud host welcoming me to his home, then pulled me into the hallway as though I were a dog on a leash.

"I know, I've been here before, remember?" I said as I looked at the concrete walls around us.

"You're losing your mind, Essie," Austin said, preoccupied by the detailed job of ensuring that his suit was lint- and wrinkle-free. "You've never been here before."

"I have," I said, certain of my memory. "Ellington is afraid of being down here. He will try to leave as soon as he can. He is afraid of the infected ones you are keeping down here for research."

Austin stopped picking at his sleeve and looked up at me, "How do you know that?"

"Because this has already happened..." I tried to explain, "You've already brought me down here, and there are people here imprisoned behind a glass wall."

Was that yesterday? I tried to remember, but now, I wasn't sure. Had I really been here, or had I just dreamed I had been here?

Ellington shifted his weight from one foot to another and scoffed.

"Look, I know you're scared and you should be. It feels like you are inside an ant's nest down here, and you are." I said, but suddenly, he raised his closed fist, signaling our group to hault immediately. The men tightened our circle and drew their guns to attention. Hegai stayed several steps away from me, but never out of reach. I felt him. My heart sang his name again and again, pumping hope into my veins.

Jackson.

"Are you afraid of what is down here?" I asked, surprised by my own knowledge of a man I didn't even know.

Ellington put a glove over my mouth. "Shut it, girl," he growled. He looked behind and in front of us before adding, "This disease has taken over most of our country. They don't want us, but they will kill us to get to your blood."

A rumble of screeching voices reached my ears.

"What's that?" I asked.

Fear stabbed my heart as the blood-curdling screams grew louder. My own blood began to pound in my ears and through my fingertips.

"That's the sound of the diseased inside the facility," Ellington answered with a mocking smile.

Austin suddenly looked pale.

"Don't worry, Ellington," Austin said with false bravado. "They are locked and secured behind the glass. There is no way out."

It sounded as though he were speaking as much to comfort himself than anyone else.

"No way out—you're sure about that?" Hegai said quickly. "If they smell her blood, it will start a stampede and they will kill us all."

Ellington spun around and stepped dangerously close to Austin, using the butt of his weapon as a motivator.

"I will not die for her," he said slowly, "and I will not die for your ignorance either. You have not seen what they can do. You have not been on the streets when they begin to feed on other humans. When they tear flesh from bone and leave nothing but empty shells of bodies in their wake."

Austin's face turned red with anger, and I saw his hands tremble slightly. Though he tried to be in charge, he was afraid of Ellington.

"You don't know anything!" Austin shouted at Ellington. "Your only job is to follow my orders! You are all so ignorant. You understand nothing!"

Austin walked up to an apparatus mounted on a smooth, concrete wall and applied his eye to it, as though looking into a microscope. In response, a hidden door slid open.

Ellington hesitated but followed, his finger on the trigger of his weapon. We walked through the door. I remembered this hallway, or one just like it. These were the prison cells, where the diseased had been housed behind the glass wall—or at least I thought it was the same hallway. Soon, I saw this hallway was different, lined with glass rooms, one after another, connected by glass doorways.

Austin, Ellington, and several of the guards walked down a stone pathway that led between the two long corridors of rooms while I stayed back by the exit. Each room held a classroom of children who were reading, studying, building models and small machines, and conditioning their bodies.

"These," Austin said proudly to Ellington, "will replace you in a few short months. Your days are numbered, Ellington. Soon you will be as useless as the diseased."

"You're going to replace highly trained soldiers with children?" Ellington laughed and so did his men.

Austin smiled, and it made my stomach turn. He pointed to the room of children, "These are the paramilitary of the future. Notice anything about them?"

"No," Ellington responded proudly, "They're just kids."

Austin smiled again, "Look closer."

We all looked at the children. They looked beautiful and perfect, though a bit robotic in motion. A child who looked no more than ten years old turned and caught my eye. His eyes were brilliantly blue, but odd somehow. Almost like they were mechanical and not real. Then all of the children in the glass room turned to face me as one. They all had the same eyes. I backed up until I was against the glass wall.

"Their eyes are unique are they not? Somewhat robotic, if you ask me but still, human in a way. That was an unexpected twist of combining the blood of the Aluid with the blood of the Friguscor and," he looked at me, "and the blood of the Simulacrum. They are called the Tres."

The Aluid...I had put together very little about them. I knew from watching the AR screens at the hospital that they were aliens, or at least that is what the Friguscor thought. They were creatures who were not human and had arrived on earth when the meteorite hit the ocean.

"Tres?" Ellington asked.

"Yes, it comes from some ancient story. I don't know," Austin furrowed his brow for a second. "Gilgamesh. That's it! The Epic of Gilgamesh. From the word Trestrenget. Who knows what it really means."

He shrugged, then waved at the child behind the glass.

The child raised his hand to wave back. The other children waved too, and I saw that they all had six fingers on each hand.

"The Epic of Gilgamesh," I said. "Mother had us read it, or parts of it. It's an ancient Akkadian legend about a cruel king who was trying to find the meaning of life. It's kind of an early story like the Iliad, something like that."

Austin looked annoyed. He obviously wanted to show off his knowledge, and I had stolen some of his thunder.

"Well, of course Gail would have taught you the epics. So, I guess you know what Trestrenget means?"

I shook my head, and he continued.

"In the story, Gilgamesh has a trusted friend who gets sick and dies. He does not want to get sick and die so he starts searching for some way to become immortal. That friend who died tells Gilgamesh that a three-stranded rope cannot be cut. These children are three strands of DNA in one body. In one body! They can never be cut down!"

"I didn't know you liked to read the classics," I said.

Austin sneered.

"Maybe I'm like that Gilgamesh guy. I have a trusted friend who tells me things, and I don't want to get sick and die. So, that's one of the reasons I've helped here at BaVil. And now, our scientists have found that the stories of legend were truer than we ever dreamed."

A door opened, and a man stepped out from the glass room.

"Austin?" Dr. Gerhard, dressed in a white lab coat, looked surprised. "You've arrived!"

Ellington and his men straightened their relaxed posture, as Austin stepped forward and embraced Dr. Gerhard. The embrace became uncomfortably long as the two men stood holding each other before us. Finally, they released their bond, and Austin spoke first.

"I was showing your work off to the soldiers," he said, and I saw him smile with genuine affection.

"They have been cleared to be inside the Machine?" asked Dr. Gerhard, glancing at the men.

"Yes," Austin nodded.

Dr. Gerhard smiled.

"Of course they have," he said, holding out a hand toward the children. "These children are the better you, the soldiers of tomorrow. They were produced in the Tower of BaVil, grown in the wombs of Friguscor women and raised here in the Machine."

"Yes," Austin continued, "under the careful watch of Dr. Gerhard, these amazing beings have been created!"

Gerhard smiled. "It was the knowledge of the Aluid that started this project, Austin, but if I do say so myself, most of the theory was my own."

"What do you mean produced, created?" Ellington asked, ignoring the prideful banter between Austin and Gerhard.

Gerhard cocked his head and nodded, pursing his lips together before answering, "They are the first of their kind. Genetically-engineered children. They have the DNA strands of three separate beings all braided together into one, small, child."

"Beings? You mean three different kinds of humans?"

"No," Gerhard corrected Ellington. "They are born of the Aluid, which are in no way human, created with the Friguscor, which are sub-human at best, and combined with a dash of Simulacrum, which," he turned and saw me standing against the wall, "are soon to be extinct."

He began to walk toward me.

"With the help of the Simulacrum, we were able to create a perfect vaccine, which given at the zygote stage of life, completely changes the genetic make-up of mankind."

He looked at me, "How old do you think these youngsters are?"

"About ten or so?" I hazarded a guess.

Dr. Gerhard nodded, pleased. "Yes, they do appear to be ten years old, I would agree, my dear. But ..." he held up his hand for effect. "They are actually only nine months old.

He obviously enjoyed the gasps he heard from all of us.

"Remarkable, I know. Genius, actually," he continued. "Yes, they skip the child-like years of mankind and become young adults in only one year. Of course, they are not the immortal beings we had hoped to produce. On the contrary, their life expectancy is actually pretty short due to their accelerated growth hormones from the Aluid DNA, but..."

He stopped and looked at me, his face unreadable as he continued. "But they are a beginning. We are on our quest as Gilgamesh was, and we will solve the mystery of immortality for the Tres."

An alarm sounded in the room, causing us all to look up. Dr. Gerhard huffed.

"Uggh. Those beasts are becoming my greatest problem! They can smell the blood from the Machine, and it is driving them mad! I'm telling you, Austin, I'm going to release all of them by the end of the week just to get them out of here!"

Dr. Gerhard ran down the hallway and out a door on the opposite side.

Austin turned back to us, his face pale with alarm, "We need to..." then he stopped.

All of the children in the rooms had turned and come to look out of the glass at us. One child, the first child that looked at me, raised his fist and began to pound softly on the glass. All of the others followed his lead. Their fists hit the glass, again and again, pounding out a message to me. It echoed out into the hallway and back to my ears. A constant foreboding of war drums.

"What are they doing?" One of the guards asked, "Why are they doing that?"

Austin shook his head, "I don't know."

Ellington turned and pushed past his men, "I'm leaving this place." We started hurrying down the hallway with the sound of the children banging repeatedly on the glass.

"We are done here, Austin," Ellington said once we stepped out back into the originally hallway. "I'm taking my men, and we are going!"

"We need to get the girl out of the hallway and into a secure area." Hegai cut in.

Ellington shifted his gaze away from Austin to Hegai, "Lock her up while we make sure everything is secure. At least that way we aren't with her if something goes wrong."

The guard to my left pulled me forward, "Come on."

"Wait," Hegai said joining my side, "I'll back you up." My whole body felt the relief of having him beside me.

Ellington agreed with a nod, "Find a place to lock her up while we find whoever works here."

Austin was seething as he snapped, "You're not in charge here, Ellington!"

"Sir," a voice from down the hall called out.

Several military soldiers were marching towards us. We moved quickly to meet them at the other end of the long triangular hallway. Their uniforms were very different from the guards with us.

As they approached, the large man in the front said, "Captain Koch, sir" he introduced himself and continued, "You are the visitors expected from the Towers. She said that you would be arriving tonight."

"She? What's going on here? What was that alarm?" Ellington asked, but the soldier did not acknowledge him.

"Has Absalom arrived?" Austin addressed Captain Koch, ignoring Ellington, too. Austin was obviously glad to have regained his prized position of authority.

Captain Koch nodded.

"Yes, he has asked to see you." He looked as though he would say more, but a loud barrage of screaming erupted in the corridor. It was a muffled, but clear sound of people shouting and screaming. Every hair on my body came alive. My tseeyen burned a warning all over my skin, and I fought the urge to run and hide.

"What is happening down there?" Ellington asked. "Why are they screaming?"

The soldier turned slightly but did not relax his perfect posture as he spoke with a slight sneer, "Afraid of the animals behind the cages?"

It was then that I realized how physically large the new band of soldiers were—and how young. Each one was at least a head taller than every man in our group. They wore no masks revealing very peculiar facial features, almost inhuman. Their wide, angular eyes were strangely blue and seemed to take in everything around them in a single glance. Most seemed to be barely teenagers.

With a shock I realized they were Tres, like the children we had just seen.

"I want to take the girl to see the Machine now. Dr. Gerhard has arranged everything with Dr. Murphy. She is waiting on us now," Austin said to the soldier.

"Yes," said Captain Koch, "but there has been a change in the schedule. I am sure you aware of the chaos that has erupted topside."

"You mean the virus. Yes, I am aware—"Austin began.

"No," said the soldier, "the Vanishing."

Austin looked momentarily dumb before regaining his self-important demeanor.

"I'm not sure I am following," he said. "It's been very busy at the Tower and—"

"People are missing," Koch explained.

"Missing?" Austin repeated, still not understanding.

"It's not a lot of people, but enough," added the soldier. "They vanished during a massive lightning storm at dawn. At least that is what has been reported. "

"Lightning storm?" Austin shook his head and raised his hand as if to slow down events he didn't understand. "What people are missing? Who is missing? And from where?"

Koch's face was void of any emotion as he laid out the data, "From everywhere. There are no bodies, no evidence of transport. People who were here yesterday are simply not here today."

Austin rubbed the bridge of his nose. "I need to see Dr. Murphy," he said.

"Dr. Murphy requests you wait until morning," the soldier replied.

"I have come on short notice to see them, and I expect to," Austin began his argument but was quickly silenced by the soldier.

"Sir, Absalom has given orders that you are to wait until morning. As I stated before, the disappearances topside have added to our work tonight. For now, he requires your assistance. He has returned with some more of the pieces for the COL, and Dr. Murphy is preoccupied by the final push to complete the in-house inoculations."

Austin's eyes widened with wonder and maybe a bit of fear, "The Cathedral of Light? Of course! Yes, will you take me now?"

The soldier narrowed his eyes at Austin, "From now on it would be wise to refer to it as the COL. Follow Captain Koch. He will take you where you need to go."

"What about the girl?" Austin asked the soldier. "This is Essie. She is a patient of Dr. Gerhard and—"

"We recognize her from the information blips," one of the soldiers spoke out suddenly. "We've seen her."

Captain Koch looked at the soldier with cool, calm disapproval that seemed more like a slap in the face. The younger soldier righted himself into attention and looked forward at the adjacent wall.

Koch said, "Absalom has left instructions for her care. We will deal properly with the Simulacrum," he promised without a hint of emotion. The captain turned and walked down the hall.

Information blips? Those were short commercials put out by the government to keep the Friguscor population informed.

"What information blips?" I asked Austin.

Austin dismissed it.

"We've been using them to educate the population about the inoculation. It's not a big deal."

"You filmed me?" I looked at him, feeling the ache of deep betrayal. "When did you film me?"

Without another word or thought, Austin followed like a dog, nipping at the captain's heels all the way down the hallway.

As soon as Austin was gone the soldier turned toward Ellington, "Follow us."

"Wait," I said and Koch looked at me for the first time. He looked at me with nothing in his eyes, as though I was an inanimate object that had somehow learned to speak. I continued, forcing myself to ask the question, "Why are those people screaming?"

Captain Koch did not even blink before he said, "Because of you. You have the blood of the Simulacrum in your veins, and they have the disease in theirs. For now, they are useful for research, and when the research is finished, they will be terminated."

Simulacrum. My throat tightened. Simulacrum. I felt suddenly naked. Completely exposed.

"Everything is known here," the soldier saw the surprise on my face and it pleased him. "You can no longer hide. We will find you all. Every last one of you." He drew out his last sentence for effect.

It worked. My jaw trembled. My heart beat faster. I couldn't hide the fear on my face. The soldier stared at me intently for a moment, and finally he smiled. But it was not pleasant at all.

"It is the end of you all. You don't belong here." The soldier turned abruptly, with robotic, precise movements and began to march forward.

Ellington caught my eye. His mask was still up, and I saw a new awareness in his eyes.

"Y'all," I called back unable to hide the tremble in my voice.

Koch stopped and turned back to me, "What did you say?"

I swallowed, "Here in the south we say 'y'all' not 'you all.'"

Captain Koch looked at me for a long moment and then turned away again. Under my breath I whispered what I had planned, before I lost my nerve, to say out-loud, "And that's how you know, you don't belong here."

Ellington stepped away from me as though I had the plague, and spoke to his men, "Take her to a cell, and then we are leaving this place. I don't want any part of this."

"Sgt. Ellington," a voice called from where the soldiers had gone, "You and your men are requested to come with me."

"We were just about to head back to BaVil," he said quickly, changing his plans on the spot, "We are needed back as soon as possible."

"No," said the soldier, "You are needed to report to the ward first. All soldiers must be vaccinated tonight. We don't want to take any chances."

Ellington looked somewhat pale but answered, "Yes, sir. Right away." Turning to Hegai, he continued, "Take her to the cell. I'll try to have someone relieve you soon. The rest of you, with me."

Somehow, I fell asleep inside the tiny, white cell. The lights stayed on permanently. I knew the walls were recording my every move, every sound. So, I found that sleep was the only true escape. At least there they could not hear me.

Sometime in the night, or maybe the morning, I wasn't sure, I awoke. The lights in the room were off. It was completely black. I looked toward the door. It was the door opening that had roused me from sleep.

"Hello?" I whispered, but instead of a voice, I heard the manual locks on the door twist into place. In the darkness, I could barely make myself breathe. I waited as someone moved toward me.

"Ausley," Jackson bent down before me, positioning himself on his knees. "It's me. Don't be afraid."

"Jackson," I touched his unmasked face with trembling fingers. "How did you get in here?"

"The power has gone down. There's been some disturbance, and the entire city is off grid. I've locked us in; we are safe right now, and besides, all the keypads have the same entrance code here. 22845...I guess it's because if you are down here, you are here to stay. No one seems to escape this place."

"Can they hear us?"

"No," he shook his head. It was dark in the room. I could barely make out where I ended and where he began. It was the kind of darkness that caused your eyes to hurt as they strained for any glimpse of light.

"What kind of outage could cause an entire city to go dark?"

He adjusted his weight from his right knee to his left. "The outside world is in chaos after the disappearance of so many people. People are afraid, and it's war on the streets."

"What?" The dark around us suddenly felt heavy.

"The lightning storm, it has knocked out all electricity. It didn't happen all at once; it's been more of a domino effect. Airplanes quit working mid-flight, hospitals went dark until their generators started up again, doors won't open at stores and houses. It's crazy out there!"

"What do you mean all electricity?"

"Ausley, this was something," he paused, searching for words. "Something that has never been seen before. I saw it on the AR screens before the electricity went off. There was no thunder, no clouds, nothing to warn anyone. Meteorologists have no explanation; it wasn't detected on any radars."

Jackson paused, and then painted a picture that I could see even in the darkest of rooms. "Ausley, it happened right as the sun started to rise. Almost as though the sun was the trigger. As the first sliver of light cut across the dark, a purple hue fell across the ground and then electric light streaked from the sky. There were thousands of lightning bolts, each one a brilliant flash of beaming light, spreading like pulsing tentacles across the purple sky. Pure white light zig-zagged so quickly that it blurred in the camera's lens."

I imagined the beauty of such an inexplicable scene.

"But what I couldn't stop watching was not the lightning itself, but how it spread," Jackson continued.

"Spread?" I asked.

"Ausley, when lightning emerges from a cloud, it usually spreads across the sky in one or two separate bolts, and then strikes the ground. This lightning looked as though it was upside down. I mean, it spread first all across the sky and then made direct lines to the ground, all at once! And it seemed to bounce back to the sky!"

I struggled to understand, "Wait. What? Lightning does not bounce back; the voltage is discharged when it hits the ground!"

"Yeah, and it didn't happen everywhere," he began to explain, "I mean, it seemed to be in focused points around the world. At least that is what they are reporting. And one of the main places was just north of Atlanta."

"Atlanta?" I whispered, "But why?"

"I don't really know," his voice sounded strained, "My mother, she used to tell me that we had family north of Atlanta and that if I ever was in danger I was to go there, to find my grandfather, Apex."

"I've never heard of Apex."

"You wouldn't" said Jackson. "My parents kept a secret. Something that I knew was never to be discussed. My family north of Atlanta; they were all descendants of Abram and Moses."

"Abram? The foreman at Red Oaks? The one who worked for my great-grandmother, Vera during the Civil War?"

"Yes," he said softly. "Atticus must have known. The day I met him in the library, I was afraid he knew our secret, but I wasn't sure. He was so proud to meet a descendant of Moses. He must have known all along what I was."

"What?" I leaned closer, "What are you saying, Jackson? What did Atticus know in the library?"

"Our family has a secret we have always kept about Abram. I never really believed it. My mother was so afraid for anyone to find out, so we never really discussed it. She finally told me, and I didn't know what to think. When I got older, I wondered why I never saw my grandparents, her parents, and finally she said I deserved to know. Besides, it was her obligation to keep our heritage alive. You know that Abram was a slave who was purchased by Ernest, Vera's father."

"Right."

"But, my mother also said that Abram had been different when they bought him. That he had been—Friguscor."

He paused. Even in the dark he must have sensed my doubt.

"Friguscor!" I cried. "What are you talking about, Jackson? "

"My mother, she's—it was the lightning strike, Ausley. That's when I knew it was all true. The moment I saw it, the moment I heard them calling it the Vanishing and naming who was missing."

"Jackson, you're not making any sense. Just tell me!"

"Ausley, my family that lived north of Atlanta, my grandfather Apex was," he swallowed, "was Boged. Like Damara, the girl you gave your blood to back at the Towers. He was Boged."

Damara. Her name brought back the memory of the girl in the hospital who had just given birth to a baby she would never see. A baby the Friguscor had killed. My neck throbbed as I remembered her teeth cutting into my skin as she drank my blood. Three days later, she had been Simulacrum. But Jackson?

"You are Boged, not Simulacrum?" I asked, thoroughly confused, "and you think the people who vanished were all Boged?"

"Yes," he said as though it was something altogether sacred.

We sat in silence.

"What does this mean?" My words broke through the thick darkness.

"I don't know," he answered.

My mind was racing, "But, it can't be ... if the Boged were the ones that vanished ... and you're Boged, why wouldn't you be gone as well?"

Jackson sighed.

"I've thought about this for the past four hours, and the more I put the pieces together ,the more positive I am. You see, I am not full-blooded Boged. I have pure Simulacrum blood in my veins. If my mother was right, if her father was Boged, and her mother was ..."

"Her mother was Simulacrum." I said knowing that to be true. And among the Simulacrum, linage passed through the women, not the men. Jackson's mother, Rosa Westbrooke is Simulacrum, so Jackson would be too, even if James, his father, was Boged.

Jackson looked at the door.

"I thought I could get you out with the electricity down," he said, "but they have generators going down here. It keeps the security fields up, but it's not enough to operate any of the elevators to get topside. And the people in here can smell your blood. I'm not sure the security glass will hold for long. For now, we are safer locked in here."

"Why can't they smell you?"

He smiled, "Maybe it's the suit, but I think it's more. I met a man, or maybe it wasn't a man. He was down in the basement of BaVil and he reminded me of the giants of old from the Histories that Veralee was always reading. He told me where to find you and they never found me. I honestly have no idea how it has worked for this long."

We sat still for a long, long, time until I could no longer keep silent.

"I knew it was you," I whispered, "I ... it just had to be you." Tears began filling up my eyes, and running down my face, "Why did you come for me?"

"At first, it was ... at first it was because you have always been like my sister, and ..."

The word sister cut me, left my heart dangling.

He couldn't see the pain on my face, so he continued.

"But as I watched you, I watched you almost die and then fight back, and then you changed the girl, Damara. I was so mad at you that day. I wanted you to leave, to go back home."

He stopped and considered his words, "But you didn't. You stayed. Ausley. I'm sorry that I wasted years watching Veralee. I'm sorry that I never truly saw you," he placed his hands on my face and brought his mouth to my ear, "While I was watching her, I almost missed the most beautiful woman in the world. I almost missed you, Ausley."

My eyes closed, and a million questions drove their way through my mind. Here, in the dark, the doubts were washed away as he whispered three simple words.

"I love you."

His words wrapped around me and raised my mouth to his.

"I love you; I always have," I whispered back.

"Will you bond yourself to me?" Those words seemed out of place, as though they were for a different time, a different place all together. Those words were meant for Red Oaks, for sweet tea and warm summer nights. Here in the cold, brokenness of now, those words felt useless, but still, they warmed the very soul of my heart.

As though he understood me already, he added, "I know that we cannot stand before the Oaks, and I know that I cannot wrap the cord that burns us together around our arms. But I love you, Ausley, and I want to be with you for the rest of my days. I want to know you are mine. The Eiani will honor our bond. "

With trembling fingers, he placed my tseeyen on top of his. The beat of his heart was unmistakable. The electricity undeniable.

"Yes," I whispered, answering every question his body was asking. "I will, from this day to the end of days."

We did not know the vows spoken under the great Sacred Oaks by those who had come before us. We did not know the secret ancient words they whispered to each other as they vowed their lives, bones and flesh to one another, but we knew the words in our hearts and so in silent agreement we vowed what we could, what we knew to one another.

"I will protect you, with every fiber of my being. I will die to see you home again, Ausley. I will love you until the end of days and beyond. I choose you, Ausley, to be my bondmate, until the Door opens and time dissolves into eternity."

"And I choose you, Jackson," I started to cry, and he kissed my lips with such tenderness that I forgot how to speak, "I ..."

"I know," he said kindly, "for it is in me as well."

Gently he fumbled with his shirt until he pulled it from his body. Immediately I felt the heat of his skin. In response, I pulled the shirt from my back, and we sat in the dark together. He placed a hand, hot as fire over my beating heart. I felt his words burn down through my spirit, uniting us with the mysteries of the Eiani. He covered my mouth with his and for a single moment, I felt a happiness flood through me that I had never known. "Jackson," I said his name as he laid my head back.

"Please," he said gently, "forgive me for being a fool, and do not ever doubt my love for you again."

I ran my hand bravely down his naked back as he kissed my face, my neck, and finally my heart.

Tears melted together, as the blood of the Eiani burned us into one.

Adair 1:6

The soldiers gathered the branches, and the breath of Ruach brought forth the fire. We sat encircled around the fire beneath the ancient oaks, listening intently to Ruach, thankful for his protecting presence. He was the only Archaon told to stay behind at Red Oaks. Achiel and the others had gone to war below the earth, at the City of Baryiach. The reddish glow of the blood moon and the flames of the fire tinted our faces, or maybe it was the seriousness of his words.

"Time has shifted," the great Archaon spoke, and the fire responded to his voice, flickering towards his rhythmic cadence. "What was not so yesterday, is today."

"What do you mean?" Eliezer, the brazen Chief Warrior of the Simulacrum Council, spoke first, "What do you mean, 'time has shifted'?

Ruach turned his giant head toward Eliezer, the firelight flashing brilliant light across his inhuman, catlike eyes that reminded us all of the great power behind his gentle voice.

"Yesterday time walked steadily toward its goal. On this day, it still moves forward, but with greater speed." He looked around and realized that we were still confused, "It is as though the same arrow has been retrieved and placed on the taut bowstring and released once again, though in the repeat, it has changed its course. "

I looked at Phineas, who in return looked at Ruach, Eliezer, and then back to me. It was obvious by the look on everyone's face that we still did not understand. Phineas adjusted his feet, and then looked as though he would speak, but he was preempted by Mattie.

She sat with her posture as straight as a Victorian Duchess, just like Mother's, and said, "He means that time is different today than it was yesterday. Time has somehow been altered and now, time is speeding up."

Ruach nodded in agreement. "The Guardian sees well."

Eliezer shot a confused look at Mattie. "The Guardian?"

I looked at the woman who just yesterday was my little girl. Time was speeding up, I thought. Is that why I feel like I can't catch up, like I am missing a lifetime with every passing hour?

"Yes," Mattie answered firmly. "I am now the Guardian of Red Oaks. My grandmother, Gail, sleeps."

"Sleeps?" Eliezer stood to his feet in shock, as he searched the faces around the fire for the one he would not find.

Tears formed on the edges of my eyes. I wiped quickly at them. From across the fire, I could see Eliezer fighting the same overwhelming emotion. Though he was hard headed as brick, Eliezer had been Mother's friend for longer than I had been alive.

"Gail has fallen," I said in an official tone, using it to hide my true grief, "The Guardian of the Gate of Red Oaks is now my daughter, Mattox."

"When did she ..." Rosa Westbrooke's voice broke, ending her question.

I should have told her before, but there had been no time. Rosa was mother's best friend. She had been a second mother to me most of my life, and now, her only son, Jackson, had been missing since that horrible day we came home and found Ausley and Daddy gone and the big house burning. Jackson had taken Nathan and Mattie to Veritas Hills, the Westbrooke's home, and then left, saying he had to check on something and had not been seen since. Rosa had no idea where her only son had gone and it was tearing her apart, though she would never admit it aloud. And now...how could I break Rosa's heart further?

"How did it happen, Adair?" Rosa asked, tears streaming down her face.

"She ...," again I felt the overwhelming loss of words, as though someone had erased the message from my brain. I dropped my head into my hands and silently let tears fall.

I looked up at them and tried to explain.

"Yesterday," I began, "my mother was awake, and today ... she is asleep. Her body is there in the house; the physical evidence of her is there ... when I woke up this morning, just before the lightning strike, she fell asleep."

"Do any here remember the hours of yesterday?" Ruach asked.

Yesterday my mother was alive. Yesterday Nathan was here. Yesterday I carried my little girl on my hip. Yesterday, the Boged had arrived. Yesterday I had learned that Veralee was changing people in the streets from Friguscor to Simulacrum.

Yesterday ...

"No," Ruach shook his head and looked directly at me. "These are not the things of yesterday."

Everyone in the crowd grew increasingly uncomfortable as he read the thoughts within the vaults of our minds.

"We hear your thoughts, but you think of days past; you cannot remember yesterday, for yesterday has been rolled like a scroll and will be your tomorrow."

No one dared to speak as the giant continued, lulling us with his songlike cadence.

"We see you do not understand the truth we speak. We will tell you of days long ago and of nights forgotten by man. The Archaon, we ancient ones, have the memory of the trees. Our roots are planted not within the bloodstained soil of this earth, but within Paraclete himself."

As Ruach began to speak, the forest seemed to press in around us. The trees went silent heir branches bowed a little lower than they had been earlier today. The sounds of the night, of the grasshopper and the cricket were hushed. They, too, waited to hear the words of the ancient creature before us.

When were you born, Ruach? The question floated across the expanse of my mind, and I felt his answer meet me there as he spoke without words, "We were not born, as are the sons of man. We came forth from the breath of the Eiani, in the beginning with the heavens and the earth, before the darkness spread over the face of the deep and all was without form and void."

"Oh," I spoke aloud, though Ruach had spoken inside my mind. He was watching me from the corner of his eye, bidding me to understand.

"Listen, Children of the Blood, to your History and remember the power of the Eiani. Before the time of the Simulacrum, was the darkness of the Friguscor, and before that, there was the time of the Original Men. When the Friguscor finally came to wipe the memory of the Original Men off the face of the earth, they marched to the City of Light to battle against the last warrior, Hizkiah. The Friguscor Prince led his army forth to drink of the blood of the Original Men and consume all that they had. With great strength and a mighty army, this prince, Sennache, the enemy of your people, rode from the east toward the great city of light. With the power of the night on his spear and the words of the dead on his lips, he conquered all within his path. Terror preceded him, and death followed closely behind. As his army advanced, Sennache sent messengers ahead to Hizkiah to deliver threatening words of discouragement and death. Hizkiah, forgetting the power of the Eiani within him, thought all was lost and fell ill, headlong into his bed. Still, he begged the Eiani to spare him the sleep in the Tombs of the Forgotten.

"As Hizkiah mourned in his bed, the Eiani sent a Wakeful One, an ancient being with words drawn from the River beneath the One Tree. With a voice as powerful as the wind and thunder, the Wakeful One delivered his message: 'Hizkiah, Son of the Blood, chosen by the Eiani for such a time as this, hear the words spoken across the waters of the One Tree. You grope for the wall like one born blind; You stumble at noon as in twilight. Your strength is poured out as wax. You moan and cry out for help, though you have closed the door with your own hands. But, the Eiani has heard your cry. You will not die in your bed, but will fall with a sword in your hand, leading the last of your men to battle.'

'Then all is lost," cried Hizkiah, "For we are the last of the Image-Bearers.'

'What will come for you has already been written, but the promise of the One Tree is true. The Image-Bearers will never again be wiped from the face of the earth.'

"The Wakeful One rose and hovered over Hizkiah's body. He blew into the king's nostrils, exhaling the words of the One Tree into the failing body: 'Your house shall not be forgotten for memory never ends,' said the Wakeful One. 'Your city shall be rescued, and you shall not sleep with the Forgotten. Years shall be added to you, for on the third day a deliverer shall come.'"

As Ruach spoke, I could not help but imagine my mother. Why had the Wakeful One not come for her?

Ruach continued: "Hizkiah did not trust the Wakeful One. He begged for a sign that all that was spoken would come to pass."

"A sign?" Eliezer sneered, "After seeing such a creature! How could he not trust what was right in front of his eyes?"

Ruach continued as though Eliezer had not spoken a word.

"The Wakeful One was prepared for Hizkiah's distrust and had an answer from the One Tree. He told the fearful king: 'On the stairs of Ahaz, you shall see the shadow of the sun regress ten steps. Darkness will be rebuffed, even as it progresses. The sun will march back three days for the healing of Hizkiah and for the rescue of the City of Light.'

"Then the Wakeful One breathed once again into the body of the king. For two days, even as the darkness spread across his boundaries and wielded swords against the men of blood, Hizkiah lay as one who had fallen asleep. When he awakened, the armies of Sennache surrounded his walls and blocked his gates, but Hizkiah did not fear. He was healed and his body refreshed, just as the Wakeful One promised. During his time of wakeful slumber, he had seen the sun spin backward for three days. He knew the words spoken by the Wakeful One were true. He rose and readied himself for battle."

"The Steps of Ahaz?" Eliezer spoke with disdain, "This is not our prophecy; we do not speak these words. These are the words of the traitors, of the banished ones! Why would you speak them here? Why now?"

Ruach's glare was dark and angry as he turned toward Eliezer.

"Truth is not determined by men. Your life is but a breath, a shadow of what is to come. Why does your kind always believe they can determine what was, or what is to come?"

"The traitors?" Phineas eyed Eliezer. "You mean the Boged?"

"Yes," Eliezer said fervently.

"They are all gone," Phineas told him. "They have vanished."

"Vanished?" Eliezer's second in command, Jonathan, spoke for the first time. "What do you mean?"

"The Seventh has fallen, and the promise to Hizkiah is fulfilled," Ruach spoke as a wandering troubadour singing his truth: "Time has been restrung on the bow and released once more."

"The Seventh has fallen?" Phineas asked quickly, "What Seventh?"

Ruach's eyes looked as full of compassion as the ocean was full of water, "The Seventh GateKeeper has fallen. Edwin, the Son of the Blood, has fallen."

Ruach nodded once and then sat silent.

James Westbrooke stood at this news, "Edwin has fallen?" He closed his eyes and took a deep breath. "These are indeed dark days." He walked to Miss Rosa, sat by his wife, and put a protective arm around her. Miss Rosa placed her head against her husband's chest and wept silently.

"How?" I trembled as I asked the question. I already knew about Daddy. Mattie had told me and Phineas, but I needed to understand more.

"How do you know?"

"We saw him fall beneath the earth, in the City of Bariyach. Though your grandmother's sister tried to stop it, these things were written long ago. They cannot be quitted any more than the ocean can quit the tide which pulls it to and fro."

"My grandmother's sister ..." I shook my head. "That makes no sense. I don't understand, how did he fall? How did he?"

"Beneath the earth, in the land of the Rephaim, the Dead Ones, the Seventh of the GateKeepers of Red Oaks, was slain by the hand of Uziel. When the Seventh GateKeeper fell, the life of the Seventh Guardian faltered for they were connected as no other bonded pair before them."

"You mean Gail fell because Edwin was killed?" Rosa said before I could interject. "We don't fall asleep just because our bondmate falls."

Ruach nodded and answered. "Willingly, he took the seat of the Guardian when it was not his to fill."

"But he had no choice," I interrupted. "The Law of the Simulacrum required Mother to step down. He had to take her place; there was no other."

"The GateKeeper stood before Wisdom at the Gate of Red Oaks and opened the Gate with blood that was not his own. He did not hold the key to the Gate, regardless of the Simulacrum law. He spoke the words but spilled her blood. This act joined their lifeblood together as one. In life and in sleep."

They sleep together.

The thought brought peace to my aching heart.

Mattie spoke. "Ruach, you are telling us that the spilling of my grandfather's blood was the trigger for this? That time turned back three days when my grandfather, the seventh GateKeeper was slain, just like in the days of Hizkiah?"

The great giant nodded, pleased that Mattie had understood.

Eliezer's face showed the dawning of understanding as he said, "But his blood did not hold the key to the Gate of Red Oaks, it held the key to Seventh Gate in the City of Bariyach beneath the earth. When his blood spilled out on the earth, it opened a Gate beneath."

"Turning back time three days," I finished for him.

"But why?" Eliezer looked at me, "Why do we need three more days?"

"And why have the Boged vanished?" Phineas added.

"The fullness of the Boged is complete," Ruach answered, "In the days of darkness, what has been divided will be united and the remnant gathered. For the sake of the remnant, so that not all are consumed by the fire, the One Tree has given the gift of the Steps of Ahaz. Three days of time. Time is a gift. You have been granted three days, though now, only seven are left on the clock."

"Seven days?" my heart felt as though it froze inside my chest.

Ruach stood and spoke as a father to everyone around the fire. "Remember who you are. Time is not your enemy, as it is to the rest of the world, but to those of the blood, it is a gift. The remnant has been given three and one-half days to prepare for the war that is almost upon you. Even now, the armies of Sennache gather once more. The prince who is to come will soon march upon the Gate to destroy all things made in the image of the One Tree."

"An army is coming?" Eliezer stood again, unable to keep his seat. "When will they arrive? Do they seek our blood?"

Three warriors stood in unison with Eliezer, as tension spread among us.

"They seek the Eighth as they have from the beginning of time."

"The Eighth?" I froze. "You mean the Eighth GateKeeper?" What had the girl Tessa said just yesterday? She had said someone was coming for Phineas.

> "Why do you need to speak to the GateKeeper?" I asked, "How do you even know of them?"
>
> "Because he told me to warn you. Someone is coming to kill you," Tessa said to Phineas. "Someone wants your blood."

"The Eighth who holds the key to the Creation Gate. The Sapru, the Malachi," Ruach answered.

Who would want Phineas's blood? Who would want him to fall?

"What is the Malachi?" I asked. Ruach wasn't making sense anymore. Phineas is GateKeeper, but not a Malachi, I thought.

I put my hands to my temples and pressed in to relieve the stress which had been threatening to overcome me all day. "What are you talking about, Ruach? We do not know these words."

"You should know them. We taught them to the Original Men and then to the Simulacrum. But, in your pride, your people let them lie fallow. Your fathers buried them so that you would live as one who does not know the date nor the time."

"He speaks of the Hidden Books," A clear and unexpected voice rang out.

I turned in unison with the entire crowd around the fire to see Deena the Judge of the Council, just outside our gathering. With her stood Issachar the TimeKeeper and Meridee the Discerner, together, in full authority.

"Deena? What are you doing here? How..." I began, but noticing an absence among them, I added, "Where is Naphtali?"

The holder of the seat of Wisdom for the Simulacrum Council should be here among these leaders of our people. Deena stood silent. I pressed her, noticing the tense set of her jaw.

"Deena? Where is Naphtali?"

Issachar the TimeKeeper, the old Caterpillar as my family had nicknamed him, seemed the only one who could speak.

"The days of darkness are upon us," his words trailed, connecting one to the other as though he spoke in cursive writing, "Naphtali is no more."

"She went into the Terebinths?" Phineas asked.

Eliezer dropped his head in respect, clearly saddened by the unexpected news.

"No," I explained, remembering my trip to the Marble Caves. I had been summoned by the Council, and even then, as I stood before the remnant of the Simulacrum Council, I had been shocked by Naphtali's appearance.

"Naphtali?" I had asked her name as if it were a problem to be solved as I had stood waiting to go before the Council elders.

"We live in the days that will usher in the end, Adair," she had answered as tiny pieces of her body fell to the ground as though she was nothing more than ash blown in the wind. She was disappearing before my eyes, one small piece at a time.

"I have little time left among our people," she explained.

"What is happening to you, Naphtali?" I had asked, horrified at her appearance.

"I am connected to Wisdom herself. It is the honor I shouldered the moment I took my oath to serve. And now, my position is being abandoned," she had answered, "In the days to come there will be no place for me, or her, among the tables of men."

Regret surfaced with the memory. I should have asked more questions.

"Naphtali, the Wisdom of our people, is gone," I said to the group. "She vanished one piece at a time, blown away like chaff in the wind. And if she is gone ..." Terror rose up my back and spread its fingers around my heart. "Wisdom, the Watcher at the Gate is gone as well?"

"What did you say?" Phineas said sharply, as though he was ready to run toward the Gate. "She can't be. She is the only one to allow us entrance into the Terebinths."

"And she is the one who keeps the others outside," added one of Eliezer's warriors.

Phineas continued, "We have to enter through Wisdom, and without Wisdom, the Gate is left open! She can't be gone!"

James Westbrooke stood and immediately began walking through the forest. I knew where he was going.

"What you said is true," said Deena approaching the fire, her small frame appearing taller in the shadow of the flames. "Naphtali is no more. And though I have not been to the Gate, for we came through a tera, I am sure Wisdom herself has departed as well."

We all looked toward Ruach who once again said nothing but nodded his confirmation.

"No!" Phineas exclaimed as he realized what this meant, "Then the Gate is more vulnerable now than it ever has been before! And the Seventh has fallen as well? Edwin is gone, Gail is gone, Naphtali is gone, and now Wisdom has left us as well."

"We've been abandoned." It was Miss Rosa who spoke. I turned to see her sitting alone on the outskirts of the circle. "We've been completely abandoned," she repeated despondently. "What will we tell all of our people who came here to Red Oaks seeking a safe haven?"

Miss Rosa was usually so hopeful, so her words fell hard on the collective thoughts of our group. They felt so utterly true. A wave of despair rippled through us all.

Abandoned. We were a people who had been abandoned.

"You are Children of the Blood. Trust the Eiani in your blood. Do not give in to despair," chided Ruach.

We all looked at him and wanted to believe, but the sorrow of the day's news and the gravity of the events were quickly swallowing our hope.

"There is still more," Meridee stepped forward, the familiar gaiety missing from her eyes. She had always looked as if she was standing in the full sun, but it seemed a shadow had fallen over her lovely countenance.

"We have brought someone," she whispered, her voice weak and unsteady. She moved around the campfire, looking at each of us expectantly. "Some will want to close their ears to him but hear me now. I tell you as the Discerner for the Council, we must not allow our emotions to define truth. What we feel matters little now. It is what we believe that will determine if we survive."

In all of the years that I had known Meridee the Discerner, I had never heard such grave talk come from her mouth. It sent a chill up my spine and instinctively reached for Mattie's little hand and was surprised again as the hand of a woman wrapped round mine.

Deena spoke with authority as she commanded, "Come and show them."

Nothing moved. We looked around, and then at each other to silently ask if anyone had seen or heard anything. No one had, and no one responded.

Deena closed her eyes, bit her lip, and then said even louder, "Come; you are among your brethren here." A little softer, she coaxed, "You have nothing to fear. Let them see you."

A branch moved in the darkness. Slowly, the silhouette of a man approached from out of the night. His back was bent, his gait twisted. As the fire illuminated his face, a collective gasp sucked the breath from us. My hand flew to my mouth, as I covered the choking cries that were coming unbidden from my throat.

Before us stood a man, or the semblance of what was once a man. Hollow cheekbones dominated his bony face, and dark, expressionless eyes stared back at us. His arms and legs were mere twigs, and his gaunt skin stretched tightly across his skeletal frame. He stood motionless, a statue of horror before us. I had never seen a person so emaciated, even in my worst nightmares. The screams I held against the back of my hand began to choke me.

Deena exhaled a long breath before speaking to us.

"You know this man," she said.

All of us looked again at the shell of what once, months or even years ago, had been a man but now seemed like a skeletal display in a science lab.

Ruach stood up, his height casting immense shadows behind the fire. He came nearer to the ghost of bones, and I thought I saw a tear sliding down Ruach's cheek. Out of respect I looked down at the ground, ashamed somehow, to see such hurt.

Ruach knelt so that he did not tower over the terrified man. "Do you remember the name given to you by your mother?" Ruach asked the man with such kindness that the man began to shiver, despite the nearness of the fire.

The ghost of bones did not answer, but simply shook his head silently.

Ruach closed his eyes, as though he was listening to something from far away. Then he spoke again.

"Do you wish to remember that which has been taken from you?" he asked.

The ghost of bones looked as though he would collapse and then nodded. Ruach took the skeleton in his arms and began a low, deep chant. Words pulled from the depths of the earth, or maybe the expanse of the sky, wove into a plaintive, but beautiful song. They shook the ground as Ruach chanted them over and over.

Then, slowly, a blue light shown from Ruach's hands. Mattie stepped forward. She placed her hand on Ruach's arm, joining him in song and effort. They spoke the old language, the language of our elders, the language of the One Tree:

From the blood of the Eiani. Lay the sinews and swell flesh upon you. From the blood of the Eiani. You shall be covered once more. Breath to your lungs, from the blood of the Eiani.

As he chanted, a rattling sound began. The ghost-man's bones came together, beating against one another. Knees against knees. Arms against arms. Ankles against ankles. His teeth chattered violently. And as I stared in awe, sinews grew over the gaping wounds on his legs and arms, and new flesh stretched across him. Fat filled in his hollow cheeks and skull-like eyes. But his lungs did not move.

He looked so still in Ruach's arms, as though he had passed into the final sleep.

Ruach commanded in the old language:

Four winds, breathe upon the slain that they may live and stand upon their own feet, an exceedingly great army.

Ruach opened his large mouth and blue air rushed from him and into the broken man's body. The man's chest heaved upward, his body completely encompassed in the blue healing light from the Archaon. A mighty wind roared across the wood. Trees bent, and the earth trembled. I stood, holding on to Phineas, trying to block the wind. Ruach closed his mouth. The wind ceased, and all was still once again.

With help from the hands of the giant, the restored man stood upright. Eliezer stepped forward, his mouth open in shock. He looked hard at the man, examining him up and down. Finally, the name slipped from his lips, "Joab?"

Not long ago, Joab and Eliezer had occupied designated seats as Chief Warriors on the Council seat.

Joab stood quietly before us, taking us in. He was not completely as he was before, but more than he had ever been. Though his face was familiar, something had changed in him that even the light of the Archaon could not restore.

"Joab? Is it really you?" Eliezer grabbed the shoulders of his old friend, gripping him with great passion. "But, you left us! You went with Absalom to join his Council. Why did you leave?" Eliezer's head fell to his chest as though he could not bear to look into Joab's eyes as he cried, "What happened to you, my brother?"

We waited, holding our breath. The horror of the emaciated man we had just seen was beyond comprehension, and I feared the explanation for what my eyes could not deny. I wanted to run, to take Mattie and Phineas and never look back. I wanted to be a coward, to stop myself from hearing anything he had to say, out of fear for what his words might mean for us.

Miss Rosa grabbed my hand and squeezed it. She looked up at me, and I saw the terror in her face. I wrapped an arm around her shoulders and felt the weight of her against my body.

Joab spoke as one who had been asleep for too long, his voice low and sluggish.

"It is true. I did not even tell you my brother, Eliezer. I left like a coward in the night."

He stopped and looked at the ground, great shame on his face as he continued, "I am the great-grandson of a poor farmer from Portugal who rose to take a seat on the great Council of the Simulacrum. But my family hid a secret, and I now believe many of yours did as well."

He stopped and took note of us all with exposing eyes that had nothing left to lose. Instead of explaining what secret his family had hidden, he said, "We believed that the Law kept us safe. And we believed a lie."

"Joab?!" Eliezer spoke with great contempt, "Listen to yourself!"

"Listen to him, Eliezer!" said Meridee. "Hear what he has come to say! Do not be a fool who closes his ears." She turned to Joab, her tone as smooth as one soothing a hurt animal and urged, "Go on."

Joab nodded and tried again, "I have come to tell you, to warn you. Do not be like me. I trusted in our ways, in our traditions, in our laws. I was hard-hearted and would not listen when others tried to warn me. But, I am a living witness to the truth. I tell you, the Law will not keep us safe. Nothing will keep us safe against what is out there." He pointed into the darkness and struggled to keep his face from straight.

Eliezer started to speak again, but the others hushed him with a motion of the hand. Joab didn't seem to notice and collected himself to begin again.

"At the Council meeting, when I saw what the girl, Veralee, had done with the little boy, I spoke out against her," he said. "It was against our law, our way! And I was bound by my oath to the Council to protect our law, and by doing so, our people! She had to be wrong; for if she was right, everything I had stood for and worked for over the years was based on a lie."

At that, he looked to me with an apology in his eyes as he continued, "I could not accept that. But in my heart the struggle was tearing me to pieces. I kept looking at that little boy and thinking about him, and I tell you, it shook me to my core. We Simulacrum had refused to believe the Boged were out there anymore. We had painted them into the same corner as a fairytale myth, and we refused to even talk about them!"

Joab gained strength with each word. "Yet, the proof that they still existed and that they could change was standing right beside Veralee. The little boy was Simulacrum! I could not reason myself out of it. I couldn't deny the truth standing before me. That boy had been changed! Finally, I admitted to myself that she was right, she had found a way. I was wrong. We were all wrong, but I did not have the courage to say this to anyone else."

He looked at Eliezer. "I knew what you would think, Eliezer, and I cared what you and the others would think of me. Still, I wanted to help right my wrong, my wrong attitudes and actions. And so, believing that he was going to help the Boged and the Friguscor people, I went with Absalom. "

"The Law is the only way! You have always known that, Joab!" Eliezer was struggling with his words.

"Yes," Joab agreed, "I had always believed that, but when the child came to the Council meeting, when what I had always believed to be true was no longer true—it was as though a brick wall came tumbling down, and I had nothing left to believe."

He looked at me, the LawGiver, as though he needed me to understand.

"So, I left this life, this way, and went to help the outside world. At least that was what I thought we were doing. It seemed right at the beginning." Joab stopped talking for a moment, nodding his head at some memory.

"The beginning?" Miss Rosa ventured, almost as if she was afraid to ask.

Joab halted, deliberating over his words. "Yes, the beginning, though I can no longer remember when or how it really began. It did not take long, or maybe it was months, But, I remember the end. I remember the day we were marched into the Machine."

"The Machine?" I said, and something in me knew I had heard this whole thing before. The impression came with such clarity that I could almost remember. Deena and Joab and this name, the Machine.

"What is the Machine?" I asked.

"I'm getting to that." Joab answered. "I have to tell you all of it so you will understand."

I nodded, so he continued.

"At first, they told us we were going into a safe facility which would house us and protect us from the Friguscor. As soon as it could be arranged, we were to begin training for our new assignments as part of the work force for BaVil. They gave us rooms in a complex, and I was able to go several times to one of their training facilities and watch their soldiers train. I even toured the hospital where they were getting ready to dispense a vaccine that promised to rid the world of the Esurio."

He swallowed again, fidgeting with his hands, "Several groups were taken to work in different cities, or so they said. We never saw or heard from them again, but now I'm pretty sure what happened to them." His eyes misted with tears and several spilled unbidden down his face, "I didn't know what was really going on until they brought us into something called MSHN."

"What does that mean?" Eliezer demanded.

Joab was getting agitated.

"It's an acronym for a medical facility named after some famous scientists, geneticists maybe. Mengele, Sangar, I don't remember the others. MSHN, but they just call it 'the machine.' They told us that we were going to help inoculate the Friguscor that day. We went willingly like lambs to the slaughter, because when we got there, we found out we were the ones they wanted. Not Friguscor, but Simulacrum. Men, women, and children. By the time we realized what was happening, it was too late. Do you understand?"

He began to groan loudly.

"It was too late! The children cried, and the women screamed. I tried to fight, but everything went dark as they stuck the needle into my veins. And then, it was as if I was asleep, but living in a dream. I knew I was hooked up to something, I knew I was surrounded by my people, but I could not move, I could not speak. We were prisoners, connected to a giant machine."

We sat in stunned silence. He was breathing very heavily as he said, "They labeled us with numbers. He revealed his lower calf, showing a number, 169061, tattooed in dark ink.

We were stacked in rows and drained like cattle."

"Drained?" the word hammered into my chest. "Drained for what?"

Everyone turned to look at me, and I knew I sounded simple, but I couldn't comprehend the horror of what he was saying. Human beings did this to other human beings?

"For my blood," Joab's face reflected the horror of his words. "They kept us alive through tubes and breathing machines. Our bodies, our naked bodies hung one on top of the other like clusters of grapes on a giant machine; and they kept us alive for one reason—for our blood. They were harvesting our blood."

"Harvesting?" Miss Rosa questioned, her voice cracking with emotion. "Is ... did you see ... is Jackson there?" As she said her son's name, tears poured down her face and onto her shirt.

Joab looked at her and shook his head, "I am not sure if I know your son, so I do not know. I am sorry."

This wasn't the Esurio, because these Friguscor weren't fighting over the blood. They were calmly and systematically draining the Simulacrum. Taking their blood. I looked to Phineas and found him looking back at me. I silently mouthed, the vaccine, and he nodded in comprehension.

Days ago, we had ventured into Samson for supplies. It was dangerous we knew, but it had to be done. What we had found was a town ravaged by sickness and fear. So many had already died. Yet, there was talk of a new vaccine, something that was supposed to not only cure the disease but prevent it from developing. It was the only hope, the people seemed to believe.

Phineas asked, "Does this have anything to do with the vaccine?"

Joab shifted his weight, as if his frame felt too heavy.

"I believe that our blood is in the vaccine somehow," he said, "and they are giving it to them. To all the Friguscor."

"They are putting our blood into them?" Phineas shook his head, "But why? Why would Absalom be so stupid? He knows that it will start the Esurio!"

"They are doing it to feed the Esurio!" Joab's answer cracked through the air like a whip. There was a collective in-take of horrified breath as Joab released the word into the air.

The Esurio was an ever-present danger to the very existence of the Simulacrum. It was the reason for our laws, why we were forbidden to share the Eiani in our blood. The Esurio was the hunger for the healing Simulacrum blood, the silent murderer, the sleeping lion that lay dormant in the veins of every Friguscor. Once awakened, the Esurio devoured and destroyed until all in its path was left a ravished waste.

I felt like I was going to throw up. Absalom wanted the Esurio? I didn't trust Absalom, but this? This was complete betrayal of our people! Even Absalom couldn't be that evil. It could not be true! My mind was spinning in every direction, and I felt my skin trying to crawl off my body. I was cold and feverish. Everything in me wanted to run away screaming from this story, but I was rooted to the spot, unable to speak. I had never felt such terror and revulsion.

In an effort to deny past episodes of the Esurio—though they didn't use that word—Friguscor government had banned books with any history or photographs of past occurrences. The Friguscor chose voluntary amnesia, a type of medicine to ease their collective consciousness. But I had seen photographs of the fields of the dead during the great wars of the last century. I have been told the stories of the massacres in Africa where millions died, or Eastern Europe when women and children found no safe place to hide. The tales of the Asian prisons, the Middle Eastern and Russian genocides, the European expulsions and murders could not be erased from my memory, nor from the collective memories of the Simulacrum.

Daddy had told me long ago that the ability to rewrite history, to forget the horrors of mankind was the true reason the Friguscor had outlawed paper products. Books were destroyed, digital stories were altered, so the evil of man could be forgotten. But we Simulacrum would not, could not, forget. It was written in indelible ink on our minds.

Esurio

The inked number on Joab's calf screamed the truth of his story.

"That is not all of the horror," said Deena. "There is more. Not only is this so-called vaccine increasing the chaos around the world by setting off the Esurio, it seems that the vaccine contains more than just our blood!"

Joab blinked several times before speaking. "Yes, the vaccine is a mixture; it has our blood, and Friguscor blood, and the blood of those who claim to have newly arrived to Eretz. The Aluid."

Joab spoke in a hybrid of languages, using Eretz, the old language word for earth.

"Newly arrived? From where? Like aliens?" Rosa had regained her composure. Maybe she had taken some comfort in the fact that Joab could not say for sure that Jackson was there.

Ruach interjected, "These creatures do not have their origins in another Eretz as they have declared."

I stared at the giant, thinking about his size, his superior knowledge and wisdom.

"What are you saying, Ruach?" I asked. "Are the Aluid like you? Are they Archaon?"

"No," said Ruach. "They lie, for they are of their father, the Usurper, who was a liar from the beginning. I do not understand why you do not know of this. Is it not in your Histories?"

Deena looked shamed, but spoke up, "This knowledge is lost to our people. The books containing these stories are—missing."

The giant looked at Deena for a long moment and then said, "The time has come for that which has been sealed to be opened. "

Though he was obviously frustrated by our ignorance, Ruach looked around at the group and melded his story with Joab's.

"The fathers of the Aluid came from among us, that is true," he said. "They walked among men and taught man the way of the One Tree. But, because of their knowledge, they became puffed up and conspired to lift themselves above the One Tree. So, they rebelled against Paraclete and followed the Usurper. They looked upon the Daughters of Men and coveted what was forbidden. They did not stay in their proper domain but left their own habitation and took women for themselves. These are kept in chains in the City of Bariyach until the final battle, though the One Tree has allowed the Usurper to roam the earth until the appointed time. The offspring of their rebellion are the dead ones, the giants of the night, the children of darkness. The Rephaim."

Ruach paused for a moment to allow us to take in this new revelation. I momentarily placed my hands over my eyes. I knew this was somehow related to the deaths of my Mother and Father.

"Wait a minute! I don't understand," said Phineas. "You're saying these Aluid are the Rephaim, that they are the offspring of a union between a Watcher and a human female. Look at you! You couldn't...I mean...how is that even possible? I mean...is that possible? And if they all died, how are they now on the earth?"

Ruach did not address the "how" question, but just let it stand as fact. Instead he answered Phineas's last question, "When the rebellious watchers joined with the daughters of man, their offspring were clothed in the flesh of man, though they had the strength, the intellect, and almost the size of their fathers. But, flesh withers like the grass of the field. Today it is green, but tomorrow it is no more. The shades have no kingdom and no habitation. They have been imprisoned in Bariyach. As the Gates of Bariyach open, they are released. They seek the flesh of those who will yield to them for a habitation, for their rebellion is not yet complete."

"Wait a minute," said Eliezer, "are you saying that the freed Rephaim are inhabiting the bodies of men and women?"

"Yes," the giant explained. "The thoughts and intentions of their hearts are only evil, and they cast out all goodness."

"But, why would they mix our blood together?" I asked, completely at a loss for words. "Friguscor, Simulacrum, and Rephaim? What could come of such a mixture?"

"I have told you that their rebellion is not yet complete. They wish to eliminate the image of the One Tree and build a new kingdom, a kingdom made in their own image. But take courage, Children of the Blood, they will win many battles, but they not prevail. The One Tree sees the hearts of all men, and Paraclete scoffs from on high."

We, the image-bearers of the One Tree, stood in shock. The darkness of the night grew suffocating. We searched for answers to questions we did not understand.

Miss Rosa stood up and finally broke the silence.

"I have no idea where my son is," she said. "We have lost almost everyone we care about, and the Esurio is just miles down the road." She shook her head slowly and deliberately. "And now you are telling me that they are mixing our blood with some dead creatures and giving it like a science experiment to the Friguscor to see what they can create? We have to do something! How are we going to protect the ones we have here at Red Oaks!"

Eliezer's gruff voice broke the brief silence.

"We will build the wall," he said.

"Yes," said a warrior to his left, "we have to protect the Gate. We have to protect our people!"

"A wall?" Phineas was able to question Eliezer before I could even get the words out, "What do you mean, a wall?"

Deena nodded and caught Eliezer's eye before speaking, "I will send messengers to all the Gates that still stand. We will put out a call for all Simulacrum to come to Red Oaks. We can survive if we fight together."

"What will you use to build such a wall?" This time it was Mattox's voice ringing out.

Eliezer grabbed a stick and began to draw out a rough sketch on the ground as he spoke, "We will build a wall around the land using the Oaks of old that have protected our people since the beginning." Added Eliezer, "This must be what the Histories meant." He grew louder with excited as he said, "The words themselves say that the Oaks were born in the beginning for the end of time! We must use now, at the end, what was given to us at the beginning!"

"A wall?" I looked at Phineas, "Wait, you mean you want to cut down the Oaks? They are already a wall as they are. What are you talking about?"

"No," said Eliezer, "We have to survive, Adair; do you not see him?" He pointed at Joab, "Do you not see what is coming for us?" He pointed to Mattie and then directed his comments straight at me, "They are coming to Red Oaks. Not one will be spared!"

My heart began to pound, and my head felt dizzy, but I refused to give way to it. Instead I stood my ground, ready to counter them, but Phineas stopped me as he placed a hand on my shoulder.

Suddenly, Ruach stood, unsheathing a long-curved blade and raised it to battle position. The moment he unsheathed the weapon, it shone with a vivid blue light. The air became electrified as my tseeyen rang out in alarm.

"What is it, Ancient One?" Eliezer came to stand near Ruach, reaching for his gun and unlatching the safety. Immediately he was joined by as many as fifteen more warriors while the rest followed his nonverbal command to spread out into the trees.

Phineas turned to me, "Take Mattie and Rosa," he commanded and then joined the other men.

Mattie grasped my hand as we stood together. Deena was calm as she stood looking out into the night.

The shrill cry that came from the darkness made my face flush with heat and fear. My overtaxed heart pounded even faster and louder, my palms began to sweat. The heat of the night began to feel suffocating. We looked all around us in search of the source of danger.

Red and yellow flames licked at my back, and I turned just in time to see a beast, with claws as long as my arm, soaring over the heads of several warriors, and bursting through the fire, sinking its teeth into my shoulder as it brought me to the ground. The smell of it was as overwhelming as the pain of its teeth deep inside my flesh. The screams of terror filled every part of my mind as it reared its head back, revealing several rows of jagged, sharp fangs that looked as though they had been sewn onto the face of a woman. With her back leg, a bent and scaly thing that looked like it had once belonged to a dinosaur, she crushed my knee with surprising power. I heard the bones crush and scatter into a million pieces, but I was effortless to stop her as she reared back to sink her teeth into my flesh once more.

But before she could reach my neck, bullets began to burst all around us. The creature pulled back, being hit with force of several bullets at once, but it did not lose its steady balance. With great power, the beast dragged its spiked tail sideways, taking out several people as the razor-sharp boney spines made impact with their arms, legs, and sides. The tail swept back and forth, a swinging sword cutting through the air and flesh.

Deena was struck hard in the face and fell to her knees, her blood pouring down her chest and onto the ground. The beast lifted its head, sniffed once, and turned toward her. It pounced with little effort onto Deena's small frame, her body bending oddly beneath the weight of the beast. More bullets, at closer range were shot into the animal. It stopped and lifted its head in a powerful roar toward the onslaught of weapons, pulling its attention away from the body of Deena. But it did not drop or stop.

The beast moved her head sharply to the right, and noticing Mattie, stopped suddenly. An odd sound, like a purr came from the back of her throat. She was arching to attack Mattie just as Ruach plunged his blade of light through the beast's stomach, lifting it high into the air as though it was rat on a stake. The beast roared and screamed, kicked its feet and clawed at the air, trying to free itself. But Ruach, in one fluid motion, twisted and pinned the animal to the ground with the long blade.

I rolled to my side, grasping my neck as Mattie began screaming, "Mother!" into my ear, her hands working to stop the blood flow coming from my shoulder. I said nothing and watched as though from a dream, as Ruach pulled another blade, a shorter one from his calf greave and cut the head of the rat completely off. Her head rolled once, twice and then stopped inches from where I lay. Her jaw inhumanly open, her tongue slacked toward the group, her eyes, her cruel eyes stared lifelessly into my face.

Day 2 Boker

Separate Water from Water

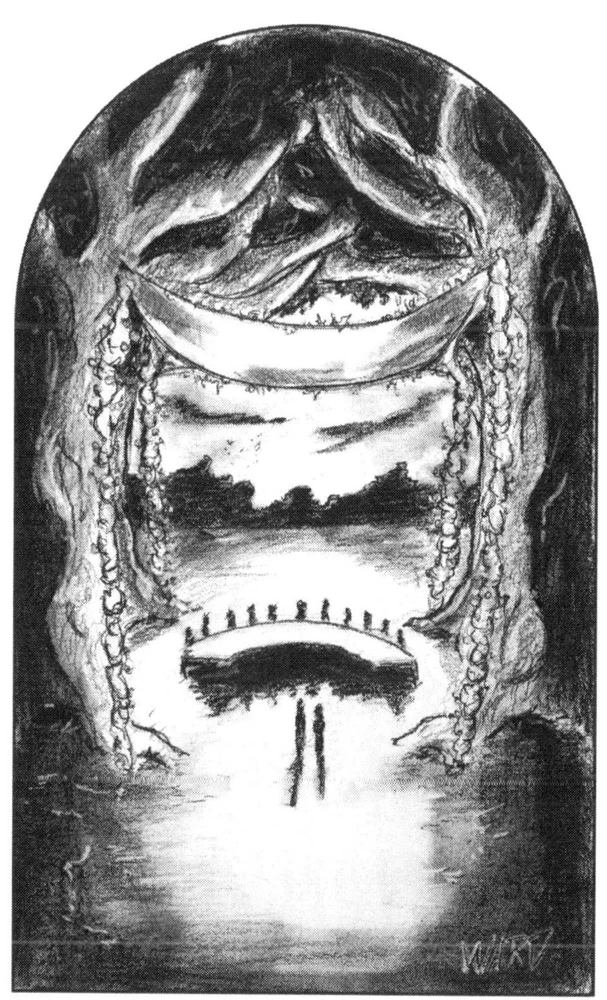

Ausley 2:1

The heartbeat of the organism they called the Machine was accelerating. I could hear it through the walls. Its rhythm of urgency burned a warning through my tseeyen. When the power was restored, Jackson stepped outside to guard the door in his role as Hegai. I remained in the room, gloriously happy for the first time since I had left my home.

When I heard someone unlocking the door, I thought it was him, and rose excitedly to meet him, hoping he had found a way out.

"Ja— " I began and stopped short as I reached the door and it opened.

Jackson was not there. In his place, well-armed female soldiers, obviously very young, ordered me to follow them. Fearful, I hesitated.

"Come," said a large soldier, with the mechanical blue eyes.

We marched down the hall, then another and another, each looking exactly like the last, turning a dozen times.

Jackson, where are you?

Finally, we stopped in front of a large door. It opened outward as if on cue. When I did not move to walk in, one of the soldiers shoved me forward into the room and stepped quickly back into the hall. Before I could react, the door closed me in, and I heard the sound of the lock as it engaged. I turned away from the door and faced a cavernous room filled with the sound of flowing water. The room was dominated by a massive, rectangular infinity pool, with dark water floating out to face a rock wall. Ten shrouded statues flanked the pool, five on either side, each with a large bowl of fire balanced atop her stone head. I soon realized the shrouds were formed by water, flowing from under each bowl and down over their feminine figures.

The water looked like it was drowning them and preparing them for burial all at once. I shivered and turned my attention from the statues to the pool.

Across the pool was a rock wall. By the rushing sound, I could tell the far edge of the pool was the top of a waterfall that dropped into unseen darkness. Wind blew from the unknown depths below, creating a breeze in the room that swayed even the heavy metal lanterns that hung on long chains from the ceiling.

An ensemble of women carrying exotic stringed and percussion instruments came from a door on one side of the room. They began to play soothing melodies that made me want to lie down and sleep.

Four women appeared silently from doors on the side of the room. Each carried a bowl, similar in size to the bowls of fire above the shrouded maidens. Each bowl was placed on the side of the pool, spilling over with spices, flower petals, oils, and other things. Without saying a word, they came and took my arms to lead me forward. I shrank back when I saw their eyes and six-fingered hands, but the strange odor in the air made it hard for me to think, much less protest. I noticed smoke was now coming from the bowls of fire. It floated out, creating a haze across the water, and I wondered if it was also causing the haziness in my mind.

"What are you doing to me? Am I to get into the water?" I asked as a woman with hair as red as fire and electric blue eyes began to take my clothes from my body. Though I protested I began to feel far away from the action. My mind was covered with a thick fog, just like the waters of the pools.

"Wait, I need my clothes," but my apparel fell softly, with my pride, to the floor. Another woman, with the same eyes, led me into the waters while the others began to float the bowls into the water beside us. Another tossed scented rose petals around me, while another woman placed floating candles on the water. The water began to heat around me. I saw that the warmth was coming from the bowls of fire which were being filled until they tipped over and poured boiling water into the pool. It had been so long since I had bathed that I did not fight the process, but instead relished the warmth of the clean waters. The attendants surrounded me but allowed me space to bask in this unexpected luxury for about an hour or so. Time felt irrelevant. With the soft music and heady incense, I fought to stay awake. Maybe I dozed, but if I did, the women kept me afloat.

The aroma of fresh, hot bread jolted me to awareness, and I realized I was famished. New attendants were bringing plates of delicacies. I recognized fresh dates, pears and apricots, grapes, nuts, and olives. There were creamy cheeses, thinly sliced meat of some type, and the hot, fresh bread that smelled heavenly. Trays of pastries that I did not recognize followed. Another poured what appeared to be a dark wine into a golden chalice. They waded into the water and presented the trays to me.

After these preparations, the women began to wash me. "I can do this myself," I tried to explain, but they neither acknowledged my words or responded in any way. They made not a sound as they washed my hair and scrubbed my body, lathering me with creamy body wash and buffing my skin with elaborate sponges. As we stood in the water together, one of the women pulled from her floating bowl a braided gold headpiece and wove it into my hair. The headpiece had a large emerald that hung in the center of my forehead. They styled my hair with braids, weaving in pearls and other jewels. Earrings of gold, studded with emeralds, diamonds, and pearls, were placed into my earlobes just before they led me out of the water.

Towels were brought to me, which were equally warm and soft. My skin was dried and lotioned from top to bottom. My nails were manicured and painted with an elaborate gold design.

Then one of the attendants left the room through the side door and returned with the most elaborate silk gown I had ever seen. In the candlelight, it shimmered a rich emerald green or gold, depending on how the light hit it. The gown had a high collar and neckline, and the back of the silk bodice was embroidered with golden thread and jewels. The front, from neck to waist, was a transparent panel of gold lace to cover my chest. The skirt was also embroidered with a similar motif front and back. Emeralds and diamonds woven into the design cast tiny rainbows of color onto the silk as light hit them. A high slit in the skirt over my right leg allowed me to walk freely but also revealed more than I liked.

Finally, one of the women put shoes studded with jewels on my feet and clasped an A-line cloak of gem-studded tulle to the tall collar of the dress. It had a full, billowing train that flowed across the ground.

"Why are you doing this?" I asked for the tenth time, "What is happening?" I tried to talk to them, to ask them what was going on, but they spoke not one word. When they did look at me, it was with obvious disdain. It was as if I didn't exist, as if I were a living mannequin to them, worth their attention only because I would display their work.

And just as I had entered, I left. The door to the hall opened and the attendants led me to the opening. They stopped at the threshold and guided me forward with a thrust of their hands. I stepped into the cold, concrete hallway. Suddenly my mind engaged. What just happened to me? I looked down at the gown and felt the softness of my skin.

"Let us go," Austin was waiting there. Then he added, "You look lovely."

I looked down at the dress.

"Why am I dressed like this?" I asked, "Why are they doing this to me?"

"You are dressed for the part you are called to play in this drama!" Austin said as he touched a piece of my hair, "I told you, we all had to do our part."

"I'm dressed like a prosti—" my eyes fell on Jackson. He was here, standing behind Austin. The memory of joining myself to him floated on the edge of my mind, touching my lips and my arms as I remembered his embrace. I wanted to run straight to him, but I was embarrassed for him to see me like this. My face flushed, but I was comforted; at least he would be guiding us forward, wherever we were going. We turned down an unknown hall that somehow felt vaguely familiar.

"Essie?" Austin snapped his fingers, "You have to focus!"

"Focus?" Rage flew all over me. I suddenly felt secure in a way I had not in so many months. Jackson's embrace from last night, the strength of his arms still wrapped around me in a way that I knew would never leave me. I longed to touch him again, to hear him speak my name as he did in the dark hours last night. It was his strength that flowed through me now.

I took my eyes off of Jackson and focused on Austin's face as I asked, "Where is my father, Austin? I know he is still alive. Where are you keeping him?"

Austin looked pale as he held his hand up, gesturing for me to stop, "Let's not talk of that now. As I said before,"

"Tell me now, Austin!" I pressed him, "Where is Daddy?"

"No!" Austin screamed, running his hand over his bald head, his fingers trembling, "That is done and over. Do not ask me again!"

He was shaking with rage, a skeleton of the man I used to know. Once, the blood of the Eiani had flowed through his veins, but now...

"What happened to you, Austin? When did you give yourself over to them?" I challenged.

"Give myself over?" His eyes narrowed in discontent as he pursed his thinning lips together, "We all have to adapt to survive, Essie."

"Maybe surviving isn't the point," I answered, willing him to hear me, and suddenly I felt as though the words filled my entire body as I spoke, "You can win the whole world and still lose in the end. And if you are against the plan of the One Tree, you will lose, Austin. Do you hear me? You will lose it all."

Any familiarity between us was quickly evaporating as he almost whispered, "You are so self-righteous; you should look at yourself in the mirror."

"But I didn't choose this," I said, holding out my thin arms as proof of his crime.

His laugh was hollow. "Oh, yes you did. Remember? You chose it all!"

"Austin," I said, grasping my hands together to stop them from shaking, "Please, tell me. Is my father still alive? I remember what happened at Red Oaks. I remember coming down the stairs and you were arguing with Daddy and..." I stopped, barely able to form the words. My throat constricted as I spit out, "I remember it all; Absalom shot my father!"

Passion fueled my words, my heartbeat accelerated as my thoughts came faster and faster, "But he didn't fall asleep. I saw my father in the basement of BaVil. I spoke to a giant who was sitting in the room, and I saw ..." The memory of Daddy hooked up to machines and an old man who I knew was Absalom lying in the bed next to him was burned into my mind, "I saw Ab—"

"You saw nothing," Austin swung the words as though they were to be a noose around my neck. Swiftly he stepped forward, his fist clinching with rage. A low fire began to burn at the base of my spine as I remembered the last time I had been alone with Austin in my cell back at BaVil. He had punched me in the face with a closed fist as though I was nothing more than a stray dog. It was Jackson who had entered and stopped him from beating me any further.

"Are you going to hit me again?" I did not fear Austin, not with Jackson by my side. "Like you did back at BaVil? You never could take the truth, could you? That's why you stayed away so much. Daddy must have seen right through you, and you couldn't handle someone seeing the real you, could you? You've been a traitor since the beginning, and Daddy must have known it. But the thing I can't figure out is how?"

"How?" He looked disgusted.

I looked at the man before me and searched his face for an answer.

"How did it happen? You have the blood of the Eiani inside your veins; how could you become a traitor? I understand how the Boged can become Simulacrum, how the dead can come alive, but what I cannot figure out is how the Simulacrum can turn into the Friguscor. How can one who was born truly alive become the living dead?"

"You arrogant bitch," Austin said in a low, angry tone. "I hope I can hear your screams when he breaks you open."

"Even if you do," I said, matching his fierceness, "it will not be the end for me, but for you, your destruction is already complete."

He pulled back his hand to strike me, but Jackson caught his arm midair.

Jackson forced Austin's hand down as he said, "She is property of Absalom. You know the rules."

Austin shoved Jackson hard against his chest.

"Back off, Hegai, before I have you thrown out of this facility. You can't protect her anymore."

Thrown out.

Those words struck fear into my bones like nothing else Austin had said. For the first time I became suddenly aware of how dangerous this was for Jackson. As we walked Austin began ranting a long diatribe of thought, but I could not hear him. One question echoed in my mind. How had Jackson stayed hidden all of this time? How had they not discovered him? Could they not smell the Eiani in his blood?

But I couldn't.

The thought hit me. The suit covered any smell from the guards. Jackson had never lifted his mask like the other guards did, he had never taken off his gloves or exposed himself in any way that I could remember. And, he had always volunteered to stay with me, which none of the other guards had wanted to do. But still, I wondered, how?

Nervously I kept one eye on Jackson walking ahead of us and the other on Austin as I watched the about-face in Austin's emotions. Our footsteps echoed against the concrete halls as he became more and more excited. Between Austin's rambling ranting, I caught the words, "the whole army," again.

Austin continued, "The vaccine is being distributed throughout the population." Austin was puffing up with pride again as he spoke. His mood swings were incredible as he spoke with joy, "The Friguscor are being changed!"

"Into what?" My words were not so much a question, but a true accusation.

"Into the image of the future!" Absalom announced as he came marching toward us, his boots clipping against the concrete floors in a hard, cold tempo. Several men walked behind and around him as though he were a treasure worth protecting.

"Yes, the image of the future!" Austin crowed as Absalom's entourage stopped before us. Absalom was no longer wearing a suit and tie but had returned more to his old ways of my youth, when he wore the long black robe of the Seer. Today, he wore black trousers but had donned a flowing black coat that hung past his knees in sharp points on each side of his legs. The back was shorter, made of strips of thin material that hung in a jagged line and flowed through the air when he walked. His bald head was shrouded in a black hood.

"Hello, child," he said as his eyes roamed slowly up and down me. "Ah yes, my girls are worthy of their wages; look at what they have accomplished! Our little country bumpkin is now Nefertiti, Helen of Troy, and Grace Kelly rolled into one, the very image of perfection. He leaned close to my face, and inhaled deeply, "Ah, the fragrance of the garden of paradise. And when the farmer finds such fertile ground, is he not negligent for leaving it fallow?"

I recoiled as I smelled death on his breath but as he pulled back his hood, his face was remarkably changed. As though time itself had moved backward across his face, his once aged appearance was now ironed straight with clean, crisp, youthfulness. He smiled at my surprise, but I found his face cold and calculating.

The memory of him in the basement of BaVil flooded into my mind again. I had seen him lying in a bed next to my father. Almost like a desiccated animal, Absalom had been incredibly emaciated and lay absolutely still, like a corpse. He was receiving a direct transfusion of my father's blood, sucking the life from my father. He had looked as though he was dead but now, he looked younger than I had ever seen him. I would have sworn he was no more than thirty years old.

And his eyes. I shuddered.

"Yes," he said knowingly, his sinister eyes flashing, "They are the color of your dearly departed father's."

He leaned in close to my face, his hood touching my forehead. "I am grateful to his blood for giving that to me." He smiled but his eyes grew dark as he added, "Nothing is as it was, child. Everything has changed."

He leaned in one more time and inhaled before he slowly kissed my cheek. I grimaced and it took all I could do to keep from slapping him in the face.

He chuckled as if he had read my thoughts. "Yes, my dear, my youthful vigor is wonderfully restored, but alas," he continued, "is it not the mark of a loving father to sacrifice for the good of his child, and indeed, for the greater good of all? I cannot argue with the logic, but," he sighed as he looked at me with unveiled hunger in his eyes, "no sacrifice is without the pain of loss."

I had learned Absalom's way of speaking in riddles. It was a rouse. Usually, he was speaking the truth, but was twisted up into a riddle to make it become his version of the truth, which in the end, was never true at all.

"Hegai," Absalom turned abruptly from me to face Jackson, "that is your name, is it not?"

"Sir," Jackson dipped his chin in a quick, deferential nod.

"You are relieved of your post for now. I will take charge of the prisoner."

Jackson hesitated. Sweat began to drip slowly down my back as Jackson stood his ground, unmoving before us.

A man, standing to Absalom's right side barked an order:

"Report to the clinic. All personal are to be vaccinated immediately."

"Can't he stay?" I asked, knowing I should keep silent, but fear forcing my hand. "I—I have become accustomed to having him near me."

Absalom lifted one eyebrow. "As I said, everything has changed now, my dear. What you once were accustomed to is no more. It is the new day."

Absalom turned toward Jackson. "Go and see that you are vaccinated. I will take the girl from here."

Jackson still hesitated, his feet frozen to the concrete floor beneath him. Absalom moved closer to him asking, "Is there a problem?"

"No, sir," Jackson said. "It is just that I am still on duty, and my orders are to guard the prisoner."

Heat ran up my back, and I felt a wave of nausea.

Did Absalom know?

As soon as the thought went through my mind, Absalom jerked his head toward me.

I looked at the ground as I worked to control my thoughts, to focus.

Mother.

I thought of her face and forced my mind to wrap around the image of her standing in her sewing room. I felt Absalom's mind move away from me.

"I am not to leave my post until someone has come to relieve me." Jackson said.

I knew that Jackson was trying to hold the strings together, but the look on Absalom's face told me it had already unraveled.

"As I said, I am relieving you." His tone told us that he would not be challenged any further.

I gave a quick, begging look toward Jackson. I wanted him out of danger.

Go, please, go.

He answered with a short, "Yes, sir," turned on his heel, and walked away from me without another word or glance.

Relieved for the moment, I wanted to watch him walk away, but I forced myself to stare down at the ground. I knew better than to give way. I could feel Absalom's probing tentacles on the edges of my mind.

"Come," Absalom said with a flick of his wrist. "There is much to see, and today the fullness of your purpose will be complete." Austin kept close to Absalom as we made our way forward.

We walked through a grand entrance of stonework, which seemed out of place against the cold, institutional blandness of the rest of the facility. A curved walkway of impressive design descended seamlessly into a deep cavern cut into the earth. The cavern was vast enough to hold a small village within it. It seemed as wide as it was tall. Soldiers, moving like ants with clear purpose within the nest beneath the ground, scurried quickly to and fro, giving the air a tense feeling of urgency. Monotones of greys and browns gave the space an earthy feeling that felt void of fresh life or fresh air. With each step, the air become colder. Below I could see some sort of a large stone structure at the center of the ant city.

Absalom said, "Beautiful, is it not?"

My thoughts were racing. Images and impressions were hovering just at the edge of my conscious mind, just out of my grasp.

I know I've been here before. I remember this place.

"You have," Absalom said, biting the words with his harsh accent.

"Have what?"

"You have been here before, of course, because of the coiling of time. Actually, my dear, time has moved backwards three days because of the Ma'alah Achaz."

"The Stairs of what? Time has moved backwards? That is impossible," I answered. "I don't know what you are talking about."

"The Stairs of Ahaz," said Austin, lifting his head condescendingly and speaking as though he were a Seer himself. "It was the prophecy of protection surrounding the Seventh Gate. The GateKeepers thought it was safe with them, the fools. But of course, you know all of this; because you were taught the Histories by the one and only Gail Harper," he goaded, his tone full of contempt.

"Oh, wait. That's right," Austin continued, enjoying his moment. "It's on a need-to-know basis, and since you were never to be the Guardian, you wouldn't need to know!" He smiled cruelly at me and continued. "Well, you do know the Gates were created in the beginning to bring about the end of time. It is brilliant when you think about it. The women have one key, and the men were given another. Each one was just as important as the other, though each one had a distinct purpose."

He gave a short, pompous laugh.

"You're talking nonsense," I said, calling his bluff with truth. "How would you know the secrets of the GateKeepers? You are not a GateKeeper."

Austin's chest rose up and down visibly as he answered, "No, but their secrets do not die with them."

Daddy.

Absalom rushed to my mind, but I quickly hid the thought. I worked to control my emotions. I would not believe their lies. I had seen Daddy, alive, back at BaVil, but something else haunted my mind. A memory, just out of my reach which made me fear trying to capture it.

"You have so much running through your mind, my dear child," Absalom cooed. "The rewrapping of time must be pressing heavily on you, as it is on all of us. Trust me, I, of all people know how difficult the encumbrance of time can be to shoulder. It is particularly arduous now that it has coiled backwards when, before now, we have only known it to advance. This is a miraculous thing, I will admit. Certainly not what I anticipated."

He paused for a moment, and the whole company came to a halt. He shook his head as if considering options.

"Had I only known that was what the prophecy meant, maybe—but alas, we only know what we know, do we not?"

He looked directly into my eyes. "And yet, you are struggling now to grasp the fragments that lie at the edge of your consciousness."

"I don't understand. You are trying to tell me that time itself has reversed? Today is not today, but is three days ago? Is that what you are trying to say?" I shook my head in disbelief.

Absalom pulled his arms from the folds of flowing fabric to gesture, and I gasped. Both arms were covered intricately carved silver metal. One silver arm started near the elbow, and the other from his upper arm. Each ended in metal hands with pointed nails.

"Yes," he explained as he flexed the fingers. Then he pulled the metal gloves off, revealing skeletal hands. Small patches of flesh, muscle, and tendons covered his arms and hands, but it looked as though someone had thrown acid onto them, eating away most of the flesh. "It was an unfortunate event."

I could not help but grimace, "What happened?" I asked in spite of myself.

"I struggle to comprehend how the time warp has rewound some events, but not others," Absalom replied as if in explanation.

Austin showed no surprise, but stood silent, looking toward the marble and concrete structure ahead of us with nervous apprehension.

Absalom put the gloves back on, "Yesterday, I believe it was yesterday, it's hard to know where we are in time right now. Well, whenever that was, we finished vaccinating the army and began vaccinating the public. But that is not what was most important. Yesterday, if it was yesterday," he looked directly at me for effect," we killed your father."

"No," I said, fighting to keep my knees from buckling, "No."

"My hands," Absalom continued nonchalantly, "were severed when I took you to Red Oaks through a tera."

"Took me to Red Oaks?! That didn't happen," I protested as I searched my mind for any memory of that.

"Memory is notoriously unreliable, my dear. It can deceive us all," Absalom explained.

"I would remember if—" I began.

Austin shook his head, "You do remember, in a way. It's like you remember a dream or a far-off memory, that's the power of the Ma'alah Achaz."

I shook my head, "I don't understand."

Absalom clicked his metal fingers together as he spoke, "Yes, the promise given by the One Tree, the words spoken so long ago. Something most of the Simulacrum buried and forgot. Only the key itself remembered. The key locked inside the blood of the GateKeepers. Yet, there were others, not of our kind, who remembered each word of the prophecy. They knew that the fall of the Seventh GateKeeper would trigger the sun moving back ten steps on the stairs of Achaz. Three days back in time, and then seven days for the fullness of all things to be accomplished. Three, plus seven equals the ten steps on the stairs."

"An ancient way of telling time," Austin added.

I put my hands to my temples.

What were they talking about? My father was not a GateKeeper. He was the Guardian of the Gate at Red Oaks!

"Ah ... things are not always as they seem, my dear. Was not your mother Gail, the Guardian?" Absalom cooed, answering my thoughts.

I was taken aback at his accuracy. Absalom had always been good at sensing what someone was thinking or feeling, he was the Seer for our people after all, but this was something altogether more potent.

"If a book is left open, should not a reader see what is inside?" Absalom said, deflecting it back to me.

"But my mother wasn't the Guardian. My Father was!" I argued.

"And who then," Absalom continued, "was the GateKeeper?"

"I—I don't know," I conceded, realizing that something about that arrangement of my parents was odd.

"Yes, the arrangement between Gail and Edwin was certainly not the norm for Guardian and Gatekeeper," he said. "There is much you do not know, but I will tell you what the ancient prophecy foretold. It said that with the fall of the GateKeeper, the Seventh Gate in the City of Bariyach would open. But, even those among your people who remembered the prophecy did not wholly understand what it meant. For what could they have known about Gates beneath the earth when the Simulacrum only remembered the Gates above. Time, as it always does, has revealed the truth of this mystery. For the Seventh Gate of Bariyach has fallen and in response, we have all seen the sun go back on the steps of Ahaz."

"Bariyach?" I asked.

"The City of the Gates, the City of the Rephaim below the earth and, well," Austin cooed, "we've gone backward three days in time."

Knowing my confused thoughts, Absalom smiled with pleasure.

"Do you not want to know how the Seventh Gate of Bariyach fell?"

"No," I shook my head, stepping away from the two men before me. "You lie."

"Your father, my dear, was the Seventh GateKeeper, "Absalom declared.

"Gail and Edwin lied to keep the secret about Veralee!" said Austin.

"Enough!" said Absalom. "I will not be interrupted another time!"

Austin cowered, and Absalom continued.

"Yes, my dear. Your father was the true GateKeeper, and your mother was the true Guardian of Red Oaks. They concocted their story to cover the fact that the Council had removed your mother and appointed your father to the post of Guardian when he was in fact the GateKeeper. Most on the Council knew the truth but agreed to the deception for the common good. However, the gifts and callings of the One Tree are not subject to the traditions of man. The keys in the blood of the GateKeeper and Guardian of the Gates are mirror-images. The key in the Guardian's blood opens the Gate to the Oaks of Mamre. The key in the GateKeeper's blood opens the Gate to the city below."

"If what you are saying is true, then my father is still alive in BaVil! You still have him hooked up so you can live off his blood!" I felt heat rising in my throat.

Absalom remained calm, "Yes, logic would dictate the truth of your version. However, as I said, I cannot account for the reversal of some events and not of others. Your father has fallen, and his body lies beneath the facility of BaVil. His blood was the trigger for the Steps of Ahaz. He could not return, for if he did, the recoiling of time would not have occurred, and the calendar would remain paused. His death was foreseen and inevitable. My arms remain injured and only partially restored. I do not have the explanation, and for some reason, my vision on this matter is partially obscured as well. I need more information."

Reaching into his robe, he produced a book and thrust it toward me. "Have you ever seen a book similar to this one in your father's library at Red Oaks...Or anywhere else, for that matter? Perhaps if we could find this book, we might be able to reverse these events. Perhaps in the book, there might be some way we could prevent the unfortunate events that have befallen your whole family. Restore what has been lost to you...your sister, your father, your home..."

The book had a beautiful engraving of a peculiar star on the front. It opened from the left instead of the right. Hope flickered in my belly; was it possible that these horrific things could be reversed as though they never happened? Could this book really have some secret knowledge?

I reached for the beautiful book, but when Absalom saw no recognition in my eyes, he quickly retracted it.

"Think carefully, my dear. It is very important, more than you know. Are you sure you have never seen one like this anywhere on Red Oaks? It has information concerning the Gates below the earth, and the coming days."

Hope dissipated. Absalom was toying with me, "No, " I spit. "I've never seen that book before. I would remember that. Besides, there are no Gates below the earth," I said emphatically, unable to stop myself from trembling before him.

He pushed forward, his voice becoming darker.

"Pity. I believe the matching book truly does offer us knowledge we need for the days ahead. We will not abandon our search for it. Regardless, you speak of things that you do not know, and I tell you of things which I have seen with my own eyes. Below the ground, where the death of the Friguscor reigns, there is a City of Bariyach, where the dead ones rule!" he said.

The air shimmered, and suddenly I saw his words come to life before my eyes. No longer was I standing before Absalom. I stood before a large Gate made of the bodies of men and women. People, stacked one upon the other like timbers, were molded together to form six large pillars, three on each side creating the doorframe for a monstrous bronze door. At the top of the door was a keystone that must have been more than fifty feet across. The men and women looked dead but screamed as though still alive. They clawed at one another, pulling flesh from bone and devouring it.

There was no wind. No air moving at all, as though I was in the deepest recesses of the world, at the bottom of a dark ocean. From behind the Gate came a terrible roaring. The blackness grew, and the pillars shook. The bronze door heaved forward but did not give. A great beast pushed against it. How I knew it was a beast I could not tell.

It cannot hold.

Abject fear struck me, and I had to force myself to breathe as the thought came to me.

The Gate cannot hold for long.

I felt something warm and looked down. Blood soaked my bare feet. The groans and screams of the dead assaulted my ears. I looked up. Above me hovered statues of large winged giants with great swords and shields. The smell of rotting flesh overwhelmed me, and I fell to the ground.

Suddenly, a hand thrust up through blood pooling on the ground and grabbed me. I kicked and fought to free myself, but as I struggled the creature that held me gained leverage and rose from the ground. It was a woman wearing a twisted metal crown. Getting hold of my other arm, she held me fast, and I was forced to my knees, facing her. Her dead eyes opened, and in them I saw my own mirrored image. She opened her mouth and vomited a fish which landed on my lap.

"NO!" I screamed as I fought to free myself from her grip. My eyes closed tightly as I kicked to get away from her. Blood splashed up into my mouth and then, suddenly, I heard Austin calling my name.

"Ausley?" Austin called again, "What are you doing?"

Panting, fear rushing through my body, I opened my eyes and found myself on the ground with Absalom standing over me.

"Did the blood which touched your tongue taste of home?" he hissed. "Could you taste your father's blood in the blood of your people that is being poured out even now, as an offering before the Eighth Gate? That which you saw was the Eighth Gate, the final Gate left to be opened. Yesterday, we spilled your father's blood and opened the Seventh Gate of Bariyach."

Tears ran down my face, but no words came. No amount of denial could cover what I had just seen. Everything in my being knew it was true. The Gates of Bariyach were real, and my father had fallen asleep.

A loud boom filled the air, as though canons had been fired into the air.

Absalom shifted his attention.

"They are almost here," he said to Austin. "Get her up and bring her down."

Austin dragged me to my feet. My mind felt disconnected from my body. Fear began to paralyze me, but Austin forced me to move down the walkway.

We stopped at the entrance to a large courtyard of stone. Before us were stone steps that led to a giant U-shaped structure I was sure I had seen before. It was decidedly Greek, with smooth marble colonnades on three sides. Large marble steps filled the center of the U, and at the top was a stone table, like an altar of some sort.

A shapely woman came halfway down the stairs. She moved silkily through the air, and I knew immediately I had seen her before as well.

"Rahab," Absalom said, his voice thick with lust.

Her name echoed in my mind

Rahab, I know you.

Rahab smiled back at Absalom. She was larger than any woman I had ever seen. She wore a striking red gown cut to the waist like mine, but without any lace cover in the front. Her flawless skin and large, full breasts were completely exposed. As she spoke, she kept her eyes fixed on Absalom and dragged her hand seductively down her chest until rested it upon her right hip.

Then she spoke.

"The Kings wait anxiously for the bodies of men."

"They are almost here," Absalom answered.

Then she turned her attention to me. With her nose turned slightly up and her mouth gaping open, she appeared to be tasting the air as she descended the remaining steps.

"And the girl? Will you offer her to them?"

"No," Absalom said. "She is for another."

Austin stepped back quickly as Rahab came near, his face a mix of pleasure and terror.

Rahab came straight for me, gripping my face in one large, strong hand.

"Do you remember my voice?" she asked. "Of course you do."

She leaned in and pressed her lips on mine.

"I never tire of the smell of honey or the taste of it," she said breathily, her lips quivering. "I could get drunk on the taste of your blood."

Fear pressed against my windpipe, taking my breath away. She smiled as though she felt it too, or maybe, it was an unseen hand of her own that clutched my throat as well.

"Be a good girl and you can win a crown too—Daughter of the Blood." She laughed and turned back to Absalom. The memory of the dead woman who wore my face and a ruined bloody crown brought on a wave of nausea.

"You do not have much time," said Rahab, as a pounding sound grew in my ears. "Look, they bring the bodies of men even now."

At the top of the stairs, dark figures began to emerge from behind the pillars.

"They are here!" she gasped as she hurried back up the stairs. "If you do not want to lose her, take her from this place! Once the Kings have entered the bodies of men, they will feed on whatever they find."

The ceiling opened like a giant door. A red blood moon hung high above, casting a spellbinding light down into the cavern. At first all was silent. But then, as fast as a moving train, the sound of beating wings entered the room. It rushed toward us, heavy and fast until the first bird swooped through the opening, circling high above all of us. A second, a third, and then a fourth until as many as twenty giant birds circled the ceiling. As they came lower, I realized they were not birds at all; these creatures had bodies similar to birds but faces and features of human women. Beneath their wings they had human-like arms, and I saw that each carried something in those arms. As each creature flew in, it dumped its burden, creating a heap in front of the stone structure, a moving heap from which came moans and screams of terror.

"Those are children!" I gasped in horror.

Absalom smiled as he turned and pulled me away.

"Yes, children are always the sweetest."

"Those are children," I repeated, trying to take in what my eyes revealed. "What are you going to do to them?"

"Come," Absalom commanded me, pulling me from the room now filled with the screams of children who were waking to a nightmare, "You must not be here when they enter their bodies."

We left the cavern-like room through a side door, and I was ashamed of the selfish relief I felt when the large steel doors slammed shut behind us. I wanted be as far from the evil of that room as possible, but still I had to ask, "What are they going to do to those children, Absalom?"

Absalom turned to me, and I thought I saw a shadow of compassion cross his face, or maybe it was simply nostalgia for what he was once capable of feeling. I could not be sure.

"When the Seventh Gate opened, the Shadows of the Kings of Old entered our dimension, our world."

"Through a machine of some kind," I said, certain without knowing why or how this knowledge came to me. "A machine that harvested the blood of the Simulacrum."

How did I know that?

"Yes," Absalom nodded, watching me carefully, "The Caldron. The blood of the Simulacrum coming from the Machine provided the power to open the bridge between the dimensions. The blood of the Simulacrum not only created the vaccine, it brought the dead into the light. But, they had no physical body as they appeared. They were still of the dimension beyond ours. With those children, we have provided a vessel for each of them to have a dwelling."

"But what happens to the children when they—"

"It matters not what happens to these children; they are Nakusa," Absalom interrupted. He stretched out one cold metallic hand and clamped it around my arm, twisting my wrist upward. Using his other hand, he sliced through my thin skin with a needle-sharp index fingertip. My heart hammered in alarm.

"What are you doing?"

I saw that we had stopped in front of an ornate antique door. Absalom smeared my stolen blood on the door. The door was so out of place against the concrete walls that I was sure it must lead to another world.

I looked helplessly toward Austin, hoping in vain to find the protector I had once known. Instead I found only a mask of nervous apprehension covering over his hollow face. By the tension in his arms and the heaving of his chest, I knew that he still cared, but in his eyes, I saw his heart. He did not hate me. He simply loved himself more.

"Austin?" I cried out in alarm and confusion. I should have realized he would abandon me.

He whispered, "Don't fight. You'll only make it worse for yourself." Then he stepped away, disappearing into the shadows.

Absalom had already slit his own wrist and was now smearing his own traitor blood over mine. As I watched, the door turned to water. A ripple began in the center and spread out to the edges, consuming the door.

Absalom looked at me and smiled to himself, "With your blood, and the blood of your father in my veins, we have access to a tera. Though you cannot open a Gate, you can still open a tera."

I had no time to scream, no time to ask any questions. Before I could even pull away, he pulled us both into the tera, beneath the rushing waves of the River. Water filled my lungs and we twisted together for no more than a second, though it felt like an eternity.

I burst forth, breathing in the cold, damp air above. Absalom stood up, water dripping from his coat and pants.

"Come," he commanded. "Get out of the pool."

As I stood, I realized that we were in a rectangular stone pool of water in a long hallway. Burning torches were mounted high above us on each side of the hallway. Absalom pulled me roughly from the pool, cutting into my already bleeding wrist where his metal fingers gripped me.

"Where are we? Where have you taken me?" The smell of honey drifted through the hall and I felt as though I was close to home.

Absalom stopped and faced me, water dripping from his hair as he spoke, "These are the Tombs of the Forgotten. The ending place of your ancestors. I thought it a good place, a fitting place, for your new beginning."

"What new beginning?" I asked, fear dripping from my words just as a drop of water falling from my chin landed upon my chest. Absalom followed the drop of water with his metal finger, letting his hand rest on my collar bone. His touch sent alarm down my arms. He noticed the vibration of my tseeyen and smiled sideways before licking his lips.

"Death and new life. Both are new beginnings, wouldn't you agree, my dear? And here, behind these walls, you are surrounded with the only legacy your family has: death."

Fear boiled in my stomach. I looked around for an escape and saw doors down the hallway. If I could just get to one of them. Absalom laughed with satisfaction.

"Well, it would almost be fun to see you try, but I think not!" He clamped down hard on my arms and leaned very close to me. "I will give you new life." His eyes were darkened by the unmistakable taint of desire, but it was the cruelty that truly scared me. He was enjoying the taste of my fear. He took a deep breath, smelling my skin and my hair.

"You smell like her, you smell like Chauvah. And the fear in your eyes, just like Chauvah." He slithered the words across his lips, letting them linger on his tongue, and then unexpectedly stepped back.

"But, I have brought you for another," he said.

"Another?" I was not sure what was happening. Was this real or was it a dream?

"My son," he smiled.

I pulled hard for freedom, feeling his metal fingers cut into my skin.

"Your son?" I swallowed, my heart breaking apart, "Let me go, Absalom, don't do this."

Absalom forced my feet forward, and with impossible strength, dragged me by several doors.

"Absalom, you're hurting me! Please, don't do this!" The walls around me seem to be closing in as panic soared through my veins. "Absalom! Let me go!"

At the open door, Absalom sent me sprawling into a cold room cut from the bedrock. In the center was a great stone table that could have once held a sleeping body. The air was charged with energy, electrifying every sense in my body.

"Do you know where you are?" asked a voice as smooth as polished quartz. Like an animal, I shifted on all fours toward the sound of the voice. A beautiful creature leaned into the shadows just behind the stone table. He was against the wall, arms crossed leisurely over his broad chest. I could see only part of his face, while the other seemed lost to the shadows in the room.

Behind me, Absalom slammed the door as I ran toward it, pulling at the metal ring with all of my strength. My fist ached as I banged on the door, screaming for help.

"Do you know where you are?" said the beautiful creature again. His voice was calm, but cold. I turned, keeping my back cautiously against the wooden door.

"Where am I?" My breath caught in my throat; I was suddenly very cold. The thought of Jackson slammed into my heart, pounding a silent plea that he would never hear.

"Do you know what you hold inside of you?" The beautiful man, with blazing blue eyes, and silver hair stepped forward one small step and hovered between the light and myself, casting his shadow over me. Fear pulsed like lightning through me but I refused to draw attention to it and instead stood still, forcing my hands beside me and my thoughts to a position of attention. My tseeyen began to send strong signals of alarm up and down my arm.

"You have a message system. An intricate book written over six centuries ago in a little garden far away from here, in a language which had never before existed."

"A message?" I forced my mind to think only of his words and not of Jackson, for my thoughts were not even safe here, "What do you mean? The Eiani?"

His eyes narrowed and a sly smile that was not friendly at all slid across his perfectly shaped lips.

"No, that came later. The message I am speaking of is the greatest piece of technology your kind has, and yet you value it so little."

Blue light immediately appeared in his open palm; it thrust upward and twisted into a double-helix that spun on the tips of his fingers. He continued, "Wrapped within a single strand you will find the whole of creation, the plan of the beginning, the plan for life. Here is the plan for immortality, written by the one who called you out of the dust."

I had heard a similar speech before by Dr. Gerhard, "You mean DNA." My voice trembled.

"Of course," His speech was as perfect as his face. He had no accent, nothing but polished words that sounded to my ears as melted butter tasted on the tongue. "We could not read or even understand the language at first. It was baffling. Though we watched as the dust was gathered together by the word of his mouth, we had no comprehension of the meaning. Though he did not speak in secret, nor in the dark, he spoke forth words that had never been. We tried, but we could not reproduce them."

He stopped for a moment as though savoring a memory before adding, "Sometimes when the night has set across the earth and the children of men sleep, I walk in their midst and try to speak the words, but the dirt will not obey my calling."

"The dirt?"

"Yes," he cocked his head toward me, answering with surprising patience, "We cannot speak the language of your DNA. We know it not, and though we try to hold it," he bent, scooping up sand from the floor and lifted it before me. I watched the sand slip between his six-fingered hand as he added, "we cannot."

His eyes did not leave my face. They were blue. So blue that I was sure they would be visible from across the ocean on the darkest night of the year. They were also more beautiful than any eyes I had ever seen, but the beauty was just a mirage. Somehow, I knew just beneath the color lay an unquenchable bloodthirst.

"I don't know it." I said quickly, my entire body beginning to shake, "Just because I have DNA does not mean—"

"No," he cut me off. "You do not, but it is inside of you. Your very flesh and bones tell the story of the message with you."

I realized what he was saying, "You mean the image. I am Simulacrum, an Image-bearer of the One Tree."

He clapped his hands together slowly in mocking praise.

"Yes. Now you understand. In the beginning of all things, we watched as the One Tree spoke new words and called everything that is from nothing. We stood on the edge of it all and watched with wonder. But we soon found we cannot creatio ex nihilo, though we can creatio ex materia."

"Simulacrum are the same. We cannot either."

"Exactly."

He cut his slanted eyes toward me, and fear skittered like spider legs down my neck.

"Neither of us can create out of nothing, as was done in the beginning, but together we can create out of what is."

He did not come near me but remained where he was, leaning against the stone table. Though he was still, I could feel his presence becoming stronger in the room. Fuller, more energetic.

"What do you want? Why did you bring me here?" I asked again.

"Do you not recognize where we are?"

He was toying with me, and he was enjoying himself.

"I've never been here before," I said.

"Of course not. Your kind does not know your yesterdays, though you are the keepers of the Histories. You have the written knowledge."

He pushed off where he had been leaning against the stone table and began to walk around, sliding his fingers in the dust around the edges.

"These are what your people call the 'Tombs of the Forgotten' where those who have died are placed. I have always liked the name, for it seems to be a good name for your people as a whole. You are all Tombs of the Forgotten. For though you do not know it yet, your future is only death; soon your people will be all but forgotten by the race of men and the home they called earth."

He slapped his hand down on the table.

"Here, a body once lay. And yet, this tomb is empty." He came around toward me, "I will tell you a secret. I come here often." His voice grew darker with each word. "I come here, and I lie on this stone table."

He backed up several feet, his eyes never leaving mine as he lifted himself easily onto the table. He lay his head back.

"And I stare up at the paintings on the wall, and I wonder. Where did the body go, and when will it return?"

"What body?" I felt like the room was closing in around me, though I knew it was not the walls that were coming closer, but the darkness from this beautiful yet horrible creature.

He sat up and looked at me.

"Beged," he said.

"I do not know a Beged."

"Never a more honest statement. Of course you do not. That was my father's greatest work."

"Your father?" I asked, "I don't understand. You are clearly not human."

"Hmm, not human?" he was playing with me the way a cat played with a mouse, "I guess to you, I might be 'not human,' but I assure you, I am in part as human as you."

I looked at the giant man before me, with skin so smooth it had not even a single wrinkle. He saw my doubt.

Without hesitation he pulled his shirt from his body, revealing a wall of muscular art before me. He smiled in satisfaction, sensuality dripping from his words as he added, "I may not be entirely human, but I believe that makes me better, superior even. Would you not agree?" His chest was not like other men. The muscles were more defined, not in the over exaggerated way of a muscle-builder; it was as though he had more muscle groups than a human.

"What are you?" I asked aware of the sensuality that dripped from his very presence. I thought briefly of Jackson but pushed him away from my mind as fast as I could. My thoughts were not safe here. I was not safe here. I did not know what this creature in front of me was capable of doing, but I had to get out of this room.

"I am Uziel, I am born of the Archaon and of man."

"The Archaon?" I shook my head, "How can that be? The Archaon cannot bond with women."

"They can," he smiled a sickening smile, "and they have. My mother is Rapha, and she is a child of such a union. She was born during the golden age of mankind, when the Friguscor rooted out all of the Original Men and ruled the earth in darkness. Many things born in those dark days till exist in the shadows today. My mother's father, Samyaza, was an Archaon, one who had left the service of Paraclete long ago. Her mother, Shamhat, was a rebellious Friguscor woman. My mother is Rapha and my father...well, he was what your Histories call a Primogene."

"A Primogene?" I questioned, "No, that is impossible."

I saw a glint of enjoyment in his eyes as he said the word, as though he was enjoying these moments with me. A Friguscor woman was one thing, but a Primogene? Impossible. Primogenes were the original twelve men and women, who after four hundred years of silence drank of the blood beneath the One Tree and became Simulacrum. This was after the race of the Original men had all been destroyed by the Friguscor men. Those original twelve were led through the desert by the Archaon to find the One Tree. From them the Simulacrum were born.

"Yes," he asserted.

I shook my head and with as much courage as I could and said, "I don't believe you. There is no Simulacrum man who would bond himself to a—" My hands were shaking now, and I tried to control them by holding them tightly together.

"Rephaim," he whispered.

"I don't know what that is either."

"Of course not," he said again, and it was demeaning. "As I said, the Rephaim or Rapha, are what your Histories call the children of the Dead Ones. They are the children of the Archaon who tired of the strangling choke of the One Tree upon their neck. They discovered the beauty of women, through the guidance of the Father."

"Who is the father?" I asked in disdain.

His eyes grew dark, "We do not even speak his name." He bowed his head respectfully as though some unseen person was listening before continuing. "A great war broke out in the horizon between the two trees."

"So, you believe in the two trees? The One Tree and the Tree of Shadow?"

"Believe?" he laughed. "Your kind always uses such nonsensical words. What does belief have to do with what is? The battle raged between the trees, and our Father faltered for he knew not the language of the words that can call into being what is not. But that was long ago, and now, we have found the path forward. Seven gates have fallen into our hands, and soon, the Eighth will be delivered. And when it is, when the Eighth falls, we will finally possess what we have longed to master: the language of creation."

"You want to create?" I asked carefully. "What do you want to create?"

"Do you not see? As long as the message is inside of your DNA, it will always enslave you to the image in which you were created. But, I will create in my image."

The room began to grow darker. The torches on the walls flickered with the power coming from Uziel's voice.

"I will ascend above all the stars. I will be set on high." As he stepped deliberately closer and closer to me, the walls began trembling, small rubble coming loose as his words echoed off of them. "I will go beyond the clouds, " his blue eyes turned to a blaze, "and I will make myself greater than he who has tried to defeat me."

I tried to turn away and escape, but he caught my wrist, and twisted me back toward him.

"Please, let me go!" Tears began running down my face.

"Would you not want to stay here, with your people?" His strong hand began to tighten on my wrist, which he bent backward.

"Please, you're hurting me!"

He cared little as he pulled me closer, grasping my back with his other arm. He whispered into my face.

"I enjoy the smell of the bodies in these tombs. It is a fragrance of victory that I find most pleasing."

"Will you please take me back?" I said, unable to restrain my tears. "Please, just let me go."

"No," he said plainly and then stepped even closer to me. With one large, six-fingered hand he lifted a long blonde curl from my shoulder. "Your hair is golden like the sun." He grabbed my waist and pulled me sharply into him, dropping the hold on my wrist as he asked, "Has anyone ever told you that?"

Instinct roared in my head and my tseeyen burned with alarm. Pushing with both hands, I tried to free myself from his embrace but found I was like a small child against his power.

"We cannot create ex nihilo, but we can create ex materio," he said, and with those words he spun me around, tossing me as though I was a doll on the stone table. Before I could move or react, he was on top of me, pushing up the skirt of my long dress ripping apart the beautiful embroidery. I knew what was happening, but I could do nothing to stop it.

"Creation is the most powerful tool in this world," he said, the smell of death coming from his beautiful face. His skin was as cold as though he had been born to ice and death.

"Please don't do this," I begged, but his only answer was what I dreaded to feel.

I beat on his chest, and tried to free my legs, but against the power of him, I could not save myself. As the moment began, as the pressure ensued, I gave way to a hidden place in my mind. I turned my face away from his, and closed my eyes, tears wetting my cheeks as the feeling of helplessness pulled me under the weight of his purpose.

Veralee 2:2

"Easy," a warm voice floated over me, "It takes a moment to adjust."

I attempted to breathe but found myself greatly inhibited by a heavy and unseen weight pressing down upon my chest. Instead of air, I pulled stale panic into my lungs, which immediately positioned me for a war with hyperventilation.

"Easy," she repeated, smoothing the stray hairs back from my forehead the same way that Mother always did when I was a child, "Breathe in through your nose and out through your mouth. Slow your breathing. You are not going to suffocate. It is just the weight of time upon your chest. It takes a minute or two, but you can control it."

With the experienced care of a mother, she caressed my cheek and then my hair, leaving a trail of comfort in her wake.

"Focus. Feel the blood in your veins. You can breathe through it, but you must calm down first."

For the moment I questioned her verity. Under the weight of the invisible stone that threatened to crush my lungs, I was sure I would die, but then, slowly, just as she said, air eased into my lungs. I began to breathe through it, finding strength in the Eiani within my blood.

"The blood in you is more powerful than the weight of time," she pulled her hands away from my face and placed them politely in her lap. The woman's hands matched her voice, small and delicate, "See? It's uncomfortable but manageable enough."

Breathing in and out, I looked up above me. A pattern of tightly positioned logs and crudely hammered iron nails made the ceiling above my head.

Breathe, Veralee.

Each breath brought a new level of confidence.

I swallowed, gauging my ability to speak.

"Why—why is this happening to me?"

"You have come through a tera," she said softly.

"But—but I have been through one before and this did not—" I stopped to breathe again.

"It is different this time, child," she said patting my shoulder. "You have come backward, against the current of the River. Normally a tera takes you with the current, and that is hard enough to stay afloat without drowning under the great weight of time that pulls the River forward; but this time, I am afraid we have both swam against the current. The weight of time is now pressing down on us both. That is what you feel on your chest."

"Backwards? You mean we have gone back in time?" I pulled myself shakily, resting my weight on my elbows to see the woman who had just talked me away from ledge of suffocation.

"Is that what you—" but I stopped as I saw her face.

"Sarah?"

"Slow now, child," was her only response.

"It's you."

Though her face was now riddled with deep lines of age, and her eyes were less bright than I remembered, I knew her immediately.

Sarah sat back in the wicker chair, positioned to the right of the small bed where I lay. Out of breath, and hurting all over, I sat up much too quickly.

"Sarah, I've been looking for you." Suddenly dizzy, I dropped back on the bed. I sat up slowly this time and sat looking at her.

I saw careful consideration pass over her face.

Sarah folded her hands neatly in her lap and looked out the open window across the room. "I have been sitting here, watching you sleep for hours." She shook her head as though an internal thought amused her. "I thought when they brought you in, well, I thought I had found her."

"Found who?"

She raised her eyes to meet mine.

"My mother. I came in search of my mother."

"Vera?" I whispered.

Sarah nodded. The very mention of her mother caused an involuntary smile to pass over her lips. "Yes. You look so much like her, but you are not her. Yet, I know you."

She extended her open hand, but then closed it.

"Grandmother, it's me." I leaned toward her, grasping her hand, "It's me, Veralee."

Her eyes opened wide as awareness spread across her narrow face.

"It is you. Veralee. My little bird." She embraced me warmly. "Oh, my little bird."

She hugged me again, then she took my hand.

"May I," she asked. Seeing my nod, she turned my hand over to reveal my tseeyen. Her eyes met mine as she said, "A sparrow. Made of time?"

The intricate pattern that started at the base of my pinky finger and wrapped lovingly around my right wrist was a sparrow made of clock parts.

"Yes," I answered as she formed the bond between us by laying her own mark on top of mine. The connection was instant, the current thick with familial tendons that wrapped my heart in comfort.

"I remember when you were a child asleep upon my lap. I would trace the lines of your evolving tseeyen and wonder what the Eiani was forming within you. You were so bold, a wild thing of a girl, hard to control and impossible to cage. Truth be told, it scared me to imagine what you could do with all that fury in such a tiny body. And one day, when you were barely a toddler, you rose before Adair, and I took you out to walk the Kaph with me. It is an old ritual of the Guardians to walk the land each day before sunrise. To ensure protection and peace upon the land. That morning, you wore a pink nightgown with white lace around the collar. I remember, because I had sewn it myself for Adair a few years before. Your hand was cold as we walked through the fields. And I looked down at you and wondered where you came from."

She leaned closer to me as she spoke, revealing the grief hidden behind her steady voice, "I feared what you could do. Gail had given you the blood without a thought. And though I loved you because of her, I feared what your existence could do to our family. Gail had broken the Law, and the Law, above all else was what defined our way of life. I was bonded to the Judge of the Council, and you were the only evidence of our crime."

She swallowed and tears formed around the edges of her eyes, but she spoke with contemplative reserve of one who was not only willing but ready to confess their crimes, "I walked you too far that morning, but you never cried. You were too curious for that, too stubborn as well."

She gave a soft apologetic smile, "I picked you up, and with you on my hip, I walked to the edge of the land, where one more step would have brought us into Friguscor territory, and there I stopped. I sat you down on the wet grass." She closed her eyes, shame coloring her cheeks, as loose tears fell down her cheeks and onto her shirt.

"I thought of leaving you there that day. It's not that I wanted to harm you, it's just that I thought that if you could just go...if you could just exist somewhere else, then we could remain as we were, as we always had been. No one would ever have to know what Gail had done. A mother will do anything to protect her child. So that morning, I let go of your hand. You toddled eagerly around, fearing nothing. As I stood in the midst of the morning light, tears streaming down my face, I screamed into the air. All the frustrations, all the fears, all of my weakness leaving my body at once. I don't remember how, but the next thing you were in my lap, and we were sitting on the ground together. That was the first time I really noticed your tseeyen. In desperation I placed my tseeyen on top of yours, and that's when I knew." Fresh tears fell from her face, "You were a part of me. You had Gail's blood in your veins, and I could feel you as though you were my own, as though you had always been ... family. From that moment on, I knew I would do anything to protect you." She wiped her face with her small, gentle hands.

"Can you ever forgive me?"

"Forgive you?" I shook my head in protest. "I should be the one asking you for forgiveness. Because of me, you were banished for a crime you did not commit. You've been exiled from your family, your people, your entire way of life, because of me. I am the one who needs to be forgiven, not you."

"I need to tell you something about how you came to be with us, how you came to be Simulacrum—" she began.

I stopped her, "You've already told me."

"What?" her eyebrows raised together just like Mother's always did.

"When we met in the woods. You told me about how Mother found me beneath the house."

Her face was blank, registering no recognition. I tried again, "Remember, when Rhen brought me to you in the woods, just a few nights ago."

I realized suddenly how far away a few nights ago really was and with the time warp, that might not have happened for her. I wasn't sure how the time warp worked. I seemed to be able to remember the prior events, but judging by the reactions of Napoleon and Zulika, maybe others didn't. So, I added, "Or maybe a long time ago, but you protected me by giving up ... by giving up..." I couldn't bring myself to say it, so I said, "...everything."

"I have no memory of these things. I don't know what you are talking about, child. I have never met you in the woods, Veralee. I know Rhen well; I have trained him in the words of the book since he was a child, but," she stopped and looked down at her lap.

I followed her gaze and saw what she protected beneath a white cotton kerchief.

"You have the book," I smiled. The one I had lost, not once but twice. The Eiani was protecting it, I thought with satisfaction.

"It has been mine since Richard fell asleep; it is why I have stayed with the Boged for so long. I had to find a place to protect it," she answered. Suddenly the amount of time and space that had fallen between us felt evident. There was so much we did not know about one another.

"How did you come to know of it?" she asked.

"You gave it to me. The night I met you in the woods." I watched her face. Her eyes narrowed as her lips tightened.

It was not distrust that I saw in her, but confusion, genuine confusion.

"I do not remember giving you this book. Why would I do that? I have dedicated almost seventeen years to protecting it. When the Boged vanished, Zulika was the only one from the Council of the Boged left behind. She had always had two faces. One for the light, and one in the dark. Once she had complete power over all that was left, she began searching for anyone else that was left behind. The adults and all the young children were gone; only the older children were left. She gathered them all into the great hall.

She also wanted this book; I'm not sure why, but she was obsessed with finding it. She didn't know I had it, and I knew I had to keep it from her. She sent Rhen's brother after me. In the midst of the chaos, I ran to the Hall of Teras hoping to find the right one..."

"The right one?"

She looked back out the window, "Yes, the one that would lead me to my mother. Vera, your great-grandmother."

"Why would you go through a tera to find Vera? She's in the Alabaster City, where all Simulacrum go to retire once we have reached our 110th year."

"That's what I believed for years," Sarah suddenly sounded her age, her voice heavy with regret. She continued, "Until two days ago, when everyone vanished, when Zulika started searching for the book, and when the dreams began."

"You have been having dreams about Vera?"

"No," she shook her head. "She is dreaming of me, and it is her dreams that I see when I sleep. My mother is not in the Terebinths nor in the Tombs of the Forgotten where Richard and my father sleep. She is speaking to me."

I see her dreams.

Suddenly the edge of a memory surfaced. Sarah as a little girl, with light blond hair, a melody on her tongue, running through the greenhouse where I sat speaking to Vera in a dream. And I heard her voice, the voice of my true mother, whom I had never met, speaking to me from across the vast canyon of consciousness.

We are a divided people. Instead of fighting the beast, we devour our own children. You must gather the child back to the Father, rejoin the joint and the marrow that was separated long ago.

"It can't be," I swung my legs off the side of the small bed and tucked my hands firmly under my thighs, feeling the cotton of the quilt beneath me. "We can't speak to each other through our dreams."

"No?" Sarah gave me a knowing look, almost as though she knew my inner thoughts. "What is the most important part of dreaming, Veelee?"

The use of my familial nickname made me feel small against this fierce yet gentle woman.

"Hearing. You taught me that hearing is the most important part of dreaming."

She came close to me and touched my cheek, just as Mother always did when sharing something of great importance.

"Hearing is the most important part of it all."

"I don't understand." I said, frowning.

She nodded, "Our people have not been forthcoming with the whole truth. There is much you do not understand." She lifted the cotton kerchief from her lap, revealing the ten-pointed dekeract of gold and silver that laced the front cover.

She frowned, "This book has not been out of my possession for seventeen years. I have guarded it with my life, as Richard guarded it with his. Perhaps you have been dreaming, Veralee, of this moment. Perhaps the Eiani is passing the responsibility to you. It is a sobering responsibility. This book must not fall into the wrong hands, and there are evil people who are searching for it. It must be protected, with your life, if necessary," she said laying the book onto my lap. "This is one of the two hidden books."

"No, I was not dreaming. It happened, but so much has transpired since that night I wouldn't know how to tell you about everything. But, as far as the books, I know that Deanna the Judge of the Simulacrum was dragged through time as a little girl when she chased these hidden books into a tera. I also know that Achiel went to great lengths to bring this book back to me when he pulled me from the Gates of Bariyach, and I know that they were never to be given over to the Rephaim, the Dead Ones. But what I don't know," I looked at her hopefully, "is why. Why are these so important?"

Sarah looked bewildered. "You say I gave you this book, though I do not remember it. But now you are telling me I gave you this book and did not tell you what it was? I can't imagine that I would do such a thing."

I remembered that night. The night that Rhen had led Atticus and me away from the Boged and onto one of the old Friguscor trains. We had waited in the forest for a woman who had asked to see me. It had turned out to be Sarah, my grandmother. She had given me the book just before she had given her life for mine.

"There was not much time when I met you, and then we were separated." I let the word fall softly off of my tongue.

"Veralee, when did this happen?"

Her question amazed me. She did not doubt me, or drill me for details, she simply believed. What kind of woman simply believed the word of a girl she had not seen in over a decade? Her tseeyen was still visible. It was one of the simpler pictures I had ever seen. A single violet surrounded by what looked like echoing round parentheses. There was my answer.

"Days ago?" I struggled to really know the right answer, "I'm not sure actually. I was in the Gates of Bariyach, and they had Daddy and—"

"They had your father?" Her eyes widened, and her voice dropped to an almost in audible sound, "Did he fall? You must tell me, did he fall, Veralee?"

My eyes filled with uninvited tears. I pushed my tongue to the top of my mouth and looked up to the ceiling of this little room.

She leaned back in her chair.

"So the Seventh has fallen. And the clock has been rolled back. The Stairway of Ahaz..."

"Wait, but how do you know that? Daddy told me just before he ..." my voice cracked. "He told me that the sun would move back ten steps when his blood fell to the ground."

"Three days," Sarah said quickly, "The prophecy of the Stairway of Ahaz tells of the sun rolling back three days, and then the clock begins ticking again. There will be seven days for the completion of all things. Ten steps, three days and then seven. So, in our normal time, the time we come from, the clocks have rolled backward three days, but here, well, we have gone back much more. That was probably what happened to the tera."

"What is the Stairway of Ahaz?"

"It's all in that book," she pointed to the book again.

"You are awake. Good!"

I turned to look at the person who spoke from the doorway. The dark-skinned man I saw was the same one who had tied my hands together.

"I am Yaholo. The Guardian of the Gate and the GateKeeper ask you to come. Please, follow me and I will take you to meet them beneath the branches of the trees."

My heart ached for a moment as I remembered falling into the blackness in the field when Yaholo had tied my hands. In the midst of my fainting I had imagined hearing Atticus's voice.

Atticus. Where are you?

Sarah stood.

"Come, Veralee," she said. Her bearing was regal, though she walked with a slight limp as she walked toward the door. Quickly, I put the book inside the bag, slung its handle over my neck, and tucked the bag safely beneath my left arm. Sarah waited for me before clinging to my arm for support. In my ear she whispered, "Keep it hidden."

Following Yaholo, we walked down narrow, wooden steps. The air within the log-cabin had a distinctly blended smell of fire, soot, men and food. The stairs creaked loudly under the weight of every step I took. My legs were heavier than normal as we went out the front door and crossed a small yard surrounded by a simple wooden fence where chickens pecked the ground in search of a midday meal. Several deer hides were stretched over cane stalks to dry in the sun, while two fat hogs lay sleeping in the cool, sandy dirt.

"Where are we exactly?" I whispered to Sarah.

"Red Oaks, of course," she answered.

The sun was high in the sky. Trees were lush and green, and the air tasted of the dustiness of harvest season. Fields ready for harvest stretched out on both sides of us as we walked. Yaholo led without turning once to look at us, nor slowing his pace to accommodate our speed. Soon we entered the woodbine and arrived at a clearing where the odor of nearby cattle drifted through the country air.

From small children to old men, people were scattered around a fire that burned at the center of the clearing. The children wore little to no clothing, while the women were dressed in an array of long skirts with simple blouses or tan dresses that came just past their knees. The men stood or squatted, laughing and speaking in low voices. Some smoked long-stemmed pipes, which they shared with one another. To one side of the rounded assembly sat three men playing drums of varying sizes; the drums were made of deer-skin stretched over hollowed-out sections of tree trunk. The children laughed and clapped their hands with the rhythm. The feeling of family, of being with the Simulacrum pulsed through my tseeyen. These were my people. This was my home.

Suddenly I remembered that I had come through the tera with Napoleon. Where was he?

"Where's Napoleon?" I whispered to Sarah.

"I have not seen him, but I have heard that his heart is failing. The weight of time is drowning him."

"What?" I questioned in alarm.

But I had no time to question her any further. Our arrival fell like an axe, splitting a path between the people and with our every step, chipping away the joy of the gathering.

A small girl ran up to me and put her hand in mine, but was quickly pulled away by a worried mother. Sarah caught my eye and gave me an apologetic look. A nervousness, a slow creeping feeling of distrust passed from their faces to ours as we followed our guide past the unfamiliar faces. As we approached, they parted on either side of us, looking me in the eye with such intimacy that I often found myself looking down to avoid eye contact. They seemed to be questioning me without words, silently asking me why I had come to their land.

"Why are they angry with us?" I whispered, pulling nearer to Sarah.

"We have not arrived at a good time for our people at Red Oaks," she said, sighing. "They are in the middle of a great war with the Friguscor over the rights to the land, but even more, their eyes can tell them that something is different about us."

By us she meant me. She touched my clothing and then took a strand of my hair in her hand.

"I'm afraid you would not blend in anywhere, except maybe in a cotton field."

She was right, not only was I the only woman in the group of people wearing pants—I had the distinction of having shining white hair.

Like waves in an ocean, they pulled back from us, until we came to the end where several men were congregated beneath a large canopy between four great trees. The oaks that were larger than the grasp of four grown men created a pillar on each side, creating a perfectly symmetric square beneath reddish brown branches that were woven together and covered in long sweeping leaves braided together in a burning red.

In the center, beneath the canopy, men and women sat in a semi-circle around a large oak table. They obviously valued age, as the youngest men and women sat on the outsides of the half-moon shape while the oldest were conspicuously positioned in the center. Sitting in what seemed the seat of honor, a man with flaming red hair was in the middle. Though his skin was much lighter than the rest of the people, he was dressed in similar fashion.

His voice, though not loud, was full authoritative thunder as he greeted us, "Lignum Vitae."

"Et Sanguis est essentia," Sarah answered with a respectful curtsey. I awkwardly tried to follow her lead and did the same.

"Please sit and eat," Yaholo said as he motioned to the open chairs.

Bowls of clay holding flat cornbread and honey, deer jerky, pears, dried peaches, and golden scuppernongs sat beside cups ready to be poured with what was probably wild muscadine wine. My mouth began to water as my stomach churned from hunger.

"Please, sit and eat," said the man before us. He was muscular, but square. His shoulders were squat but held high above his small, powerful frame. His fiery red hair sat atop his head like a tuft of autumn moss. Around his waist, carefully tied over his tan pants, was a beaded belt of white, black and red. Spectators stood behind him, staring intently at the proceedings through every side of the canopy.

"I am the GateKeeper, Liam McIntosh, Chief of the Poarch Creek Indians, and this," he motioned to stunning woman who sat on his right side with velvet black hair and eyes as sharp as a crow, "is Sehoy, Guardian of the Gate of Cate Eto, Red Oaks; daughter of the GateKeeper, Chief Opothle and the great Guardian Eyota; mother to the Guardian to come, Barthenia."

To the left of the chief sat a younger girl, who appeared to be about my age. She bowed her head slightly as he said her name.

Sarah lowered her head in polite reverence with each introduction, but even sitting down I struggled to wrap my mind around what was happening. Barthenia, the Guardian to come? Sehoy and Liam? These were my ancestors from generations past.

The girl sitting across from me with jet black hair like her mother's and eyes as silver as the moon, sat watching me with me a quiet wisdom in her gaze. Her hair was braided with feathers falling down around her chest. Her square jaw and high cheek bones made her face a work of art. Fine dark lashes fluttered over her eyes.

Nostalgia passed over me. I was somehow walking through a living dream. Yesterday I would have been shocked to meet Barthenia, who I had always believed to be my great-great grandmother. But today I knew more than I did then. Barthenia was Vera's mother, which would make the small-boned woman sitting before my grandmother. These strangers, whom I had never met, were my family, my lineage. How far back had the tera brought me? Sehoy was the Guardian of the Gate in this time. Sehoy, the legend, who had before now only been known to me by name.

Sehoy spoke.

"You are our kind, and we honor the blood in your veins; welcome to the Red Oaks. Tell me," she turned her lovely face toward me, "how is it that you have come to shine like a star?"

Sarah looked at me, as if she wondered as well.

"I have met Paraclete face to face," I answered simply.

Everyone at the table looked momentarily stunned, but Sehoy's eyes shone with rich fascination.

"Remarkable," she said. "You speak truth?"

"Yes," I answered simply. It was true.

Voices whispered all around me. Bright eyes stared like stars. They began to press in, to look at me as if I was something sacred. I felt awkward, uncomfortable with admiration, eager to distance myself from their thoughts about me.

"It doesn't mean anything. It just happened."

"It means nothing?" Sehoy questioned me. "How can you say to meet Paraclete means nothing?"

"No," I immediately tried to explain. "I mean, it doesn't mean anything about me. He was the one who mattered, not me. I was simply marked by his presence, that's all."

"And where did you meet him?" Liam asked this question.

All around me, people seemed to be holding their breath, waiting for my response. Hesitantly, knowing what my response would mean, I said, "In the garden, in the horizon between the trees."

"So, you have seen beyond this world," Sehoy paused and looked closely at me. "and you are not from here either. You are far from your rightful place on the banks of the River. I have seen the tera that brought you here with my own eyes. It is unlike any other; its shape is inverted. Instead of the pull moving into the tera, the waves appear to lap outwardly, as though the tide pushes it toward us instead of pulling the waves into it. I have spent many nights under the moon, watching it and thinking upon these things in my heart. What has created such an aberation and why? That is how we found you so quickly after you arrived. Yaholo and Bula were watching to see if anyone would come through once more after the arrival of Sarah the day before. I ask you now to speak truthfully before me. Have you come against the current? Have you come up the River?"

I knew little about teras or how they worked, but I didn't have to know much to know that Sehoy's voice held a nervous warning beneath its calm tone.

Sarah nodded as she answered, "Yes."

A hushed awe fell across the crowd.

Barthenia spoke, her voice light as the wind.

"But you cannot. Teras only move forward or parallel. They do not move backwards. They have not the ability to go against the current of the River."

Everyone looked to Sarah for an answer, including me.

"I have little explanation for you," Sarah said, "but what I tell you is true. We come from a time when darkness is casting a long shadow across the sun. The Seventh GateKeeper has fallen. Time, it seems, has become flexible, coiling around the promise of the Stairway of Ahaz."

"The Stairway of Ahaz?" said Sehoy, "Do you speak of Ma'alah Achaz?"

"Yes," said Sarah boldly, "The promise for protection. I believe I opened the tera at the exact moment that the sun rolled back on the stairs, and that would explain why the tera went backward and not forward. But how do you know that name?"

"How do you know of the Ma'alah Achaz?" said Liam, leaning forward and looking directly into Sarah's eyes. "How do you know of these things meant only for the ears of the GateKeepers?"

"I am Sarah of Red Oaks," she responded without hesitation. "I too was once a Guardian of these lands, or I will be in the days to come."

Sehoy spoke again.

"You have put us all in great danger by swimming against the current of the River. These ways remain closed to protect the time of the beginning."

"To protect the beginning?" I said trying to keep up, "What do you mean?"

"The River runs in one direction to ensure that the Nechas, the evil one, who crawls on its belly until the end of all things, cannot go backward but must go only to his ultimate destruction in the fires of the end," Sehoy answered. "Or so my Puca, my grandfather, used to say when the council fires would burn low in the night, and I would drift asleep listening to their stories as a child."

Then she stopped and looked at me with wonder.

"Girl who has been face to face with Paraclete," she said. "What is your name?"

Before I could answer, another voice spoke my name as a question.

Veralee?

I froze, my eyes widening. I knew the voice. I turned around and then round again, looking for her, but I couldn't see her.

Sehoy asked again, "What is your name, girl?"

My mouth felt dry. I stammered, trying to answer her, but then, for a second time, I heard Adair's voice.

Veralee!

"Adair?" I whispered as I heard her speak.

Come home to us, Veralee, come home.

It was as if Adair's voice rode on the wind. It sounded so very far away, yet somehow I knew she was right there, in the forest where we stood.

"Will you not tell us your name?" Sehoy asked again.

"Veralee," I answered quickly. I tried to focus on the faces looking curiously at me. "I am Veralee Harper of..." I looked around and realized that they weren't going to understand this, "of... Red Oaks."

What was happening here? I could hear Adair calling me from far away.

"Of Red Oaks? What are you doing here on these lands? And why did you bring a Friguscor through a tera?" Now it was Liam who asked the question. I heard an uneasiness in his question. "Why would a Simulacrum travel with the enemy?"

"I was looking for my grandmother, Sarah, but I did not mean to enter the tera. I was pulled through. The enemy?" I realized she meant Napolean. I remembered him groaning when we came through the tera. He was Friguscor, and he had refused the blood of his parents at the Elektos.

The words felt like old tethers pulling me back under the burden of the Law of the Simulacrum. I had begun to remove that burden from my shoulders, one Boged at a time. Each Friguscor person with whom I had shared my blood had loosened the bonds of the Law, but here, I felt its heavy yoke again.

For most of my life, I had been taught to avoid the Friguscor, that they were unsafe and unclean. In many ways, this was true. One drop of Simulacrum blood, and the Friguscor developed the Esurio, the thirst for our blood that ultimately caused them to devolve into animals killing anything and anyone in their way. Many times in the history of man, the Esurio had broken out in the Friguscor and our people, the Simulacrum, had been killed by the thousands. Several times we had been almost wiped off the face of the earth. This Law against sharing our blood was created to protect us.

But hidden within the Friguscor, like gold hidden within the dirt beneath a river, the Boged existed. The Boged were Friguscor with a lingering memory of the Eiani tucked down inside their DNA. One drop of Simulacrum blood transformed them into Simulacrum. But since we did not know how to identify the Boged from among the Simulacrum, our people had quit trying to find them. In fact, our councils had passed the Sacred Law, which strictly forbade anyone from sharing blood with a Friguscor. The penalty for violating the Law was banishment from all things Simulacrum. A person who was banished would be cut off from family and friends, cut off from any communication or contact for ever. Banishment also meant never again convening at our sacred gathering place, the Terebinths of Mamre, and thus would not be able to eat of the basar fruit for sustaining nourishment. Without the basar fruit which revitalized Simulacrum bodies, even Simulacrum would eventually die in the Friguscor world. And they could not go to the Alabaster City to be with their ancestors.

My mother, Gail, had violated the Law, when she had changed me, or so she thought. Charges were brought against her by the Council, and she was sentenced to banishment. Because Adair and I were so little and needed our mother, my Grandmother Sarah had invoked Padha, our tradition which allowed her, an innocent person, to assume the punishment for my mother. Grandmother had been banished in place of my mother and my mother...she had been banished because of me.

When Atticus and I had come to the Boged Caves the first time, I had learned, in a stunning irony, that my Grandmother Sarah had been living there with the Boged. When the Simulacrum had driven her from the protection of their community, the Boged had taken her in and provided for her.

In true family tradition, I had also been banished because of breaking the Law. But banishment, and Paraclete, and taught me something the Simulacrum had yet to learn; how to identify the Boged from among the Friguscor and so avoided giving anyone the Esurio. What if long ago the Simulacrum had stopped wasting all of their efforts to uphold the Law and had put their resources into learning how to find them? The Simulacrum could have changed the Boged and given them the gift of the Eiani, and their enemies would have been fewer, but in their blindness, they had refused. They had allowed their fear of the Esurio to override their concern for others who were living and dying without the Eiani. They had retreated into the safety of the Law and built their whole society around it.

If the law is the master of the government, then the government is its slave. Plato's words from the Republic finally made sense to me. The Simulacrum had long ago become a slave to the wrong master.

Liam's voice drew me back, "The man who arrived with you, the Friguscor; his time is limited. He will not last another day."

Napoleon was dying?

"Where is he?" I asked urgently.

Sehoy motioned to her right, and the crowd parted. Two men carried Napoleon through the opening and dumped him on the ground. He groaned as he fell in the dirt. I rushed to him and rolled him over to listen for his heart beat. I heard the tell-tale sign that I had learned identified him as Boged: his heart was trilling, ready for the blood.

"The Friguscor cannot endure the hardships a tera presses onto their bodies," Sehoy said. "It is made worse because he has moved through this kind, the kind of tera that should not exist. You two can maintain, for a time, but it will end his days quickly if he stays here."

"Your time is limited here as well," said Liam. "You cannot remain where you do not belong."

"And you do not belong here," Sehoy added, "so why then have you come? Why have you opened up a path that could be followed by the Dark Ones?"

"You can't just let him die," I blurted out.

"Let him die?" Liam challenged. "We did not bring him here to this time. And we cannot keep him alive if we so desired. He is Friguscor—"

"You could save him," I interrupted.

"Save him?" A man stepped forward, and I knew him instantly. Though he was much changed since the last time I had set eyes upon him, he was still unmistakable. Even beneath a different robe, his bird-like fingers were folded in a steeple over his mouth as he stepped forward respectfully.

He put a gentle hand on Sehoy's shoulder as she made the introduction, "This is Absalom, the Seer for our Council."

I recoiled from his presence, feeling like the snake might strike at any moment.

In less than a second, he answered, "Though they may not be able to see it, I can. You both wear the mark of one who has been banished."

All heads jerked back to us as the word "banished" fell from his mouth.

Sehoy examined us, "Is this true? Have you been banished from our people?"

"Yes," I answered honestly, keeping my eyes on Absalom but feeling for Napoleon's weakening pulse. Absalom did not seem to know me, which was good, but still, how could he not know me?

Barthenia locked her eyes on mine, studying me intently; then she tilted her gaze to the right where a young man stood watching her with equal eagerness. He looked like he was in his twenties, of medium build, but taller than the others and of very different coloring. Wavy blond hair fell over the soft blue eyes that exchanged telling glances with Barthenia. They spoke without words, and I recognized the message in their eyes, for I had said the same to Atticus many times.

The atmosphere around me was charged with distrust. I knew I could not help Napoleon right now, in front of so many people. "Hold on, Napoleon," I whispered, noticing Absalom's eyes narrowing in on me.

"You have come against the current through the River to us. And now you admit that you are both LawBreakers?" Liam was growing increasingly angry. "Why have you come to us?"

"I have told you," Sarah interjected, "the Stairway of Ahaz opened and—"

Words failed her. I could tell the story was falling flat, so I added, "I was being chased by the Rephaim or something like it. We fell through the tera that was already opened."

Sarah raised wide eyes to mine, and I knew I had said too much.

"You were being chased by...the Rapha?" Liam looked to Sehoy, who looked at us and asked, "What are you saying, girl?"

I kept my eyes on Absalom, who looked like a man slowly coming awake before me.

"The Rephaim, the Dead Ones," Absalom said with smooth, long words. "You say they were chasing you in your own time? Why would the Dead Ones chase a banished girl?"

Immediately I worked hard to put a shield in front of my mind. He was probing with his tentacles, trying to learn more.

He smiled at me when he hit the wall in my mind.

"You have met Paraclete face to face," he said, his eyes triumphant, "and you say the Stairs of Ahaz have turned back time, but these are old wives' tales. Tales that the Simulacrum do not tell. And now you are here, swimming up the River of time which has never been done before. How interesting you are, Veralee Harper of Red Oaks."

Sehoy contemplated these things silently and finally asked, "Sarah, you say you are a Guardian to come, and yet you have been banished. Why would a Guardian be banished from land she is sworn to protect?"

Sarah looked down for a moment, considering her words, and I felt as though I was back in front of the Council again. I was tired of this conversation, tired of the Law, and tired of having to defend what I knew was the right way to share the blood of the Eiani. We had both been banished for the same crime.

Except Sarah had never actually broken the Law, and it turns out, neither had my mother. I was not Friguscor as they had thought, but as Vera's biological daughter, I was Simulacrum...or something. The thought rushed to my mind. I have no idea what I am.

Regardless of what I was, I had broken the law when I had given my blood to Nathan.

Sarah was innocent, but I was not. I could not stand to hear her defend herself against a crime she had not committed, so I spoke before she could.

"Sarah was banished because of me, and I was banished because I broke the Simulacrum Law. I shared my blood with a little boy who was dying on the streets of a town called Montgomery. He was Boged, and now he is

Simulacrum. When the Council discovered my crime, they banished me from my own people."

Everyone turned and looked to me with shock and disgust. Voices erupted as everyone began to shout. Barthenia sat on the edge of her seat, interest warming her brown cheeks to a rosy red. The young man with wavy blonde hair who had been watching her stepped forward and put his hand on the end of the large table as if to steady himself.

Finally, Liam raised his hand and silence fell once more, "You have come through a tera that should not exist; you have brought the Friguscor man, our enemy, onto our lands, and worse still, you tell us that the tera could bring the Dead Ones upon us. But now, now you tell us that you also are a Law-Breaker who cares nothing for the Law? Who has sent you here? These are days when the wars are upon us, when our lands are being threatened, and when the Aiyendalet has just appeared at our threshold not a fortnight ago? What darkness have you brought upon us?"

I froze, hearing nothing more of what he said. Only Aiyendalet.

Sehoy added, "War is coming to our land with the rising sun. A battle for the Gate is beginning; why would the Eiani allow you to come here now?"

"Yes," Absalom added with hungry eyes. "Why?"

Everyone went silent as they looked to me for an answer, but I could not speak.

Aiyendalet.

I saw and hear nothing else.

Was it true? Could he be here?

Liam had said that war was coming to this land. Atticus had told me that when he was moved down the River, he usually arrived at a new destination on the eve of a battle. As the Aiyendalet, he had been charged by the Man of Words to watch for, and lead the people to, the Door when it appeared. I felt short of breath again, and I looked at every face, searching for his.

The man whom Barthenia had been watching and admiring took full opportunity of the break in conversation and suddenly stepped forward from the crowd.

"I—I am—I am here to ask for Barthenia," he stammered as all eyes turned to the strange man with the strange question.

Liam turned toward him and slammed his hand down on the wooden table.

"No! I have given my answer."

I was barely aware of what was going on before me, lost in a dream.

Aiyendalet.

Everything around me was in motion, and yet I was frozen by those words.

Barthenia broke her silence.

"He is the answer!" she said with surprising boldness. She turned to her father, "He can protect the land! His name alone, the name of a white man. It will protect the land. Father, we are losing our land. It is not right, but it is the reality we must acknowledge. You know it is true!"

"Silence!" Sehoy shouted, demanding obedience of her passionate daughter before she turned to address the man waiting for an answer. "You have heard our answer. You cannot bond yourself to our daughter. You are not Istichata, or as you Europeans call us, Creek Indian. You are not a Guardian, and you are not for her."

"Not for her?" The man began to question the wisdom of such a statement and for a moment I saw him as he was. A white man, with blonde hair and blue eyes, dressed in clothing that seemed to come from the other side of the world compared to the Native people around him.

"Who are you to say who is for me?" Barthenia stood now, and the fire in her eyes set the entire assembly ablaze.

The passion in Barthenia's voice drew my eyes and my focus back to her. Her parents and those around her could only see her obstinance, but when I looked at my grandmother, all I saw was her fierce boldness.

"Do I have no voice? Am I only a prized pony to be led by the reins for show?" she demanded.

Everyone stood silent. Mouths hung open as they looked to the young girl with a woman's courage.

I could not keep my eyes off of her as Chief Liam asked, "Do you dare to defy me?"

"I do not wish to defy you, Father. I wish only to follow the path that the Eiani has placed before me. "

"What path, Barthenia?" Sehoy asked.

"This man! He is my way forward!" Barthenia looked toward the young man. They stared into each other's eyes for assurance. They were walking the same tightrope, and if they looked away from each other, they would be lost to the world of doubt and unknown below.

Chief Liam looked from Barthenia to the man with the blue eyes. The voices of the crowd had risen from a low murmuring to a growing current of shock and fear.

"She cannot bond herself to a white man!" said several young warriors, "That is not our way!"

"What of the ways of the Creek? Shall we forget them so quickly?" called more people.

"We are losing everything! Shall we also lose our princess to the white men?" echoed so many others.

Liam took it all in, and I saw it added another weight to his already overburdened shoulders. He heard the alarm growing in the crowd around him, but he kept his eyes on Barthenia as though she alone could steady him. Pain was evident on his face. The pain of a father who could not give a beloved daughter all that she wanted. He sighed as he caught Sehoy's constant gaze.

After a moment, Sehoy shook her head in a slow, but unmistakable, silent denial.

Barthenia's shoulders fell as she tried to control the agony that tore from her chest, erupting over her face with large, wet tears.

Liam watched his daughter's grief, and I saw conflict flicker across his face. I thought for a moment he might change his mind and grant her request. Instead, he squared his shoulders and spoke directly to the crowd, "These are uncertain days, dark days. The blood moons have begun. War is as certain as our future is not."

Liam looked out toward his people, who gathered closer to their leader.

"I speak hard truth to you as your leader. The sun is setting on our way of life on this land. Twilight is falling upon the way of the Muskogee Creek, of all the native peoples, the way of our parents and grandparents."

Disbelief welled up in their eyes as they listened to their Chief speak such words. Women began to cry softly; men began to shift weight nervously from one foot to the other. The heartbreak was as tangible as the sun on their faces.

Liam paused to look to Sehoy as though she might speak next. But she was silent, standing before her people without an ounce of fear in her face. She looked like a pillar of fortitude, her head held high, her shoulders set against the coming storm. She was the Guardian of the Gate of Red Oaks. Liam, like all the rest of us, visibly swelled with strength from Sehoy's presence.

"But we must not lose hope," he continued. "For though we are of this land, of this soil, and of these rivers, though we have birthed our children and buried those who have fallen asleep beneath these grounds, we must remember who we are. We are the Image-Bearers; we are Simulacrum before we are Creek. We have the Eiani in our veins; we are Simulacrum before we are mothers, fathers, Guardians, or Keepers. We are Simulacrum above all else."

Liam stepped closer to the crowds, placing a hand on an older man's sunken shoulders. He faced the man and spoke directly to him, "Hear me in your hearts and know that my words are true; let the ways of the Creek die, let the love for yesterday die as well, for today or maybe tomorrow, we will walk through the Door and live forever in the presence of the One Tree. On that day all that was will be but a forgotten memory. Dry your tears. Set your faces toward the setting sun. We must not mourn what has already passed away but instead fight for what has always been. The Eiani. The Image inside of you and me!" Liam picked up a small child in his arms, pulling him affectionately to his chest as he continued, "Our brothers and sisters, and above all, the One Tree. Let yesterday die quietly, but let us fight for what comes tomorrow!"

Slowly they began to nod in agreement with their Chief. I understood so little of these people, my own people. They were losing everything. History would not be kind to these brave faces, to these women holding babies, to the men holding those same women. I found myself looking back at Barthenia in all of her agony, and I suddenly understood Sehoy and Liam in a way I had not before. Their people were losing everything, and all they could preserve of their way of life was their daughter. Whether I agreed or not, I understood. As I looked at Liam's face, I could not help but remember my own father's face at the Council meeting the day I was banished.

"Have mercy on her!" my father had cried out, begging the Council for a privilege they would not, could not afford me. The Simulacrum of my time were just as nervous as the Simulacrum of this time. They too had feared the unknown, the ever-present darkness that was threatening to destroy all we held sacred.

The day of my banishment, the Council was also trying to preserve the end of an era. I remembered the faces of the Council members: Issachar, Deena, Meridee, Eleizer and Joab. They must have known it was the end of our time, that dark days were coming for our people and in the end, we would lose everything just as the Creek people would. But, they had not fully grasped the reality of that either. Because suddenly, standing two hundred years back in time, I saw what I had never seen before. They could not stop what was coming for the

Simulacrum any more than these people would be able to stop the history that had already been written. For it had all already been written.

"We have not been abandoned," Liam was saying. "The plan from the beginning is still at work; the presence of the Ayindalet proves that. The One Tree has sent him to us in the day of our distress. Ayindalet, step forward."

He walked out from the trees, just as he had done the night I was heading to Montgomery. He had been there, waiting in the dark for me then, and now. Now he was here again.

"Atticus!" I yelled, unable to contain myself. My heart burst forward, dragging me toward him, "Atticus!"

His name filled my entire heart as I threw my arms around him. I pulled back to see his eyes, his green eyes.

"It's you!" I began to cry. "I thought I had lost you. I thought—"

He held my gaze for a long moment as electricity burned between our tseeyens though they did not touch. But after a moment, Atticus pulled back from me, taking my hands from his neck and clasping them between us. He shook his head, his brows furrowed, and his green eyes staring blankly at me.

"How do you know my name?"

"You know these women, Ayindalet?" said Liam in an accusing voice.

"No," Atticus answered, taking a noticeable step away from me. "No, I do not know her." And his words felt like hammer inside my chest.

I do not know her.

I started toward him. How could he not know me?

But I was interrupted by a loud thundering sound followed by an eruption of Creek battle cries and the sound of hoofbeats. Warriors came galloping in on powerful horses, throwing up dust as they approached. The battle cry sent panic through my veins.

One rider pulled his horse up short near the table.

"Chief Liam, they have crossed into the lands. They have gathered more than we expected. It has begun. War is upon us."

"More?" Liam answered, his voice strong but still full of concern. "Bring my horse!"

The atmosphere of war spread immediately through the air.

Drums began in the distance, and for a moment I did not know where I was. I felt suddenly stuck between two worlds that were colliding into one moment.

"Atticus?" I ignored everything and focused on him, but he was just swinging into the saddle of a horse.

"Take shelter, ma'am," he said.

I grabbed the reins and yanked hard.

"I want to go with you!" I cried.

He sat straight on his horse and looked down on me, still recognizing me.

"Would you leave your companion?"

I had completely forgotten about Sarah.

In my moment's hesitation he pulled the reins from my hands and clicked his heels into the horse. In the noise and chaos, he galloped away.

"Sarah?" I turned to see her standing nervously against the treeline.

Sehoy commanded someone to bring her horse. The response was swift, and soon she too was mounted and ready to ride along with Liam.

"Barthenia, stay with them until I return," she said. "Women, take the children to your homes. Every man with us!" Sehoy was a warrior, and the sight of her on her warhorse took my breath away.

Before she rode away, she turned her horse's head toward me.

"This is no place for you," she said. "Leave, return to your own."

She rode away before she could hear me say softly, "But you are my own."

The dust swirled around us as the leaves of the Oaks began to fall to the ground. Women were running through the trees with children on their hips. But I couldn't move. A familiar sound found my ears. A small trill, a beating heart. It was Napoleon's heart, calling to me. I had learned to hear the Boged in his blood calling for the Eiani. The world around me began to spin. And in the midst of it all, I heard the call of Paraclete from within me.

Gather what has been scattered, for the way is in your blood.

Sarah leaned into me, touching my arm,"Veralee, we should go back."

But her voice already sounded miles away. I walked toward Napoleon who was lying in the dirt as though he was nothing more than a discarded blanket.

"Don't die," I whispered as I dropped to my knees and pulled Atticus's blade from my pants. "Not yet; you are Rhen's brother and he risked his life to save me, and now I owe you the same."

Gather what has been scattered.

The blade burned as it always did when it cut through the skin, and the blood was just as reliable. It came quickly, flowing from my veins into Napoleon's gaping mouth. For the way is in your blood. Napoleon sucked in a precious breath of life. With two strong hands, he grabbed my wrist and began to bite down hard. The pain was intense as he sucked down my blood, gulping as though it was air to his lungs. My vision blurred, as I tried to pull away from him.

Then the man who had asked for Barthenia was standing before me. With great effort he loosened Napoleon's grip, but he had underestimated the fight that would come from Napoleon. As my eyes closed to the darkness around me, I heard them wrestling in the dirt.

Then I heard a familiar voice coming from the darkness. It was Absalom.

He bent down, bringing his lips to my ear as he whispered.

"We see you."

Adair 2:3

I shook my head. No.

"Sure, you don't," he was smiling, but there was worry in his eyes.

He took a quiet but confident step toward me and gingerly kissed my lips. His hands found their way to my face. Softly, he cradled me as he kissed me.

"I love you, Adair," he said, the sweetness of his breath lingering in the air. "Ruach has done his best to heal the wound."

Gingerly, I felt the thin, pink skin on my neck where the creature had attacked me.

"And I've asked, but he does not know why you still cannot speak." His jaw tightened, but still he smiled. "I believe the Eiani will heal your voice; it may just take a little time."

I nodded, wiping a tear from my cheek.

"You're strong," he said. "You'll be back to yourself in no time."

Neither of us believed that.

"Listen, I let you sleep because the wound is still delicate. You lost a tremendous amount of blood last night. I thought you might..." He looked up at the ceiling, and then laughed a short, nervous laugh. "Oh man, this is hard. Listen," he paused, and I tugged at his shirt, impatient to hear his words. "You have to listen to me. The wall. They started building the wall last night."

My eyes grew wide. My mouth twitched but did not move.

He understood me and answered the question I couldn't ask.

"The Simulacrum are pouring in. Meridee the Discerner, told me that two more Gates to the Terebinths of Mamre have fallen!"

This was devastating news to hear that our sacred gathering grounds were in danger. Our people and our governing council met every seven years at the Terebinths, which existed in a dimension beyond this world. Who or what could be successful in attacking that sacred and—we had believed—secure place. I wondered what this meant for the Basar, a fruit that only grew in the Terebinths. Eating it sustained, protected, and rejuvenated our bodies, so that our flesh did not wear out or contract disease like the Friguscor's bodies did.

There were twelve gates located aroung the world that all led into the Terebinths. Without them, we could not enter the grounds, we could not gather and council together, and we could not partake of the Basar fruit. It would be disastrous for us. How could this happen?

Phineas continued, "Meridee and Issachar just left to see which gates still stand. Thankfully, the one here at Red Oaks is intact; well, we think it is. Without Wisdom, no one is really sure how it will all work. Meridee was afraid that only one other gate is left. Or at least, she was sure it was standing a few hours ago. I don't know. Time is hard to guage today; hours seem to be more than they were yesterday. Simulacrum are still pouring in here, and every able body that arrives is given a tool and weapon. Eliezer has commanded them to build the wall. And they are. They work, young to old, to preserve the Simulacrum way of life."

With his help, I rose from the bed and looked out the tall windows. Horrified, I pointed to what I saw outside.

He stood beside me at the window, watching the activity with me.

"Fear is powerful, Adair. Those beasts that arrived last night, they were not just a hunting party, they were scouts." He was lost in the recollection of the horrific drama of last night at the campfire, "I've never seen anything like them, Adair. They were obviously not something that the Eiani created. They were like Frankenstein monsters, pieces of different animals and humans all stuck together! They jumped like gazelles, ran like leopards, and had the teeth of bears. And their claws...."

I pulled on his arm to stop. I rubbed my neck; it was aching again. I couldn't take anymore.

“I'm sorry, Adair. I'm so sorry for what happened,” He put his arm around my shoulders and pulled me close. “But, those things...it was like they were made to hunt us. Our people won't forget that. We've all lost so much already. Many have missing loved ones, and no one has any idea what happened to them. Thousands more Boged just disappeared...disappeared with no trace! And most have lost their homes, their Gates, and the safety net of the very thing that has protected them for centuries."

The Law. I knew what he meant. The Sacred Law that had defined our way of life for centuries. It promised that if we did not share our blood, then the Friguscor would not recognize that we were different from them. We could hide in plain sight, living side by side in the same cities, towns, and villages, conducting business, attending the same colleges, and being neighbors. The Law had protected us from the Esurio, the hunger in their veins, but now, despite all of that, the Euserio was an epidemic. And now, it was just down the road; it was only a matter of time before they came for us.

"And now," Phineas looked at me sadly, “If what Joab says is true, the Law is finished. It is totally irrelevant. It can't protect any of us if they are giving them our blood in a vaccine. So, these people are desperate. They'll try anything that has any hope of protecting what they've got left. I might not totally agree with the tactics, but I understand how they feel. "

The Law is finished.

His words echoed in my mind. If the Law is finished, then what becomes of me, the LawGiver? Am I finished as well?

“You need to realize,” his voice held a warning, “they are not using just any trees to build the wall, Adair. They are cutting down the Red Oaks. They feel like the oaks have an extra protection built into them from the Eiani. They think they will be stronger and more solid than any other material.”

Cutting down Red Oaks? I rubbed my eyes, feeling suddenly strong despite my wound. I wrote on the small chalkboard: “Our trees...my home!”

He nodded and then looked back at the ongoing work outside the windows. "I get it, Adair. I was totally against it at first. But, after everything that's happened, I'm not so sure. Maybe this is the right thing to do, Adair," Phineas looked at me with the most serious look on his face that I think I'd ever seen. "Maybe this is what they were meant to do all along, and we just didn't see it this way. Think about it, are they any less useful as a wall of wood than they were as trees?"

I shook my head in protest. No, no, no! I shouted in my mind. They were placed there for a reason! I wrote, "No!" on my board.

"Adair," Phineas added, "the people have a mind to build that wall, and they are going to defend the land no matter what it takes. Deena's strength is failing. She is not recovering from that attack last night. I really don't know how she survived at all. But even before the attack, she had become a weak Judge. Naphtali and Wisdom are gone, and the others are not strong enough to lead. There is too much uncertainty. We will not be able to stop whatever army is coming, and I don't believe we will be able to stop the building of this wall either. Even now, Eliezer has them working on the wall with one hand and holding a weapon with the other."

He paused to let all of that sink in before he continued.

"Besides, I have not told you everything."

What more could you possibly ...

"Do you remember the night I went with Ruach, the night it was raining? I'm not sure when that was now because of the Stairs or the rolling back of time or whatever that is. But do you remember that I went into the forest with Ruach and a storm had rolled over the land?"

I confirmed with a nod. I had waited for him to tell me what had happened that night. He had been injured but so far, had refused to tell me what had occurred.

He looked down briefly at his chest as he said, "Adair, someone came through the tera that night, and I didn't have the heart to tell you that it was—"

Suddenly several short, broken blasts came shooting through the air.

My face asked the question that Phineas answered, "Yes, those are the rams' horns from the Terebinths. Some of the others brought them when they arrived. It means more have arrived."

"Mother?" Mattie's voice floated up the stairs with an edge to it. "Y'all should come down! Someone is here."

As we reached the door to my room, I heard Eliezer's familiar voice from downstairs, "You are the Guardian of the Gate now."

Phineas held a protective hand around my waist and helped me as we made our way slowly down the grand stairway. Mattie was standing at the open front door with her back to us.

I heard him before I saw him as he said, "No, it is good you bring your mother and father. For your mother is the LawGiver, and your father is still the GateKeeper of Red Oaks, is he not?"

"Yes," said Mattie, her voice strong.

Phineas interrupted, "Inman?! How are you here?"

I had not seen Inman, Absalom's messenger from the city, in weeks. Tall and slender, he seemed more muscular than before but still sported the bald head of the Friguscor.

Though he was Simulacrum, he had left with the defectors, those who had followed Absalom into the city after the last fateful Council Meeting in the Terebinths of Mamre. It was that decision that had ultimately led so many of our people to what Joab had called The Machine.

"He came through the tera," Mattie answered her father, forestalling whatever Inman was about to say.

"The tera?" Phineas inquired, giving Inman a look of distrust.

"Ruach found him traversing the land." Mattie answered as though she was listening to Ruach's voice from the forest.

"Yes, I had to come quickly, and I did not travel lightly," Inman spoke with sincerity. "I came to warn you of great danger. You have no idea what is coming."

"Oh, we have an idea," Phineas said, pulling a long, clawed finger from his back pocket. "A creature found its way here last night. It was half animal and half ..." he shook his head in disbelief, "half human. It attacked many of our people." Phineas looked at me with pity in his eyes.

"Yes," Inman said, bowing his head slightly. "But that is only the beginning, there is more. There is ..."

"The Machine?" said Eliezer.

Inman was caught off guard by Phineas's knowledge.

"How do you know about the Machine?"

"Joab told us," Mattie said. "He arrived last night, just before the monster. It must have been hunting him since he escaped."

I looked at Mattie, unable to hide my surprise. I had not connected the beast's appearance with Joab. She smiled at me as our eyes met. Though my heart swelled with pride at the woman she was, my heart still ached a little for the loss of the sound of her little voice echoing through this house.

"Joab?" Inman looked around, meeting each set of eyes trained on him. "He has returned?"

"Yes," answered Eliezer.

Phineas helped me across the marble floor. I motioned them in.

We worked our way into Daddy's library, and Phineas helped me into Daddy's chair. It felt odd and yet comforting to take his place behind the desk. Eliezer and Inman followed us into the room.

"Daddy, can you get Joab? I'll get Miss Rosa to help me bring Deena," Mattie said when they got me settled.

Phineas nodded and left to find Joab while Mattie left to find Miss Rosa. Inman noticed me then.

"You have been injured," he said, concerned. "Was it the beast?"

I nodded, and he saw that I could not speak so I motioned to the chalkboard in my lap.

"I need to apologize, Adair," he said with smooth, warm words. "for the last time we met by the far gate. It did not end as well as I would have hoped."

I reached down and scraped out one word on the chalkboard, "Ausley." His eyes dropped away from mine, and he did not immediately speak. I tapped my finger to her name.

"Your sisters," he said quietly, as though he was speaking the names of the dead. "Your sisters have both been taken by the Machine. I am so very sorry, Adair."

I collapsed against the back of the chair.

"No!" My lips moved in a silent scream, and then I leaned my head forward into my palms. I felt as though I might fall to the floor.

Eliezer looked bereft as he half-leaned, half-fell against the wall behind him.

"Oh, how dark can these days grow?" he whispered.

Phineas and Joab walked back in. Phineas saw my distress. Immediately he came to me, but looked accusingly at Inman as he asked, "What is it? What has he said to you?"

Inman shook his head, "She asked about her sisters," he began to explain. "I am so very, very, sorry but they are both inside the Machine."

"What?" Phineas lamented. "No doubt it was Absalom who put them there," Phineas said bitterly. "Veralee did not deserve this, but Ausley made her bed."

Deena could be heard from the entry way, her frail voice accusing Inman before she even entered the room, "You!"

With Mattie on one side and Miss Rosa on the other, they helped the frail woman into the wing backed chair by the fireplace. Deena looked like I felt. My insides were tearing to pieces, my heart was threatening to explode, but

Deena, the tiny woman who was the Judge of the Simulacrum Council, looked as though she might fall asleep before the end of the day.

"Deena," I mouthed her name, as if it could somehow strengthen her, but she held up a cold hand, refusing to be coddled by anyone.

"Explain to me, how you, who have sided with Absalom, can expect to come to our lands with no retribution?" she said. "Speak truth to me, boy, or it will be the last words you utter." She spoke with difficulty, an audible wheeze in each word.

Why had Ruach not been able to heal her? I wondered.

Joab stepped into the center of the room. He was dressed in the ceremonial dress of the Simulacrum warriors. A large white tree was emblazoned his leather breastplate, and gold aiguillettes formed of chains of oak leaves hung on either side of his shoulders. More chains of oak leaves circled around to fasten a scarlet cloak onto his back. Golden arm guards scrolled in gold filigree protected his lower arms to his elbows. Beneath it all he wore a chain mail shirt.

"The chain mail of the First Men," Inman said thoughtfully. "It was said at one time that it could stop the fiery arrows of the enemy. It is good to see you, Joab. I see you got out unscathed."

"Out?"His voice sounded ancient. "No, you are mistaken. My body is here, but I assure you, I still hang with my brethren, naked and exposed on the hooks of the Machine."

"Have you seen my Jackson?" Miss Rosa broke in. "Have you seen my son? Have you seen him?"

Inman shook his head, "Ms..." Inman faltered, not sure of Miss Rosa's name.

"Mrs. Westbrooke to you," Miss Rosa answered disdainfully.

"I'm so sorry your son is missing. Most of us have lost friends and loved ones. Please, I cannot tell you anything of him. I can only imagine how painful this must be for you. I am truly sorry." Inman sounded sincere, and Mrs Westbrooke's face fell, but I could tell she did not trust him compeltely.

Inman dropped his head and covered his eyes with a shaking hand, "Joab, Mrs Westbrooke, I do not pretend to understand what you have been through," he said. "But I assure you, I am here to see it does not happen to any more of our people."

"Why did he do it?" Joab spit out derisively, "Why would Absalom do this to his own kind?"

Inman jerked his head up to face Joab, his face showing genuine confu-

sion.

"Absalom? You believe Absalom is behind such evil?"

Joab's cheek twitched up toward his right eye as he said, "It was he who led us into the underground facility. He said we were going to help. He said..."

"That is what he was told," Inman interrupted, becoming solemn. He looked at Joab with compassion. "Absalom has his faults, for sure. He is so passionate about his ideals that he can come across as abrupt. But, friends," Inman looked around at us," he is not cruel. How can you believe he would do this to his brothers and sisters? No, he is not the mastermind of this horror."

Joab looked momentarily perplexed, but then shook his head.

"It was he who led us there," he said emphatically.

"Yes," Inman said, falling back into the chair, "If anything, that was his fault: he believed the Friguscor, and for that mistake he is paying dearly."

"How?" Joab raised his rusty voice. "How does he pay for what he has done?"

"By living a life of sacrifice. By living every day under the torture of that facility, hoping to find a way to free them. That is how you got out, is it not?"

"How I—?" Joab stopped, looked as though he was pushing bile back down his throat. "I'm not absolutely sure how I got out. It was a ... a guard who helped me out. I do not know who he was, but he was not Absalom!"

Inman sat on the edge of his seat.

"Joab, Absalom was behind your release, and he is working still to free others. If he is discovered, no doubt he will find himself hooked up to the machine. Absalom puts himself in danger every day to do this, but he is willing to take the risk for our people. Soon, you will see more return. I myself brought back someone whom you all had given up hope of ever seeing again. Through the help of Absalom, I was able to get her out."

"Who?" Deena demanded, her fingers digging into the armrest of her chair, "Who is with you?"

"You can come in now," Inman said as though he was coaxing a baby bird, "Please, let them see you."

I turned toward the large, oak doors in the foyer, which I could see through the double library doors that had been left wide open. A cool breeze, which had little to do with the weather and everything to do with the silhouette in the doorway, chilled my spine. I steadied my trembling hands on the desk and rose from the chair, supporting my weight on one leg.

The gaunt woman in the doorway did not move but stood leaning against the doorframe, enveloped in a black wool wrap.

Miss Rosa gasped audibly.

"It can't be," I thought. The woman stared back at me. Her lips were as dry and brittle as her gangly arms and legs. Above her wrap, I saw that her collarbones bridged deep hollows only seen in people close to dying from starvation. Tired did not describe the vacant stare of her eyes; it was more than that. It was an absence, a body with no soul.

She walked unsteadily toward us, clutching the wrap around her with bony fingers, as if it could protect her from the harshness of the world.

Phineas and Miss Rosa went to her. Phineas wrapped an arm around the woman's shoulders, and she seemed to almost fall into him with relief. Delicately they placed her in the chair that Inman offered freely with a warm smile of sympathy.

Her eyes were on me as Phineas asked, "Agatha? Is it really you?"

Agatha Dupree had always been a mystery to me growing up. She moved like water, smooth and direct and seemed to command attention whereever she went.

Agatha nodded once and with a trembling voice that we all had to strain to hear said, "I was, at one time long ago."

Miss Rosa said, "Rest for a second, Agatha." She rushed out and came back with a glass of water. Agatha drank thankfully.

"What happened, Agatha?" Miss Rosa asked, going to kneel beside her.

I was struggling to hide my shock and grief. This was a shell of the beautiful, intelligent, witty woman whom I had known all my life.

"Why did you go with Absalom?" Rosa asked sadly,

Agatha's eyes looked confused, but somehow steadier than Joab's. Joab came to stand beside her, a wall of witness to the rest of us.

"I did not go with Absalom," she began, mildly offended by the inference. "I was taken by the Dark Ones."

"Taken? When?" Rosa responded, surprised at this revelation.

Agatha pulled the wrap closer to her throat, cocooning herself in the chair with those who loved her by her side. She breathed in deeply. Her eyes closed for a long moment and then finally she said, "I did not go to the meeting with the Archaon. I left with Sonith the LawGiver in the chaos of the next morning."

"Why?" asked Phineas, "Did you not believe Veralee when she said the Archaon were coming?"

Agatha looked to Phineas and with no room for doubt in her voice said, "I have always believed Veralee. From before you could even imagine. I did not doubt her word. I knew that the Archaon would come, but I could also see the division that was growing deeper among our people."

She stopped for a moment, took another sip of water, and gathered strength to talk again, "I sat at the Council meeting as all of you did. I watched the trial of Veralee and the boy whom she saved. I saw that Austin, in his...," she breathed in again, "naivete thought he was finally going to win his personal battle against the Law, and he did not mind sacrificing Veralee to do it. He had argued passionately against the ban on giving our blood in the past but had never convinced anyone that he was right. He was, and is, a fool. He did not see the hands working behind the scenes, but I watched Absalom that day. I watched as he twisted and spun words into buttered gold and convinced the people that Veralee had to be banished."

Agatha looked around at us.

"I agreed with him; there was nothing to do for the girl. It is the way of our Law. But something dangerous was hiding just behind the truth. Rebellion so often hides just behind the truth. So, with Sonith by my side, we left the Terebinths, carrying that which could not be lost again."

Deena looked sharply at Agatha.

"Quiet, Agatha. You are much distressed," she chastised.

"No," Agatha said plainly, "I see more clearly now that I ever have before."

"Keep to your oath," Deena warned. "Remember, you have sworn your life."

"I remember," Agatha said without a second thought. "I have been remembering since I was pulled off that Machine and set free. And tell me now, Deena, as you look at me, what are the oaths of men compared to the words of the One Tree? We were wrong, Deena, wrong!"

Her words were more than an accusation, they were the slamming of a gavel, the closing of the subject, the judgment long awaited.

"We were wrong for keeping it in the dark, for what is done in the dark always comes to the light."

Joab put an assenting hand on Agatha's shoulder. She obviously felt his tacit agreement.

"Death has a way of redefining life," he said. "This truth is something that I did not grasp before, but now I will speak openly and leave nothing to the dark. The Archaon warned me, at the meeting in the Maqom, but I did not heed their words. I paid for my ignorance."

Joab, unlike Agatha, had journeyed to the meeting with the Archaon at the city of the Original Men inside the Terebinths of Mamre, just after the Council had banished Veralee. Veralee had tried to tell everyone that the Archaon had come and requested to meet with the Simulacrum at the Maqom, the meeting place in the Original City, but most did not believe her. Absalom had convinced most of the people that the Archaon would not seek out a girl, and a lawbreaker at that. Drums of war had been sounded by the GateKeepers outside the Terebinths, warning us that something catastrophic had occurred in the world of the Friguscor.

Out of fear and disbelief, most fled the Terebinths without meeting the Archaon. Those who followed Absalom's advice into Atlanta eventually ended up in the Machine. Joab had attended the meeting with the Archaon and challenged Achiel, the leader of the Archaon, asking why the Archaon had left the Simularcrum alone for so long and had stubbornly refused to listen to Achiel's response.

"Why are you amazed that what has been promised has come?" Achiel had asked us at the meeting. "We have sounded the war drums because the days of night are upon you. The gates below have opened and the Rafa have returned to seek a place above men. The wars of the last days are upon us."

He looked at each of us as he spoke, willing strength into our souls.

"Though your number be few, we will stand with you. We leave for the Gates of Bariyach, for the earth groans and calls out for vengeance."

"Leave?" Joab had cried out. "The Gates of Bariyach? Beneath the earth? What do those have to do with us?"

Achiel had looked at Joab with something like anger in his eyes.

"Wisdom save you from this woman," he had said. "Surely she will lead you to the house of death from which none will return. Give careful thought to the partner of your youth."

Joab's glare had remained defiant, and Achiel looked at him for a brief moment more, as if offering a chance to reconsider. Finally, he said:

"Go, do what you will. But, woe to him that hath ears, but will not hear."

At the end of the meeting, I had a vision of Red Oaks burning, and we had all left in a panic. Joab had disappeared, and later we learned that he had gone to join Absalom and had accepted a seat on the Novus Council.

Ruach had healed Joab. Agatha put a reassuring hand on top of Joab's.

"I left with Sonith," she said, looking at me, "to protect one of the Hidden Books preserved by the Inner Council of the Simulacrum since your grandfather, Richard, was Judge, Adair."

At the mention of my grandfather Richard, I remembered his body sleeping in the Tombs of the Forgotten, beneath the Marble Caves of the Simulacrum. Deena had warned me that many secrets that now slept would one day come to light.

There, in the Tombs of the Forgotten, beside their lifeless bodies, she had told me about Ernest, my great-great grandfather and Richard. During the Civil War, Ernest had secretly been changing Friguscor into Simulacrum. According to Deena, it was this act that caused him to fall in the fields of Red Oaks, at the hands of the Council's decision. Richard, who was Chiam Arukim, a man who lived for centuries without going back to the Alabaster City of the Simulacrum, had agreed with the Council's decision and allowed Ernest to fall. She told me Ernest had fallen at Absalom's hand and Richard's command. In turn, Richard had also been murdered, but Deena had not known by whom or why. I knew they had to be connected somehow.

Deena had also warned me that Absalom would not allow a peaceful divide in the Simulacrum and that he would stop at nothing to get his way. She had said that we must keep the secret of the keys hidden. Then she had left me with the warning that Absalom might be insane enough to reveal everything.

After she left me alone with the bodies, I had met Uziel, who also spoke of secrets. His image would be burned inside my mind forever.

"Hidden books?" Mattox asked.

My daughter's voice brought me back from my memory. She glanced at the Histories that surrounded us in the room; I followed her gaze.

"We have the Histories," she said. "What books are hidden?"

In answer to her question, I heard Uziel's voice, echoing in the Tombs:

'The pages of a lost book have been hidden, and yet, your family lies sleeping in the Tombs. More will soon join them, for the war is far from over. We must all find what has been hidden."

"A book?We have to find a hidden book?"I asked.

"Or a key," he said...

"No!" Deena insisted, holding up a hand. "Do not speak of these things! Agatha! Joab, remember yourself!"

Deena looked to Eliezer for support but found only an arched eyebrow and a stern jaw.

"You speak of the Hidden Books?" Eliezer asked sharply. "No one has ever held those books. They are but rumors from the traitors, a lie from the enemy during the Dividing Wars."

Agatha rebutted, "It was no lie, Eliezer. It was a secret, forged in the flames of blood and rejection, but hear me this day. The books exist, and their words are true. Deena herself will tell you they are real, for she has given up much to preserve the words written before the foundation of the earth inside the pages of blood. Have you not, Deena?"

All eyes looked back to the small woman who suddenly seemed to be made of steel doors. Her lips were closed tight as she seethed in the chair.

Inside I was speaking, but no one could hear me. As the LawGiver, I had pored over our Books of Histories, and I knew they were like a bucket with a hole in the bottom. Something was missing.

Agatha nodded at me, as if she knew what I was thinking.

"The knowledge of the Hidden Books of our Histories was given to Richard, your grandfather, when he bonded himself to the Guardian of the Gate, your grandmother, Sarah, and became the GateKeeper of Red Oaks. He kept the books hidden and protected them for years."

"Who gave them to Richard?" Phinieas asked. "As the GateKeeper, I have never been told of any hidden books."

"I do not know where they came from," said Agatha, "only that Richard had them and kept them safe."

"From whom?" Eliezer still doubted. "Why would we keep a book of the Histories hidden from anyone? They are on display for all to see." He waved his hand toward the books on the shelves in the library.

Joab answered bleakly, "He kept them from the Council of the Simulacrum."

Deena looked like she might be sick. Eliezer was obviously angry.

I remembered Deena's words to me in the Tombs of the Forgotten.

I picked up my chalkboard and scribbled one name, my grandfather's. I held it up for them to read.

"Richard?"

Deena shook her head; her lips remaining tightly closed.

I turned to face Agatha and pointed to the name. She nodded.

"He had the books and protected them until he fell," she said. "That is when we separated the books. One went with your grandmother, Sarah, and the other was protected by the LawGiver."

"Why are these books so important? What do they say?" Phineas asked.

"I'm not entirely sure," Agatha said apologetically. "Most of the pages are Hidden. That is why they were called the Hidden Books."

"How were they Hidden?" Mattie asked, and I listened carefully for the answer.

"The legend says that the books were written by the pen of an Original Man with the blood of one of the Primogenes," Agatha said. "Some of the pages, the ones at the beginning are legible. They tell of a story that to us would seem impossible. It tells about the Simulacrum in the early days of the Primogenes, and a wall of doors in a place called Ariel that fell flat when a Primogene was killed. The Primogene's name was Beged. But the rest of the pages ..."

Short of the breath from the effort of her speech, Agatha had to stop for a moment, then finished by saying:

"The rest were blank."

"What is so important about blank pages in an old book?" Eliezer asked.

Agatha leaned close. "Remember, Old Warrior, just because you cannot see something, does not mean it is not there. In those blank pages are the mysteries of the end. And I believe that in those blank pages is a map that leads to a secret gate, hidden within the Terebinths of Mamre."

"Beged? That is traitor's rubbish!" cried Eliezer. "Old wise tales from long forgotten stories carried down from the Dividing Wars!"

"Richard fell asleep on this land protecting what you call traitor's rubbish!" Agatha persisted. "Why would such a man die for anything but the truth?"

"Richard did not fall because of some books," Eliezer said in disgust.

"Then why did he fall?" Agatha shot back.

Eliezer shot back, "Maybe it was punishment for what he did to Ernest Weekes, the father of his bondmate, Sarah."

I knew he was talking about my great-grandfather, who had been the GateKeeper with the Guardian of the Gate, Barthenia who was my great-grandmother.

"No," Agatha said sharply, "Richard did not know about the books when he ordered the death of Ernest, and it was more complicated than that. It was the decision of the Inner Council to pass judgment on Ernest after he would not stop..." she faltered for a moment.

Phineas finished her sentence, "Changing the Friguscor into Simulacrum?"

"How do you know this?" Mattie asked, her face void of judgment. Immediately I felt heat rising up my body. I did not want to say too much and betray Rosa. The memory of Rosa telling both Phineas and me her family secret surfaced slowly. It was more like the memory of a far-away dream than anything solid. When had she told me this? I could not place the memory, though I knew it had happened.

"Because I am a descendant of those whom he changed," said Miss Rosa, breaking hundreds of years of silence all in one moment. "I have Boged blood through my great-grandfather Moses who was the son of Abram, but through my mother's lineage I am also Simulacrum. I am from both. A child of two worlds. A two-stranded chord."

The room was silent with shock.

Rosa looked to Mr. Westbrooke who was leaning against the wall on the side of the large windows which faced the lane of giant Oaks outside. During all this conversation he had been so silent I had not even realized he was in the room.

Mattie was the only one who dared speak.

"Let me see if I am understanding this correctly," she said. "Richard, who was the Judge of the Council, agreed to the murder of the GateKeeper Ernest, because Ernest was changing the Boged which was and is against the Law of the Simulacrum Council. But then, someone murdered Richard, so why did Richard fall?"

The air shimmered, and another memory came back to my mind,

'Richard!' my grandmother had cried out, "What have they done to you?"

"You came,' he gasped for air, "I hoped--"

"I felt you fall," Sarah had moved close to him, cradling over his body.

"Listen,' he gasped, his breath ragged, "Even now my eyes grow heavy with sleep. Listen to me, my dear one. Stay the course with the Council, but if it goes awry, if the worst occurs, go to Veritas Hills. James Westbrooke says he can get you to a safe place."

He gasped and then opened his eyes wide, "It's time, Sarah. We need to go home."

'Home?" she had looked bereft.

'Come with me, we can go home now.'

'No, Richard, I can't go right now. You go on ahead of me, and I'll see you when we wake."

He had opened his eyes one last time and said, 'Tell Adair. Adair will avenge my blood; tell her to bury the dead so that none can find him."

I swallowed with great pain. Why would he have said this as he was falling asleep? I had never killed anyone, nor could I! But still, in the back of my mind, there was a picture of me with blood on my hands, and a body in the foyer.

Adair will avenge my blood; tell her to bury the dead so that none can find him.

Mattox was staring directly at me, and I had the feeling she could see the invisible blood on my hands.

"Richard fell in the woods, by the hand of an unknown murderer," Agatha said. "Adair, has Ruach shown you what happened to them? I sense perhaps he has."

I nodded and she pressed, "Did you see who felled Richard?"

Agatha had always been able to sense things, not as much as a Seer would, but still she had a gift.

I shook my head.

"Soon after this, Sarah was banished, and with the book in hand she left Red Oaks and hid," Agatha continued.

"Where?" It was Eliezer who asked. "Where did she hide with the mysterious book?"

"With the Boged," answered Mr. Westbrooke.

"Do you know about the Vanishing?" Inman had been listening quietly to this conversation and addressed his question to Mr. Westbrooke. "The Boged have vanished."

"I assumed when they vanished from here, that all the Boged were gone, at least all the Boged who had no Simulacrum blood in them," Mr. Westbrooke answered plainly.

"You are right," Inman said and rose to walk around the room. "We have been discussing the events of yesterday as though they are still here with us today. We need to focus. Everything has changed. The entire country is in chaos. You can't imagine the state of things outside Red Oaks. Something happened; people vanished in a freakish lightning storm."

He looked at each of us as if sizing us up. "That is why I have come today. It is why I brought Agatha back. I have come to make sure you do not end up as the Boged."

"Ruach told us they had vanished because their season had ended," Phineas said, his eyes challenging Inman.

"The Boged," Inman looked up at Mr. Westbrooke, "are all gone. They have vanished off the face of the earth entirely."

"Good," Eliezer said gruffly. "The traitors have existed for centuries, and we are all better off without them. Maybe the One Tree finally gave them what was coming to them. The Warriors not only protect our people from the Friguscor but those who came before me had to keep our people safe from the Boged as well. We will not repeat the early days of the Dividing Wars."

"The Dividing Wars are history; that is in the distant past that is better forgotten," Inman interjected smoothly. "The point is today. My brothers and sisters, we must focus on today!"

His voice grew in passion and volume as he exclaimed, "Listen and hear me. Clearly what we have discovered today is that there have been years of discord among our own people. Lost books of our Histories are somewhere that contain pages which are blank, yet Agatha tells us those blank pages hide secrets. It seems that secrets have been more common than truth, and a Judge ordered the murder of a GateKeeper over them! Things were not as easy or good as we were led to believe."

He looked at me, and when I nodded in agreement, he continued.

"But I am here to help. I know you will struggle to believe me, but Absalom is not our enemy, and I am not your enemy either. I am you, and you are me. We are the same. I have come to help you, to keep you safe, not to hurt you. I brought Agatha as a sign from Absalom. It was he who managed to get her out."

He walked around the room, addressing each person in turn.

"Absalom sent me to warn you, to tell you that the Friguscor who run BaVil want to destroy us all. They know about us; we no longer live in the shadow. They know about the Simulacrum; they know that our blood is different. They are the ones running the Machine and sending those monsters to Red Oaks and spreading the Esurio."

"Why are they spreading it?" asked Mr. Westbrooke. "Why spread the Esurio if they want our blood? Why kill us off if they want our blood?"

Inman stopped and wiped his hands on his pants. I could see that he was shaking.

"To kill unwanted Friguscor as well. There are too many people on the planet and not enough resources. They are using the Esurio to decrease the population to numbers which the earth can sustain."

He stopped and held out his hand to us.

"But that is not why I came. I came to warn you that an army is coming behind me. They know how many Simulacrum are here. They are coming for you."

"An army? What army? We are building a wall." Eliezer said suddenly.

"How can we help you?" Inman asked, "I saw the wall as I came in, but you will need help to finish in time."

"Help us?" Mattie looked at Inman, "The last time we saw you, you seemed to be threatening my mother. You told her that she had chosen a line, and we were now on opposite sides of that line, if I remember correctly. That sounds a lot like saying we were enemies. You sided with Absalom and started a new Council which ended in our people being hooked up to machines and drained of their blood. Now you waltz in here and expect us to believe that you want to help us? Are you mad, or do you just believe we are?"

Deena spoke. "That is the most reasonable thing I have heard said during this entire meeting."

Inman dropped his hands to his sides with defeat and apology in his voice.

"You are right. I was arrogant and full of the passion of youth. I did not see clearly, and I helped put our people in great danger. I was wrong, but now I know better. Can't you find a way to forgive someone who naively broke the trust of our people?"

He was looking directly at me, his eyes saying more than his words.

"Can you find it in you to forgive me for following my passion? Would you forgive me if I was your sister?"

"Cheap shot, man," Phineas said without blinking. "Veralee didn't lead our people into the slaughter house of this machine. She saved a boy's life. It's completely different."

"Is it?" Inman had no argument to his tone but sounded genuine as he added. "Maybe it is; maybe in the eyes of the Law I have done a more grievous act than she."

At the mention of the Law, all eyes turned toward me. They were waiting for my reply as LawGiver, as they should. My hand went quickly to my necklace. I fumbled the pendant through my fingers several times. Quickly, I turned and reached to grab a nearby book. I knew it well by now. I had read it over and over. A month earlier I would have had no idea what was in this book, but now it was different. I was different. I was the LawGiver. and I had a responsibility to my people.

My hand flipped freely through the pages that held the voices of those who had come before us.

I pointed to the page, and Mattie read, "The Law is the collective thought of our people, our rules and regulations to order our lives on this side of the Door."

My hand stopped on the page that laid out the punishment for Law-Breakers and the exceptions like Padhah. I looked up to Inman, a fire burning in my gut against him as Mattie read and then summarized by saying, "The punishment is clear for those who break the Law. It is banishment. The question is, did you break the Law of the Simulacrum? Did you share your blood in order to help them make this vaccine?"

I patted Mattie on the back and nodded my agreement.

All shifted as if they were one body to look at Inman. He looked at the ground, his lips pursed tight into a thin line of nerves as he said, "Yes."

"Then the punishment is clear." Mattie responded without breaking eye connection with him, "Unless you have someone who is willing to pay Padhah for you, someone who is willing to exchange their innocence for your guilt by going into banishment for you."

Inman looked up, his eyes slightly misty, as he said, "I do." His shoulders fell, and he looked like he was fighting an inner war none but he could see. "I don't want to do this, but he said it would come to this."

"He?" Deena asked. "Who?"

Inman drew out a chord from his jacket. It was bright as the sun, shining with the light of the Seer.

"Absalom?" Deena narrowed her eyes. "He has given you the chord of light fashioned by the Archaon? But that is his to keep as the Seer! It allows him to see even in the dark. Why would he give that to you?"

Inman held it up so that all could see the magical chord which had been forged when the Council was founded by the Primogenes.

"He told me there would have to be a sacrifice, an innocent life to substitute for my crimes, and he told me that it would have to be him."

"Why would it be him and not you?" Phineas asked.

"Because he cannot leave BaVil. He is too ingrained there, and he believes he must stay to see that our people, that our way of life is not extinguished from this earth. But I can move between these two places, and I can help. I am here to help you!"

Obviously not yet convinced, Phineas asked, "And just how is it that you are able to move between our two worlds?" I beamed with pride at his perceptiveness as he added, "If they are capturing our kind and putting them in a Machine, how are you able to be with them and not be taken?"

Inman looked at Mr. Westbrooke who was watching him intently, though so far, he had said nothing. Inman pulled something from his other pocket. It was a syringe that had a soft blue tint to it.

"With this," Inman said showing it to us all. "This is the vaccine that they are giving the Friguscor."

"How does that help you?" Eliezer asked, truly curious.

Inman pulled up his left sleeve and plunged the needle into his vein as we all stood by in shock. Without any explanation he emptied the contents of the syringe into his bloodstream, and then withdrew the needle. The syringe fell to the ground as Inman swayed slightly and leaned over to steady himself on the large oak desk. He shut his eyes and moved his head from side to side as though he was working a cramp out of his neck.

"What are you doing?" Eliezer asked, alarmed. "Why would you--"

But Inman help up a hand to quiet him. Then slowly, he raised his head toward Eliezer and the ones on that side of the room. Their eyebrows flew up in utter surprise, but it was not until he turned to look at me that I realized why. His eyes were blue, crystal blue, and they looked more mechanical than human.

Suddenly an impure fragrance wafted through the air. I put a hand up to my nose and fought to keep from gagging.

"It is the smell of their death," Inman said slowly, smoothing out each word with his tongue. "When we take the vaccine, it covers us like it does them for a day or so. The vaccine takes three days to transform the Friguscor. It works by finding its way through the bloodstream into the DNA; it attaches at a specific spot of the strand where it then alters the DNA. But it cannot attach to our strand for we are shielded by the Eiani, so the vaccine is quickly rejected by the body and expelled. But for a day or a day and half, it covers the smell of the Eiani and makes our eyes appear to take on the change. For the rest," he pulled a pair of gloves from his pocket, "For the rest I can wear gloves."

"The rest of what?" Phineas asked.

Inman raised his eyes again, "When they take the vaccine their eyes become this crystal blue color. Plus, they get stronger and grow larger. Much stronger! I'm talking about an almost inhuman strength. And," he emphasized, "they develop another finger so that they have six fingers on each hand instead of five. That is the truest way to know that the DNA has been changed. You see this mark on their hands, and you know the mind has been changed as well. So, Absalom had gloves made for me, to allow me to play the part."

Six fingers. The giant in the Tomb had six fingers. What was he?

We all waited. His words echoed through our doubts and questions and fears.

"They are creating monsters," said Joab slowly, trying to absorb this disturbing revelation.

Inman pushed his advantage.

"Yes, and this army is coming here to Red Oaks! They know you are here, and they are coming to round you up and take you to the Machine."

He turned to make sure all eyes were on him, and he held up the cord again.

"Listen to me! You have maybe two days before they will be here." The cord glowed like lightning in his palm as he said, "Let me be cleared of my crime. Let me enact Padhah, and for the sake of all of you and all our people, let me help you!"

I threw my hands up in frustration and flipped the page over twice and pointed furiously at the scrolled letters.

Mattie read and then looked up at Inman.

"According to this, Absalom does not meet the requirements to pay for your crime. The book clearly states two essential stipulations in order to enact Padhah. You must be related by a blood-bond and the one enacting Padhah must be innocent of the crime of breaking the Law. Absalom is neither of those for you, so you see you cannot enact the right of Padhah."

"Actually," Agatha leaned her head against her palm, "Inman is related by a blood-bond."

Eliezer continued, "Inman is Absalom's son."

I looked at Inman in disbelief.

"I thought you knew," he said slowly.

"Wait a minute!" said Phineas. "You've only been around for a few weeks. You never came with Absalom when he came to the house. I mean, I saw you in the Terebinths, but that was all. If you are his son, why have you only recently appeared? Where were you this whole time?"

"I lived with my mother in the Middle East," he said. "When my father traveled here, I did not come. I was raised separate from others. We lived a very private life, much like you yourself do, secluded from the cities. My father wanted to keep his family out of any drama with the Council, so we went quietly to the Sacred Oaks and stayed in the background," he answered.

Suddenly I thought of all the times I had realized how much Inman was like Absalom, and I knew it must be true.

Mattie spoke up, undeterred by the revelation of Inman's lineage, "Even if you are his son, you have a problem with innocence. Is that right, Mother? Was that not the second requirement for Padhah?"

I looked down at the book, knowing the answer already, but needing a moment to regroup. I hated being taken by surprise.

I nodded my head.

"But he has not broken the Law," Inman said with a plea in his voice. "He has not given his blood ever."

"No," Joab said hotly. "He gave mine and hers instead."

Agatha straightened her back. "Though it was Absalom who helped me escape, I do not trust him. I never have, but it was he who helped me get out."

Deena spoke up, "Never trust Absalom. He is only out for himself. I don't believe for a moment that he got you out, Agatha. Not unless getting you out was part of his plan...to get us to trust his son! Inman, you are a Trojan horse! Don't listen to him!"

"Please, you must listen to me," Inman turned to Deena. "I know you and my father have had your differences, but we are talking about the survival of our people! This is worse than anything we have ever faced, including the Dividing Wars! Joab and Agatha, you have seen the Machine; you are witnesses to its horrors and to the cruelty of the Friguscor who devised it. Phineas and Eliezer, you have faced and fought the hybrid beasts these evil people are devising to hunt and destroy us! Now they are building an army, stronger than anything you have ever seen, to come against us! I am telling you, our people are in grave danger of being wiped off the face of this earth! We have to work together; we have to put aside our petty differences or we will not survive."

He turned to Eliezer, "You are saying you are trying to build a wall," his smooth voice uncharacteristically rough,"and I can help you. I have brought help to—"

"That does not matter," Mattox interrupted. "You are trying to split hairs with the Law, and that does not work. Absalom is guilty, and that is obvious."

"And Inman," Phineas said, "How is Absalom doing now that he has no hands?"

Inman looked shocked and was quiet for a moment. Finally, he asked, "How do you remember something that has no longer happened?"

Phineas crossed his arms in front of his chest.

"Oh, it happened, Inman. Ruach brought me to the tera that night, and we found Absalom and Ausley. I tried to get Ausley to stay, but she fought me and insisted that she had to go back. She cut me with my own sword just before I cut Absalom's hands off."

Inman swallowed hard, before saying, "Phineas, Absalom came with Ausley to see if they could get help from Wisdom who stands at the Gate. That night, after you tried to make Ausley stay, she told me she had hurt you. She didn't mean it. But she had to go back, she had to—""

"Why?" Phineas raged. "She was home! Why would she go back?"

"Because she knew that if she did not go back, there would be no hope for Jackson," Inman explained. "I'm sorry, Mrs. Westbrooke, I didn't directly answer your question earlier because I had hoped to save you this news."

Miss Rosa gasped and grabbed hold of the winged back chair to steady herself. Mr. Westbrooke put an arm around his wife.

"Or for your father," said Inman, not missing a beat. "Ausley had to go back. She was trying to get Jackson and your father out. Jackson was disguised as a guard in the facility. If Ausley and Absalom had not returned to BaVil, the powers that be would have found Jackson hiding as a guard, and they would have killed him and your father."

He looked at me with pity in his eyes, "Sadly, Ausley was not able to stop the death of your father, and in the end both she and Jackson were discovered and taken to the Machine. Absalom is working even now to get them out."

Silent tears fell down my face. Ausley, Jackson, and Veralee were inside of that heinous machine, Daddy and Mother fallen. A monster army heading toward Red Oaks. I closed my eyes, and Phineas came to stand by me. Mattie placed her hand on my arm in support.

"And has this army had the vaccine?" Eliezer asked, resuming his role of Warrior, and addressing the problem at hand.

"Yes," Inman answered.

"So, they are no longer Friguscor, but some kind of hybrid combination? Is that what you are telling us?"

"Yes," his voice was calm, smooth, and direct.

"Then we have to build this wall, and we have to build it quickly," Phineas said.

I looked at him as though he had betrayed me personally. He did not look back at me, but only at Inman.

"I thought I was protecting Ausley," he said.

"She knew that," Inman said his head bowing slightly. "You just didn't have the full picture of what was happening, and it happened so fast, she didn't have time to tell you. Just like now, but I'm trying to make it clear. They are coming for us, and they mean to destroy us...completely."

Everyone seemed to be agreeing, but I was protesting inside my head.

We have never cut these trees. The Eiani gave us those trees!

Eliezer said, "And we have never faced an army such as the one which is coming."

The picture of Red Oaks blazing with fire burned behind my eyelids. In a vision the Archaon had shown me, I was standing by the river bank trying to help our people as the Red Oaks burned down around me.

Deena held up her hand and pointed to Mattie.

"You are the Guardian," she said, "So your vote will be heard here." With that Deena said, "I call this to a vote of the Simulacrum Council."

Inman as if on cue, stood and held out the chord for all to see once more. Deena said, "All who approve the payment of Padhah for Inman's crime, let your voice be heard."

"Aye," said Eliezer.

"Aye," said Phineas.

"Aye," said Deena.

Joab breathed out pure frustration and looked at Eliezer, "Nay."

I looked at Mattie, who looked to her father and then at me. She closed her eyes for a moment and then quietly said, "Nay."

I shook my head vigorously to indicate my negative vote.

In a raspy voice, Deena said, "James. You are called to break the tie. You served as a GateKeeper at one time, and we ask for your vote now."

Everyone looked at the quiet man whose face was marked by undeniable sadness.

"I do not wish to weigh in, but if I am called by my Judge, I will serve."

He looked at Inman and shook his head. Then he turned to Eliezer and said, "Take the boy's chord and build the wall quickly, for the days of darkness have come."

Eliezer stepped forward and with his right hand, grabbed hold of the chord offered by Inman. But he jerked his hand back and cried out in pain as though a viper had bitten him.

"It burned me!" Eliezer said cradling his hand.

Inman looked not quite apologetic.

"Yes, the chord of the Seer will do that if not handled with care."

Day 2 Erev

Veralee 2:4

Behind the barred door, outside on the fields of Red Oaks, sounds of thunder and battle blurred into one indistinguishable cry until finally, an unnatural silence fell across the land. The sun slipped down behind the trees, and finally the door opened. Barthenia came quickly inside, shutting the door with care behind her.

"Lignum Vitae," she half-whispered. She did not wait for a reply, but continued briskly, "We have but little time, I have obtained the key to your door." With trembling hands, she presented the heavy iron key, "You need to change, and I will make sure our path is clear." She was breathless as though she had been running, "The war has begun, and it is clear from this day that we will not win."

I rushed to her, the first person Sarah and I had seen since they locked us up in the small shed, "Have you seen Atticus?"

"No," Barthenia said in a rough whisper. "I will not bond myself to him."

"Bond yourself to him?" Shock must have been more than evident on my face as she hurried to explain, "It is my Father's plan to bond me to the Ayindalet. To give the people hope for our future. And though he means well, the Ayindalet cannot save this land." Barthenia took a deep breath and added, "But I can."

While stuck inside, I had tried to organize the events of yesterday in my mind. Number one: Time had successfully completed a backbend. It had coiled up around itself like a strand of DNA. But was it now straight once again, marching forward in only one direction? I thought so, but I couldn't be sure. And, had everyone's path changed now that time had reversed for three days?

Were all events that had happened in those three days erased? Were these "new" three days a blank slate to be filled in an entirely different path, so that all that had happened in my life thus far, uncertain in this new future? I had more questions than answers, and it was messing with my mind. That brought me to my next point I had been pondering.

Number two: Atticus did not know me, because he had yet to meet me in his linear line of time. For me, I already knew Atticus because our meeting had already happened, but for him, our meeting was still yet to come. Did that even make sense?

Now Barthenia announced that her father was planning for her to bond with Atticus! But, in my future, she was my grandmother, and she had bonded to Ernest. If she didn't marry Ernest, Vera would never be born .... and neither would I. My head was beginning to hurt.

Barthenia didn't know she had just dropped a bombshell on me and was continuing, "The Creeks have arrived from all over, even some from Georgia and the Florida Territories," Barthenia continued as she opened a deer-skin bag with beads dangling from the bottom. She poured the contents of the bag onto the floor.

"Territories?" I asked.

Sarah explained, "Alabama is not yet a state, Veralee. That will not happen until 1819."

"1819?" Barthenia paused. She held a dress, wadded against her chest as though she was waiting for something to pass over her.

"Put these clothes on," she said

The thought of a corset repelled me.

"I'm not wearing pantaloons," I said before I could even think better of it. The two women turned to look at me. I offered a weak smile, adding, "It's too hot in Alabama to wear pantaloons."

"Thank you for the clothes," Sarah replied, full of genteel manners.

"It is better that you are less ostentatious," Barthenia said, aggravation tinting her voice. We have many Friguscor coming toward the land. You should be dressed as..."

"As though we belong in this day and time," Sarah finished for Barthenia.

"Yes, that is right, thank you," Barthenia answered, obviously appreciative of Sarah's understanding.

Barthenia was quiet for a moment. She reminded me of a young deer, timid and shy, always aware of everything around her and ready at any moment to escape in flight. Finally, she answered, "We are in the middle of a war for independence."

I did the mental math quickly as I dressed and asked, "I'm sorry, but the American War of Independence ended in 1787; you said yesterday that we were in 1814. Why would you still be involved with the Revolution?"

"Not the Revolution, we are in the middle of a civil war between the Red Sticks and the White Sticks, two factions of the Muskogee people."

I remembered Liam's gallant speech to his people, and compassion rose up within me for these people. Civil war was something I understood. Even though I had not actually lived through the American Civil War, I was Southern, and that was as close to it as you could come. I looked at Barthenia and realized this would not be the last civil war she would be suffer. One day Thenie and her daughter Vera would have to protect Red Oaks through another Civil War.

"A civil war? Over what?"

"For decades, as long as I can remember, the white man, the Friguscor man, has come to our land. Most from across the great waters, and always with different tongues. Years ago, at the Council meetings within the Terebinths, we learned that the white men of France, Britain and Spain had designs on the land here where we live, and that large numbers of them were coming across the seas. Our focus became singular in nature. The Gate. Red Oaks had to remain in

Simulacrum hands. For years we have used the strong bond of the Eiani to protect the land as best as we can and for now, the Gate is safe, the land holds. But, something in this new war frightens me. I see a darkness rising on the horizon. The trees have warned us of a coming battle. The blood moon speaks of dark times. My father, Chief Liam, sees the coming tide; he knows the change that is inevitable, and he is trying to protect the lands and the Guardian the only way he knows how."

"And how is that?" Sarah asked.

"Through the power of our people. By bringing the Creeks together."

"But why get involved with them?" Sarah asked her, "I mean, why get involved with the wars of the Friguscor? They have always slain each other; Simulacrum do not get involved with the inner-workings of the Friguscor men."

Barthenia answered, "This war between the Creeks, though it was flamed by the pressure of the Friguscor to take the land, was started from within our own. The Red Sticks, are led by one called Osceola. He argues for a return to the old ways, to fight the white man and to keep our lands by force. But, Father, Chief Liam, does not agree. He sees what he calls the writing on the wall. He believes that the age of the Creek in these lands is over, but the age of the Simulacrum is still at hand. The most important thing is the land. We must at all cost keep the land and ensure that it does not pass into Friguscor hands."

"So, you will not fight with the Red Sticks?" Sarah asked.

Barthenia answered with a tight and steady gaze, "It began with Osceola and the tribes of the Creeks, but now the war involves the Americans, and they want the land just as much as the Creeks. After a group of Red Stick traders were attacked and murdered, they took revenge last August at an American fort called Mims. The Creeks killed many Americans there, women and children, too. Now, a white chief from Tennessee, called Stabbing Knife, his white name is Andrew Jackson..."

"Andrew Jackson," I said quickly, "you mean Stonewall Jackson, the seventh President of the United States?"

Barthenia's eyes narrowed, "He is no President; he is an Army general, and he has no love for our people. Madison is the President to the Americans. But I see this name, Jackson, lives in history for you?"

"Yes" I said trying to navigate this conversation without hitting anymore rocks, but failing terribly as I said, "He was our seventh president."

"Our?" She seemed confused. She leaned forward, "You are Simulacrum." She looked to Sarah, "and you are Guardian of Red Oaks in the years to come." Sarah nodded as Barthenia continued, "and yet you speak as though you have a president, as though you consider yourself an ... an American?"

Unsure of her meaning, I answered with a simple, "Yes."

She looked down at her hands and then back to me. Her eyes revealed little of what she was thinking. and yet I saw a sadness there that her calm face could not deny.

"Have I said something to upset you?" I asked.

"No." She shook her head and gave a long, heavy sigh.

"Sarah, you have said you are Guardian in the days to come, and yet you have little to no Creek in you."

Sarah stood silent, unsure of how to answer.

Barthenia was silent as well, but finally, with pain in her voice said, "If Stabbing Knife becomes a president to these United States, and you call yourself an American, then it is certain. The Red Sticks will lose this battle against Stabbing Knife on the Tallapoosa River."

"The Battle of Horseshoe Bend." I whispered under my breath. Out loud I said, "What do the other Creeks want with Red Oaks?" I asked.

Barthenia looked toward the single window in the room as she said, "They want my father to lead them. They want a leader for the White Sticks."

"Will he become entwined in the Friguscor wars?" It was Sarah who asked this time.

"Sometimes only a single path is before you, and you have no choice but to walk upon it. We must protect this land, and for now, leading the White

Sticks may be the only way against Osceola and the Red Sticks. But that is my father's path. Not mine."

She stood, "Dress, and I will be back for you shortly."

"Where are we going?" Sarah asked as Thenie moved toward the door. She stopped and looked at me, "You gave your blood to the dying man, a Friguscor man. There is someone who needs to speak with you."

"Who?" I said quickly; I did not want to speak to Absalom. The thought of him made my tseeyen vibrate with warning.

"I would not take you to him if it was not safe," Thenie said as though she understood. She stopped at the door and looked back, "I am your friend, Veralee. You will have to trust me now."

With that she left.

No, you are more than a friend, you are my grandmother, I thought.

Sarah turned to me, "Veralee, we must be careful even among our own while we are here. What we tell them could affect the outcome of their decisions."

I pulled off my shirt and pants as I said, "We can't change any of this, Sarah, what has happened has already happened, so whatever we do is already a part of this plan."

"Maybe," Sarah said pulling the dress over her head in one fluid motion, "Or maybe not. We don't know what we could influence or change, and besides, I am here for a reason."

"Why are you here, Sarah?" I said, matching her urgent tone as I stepped into the dress, "Why did you come here?"

Sarah stopped working on her dress and said, "I fled to the Hall of Teras after everyone vanished. Zulika was searching for me; she thought I might know something about the Hidden Books. I don't know how she knew I had it, or even if she really knew, but one thing was certain, she was dangerous. I knew I had to keep the book from falling into her hands. So, I was trying to get to Red

Oaks. Even though I was banished and they could kill me if I returned, I had to take the chance in order to warn them."

"Warn them of what?"

"Before time moved back, something was stirring among the Boged. They had been watching the sky for signs that were written in their Histories. They believed that something was coming. They were searching for the Nikud, the star that would lead them back."

"Yes, they called me that when I first arrived," I said. "I mean the first time, not the second time, or—ugh—" I stopped trying to explain, because I was confusing myself.

"Correct," Sarah said, "And the Nikud was to be a light that would lead them back. They believed that they were never meant to be separated from the Simulacrum. That it was a great tragedy that split us in two."

I remembered Apex, Callie, and Zulika the first time I had met them. They had been gracious and had fed and housed us, but they clearly were not happy with the idea. They believed Atticus was a traitor to the Boged, and Rhen had told us they planned to kill Atticus and make me stay with them against my will.

"But the Boged can't stand us. They don't like us at all."

Sarah said, "That is not true at all, Veralee. You understand little if you believe the Boged hated us. They wanted to be brought into our world, but rejection was the axe that split them from us. And eventually rejection turned to bitterness. Bitterness can look like hate, but if you see it for what it really is, it simply a child standing in the rain hoping that his mother will soon come to bring him home."

Sarah stopped and then said, "Turn around, and I will lace you up."

Sarah continued as she fastened my dress, "When they started searching for the Nikud, I began searching as well. I had one of the Hidden Books, so I knew the time was near. I sent Albert out to look for the one who could not only change the Friguscor into Simulacrum, but who could also find them."

I remembered Albert. He was the man in the hooded sweatshirt who followed Atticus and me through the streets of Atlanta. His life had ended in Agatha's bookstore when the Rephaim came to kill us. He was the one who had opened the tera which had allowed us to escape. He had saved our lives.

"I can find them; I can find the Boged," I said pushing the sadness from my mind, but finding it settled in my heart.

"I saw that when you gave the man your blood. You knew he could change, didn't you?" she asked, hopefully.

"Yes," I said and turned to face her.

"Veralee, did Albert find you? Was it you that I was looking for?" Sarah, my grandmother, my sister asked.

"Yes," I said, "He found me and brought me to the Boged, but he lost his life in the process."

It hurt Sarah to hear this. Tears misted her eyes, "He was the grandson of Apex, my dear friend. It was Apex who hid me among the Boged all of these years."

"Why did he let you stay?" I wondered out loud.

"Because of an old oath," she explained cryptically.

"Old oath?" I wanted to hear more.

"Apex is Rosa Westbrooke's father-in-law. He is a direct descendant of Moses, a baby my mother protected through the Civil War until Abram, his father, could raise him at Veritas Hills."

"Apex is Jackson's grandfather?" I asked, putting the pieces together.

"Jackson?" Sarah shook her head, "Who is Jackson?"

"Rosa's son."

"Oh," Sarah smiled. "I remember him as a baby."

She touched my white hair in the palm of her hand, "The Nikud glows like a star; it leads the people who have been scattered back home again."

"But I'm not the Nikud, Sarah," I said, wondering how to tell her what at one time she already knew. "I'm not who you thought I was at all."

"What do you mean, Veralee?" she asked and furrowed her brow.

"This is not the first time I have moved against the current of the River. Achiel took me back once before. He took me to see my mother and my father back at Red Oaks."

"That is where Gail changed you; did he show you the night you were changed?"

"No," I shook my head, "Achiel took me to see my true mother and my true father."

Sarah understood. It was all over her face. "The mother who birthed you?"

"Yes," I said, reaching down to grab her hands. "He took me back to the night of the Battle at Red Oaks."

Sarah's eyes narrowed in concentration.

"The battle?" she stammered knowing what battle I meant. That battle had been a celebrated event for Red Oaks for more than a hundred years.

"I saw Vera as she tried to escape that night. She had two babies with her. One was Moses, who she held in her arms, and the other was tied on her back with an Indian cradleboard."

Sarah looked weak, but I could not stop speaking. The truth of it all came spilling out of me.

"Atticus was there with her and a man named Jeremiah. He came in and kissed the baby just before the house shook from explosions outside. Before Vera left, I heard him tell Vera that their baby would be named 'Veralee.'"

"Veralee?" Sarah said my name as though it was suddenly as foreign as another language.

"He said, 'Her name shall be Veralee, for she shall be a shelter for the truth hidden within her veins.'" I told her, remembering the look on his face, the tenderness of his eyes, and the sadness hidden just behind them.

Sarah shook her head back and forth in denial.

"Mother was not married before my father, and she never had another child. What are you talking about?"

"Sarah, the night of the battle, Atticus helped Vera into the tunnel beneath the house. The one in the library. Jeremiah dropped into the tunnel just after, but something horrible came after him. It was not the Union soldiers or Friguscor men. It was a beast. A dead one. I think the Rephaim had come to Red Oaks to fight Jeremiah that night. The last thing Achiel let me see was Atticus pulling Vera away from Jeremiah."

I thought for a moment. "The Archaon must have moved me when Vera was going through the tunnel, and I think... somehow it moved Atticus as well. We were both pulled down the River of time, but we came out on different shores. I arrived nineteen years before him, but at the same place. We both arrived in the..."

"Tunnel beneath the Big House," Sarah finished my sentence, "where Gail found you."

"Yes," I whispered. We looked at each other. Years apart, but suddenly closer than we had ever been before.

"You are saying, that you, my young girl, my sweet granddaughter, are my older sister?" The laughter in her voice came as a welcome relief.

"Yes."

After one brief knock, Barthenia, stuck her head in and motioned us out.

"Why is the Seer looking for me?" I asked as we rushed through the night.

"It is because of the Friguscor man, the one to whom you gave your blood," she answered.

Beneath us the ground shook violently. I fell onto my hands and knees. The air smelled of smoke and gun powder.

"Cannon fire," Barthenia said. She stood quickly and then extended a hand to help me up. We were nearly the same height. Wasting no time, she helped Sarah to her feet as well.

"Barthenia, where is the Friguscor man?" Sarah asked. "Does he live?"

"Yes," she said. Leading us forward at a quick pace she added, "but I have not laid eyes upon him. The Seer has taken charge of the man."

"The Seer?" My stomach turned, "Why would the Seer want him?"

Barthenia stopped walking. The moon was rising behind her. "I will say this once. Not all who bear the Image are trustworthy."

We made our way through the village with relative ease though we could not escape the constant barrage of fear and panic that the sounds of battle grated against our nerves. We could smell fires burning in the distance. Barthenia knew every turn and path to take within the trees. Once we had to stop and hide as Friguscor men rode by on horses, but Barthenia was relentless and marched us forward at a pace that would have impressed Atticus.

Finally, she stopped before a small footbridge that was no larger than five feet wide.

"Come," she motioned that we follow her down to the steep creekbank.

The sound of the creek bubbled in my ears. The forest seemed peaceful here, but every time the wind blew, the fantasy was lost. The smell of gunpowder was undeniable. Not far from here, men were dying.

Barthenia stood beneath the bridge beside the creek. She whistled a soft bird call.

Bob-white.

In the distance a matching whistle answered through the trees.

Bob-white.

A medium-framed man with light blonde hair and golden-brown eyes stepped out from the blur of foliage. I let out a breath of relief that I did not know I had been holding.

"It's you," I said slightly shaken.

"Miss Veralee," he bowed low in the genteel fashion of his day as he asked, "It is Miss Veralee, is it not?"

I recognized the man from the earlier gathering. He had been standing outside the inner circle of the canopy, and had for the most part, been privy to most of the unspoken communication in Barthenia's constant gaze. He was the man who had asked and then had been denied the right to bond himself to her.

"Yes," I said, attempting to control my nerves. "And you are?"

He turned his black hat in his hand as he answered, "I am Ernest Weekes."

"Ernest Weekes?" A smile broke across my face, and then I laughed out loud at the irony, cupping my hand over my mouth.

"Of course, you're Ernest!"

"Ernest!" said Sarah, with great familiarity. This was the grandfather that we had never met and yet so much of him still defined our lives today.

The man standing before me in buckskin breeches, a long-tailed garnet jacket over a white collared shirt, and Hessian boots. He looked a picture of a gentleman if ever I did see one.

"You're wearing the jacket," I said in true awe. Mother had made Daddy a faithful replica of the clothes Ernest was wearing now. The clothes he wore in the only picture we had of him and Barthenia.

Ernest looked quickly to his jacket and back to me.

"I suppose I am," he looked to Thenie for an explanation before adding, "wearing a jacket, that is."

"And you're English!?" I asked, wanting to confirm everything I had been taught about him.

"Why yes," he lowered his head slightly, "I am that as well. Sussex."

"How did you get here? To Red Oaks I mean?" I wanted to know.

He started to speak, but then stopped and blinked his eyes several times as though he was working out a question in his mind before he spoke. He looked from Barthenia to me with a look of befuddlement.

"I apologize, Miss Veralee," He fumbled with his hat again, "but have we had the opportunity of making one another's acquaintance before this day?"

All my life I had thought this man was nothing more than a name and figure in a black-and-white photograph. A name in a long list of names. But now, he stood before me. Flesh and blood, living and vital with an unexpected yet pleasant, British accent.

"No," I forced myself to speak, but found I was oddly breathless. "No, I guess we have not. I was just wondering how you happen to be at Red Oaks." Fishing for something to make me sound more normal I asked, "Are you just traveling through?"

"I figure that is as good as description as any," he answered. His clothes were noticeably finer than any I had seen thus far at Red Oaks. He continued with manners of the well-bred, "But I have come with a purpose. You see, this past October, at the Council Meeting, I was honored to meet Miss Thenie."

Thenie. This was the name that Mother always used when affectionately referring to her great-grandmother. Ernest must have given Barthenia the nickname that would stick for generations.

Thenie looked at Earnest with such admiration that I was sure all of her dreams and hopes were kept safe in him. Ernest returned the gesture in his own way, for as he spoke, he motioned continually toward her with a constant, lovingmanner that included her in every word. They stood before me, gazing at each other as though they were the only two people under the bridge. Though Ernest spoke to me, I had the obvious feeling that he truly spoke only to Thenie.

"My family is from Sussex. I left home three years ago to broaden our profession in the cotton industry, in search of new lands through which to increase our revenue without the heavy taxation of the British government."

I tried to think of something to say that would sound knowledgeable but only came up with, "Oh?"

"And when it was time to attend my first Council meeting, I was led by my companion to Red Oaks."

"Your companion?" I asked.

"Yes," he continued, "And that is why I have asked to speak with you. I ... I want to confide in you, something of great, well, of great importance that should anyone else discover, it would leave me in a grievous state indeed."

"Okay," I answered, a little taken aback. Where was this leading?

Thenie stepped toward me and took my hand in hers as she said, "Please, Veralee. We heard what you said under the canopy." She turned to include Sarah and added, "We heard you say you both were banished as Law-Breakers."

My eyes flashed up to Earnest's face. He stood gazing down at me.

"Have you broken the Law?" I asked without thinking.

Thenie looked down at the ground, her head lowered. Whatever he was going to say, she already knew it. Ernest swallowed and began to talk, but then stopped as though his mouth was empty of words.

"If you have, I don't care." I said. "I don't care at all, actually."

Sarah paled, but I went on.

"The age of the Law is over. I will not live under it anymore."

"No, no," Ernest said bringing his hand up to his mouth. He kept it there until he agreed with some inner monologue after which he nodded to himself. "I was born into a family of great wealth. But in every way that truly mattered we were poor. When my father sent me to America to acquire new lands, I thought of only one thing, of the riches I would build. But along the road, the man I hired to travel beside me on the stagecoach began to tell me of myself. We traveled far into the wilderness, and there he told me of the Eiani."

"You were Boged?" This was new information! No one in the family had ever told me this. Perhaps they did not know. Secrets like this would be closely guarded in the Simulacrum community.

Ernest held out a trembling hand. "In the wilderness, late one night, he gave me his blood. I remember little but waking from the dead three days later.

To answer your question, Miss Veralee, I have not broken the law, but I plan to...with your help, that is."

"My help?"

"You said you saved a boy," Thenie said, her eyes flashing with excitement. "That you gave your blood to him and that was why you were banished. Then there is the Friguscor man you call Napoleon. You gave him your blood. We have not seen him, but they say, they say though he lays as a dead man, he is alive, and he is changing even now."

Earnest added eagerly, "Will you teach me?"

"Teach you?" I shook my head, "What do you mean 'teach you'?"

Ernest became suddenly serious. "I told you, I was rich in material things, but I was dead inside. I lived as one who walked the earth asleep and then, the blood of the Eiani came and brought me to life. It woke me from the darkness. It was as if I had crawled back into my mother's womb and was birthed again into the world a whole new man. The Law states that we cannot share our blood because of the possibility of starting the Esurio, the hunger in the Friguscor. Their concern is understandable, but I will honor no law that requires mankind to live their lives inside of their graves and offer no way out of their misery."

"It's not that I wouldn't," I tried to explain. "Trust me, you are speaking words that are dear to my heart. And I will help change any we can find while I am here, but I can't teach you how to find them. I mean I know how to find them, but I don't know how to teach you to do it."

"Veralee," Sarah came toward me, her hair sticking to the side of her neck from the humidity. "Have you changed more than just the boy and Napoleon?"

"Many," I nodded. "More than I can count."

"Many?" she said in pure disbelief. "Many?"

Sarah voiced the question that hung in the air. "But, have you ever been wrong? Have you ever given your blood and the change was not into Simulacrum, but into a blood-thirsty monster infected with the Esurio?"

"No. No, well, I don't think so. The Eiani ... I just know which ones are Boged. I believe the Eiani shows them to me," I answered truthfully.

Ernest smiled and shook his head, "Then you know not only how to change men, but how to find life within the dead!"

"I know how to find them, even in the midst of a crowd," I tried to explain. "But I don't know how to teach others to do it. I barely understand it myself."

Ernest stepped closer to me, "I know something that could."

As I looked into the eyes of my grandfather ,a memory surfaced in my mind.

Riding to Montgomery with Atticus in my car, the first time we were going to see little Nathan, Atticus had told me about life at Red Oaks during the Civil War.

"But the most curious thing about the plantation was the amount of Boged living there ..."

I remembered the conversation well. It was the first time I had ever talked to anyone about the Boged. The first time I had ever heard someone say out loud that they were actually real.

"To have that many of the Boged living together on Simulacrum land, it would indicate that someone was changing them," Atticus had said.

"Yes," I answered suddenly, feeling the answer on the tip of my tongue, "If you think you have something that will help me understand more, then I will teach you."

Earnest smiled and grabbed my hands, "Thank you, Miss Veralee. We plan on changing everything."

"Everything?" I looked up at him.

He in turn looked to Thenie, "Well ... maybe not everything," he smiled at Thenie, "But at least this small part of the world."

"Red Oaks?" I asked looking at the two of them. "You wish to be bonded to each other."

Ernest eyed Thenie, and I noticed they were sharing a secret moment before Ernest concluded, "We do not plan to wait for his approval. That is our decision to make and now the matter before is pressing. Will you come and see what I have that might be able to help you? It is hidden and we do not have much time. As the sun rises tomorrow morning, Thenie and I will stand before the oaks and say the words that bond us together for all of time."

"We will take you now," Thenie said as she turned and began walking down a small path that was just visible in the foliage. "We must be quiet, and avoid meeting any others."

The wind blew and brought a voice that surrounded me.

We see you.

The voice was so loud that I stumbled and almost fell to my knees, but Ernest caught me, "Are you alright, Miss Veralee?"

I swallowed down the panicked feeling and leaned against his arm as I righted myself, "Yes," I said a little breathless, "I just tripped, that's all."

But Sarah was not as easily convinced as the young couple. She stood for a moment and looked all around us, her wise eyes taking in the precarious surroundings of the forest at sunset. Had she heard the voice?

"We must move as the deer," Barthenia directed our group, "Do not speak until we arrive."

With a nod we agreed as we worked ourselves through the dense forest. Finally, after walking for half an hour, we arrived at a place I knew well. We were at the edge of a giant field where twenty great oaks lined what would one day be a road, but by then there would be twenty- eight giant oaks. I wondered briefly when Ernest and Thenie would plant the additional four trees on each side of the road to make twenty-eight.

"It's beautiful here," I whispered as we stood looking down the peaceful field. Just beyond the hill I knew a battle raged, but here, now, it was quiet.

"We must enter the current correctly to find ourselves at the riverbank. Otherwise we will not be able to locate it," Ernest whispered in the late-afternoon light.

"There is no river here," I gestured before us, "The river is at the back of the property." I knew this land.

"Not that river, Miss Veralee," Ernest answered, "A river the eye cannot see."

Sarah furrowed her brow, "If it is not a physical river, what does it mean to enter correctly?"

"We must begin our journey at the base of the farthest tree." He pointed to the end of the massive field, "And walk all the way down."

I looked over at the alleyway between the trees and then back at Ernest, "Is this safe to do? I mean, we are going to be pretty out in the open, and the battle does not seem to be far away."

"Safe?" Thenie said. "No, I suppose not, but it is what we must do."

"We must do it just as he showed me." Ernest added.

"He?" Sarah questioned.

"We can stay in the treeline all the way until we turn the corner and move to the middle of the field," I said pointing down to our right, "And then we have to make it from the treeline to the beginning of the trees. That is when we will be most vulnerable in the clearing between the large oaks and the start of the forest."

"If only there were more trees," Sarah said, straining to see in the dimming light, "That way there would not be a gap."

Ernest shook his head and agreed, "Yes, if only there were about one, two, three, well, maybe four more trees on each side."

I smiled at him, "Yeah, if only..." But my excitement was immediately cooled as my tseeyen began to glow in the dark. I felt a warning of danger run deep into my veins.

Thenie spoke, "We will follow you, Veralee, for you are the one with the plan forward."

"Okay," I answered, covering my arm. Together we worked our way forward. I tried to heed Thenie's advice, willing myself to walk and move like a deer though my arm was screaming the warning of danger. I looked back at Thenie. She was so quiet, the leaves seemed not even to move beneath her feet. But Sarah and I were at a strong disadvantage. We were somehow heavier here in this time, and I feared that we sounded more like elephants than mice. My fears were confirmed as we turned at the elbow of the trees and began making our way toward the center of the front side of the field through which we would make our way to the large oaks. Someone was following us.

Thenie heard them first. Her cry was barely audible as she whispered, "Stop!"

The smell of rot, of putrid ruin, floated in the air. A large group of men were slipping silently through the trees.

Instinctively we lowered ourselves to the ground. Lying flat, Thenie showed us how to slide beneath the bushes.

A man stopped just beside us and motioned to his men. He was tall, lean and the color of the moon with silver hair.

"Osceola," Thenie whispered into my ear.

He turned as though he had heard her say his name. We held our breath. He stepped closer and smelled the air. One, two, three steps closer. He was almost on top of me. I could see his face from beneath the bush where I lay flat, though the air between us looked somewhat misty.

Then he looked straight at me. I froze in terror; he must have seen me! I started to run, but felt a heavy hand on my back holding me in place. I wanted to scream, but found I could not utter a sound.

"The blood of the Malachi ..." the hiss of his voice rang out. My heart began to pound so loudly that I thought he could hear it.

He furrowed his brow and mocked derisively, "Why have you come now?"

I knew he would reach down and grab me any second now.

A horrifying screech ripped through the air that I had not only heard before, but I would never forget. Chills ran up my spine. It was from one of the beasts.

When Atticus and I were trying to make our way to BaVil in Atlanta, we had happened upon a stationary train full of terrified people being guarded by a monstrous, hybrid beast. When I had recognized my Friguscor friend from college, Emmalie, among the captives, Atticus and I had tried to free them. The beast had awakened and killed Emmalie. It had appeared to be a hybrid of animal and human and had superhuman strength, human intelligence, and augmented animal speed and hunting abilities. The same beast had hunted down Sarah in the woods.

Osceola heard the roar and yelled, "Come!" to his men. All started running toward the sound. Miraculously, Osceola ran back toward his men and away from us! He hadn't seen me after all!

"They must have come through the tera," Sarah said as we scrambled to our feet.

A roar that sounded both like a combination of a woman screaming in the night and the cry of a lion cut deep between us.

Ernest exclaimed, "What, what, is that?!"

Thenie stammered, "That is no animal of this forest!"

"They are Raptors, trackers, created by BaVil. They are trained to hunt us, and they will not stop until they taste Simulacrum blood. Go quickly," Sarah said, squeezing my arm, "I will come if I can, but take them and run! Go, Veralee, and don't look back, not even for a moment!"

"No!" I protested.

But, Sarah was pushing me forward as she spit out the words, "Run, Veralee! Run! You have the key and the book! You must survive! The way is in your blood, Malachi!"

As the words fell from her mouth, I turned, grabbing Thenie's hand and burst through the hedge. My dress snagged on a bush, and I ripped it as I pulled it free, but I did not stop.

"Run!" I screamed at Ernest.

The wind rushed up behind us as we fled, helping us forward, giving speed to our flight. The forest around us began to blow with an opposing great wind. A storm was just above us, but it had no rain to give, for it was not to feed the earth but to take away. By the light of the rising moon we ran through the gap between the trees. My body was electrified with the fear of what ran somewhere behind us.

Suddenly, a rider on a horse came galloping toward us from the left, but I pushed forward, refusing to stop. Loud yelping sounds of men came from the trees and shots rang out.

"We must make it to the trees!" I screamed.

Behind us a loud, inhuman cry erupted, and I knew the beast had picked up our scent. The horseback rider pursued us. But behind him, I vaguely recognized another rider.

The first rider was Friguscor, and even in my flight I smelled the rot of his skin on the wind.

Ernest yelled, "Watch your left flank!" just as the Native American man on horseback veered toward me, a large hatchet in his capable hand. I tripped on a root and fell just as he swiped the razor-sharp weapon toward my neck, causing him to miss.

We were still a hundred yards from the safety of the Oaks.

Thenie reached her hand down, "Get UP!" I took her hand and rose, but the horseman circled back quickly and now was coming directly at us. We turned and started scrambling back to the tree line. The wrong direction, I knew, but we had no options.

A chilling battle cry escaped the rider's mouth, and I felt the heat of the horse behind me. "Sapru!" the man yelled, and I recognized him as Osceola. The horse nipped at my hair, pulling my head backward as my body began to follow. and just as I fell to the ground, the first horse trampled my leg, just missing my head. I screamed.

As the momentum rolled me over, I saw the second rider barreling toward us. He threw a dagger from an incredible distance, and Osceola's horse buckled underneath him and thrashed from the wound. But Osceola was up with incredible speed and turned purposely toward me. He began running with his hatchet held high above his head. I screamed again, and with a damaged knee, tried to move, pushing my feet into the ground and heaving myself backward using my palms and rear.

The second rider came back around. A single blade came flying through the air with such speed and accuracy that I knew whose arm had thrown it. Just as the blade hit its target, and Osceola fell to the ground I called out, "Atticus!"

But I had no time to listen for his answer for I heard the roar of the horrible beast followed by Sarah's agonizing scream. I knew why.

"Sarah!" I screamed, knowing I could do nothing for her now. This was the second time I had heard her scream her last at the claws of that beast.

"Atticus," I screamed as he rode hard toward me. His horse was panting heavily and sweat covered its brown body.

Atticus dismounted and commanded Ernest, "Get Barthenia to the trees."

He turned, looked down at me, and pulled me up with one fluid motion, "Your leg is hurt?"

"Sarah, my grandmother," I pointed behind us, "She is in danger."

"We cannot go back for her now; there is nothing we can do for her. We must get to the trees," he said. He held me upright.

Tears fell down my cheeks. I already knew that she was gone. I had felt it the moment she had fallen.

"How did you know to come?" I gasped, touching his bearded face.

"I felt you." He added, "My tseeyen."

"I knew you would come," I whispered.

With that he threw my right leg over, positioning me on the horse, before pulling himself back into the saddle. The exhausted horse obeyed as Atticus jerked the reigns with a forceful, "Hiyay!" Heavy hooves bore into the ground and rushed toward the great oaks. Forcing myself to ignore my throbbing leg, I wrapped my arms around Atticus and held on. It was the safest place in the world. Ernest and Thenie were almost there as we passed them.

"We have to get them all the way down the alley of the trees." I said to Atticus, my hands wrapped closely around his chest. For a small second, the smell of him overwhelmed me and as the horse galloped forward, I let it pour strength into my frayed nerves. The horse stopped just behind the first large oak.

Atticus helped me dismount and then dropped down to the ground with a thud.

Thenie and Ernest ran into the trees and stood, catching gulps of fresh air.

"Why are you out here?" Atticus's voice was rough.

Ernest said, "We have to get something, we–"

"The Hidden Books are here, Atticus." I said looking at him. "The books you read when you were with the Boged. When you met Zulika."

Atticus looked at me for a long moment. His green eyes staring into mine. I willed him to hear me. I know you, and you know me.

The nearness of him made my tseeyen vibrate, and I watched as he glanced curiously down at his own mark. He looked back up, and the truth was undeniable in his eyes. He felt it as well.

Take my hand, remember...

He opened his mouth to speak, but a familiar sound of horror cut him off. He, Ernest, and Thenie all turned to see what could have made such a sound.

"What is that?" Atticus asked.

The beast now stood at the other side of the clearance, stamping its heavy claws into the earth. It stretched its neck up toward the boiling sky; lightening erupted through the clouds. The trees were bending under the weight of the wind.

"It's from my time," I said quickly, "It will be slower than normal until it adjusts but also much heavier. It is a hunter. It won't stop until it has tasted blood."

"Where is Sarah?" Thenie asked.

But I could not answer her, for I knew in the depths of my bones what had happened to Sarah. Sarah had given her life for mine, again. I would not let her fall asleep in vain. Honoring her last request, I turned to Ernest, "You are sure the books are at the end of the trees?"

"Yes," he said quickly.

"Atticus, can you get Ernest and Thenie down to the end and then come back for me?"

"No," Ernest and Thenie rebutted, "No, we will not leave you here."

"Atticus," I held his gaze and pulled his own blade from my leg, "Get them to the end, and come back for me."

His green eyes burned into mine. Our tseeyens popped with hot electricity in the night air. He looked at the blade and then back to me as he said, "Where did you get that?"

"You gave it to me."

His jaw tightened as he promised, "I will come back for you."

"I know."

Ernest said, "I will run. Take Thenie!" With that Atticus threw Thenie on the back of the horse. Atticus looked to me and then turned the horse toward where one day my own home would be built.

The creature screamed into the air, filling my blood with fear. The creature had come through the tera. But how did it know to follow us? Immediately I knew.

Absalom.

It had to be. Peaking around the tree, I saw as Osceola sat up, pulled the hatchet from his neck and began to stand.

Then the trees moved with a violent wind. Before I saw him, I heard his voice.

"We see you."

Absalom was standing in the midst of an unnatural wind, his black robes flapping against himself. In his hands he held a book, with half of a Dekeract on the front.

One at a time, three beasts came to stand behind Absalom. I turned and began to run on my injured leg. The sound of the creature burned in my ears but still, I ran. My white hair ripped across my face as the wind roared around me, but still, I ran.

"Give us the Key," I heard the voice from all the way across the field. "You are the Malachi."

I was the hunted; the beasts were there for me.

Absalom opened the book and began to read, "Kakkibis samami...ana simatu awilutim..."

It became hard to breathe, my chest began to brighten, revealing the key as he read the words from the book. The largest beast stepped forward.

I willed myself forward, regardless of the pain in my leg and now my chest.

I can't stop. I have to run. I've come too far to die here.

I scrambled forward in the darkness, not knowing where my feet would land, but fearing what lay behind me more than what waited before me. I felt the ground shake behind me as the beast began to run. As I ran, I counted, I was only nine trees in, I would not make it before the beast reached to me.

Absalom called to me, his voice echoing off the trees, "You are the Malachi! They hid you in the River. I should have known it the first time I saw you. I thought you were simply another repeat of Ernest, but no... You are the Malachi! We see you!"

He opened the book and said, "I will destroy you with the words of your own father...Kakibis Samami..."

The key felt as though it was coming up my throat. I clenched my teeth together.

I heard hoofbeats, and I knew it was Atticus, coming back for me as he had promised. His horse came strong and steady toward me as Absalom called to me over and over again, each word running into the next.

"Malachi! Malachi!"

"Atticus," I screamed.

He circled beside me, and I raised my hand to him. With all the strength of his body and the support of the wind which lifted me, Atticus swung me around, pulling me onto the horse. I landed with a hard thump and grapped tightly onto his waist. The horse was breathing heavy. The wind raged around us. The beast raced to catch us. The darkness closed around us.

I buried my head into his back.

"Look!" he cried.

Before us, I saw a golden door cut in the bottom the upturned side of a large oak.

"Veralee! We must get to the door!"

"What did you say?"

He yelled the words again. The words I had heard for years in my dreams as we rushed toward the golden door.

"You must get to the door!"

Adair 2:5

Thunder erupted in the distance and though it held promise, it brought no rain, only a dryness that parched my aching throat. The call from the beast screamed at me again. I felt the weight of it upon my chest and smelled the rankness of its breath.

"Inman said he would be back by the edge of dark," Deena said, breaking me free from the memory of the monster. I steadied my breathing and slowly unlocked my fingers from the arms of the rocking chair where I sat frozen in fear. My fingers were as white as I felt. Deena was watching the treeline for movement.

Phineas and Mattie had not yet returned from investigating the condition of the gate. With my injury not fully healed, I had stayed behind, doing what I could from home. Simulacrum continued to stream into Red Oaks, seeking safe haven, just as the Boged had before. The world I knew was literally collapsing before my eyes. I sighed deeply and determined not to think of Nathan or the Boged, Inman, or any of it. It was too painful.

Instead, I had spent the last few days making a list of everything I could think to do, organizing groups to distribute food from the barns and creating work spaces for essential tasks. Food was soon going to be a problem, but for now, we would live off the harvest. Our running water had stopped at the Big House this afternoon, but, with the river running through the land, we would not run out of water. At every obstacle, we had thought of a solution; still, housing this many people at Red Oaks had me putting ten pounds in a five-pound sack every day.

Well, we had thought of a solution for every obstacle except the attitude of Eliezer; he had crews working steadily to fell our oaks and built them into a wall. If I could, I would rip down that wall with my bare hands. The massive wooden wall now stood at the end of our Oak alley.

Agatha and Deena sat wrapped in blankets beside me. They looked like old, feeble women instead of the Simulacrum of my childhood. It bothered me, but instead of showing them that, I smiled.

I moaned, as I stood up. It was the only sound I could make. Why are those men stomping through mother's flower gardens like a herd of elephants? I motioned toward the flowers with both hands.

"Adair," Deena's voice was soft but becoming more solid, "Adair?"

I looked at her and then back at the scene before us. Large, grand oaks were being dragged across the field as dead bodies to their burial place. The wall. A tomb for our trees.

"You know those flowers do not matter anymore," she said softly but sternly. "You are going to have to let a lot go in the coming days, so you might as well start with the flowers. The flowers do not matter anymore. Do you hear me? Do you understand? Let it go, child."

I would have loved to give her the tip of my tongue. Instead I watched in silent fury. I had lost my parents, my sisters, Nathan, and in many ways, my daughter. I could not bear to lose anymore.

"I need to tell you something." Agatha spoke for the first time, and we both looked at her expectantly. She had been almost silent since the meeting in the library. It had made me uncomfortable to look at her. Her eyes vacant, staring off into space as though she was somewhere far away.

Suddenly the porch trembled as Ruach came through the trees toward us. Agatha stopped speaking and looked toward the forest to watch his approach.

The giant took the fields in quick, swift, steps. His movement was more like dancing than running; it was light, swift and rhythmic as he came toward us, his long hair beating against his back.

I noticed his sword, and immediately I thought of the beast again. I could hear it screaming as it lunged for me. I swallowed hard.

Would there be other beasts soon?

Phineas had told me that our bullets had not dropped the creature that bore the face of a woman, that it was only the sword of light that had been able cut it down.

"The GateKeeper told us of your wounds," Ruach said as he came near. "We have come to offer healing to you, Agatha, the Discerner."

The Discerner?

Then I remembered. Agatha had sat as the Discerner under Richard, my grandfather.

I nodded to Deena but turned back to Agatha again and wrote,"Why did you step down?" on the chalkboard in my lap.

Deena looked at the chalkboard and answered for Agatha.

"When a new Judge assumes that position, it is customary that other Council members who wish to step down can do so at that time, or they continue to serve as the Judge wishes."

I looked at the two women and knew there was more.

Agatha sighed as though Deena exhausted her.

"It was safer for me to come off the Council than to stay," she said, pulling the shawl closer to her neck as though suddenly chilled. "Adair, the story your mother told at the Council meeting, the story about finding your sister behind the bookstore was not the true story of how Veralee came to be your sister, though it was the one told the night your Grandmother Sarah was banished, and it was the story your Grandfather Richard insisted Gail tell when the time came."

Something familiar lurked in the recesses of my mind, a memory, or a dream. Agatha reached out and grabbed my hand.

"Ruach will show you," she said.

As Agatha spoke, I saw it all, as if I had been there.

"Your mother found Veralee here in the tunnel under the house and changed her. We were all here for the celebration of Richard's life days. I did not see Veralee before your Mother gave her the blood, but she believed the child to be a Friguscor babe who was close to death. But years later, as I read the Hidden Book, I began to wonder about Veralee. And then, last year, when she came into the book store, I heard her heart for the first time. I heard it beat with a trill.

She looked at Ruach.

"The Archaon came to her first. I should have put it all together, but I was blinded by the purpose of seeing the book to safety. But the Archaon, you must have known?"

Ruach narrowed his cat-like eyes and the colors of his pupils seemed to intensify.

"You discern correctly, Daughter of the Blood.

Agatha took a deep breath and lowered her head as though exhausted.

"Richard must have known as well," she said. "He must have understood more than we did, for he came to me at my shop and made a very odd request. He asked me to step down from the Council if he should fall."

Suddenly I was standing in the bookstore watching Agatha's memory play out before me.

"Fall?" Agatha protested, "Why would you say such a thing, Richard? Who would put you to sleep?"

He was broad shouldered, handsome, and refined. His salt and pepper hair and coal black eyes shone with glints of wisdom as he said, "Agatha, I have made many mistakes in this life. Too many to count. I plan on righting all that I can by protecting those whom I love before I go. My end is coming. The Eiani has revealed it in my dreams and I know that there are those who seek to end my days. What will be will be; we cannot change the will of the Eiani."

"Why do you speak as if it is already done?" Agatha asked. "Is it the will of the Eiani that the Judge of the Council fall to the ground? Do you not have warriors who sit on our Council? Reveal those who seek your days, and you will have a long life ahead of you.

Richard leaned across the counter and reached for her hand. It was small against his wide palm.

"Because it is, Agatha. Twice I have dreamt of my end."

"Twice?" Agatha's confident look seemed shaken.

Richard nodded and continued. "I do not fear my end, for the Eiani has a plan. It is just that I give my life without complaint, for we both know I took life that was not mine to take."

"You did not know all that you know now, Richard, and besides, Ernest refused to stop even after he had been warned. You did the best you could at the time. Stop heaping guilt upon yourself. Sarah has forgiven you ..."

He stood up.

"But I cannot forgive myself, and I will not allow another death to come at my hands of my own kinsman."

"You speak of the girl?"

"Blood of my blood," he said. "She cannot stay hidden from the Council."

Awareness entered Agatha's eyes, "And you cannot be the Judge when Gail comes before the Council, so you will resign your rightful place."

"I understand, but then you must retire to the Terebinths and wait for Sarah to join you. It is not so hard."

"I shall not make it that long," he said, as though they were a certainty. "Promise me, Agatha. When I fall, step down from the Council and protect the Hidden Book. The Council is no longer safe. I fear that it has been unsafe for many years."

"The Seer?" Agatha raised an eyebrow.

"Maybe," Richard shook his head, "Maybe not. I am not sure where the rip in the seam begins, but I feel the presence." Richard stood upright from where he had been leaning against the counter and released her hand.

"But I can trust you, and I need you to protect the Hidden Book."

"Why?" Agatha insisted, "What's in the book?"

"One more thing," Richard said, without answering her question. "Remember never to read the book aloud."

"Why?" she asked. "What is in the book that cannot be read aloud?'

"Reading the books aloud brings it into present. It pulls the prophecy from yesterday and tomorrow into today. It is the power of the words. Do not read it aloud before it is time, for it is to remain sealed until the appointed day. Keep it safe, keep it hidden, and above all else, do not allow it to fall into another's hands."

As he spoke, he slid the book across the counter. It was black, bound in leather and adorned with half of an elaborate gold and silver dekeract star on the front cover.

"You have had this book the entire time?" Agatha asked in awe and wonder.

"On the night of Veralee's arrival, after Gail pulled the babe from the tunnel, and the chaos of the event had passed, and the house had gone to sleep, I took a light and opened the hatch once more. I knew the books would be there. I had been told to guard the house, the Guardian and the Gate from the darkness, but I had never actually seen the Hidden Books."

"Books? There are more than one? And you had never seen them?"

"Yes, there are two books. And, no, I had never before that moment seen either of them," he said. "I knew they were in that tunnel, for Vera herself told me. She told me the books would be in the tunnel and when it was time, to get them out."

"And how did Vera know this?"

"That was at our bonding ceremony in the Terebinths. Vera told me of a dream that the Eiani had given her many years before. She said she had dreamt for years of a girl with a crown of snow and golden fire in her chest who was running from a great dragon. In her dreams, the girl was always running up spiral steps in a tall tower, round and round as the dragon chased her, blasting fire from his mouth. As the girl ran, she grew. The dragon sought to burn and destroy the girl, but she evaded and finally became a woman.

"Vera said the secret to the hidden books was deposited in the girl. And in her dream Vera kept trying to read the words of the Hidden Books to the woman who ran on the spiral steps, but every time she got close, the woman would be moved a flight up. It was as though an unseen force was pulling the girl through a current of water. On and on the dragon pursued her, but the woman ran tirelessly as the sun turned to evening and the evening to the darkest part of night. Finally, at the top of the great spiral staircase, the woman with the crown of snow stood as the dragon approached her from the east. His great wings beat across the skies, blowing the woman to her knees. He gathered air, readying himself to burn her in flames. But Vera stood several flights beneath her, and with nothing left in her hands to help, she threw the book up, hoping to hit the beast as it flew over them both. The book, she said, turned into a great bird, a sparrow made of metal clock parts. As the dragon released the fire, the bird hovered over the face of the woman and the flames did not consume her but passed over her and she lived.'

Richard had stopped and thought for a moment.

"I thought for years that the girl was Sarah."

"Because Sarah is Vera's only daughter," Agatha said.

He nodded in agreement.

"As I lay in my bed that night, I remembered Vera's warning dream. It had always sat just under my consciousness. I kept thinking about how Vera said the woman in her dreams was a young girl who grew as she ran up the stairs. When the babe arrived, I realized the girl in Vera's dreams was not Sarah.

And with my candle in my hand, I rose and looked for the books. Inside the tunnel, not far from the opening, I found a clear box outlined in gold. I touched the top. It was like water. My hands passed through it into the box, and I pulled the books out. A voice said, 'Twice will it open, only once will it close.'

When I lifted up the books, the pages fell open. I knew that the baby who had come to us that night was the girl in Vera's dreams. So, the next morning when Gail came down with the babe in her arms, I told her we should name her Veralee for Vera had said the woman was her daughter."

I was back on the porch. Richard, the bookstore, and the memory was gone.

Ruach was almost smiling as he added, "She is a shelter for the truth hidden in her veins and the golden fire kept in her chest."

Agatha said, "I do not pretend to understand how, maybe it is simply allegorical, or maybe it is from the help of the Archaon, but Veralee is the daughter of Vera. Or so that is what Richard believed."

"By the word of Paraclete, we were ordered to protect the Daughter of the Blood, the last of the Guardians, so we took the small baby and placed her in a basket just before we waded her out into the river. We are still to guard and protect the Daughters of the Blood."

I grabbed my chalkboard and wrote, "Why the house?"

"Beneath the house is a secret," said Ruach. "The house was built upon the banks of the River."

Agatha added, "And that must have been how the books were hidden in that tunnel for so long. Because the tunnel is the bank of the River of time."

Beneath our house was some kind of entrance into the river of time? I got up and went to the door. Throwing it open, I made my way to the library. The rug sat perfectly as Mother had left it. I turned it up and saw the small door in the floor. Ruach entered behind me, covering most of the space in the room as Deena and Agatha squeezed in as well.

I tried to pull the wooden door open, but found it stuck. Ruach reached over and opened it with ease. I peered down into the tunnel. Nothing, just dirt.

Agatha sat in the winged back chair. "It is there. Just because you can't see it does not mean it is not there."

I stood and grabbed the chalkboard off the desk, "Where are the books?"

"Richard only gave me one book. He refused to tell me where the other was, for the safety of the books themselves. But the night we met in secret in the forest to decide Gail's punishment for her crime, Sarah volunteered so quickly to take Gail's place that I wondered if she had the other book. On the outside, it made perfect sense for a mother, who had recently lost her bondmate to give her life for the life of her daughter's by taking the punishment of banishment. Then I discovered that she had not gone to the Terebinths, but that James Westbrooke had helped her leave Red Oaks. Then I knew she must have had the other book."

Quickly I wrote, "Why didn't she just take it into the Terebinths?"

Deena answered this time.

"None of the Histories, not even the Hidden Histories can enter the Terebinths, for they are temporal words, words for today, that will not last beyond the seventh day. They cannot enter through the gates or they will vanish, having already been and become what is for what will be."

Agatha said, "Richard knew the book would be safer with the Boged, for the Simulacrum would never unite with the Boged."

"Yes," Deena said, "It was the duty, or part of the duty, of the Council to keep the Simulacrum separate from the Boged."

"Why?" I wrote the question and held it up. After Tessa and Nathan and Veralee. Why was it so important to keep them separated?

Deena was silent, but rocked her chair several times before she said, "Because of the Dividing Wars when the Simulacrum and Boged killed each other en masse, and because," she swallowed, "because they are a lie! A lie told centuries before to undo us, to break our way of life, to break down our Law ... all because of a liar named Boged. He sleeps today in his tomb for what he did!"

Sleeps? I remembered the tomb. The giant, Uziel had told me that the tomb had belonged to Beged. The stone table where his body once lay was empty. The bodies of Ernest and Richard lay undisturbed on the stone tables in their tombs, but Beged's tomb was empty.

Agatha spoke, "His name was not Boged, but Beged, and he was no traitor."

"He was the ultimate traitor to our people," Deena hissed. "You know our History."

"I know our version of history, for we wrote what we wanted to believe. That is why the books were deemed a danger, why they were thrown down that tera which you followed and why they are considered a danger even to this day. They told the true story. They told what really happened so long ago, when the Simulacrum felled one of their own. When they used the Friguscor to kill the man named Beged."

Ruach looked to Agatha and asked, "Daughter of the Blood, you are wise, but how were your eyes opened when you are born of those whose eyes refuse to see?"

Agatha lifted her eyes to him, "It was the Machine. As I lay as one who was dead, all of these things ran through my dreams. The words of the Hidden Book, the teachings of my youth, and even the girl. But it was when he came to me that I truly understood.

"In my dream, I was a blind woman stumbling in the dark. I fell to my knees and grappled with the ground, trying to stand. I heard someone kneel beside me and then a man's voice full of power, but also with compassion, asked me if I wanted to be healed, if I wanted to see again. I put my hands out to touch him, but I could not. "Yes! Yes," I blurted out. I heard him spit into his hands, and then I felt cool mud on my eyes. As he wiped the dirt of the earth over my eyes, I heard him say, 'From the river of the Gihon, the waters of the beginning, healing is coming to your people, so that the blind may open their eyes and once again see. Then and then only will I come. Go and stand as a light, shining in the dark.'

"Then I could see! I was healed! I looked up to see who had healed me, and I saw the most amazing sight: a man made purely of words! I woke to Absalom pulling me down from the Machine and throwing a blanket over my shoulders."

Agatha stopped speaking, trying to catch her labored breath. She looked so very frail and old as Rauch asked, "Do you wish to be healed now, Daughter of the Blood, one who has come to see though her eyes were born into darkness?"

Agatha smiled. Her smile was no longer beautiful, though it was somehow peaceful. She shook her head.

"No."

"Agatha, let him heal you," Deena said.

"No," she said again, "I will stand as a witness to all who see me. That is my last sacrifice to the blood that I can give. My face and my body will tell of what the dark ones have done. So that all Simulacrum will look on me and believe. For I am to tell them all, that we have all been born blind. We have all missed the very thing we have been waiting for."

"And what have we missed, Agatha?" Deena asked in dismay.

Agatha leaned forward and with a trembling voice said, "The Door, Deena, we have missed The Door."

The Door? I shook my head vigorously, but lightning struck inside my chest as I remembered the words of Wisdom from that day in the woods with Nathan, Mattie, and Ruach. Ruach had taken Nathan, Mattie, and me to meet Wisdom near what Ruach called the Stones of Remembrance. Wisdom had called Nathan a child of Beged and said creation, which was never meant to be divided, was longing to be reunited. Then she narrated the story of the fallen Archaon, how they had tried to erase the image of the One Tree, and then were imprisoned in the City of Baryiach, the City of the Eight Gates. She said that they would again try to erase the Image.

That was the only time in my life that I had seen a vision of the One Tree. Tears formed as I remembered the beauty, the overwhelming awe I had felt. The Man of Words had emerged from the flaming One Tree; he had formed a helix like DNA, blew upon it, and then placed it into a clay man he had formed. Wisdom prophesied that one from the line of Seth would stand forever before the One Tree, like a lamp burning against the night.

The one who carries the mantle carries a light that will not be overcome. The Image will not be erased. No power shall prevail against the One Tree's plan. Let what was divided be united, for the time of restoration is upon us...Do not fear the change that is coming. Your foundation will be shaken, but blinded eyes must be opened to see truth. For what was divided must be united, and then the second door will open.

Then, she showed me the most beautiful scene: Mattie as an adult, Phineas, Veralee, Ausley, Mother, Daddy. All of us reunited. I remembered watching the scene and saying,

"I thought we lost it all. The gates... they fell, we failed... all was lost!'"

But the Man of Words had looked at me and said, "Not one was ever lost."

Ruach had told me then that the vision was a gift to hide in my heart, a promise of what will come to hold onto when the night becomes dark.

Do not rely on the plans and schemes of men, Daugher of the Blood. They cannot deliver victory. Place your trust in the promises of old. The trees that were meant to protect, the watchers who were meant to guard, and the Eiani that was meant to redeem. Only in the ancient ways will you find what you seek.

Just before she left, Wisdom had told me, "What was divided must be reunited and then, the second door will open."

I knew this was all connected. Mattie was now an adult, just like in the vision...and Wisdom had called Nathan a child of Beged but still, I wondered.

"What do the Boged have to do with the Door?" I wrote on my board.

"The Boged are the evidence that the Door has opened," Agatha explained. "We thought they were the enemy, trying to destroy our way of life, when they were the proof that we could not believe. Maybe that is why our people hated them so. The Friguscor were brought into the fold, grafted into the Simulacrum so that all mankind would have a chance to enter through the second door, which comes at the final beginning. We believed that there was only one Door, and we were right, but what we did not understand is that the Door would open twice. Once to bring the Boged in, and twice to take us all back home. They were right, Adair, and we were wrong. That is what I have come to tell our people, and I am not to take any healing. Look at me now, girl, and see. I am our people."

She held out her hands, showing the brokenness of her body, "I am the future of our people should we choose to turn away again."

I wanted to cry out, "No!" but of course, I could not. And somehow it all came together. I knew she was right.

Agatha drilled her eyes into mine.

"The Hidden Books tell the true story." She said, leaning forward. "Don't you understand? The story of how the Door first opened is inside those books. We hid them from the people because we believed them to be heresy. They were against our Law, our way of life, and we could not have them read. So, Deena's father ..."

My eyes cut over to Deena.

Deena explained, "I was born in India, after the Mongol invasion, to the line of Judges for the Simulacrum Council."

Chaim Arukim. The lineage of Judges and TimeKeepers were given the gift of long-life.

"My father was a child of the Dividing Wars. He knew the books were dangerous to our people. He tried, like many others, to destroy the books, but he could not for they were not made of mortal things. One night, my father found me reading from the books. I read a single page aloud before he could stop me. I didn't realize it, but it opened a tera on the ground beside me. My father tossed the books in, but the pull of the tera took me as well. Five hundred years later, I emerged from the waters of the tera. I was twelve years old."

Deena's shoulders sagged.

"When I came through and realized what had happened to me, I knew my father had been right. Those books brought nothing but harm to me. So, I relinquished myself of the burden. I gave the books to a stranger with a tseeyen that matched the symbol on the front of the books, aboard the Chatham, on my way to America."

She turned to Agatha. "What you are saying is against everything we have always known. The Door has not opened yet. We still wait for it. Daily I wait for it. You are sick and weak. All you saw was a dream from the loss of blood."

"No," Agatha said her voice suddenly strong. "I tell you the truth. The Man of Words came and spoke to me. The Door has opened! The story of Boged was a lie, Deena. His name was Beged!"

"No" said Deena, emphatically. "His name was Boged!"

"That is what we were taught, Deena, for they wanted to hide the truth," Agatha refused to acquiesce.

"Why? If it was true, why would they hide it?" Deena demanded, shaking her head, and I felt the circular nature of our arguments defining everything around us. Deena kept the argument going as she shook her head. "No, you are not making any sense, Agatha."

"Because they could not believe, would not believe, that the blood is for the Simulacrum and the Friguscor. We wanted it to be just us, we wanted to keep it for ourselves, but it was never meant for that, Deena! The Eiani was meant for all mankind! You know this!"

Agatha turned from Deena to face me, "We must find the books, Adair. They will not believe without reading it in the books. The dark ones have the one. They caught me at my bookshop. I should have known better than to return there. They killed Sonith and took me and the book."

I picked up the chalkboard. Something Deena said did not make sense. These books were so valuable, they had been so well protected and hidden for so long, and yet Deena said that she just gave the books away to some person on a ship?

"Who did you give the books to?" I held up the board and pointed to Deena.

Deena sighed. "Some man I met on the ship. He ..." she looked defeated, "I was a twelve-year-old girl. His name was Jeremiah."

"The tera has opened," said Ruach as he turned and started out the large oak doors in one swift motion.

I stood up and began to run out the door after him.

"Adair, remember you are not the Guardian of the Gate!" Deena called after me.

"No," I thought as I ran, "But I am still her mother!"

Ruach met me at the steps and lifted me onto his back before I could protest. Months ago, I had found the tera and showed it to Phineas, and then that day in the woods with Wisdom, I had told Ruach about it. He had already known and said the Archaon were monitoring it.

A large crowd had already gathered when we arrived. I had no time to think of what Agatha had said for all thoughts of history were replaced by a more present danger as Inman stood before us.

After our heated meeting the other night, Inman had returned to Atlanta to get help. There he stood, and behind him, a large group of Friguscor men and women.

Eliezer's warriors stood poised to attack, their guns raised, their backs arched as though they would pounce at any movement.

Mattie stood in the middle, her golden hair shining unnaturally, floating as though it were altogether something from a dream. The light dimmed unnaturally around us. Heat lightening popped in the sky. I walked slowly, feeling the heaviness in my leg as I evaluated the scene before me.

Mattie spoke in a whisper, "Mother, Veralee is so very close to us here, can you feel her?"

Veralee? She is in the Machine, I thought.

Mattie had her eyes closed as though she was listening to something very far away.

"No," she whispered in a voice that I barley recognized as her own. She raised her arm to mine and opened her eyes. "Feel this, Mother."

She placed her tseeyen on my own and for a moment, I felt the closeness of Veralee as though she was just right around the corner.

"She is closer than we think," Mattie said, a smile skirting around her lips. "She is already here. She is on the other side of the Riverbank."

Tears came to my eyes. I could feel her, my baby sister, the small girl with chestnut hair and eyes too wide for her own good. It felt as though she was somehow standing right next to me.

"Veralee!" I called her name in my mind. "Where are you, Veralee?"

"Adair?" I heard her answer me. "I'm coming, Adair. I'm coming home!"

Then, as quickly as it had come, the moment was gone. Mattie pulled her arm away and said, "Look," A dark cloud of smoke billowed around our feet. "It's from the tera."

The smoke floated out of the tera and spread up around the trees. I lifted my foot as it floated passed me, feeling a coolness that I feared had nothing to do with temperature.

Thunder erupted in the distance again and yet still no rain.

Mattie said, "Inman you have brought Friguscor to our land?"

"You traitor!" yelled someone.

Inman held out his hands. "Listen, they will not harm you," he said. He walked slowly nearer with palms up, in a submissive gesture. "They have been given a blocking-serum."

"The vaccine?" a warrior readied his gun. "Kill them all!"

"If they had had the vaccine your gun would not be able to kill them," Inman said. "Look at them. Look!" He pointed back to the group of thirty to forty Friguscor. "I brought them for a reason," He walked beside one of the young men. "By inhibiting their higher cognitive function, we've put them into a wakeful-sleep state. They are basically machines, themselves. Trust me."

"Inman, you have lost your mind! They are dangerous," Phineas barked, shaking his head in anger, "At any moment they could harm one of us, and..."

"They will not harm you," said Inman quickly. "Watch."

Inman took a long, silver knife from his pocket and cut the flesh of his palm.

An audible gasp came from all around, but Eliezer held his men back with a single hand. Inman looked to Eliezer and seemed to ask permission to proceed. Eliezer nodded for him to continue. Inman held his bloodied hand up to the Friguscor man's nose, but nothing happened. His pupils did not dilate, and his mouth did not even twitch.

I looked to Phineas who was watching intently. He did not seem convinced.

Mattie glanced over to me, and I saw doubt in her eyes.

She did not trust Inman and neither did I, but surprisingly it was Eliezer who said, "A wall I can agree with, but this," he raised his hand toward the Friguscor, "this is madness, Inman. Take them back, before we kill every last one of them!"

Inman's eyes flashed just as the lightning popped dangerously close to the trees above.

Before anyone else could react, a woman stepped out of the tera. Her porcelain skin was flawless, free of any blemish or mark; it accented her blue eyes and long black lashes. She wore a long, fitted jacket that was tailored to accentuate her small waist and full hips. Beneath the jacket she wore an odd shirt made of some sort of clinging material which climbed up the back of her neck and covered almost to her chin.

The woman from the tera held some sort of metal box in her hand. She spoke with a heavy eastern accent.

"With these we do not have to fear anything," she said.

Inman nodded to the woman.

"This is Semira." We all looked at the woman with lips as red as her eyes were blue, as Inman continued, "She is my bondmate."

Semira looked to Mattox and bowed her head respectfully before she greeted the crowd with our words, "Lignum Vitae."

She was Simulacrum, but something was off. I did not know this woman, and I was certain she had never been to Red Oaks before, so why was Inman bringing her now?

Some muttered the reply, but most stared at what she held in her hands.

Mattox did not respond, but instead asked Inman, "What is in the box?"

"They are weapons, created by BaVil." Inman replied, his face serious. "We have them only for one night, and then I must put them back before they are missed. This way, we can use the weapons of our enemies against them. We can let them build our wall of protection."

Eliezer asked, "Weapons?"

Inman looked to Semira who obediently opened the lid of the long, metal box. A horde of something like metallic locusts poured out of the box, flying in a thick cloud just above our heads. Curiously they did not fly to the nearest tree nor begin to bite and devour one another as locusts had such a great tendency to do. Insteaad, they hovered just above as though they were tethered to the box.

"They are modified LRAD's. Long-range-acoustic-devices." Inman explained with fascination in his voice. "They were developed for communications, but these particular ones have the ability, among many other things, to project sound waves with incredible force over a long distance. That has many uses. Under certain circumstances, for instance, when strategically placed in wood that has been carefully cut to specification, they can release powerful sonic waves that travel at high speeds and can destroy anything in its path."

"What?" Phineas asked.

"Semira," Inman called, "please demonstrate." She took her cue and turned the box to face her. On the lid was a small keypad that became visible when she ran her hand above the top. She typed in a series of numbers and looked up.

"Eliezer," Inman asked, "What area will you be cutting next for the wall?"

Eliezer had a keen eye on the 'locusts' and with his weapon, he motioned just to the east of where we stood.

Inman gave Semira a nod and then, the small horde of mechanical locusts moved. As a group they levitated up above the trees. A low, vibrating sound began. We all stood looking up into the dark sky. Lightening licked the edges of the horizon.

The vibration became a hum, and the hum increased into a drumming cacophony in seconds. A flash of light and a sonic boom erupted above. My eyes were temporarily blinded, and my ears rang. Everyone grabbed their ears. The group of Friguscor fell to the ground.

In the distance, far away, I heard the sound of trees falling to the earth. It filled the night around us. I looked down at my feet. It felt as though the very earth beneath me might give way.

"It worked," Phineas said breathlessly, shaking his head from the noise.

Inman took advantage of the moment and said, "That was simply the beginning of what BaVil is capable of doing. They have developed technology that you have never heard of, never dreamt of. They have the ability to remove large groups of people by opening a tera deep into the earth. Listen, the people who went missing yesterday. The Boged. I found out that they were just the first wave."

Eliezer turned back to Inman. "The first wave?" He asked as the sound of falling trees filled the air.

Inman began to walk around the group, his voice becoming smoother as he spoke, "Those people," he pointed past the trees, "the ones who were sleeping safely beneath the Oaks of Red Oaks just nights ago, are now hooked to the Machine. Even now, they are being drained of every drop of blood to create the vaccine, and to feed the Aluid who are now drunk on the blood of your fathers, mothers and children."

"You are saying that BaVil took the Boged from Red Oaks?" Mr. Westbrooke asked and then added, "Impossible. You are simply trying to scare the women here."

Inman continued like a bull charging in a field, "I speak the truth. With my own eyes I have seen the Machine full of the Boged. And if you do not act quickly, it will be full of the Simulacrum again. You need this wall, and you need it now. With the protection I can provide, we can stop them from getting through, from taking more of you...we will embed these LRAD's into the wall. Face them outward and prepare for our enemies."

Mattox raised her voice, "Ruach has already told us what happened to the Boged. They were not taken by BaVil but were removed because of the prophecy of the Stairs of Ahaz!"

"Removed?" Inman gathered his hands together into a steeple, as he spoke, wiping his mouth before adding, "Okay. So, the Archaon have told you that the people have been removed because of an ancient prophecy. A prophecy that you've never seen, that isn't in your Histories. About the Boged. But the Simulacrum, all of you," Inman pointed to the crowd, "and I have been left behind to fend for ourselves? We are the Simulacrum, the Image-Bearers to the One Tree. You really believe that the Boged have been taken by the One Tree, and we have been left here?"

"Yes," Mattox said without a trace of doubt in her voice.

"So where did they go?" Inman said, pressing in closer to Mattox as he asked, "Where are the Boged exactly?"

Mattie did not turn her body toward him, but only her head as she answered, "I do not know!"

"Ahhh!" Inman said with a smile, "You don't know where..."

But Mattox cut him off, "I do not need to know! I do not have to know! All I know is that the words of the Archaon are true, and we must believe them!"

"We have to believe what? In ancient words that have done nothing to protect us? Look around us, Guardian! Look at our people! We are losing this race!" His words worked like rope being lassoed around the nervous crowd, encircling us together in fear and binding us into no options.

Inman abandoned Mattox and spoke to Joab, "Joab, you remember the Machine; you remember what it was like."

Inman raised his hands, just as Absalom would have done.

"Hear me," he began with a voice laced with passion and purpose, "The Friguscor have created a vaccine for their own kind. It changes them at a molecular level. Their eyes," he pointed to the Friguscor behind him, "are no longer dull and unaware, but bright like the color of gems in the sun and keen to all their surroundings, their skin is no longer dry and cracked but smooth as a stone beneath a river for a thousand years, and their hands no longer have five, but six fingers on each hand. They have superhuman strength and abilities. I've seen them with my on eyes. You have no idea what you are up against!"

He turned to the group as he talked, making sure all were listening, "The vaccine is made with a mixture. The first part is from the blood of the Aluid. They are the ones whom the Friguscor believe recently arrived, but we know are conquerors from ancient days." He caught his breath, his mouth slack for a moment as he gathered his words, "And the other part of the vaccine is from the blood of the Simulacrum, which is gathered from our people hooked to a Machine...as though they were nothing more than sheep for the slaughterhouse."

Fear gripped us all. It spread like fire through everyone, heating up as Inman continued, "Many of those who are missing, your loved ones who you cannot find, the many who just disappeared without a trace, they are lost to this Machine. You have seen Joab," Inman motioned to the man, "You have seen the truth of what I say in his eyes."

I glanced at Joab, who was visibly trembling, his face white with fear.

"And now the Boged are being drained as well. They were taken from our own lands by the long-reaching hand of BaVil."

"The rumors are true!" said a middle-aged man from Georgia.

"You have no proof that their disappearance was because of BaVil," another said loudly, "You bring only rumors as evidence."

"And you have no proof that it was anything else!" Inman said, his voice passionate, but still steady.

"It was the Stairs of Ahaz," Agatha raised her head, her body a testimony to the horror of the Machine.

"The Stairs of Ahaz?" Inman looked at Agatha, "I ask again, why would the plan of the One Tree protect a half-breed people who are against the very Law of the Simulacrum and leave the Simulacrum to suffer through the Days of Darkness? It makes no sense. We are the people of the One Tree. We are the ones who are chosen. Why would we be abandoned and the Boged protected from such horror?"

Agatha stared straight at Inman who turned to look back at her. Semira stood quietly by his side.

"Why?" he asked with anger boiling in his voice, "Why, Agatha?"

Why was Inman pushing Agatha to speak and not Mattie?

Everyone turned to Agatha. She looked broken, like a walking skeleton. She stood as a living witness to the power of the Machine.

"Because we rejected the Door," she said, her voice cutting through the night air, "Because we missed the Door."

The entire crowd erupted into hissing and chaos. I looked to Mattie who stood silently watching Agatha. She went to stand near her. I heard a million voices around me, but all I saw was Mattie standing near Agatha.

Then I looked to Inman. I was sure that he was creating this chaos on purpose. He gazed at Agatha with visible satisfaction as the crowd turned on her with shattered glass words that cut her already brittle skin. Agatha was a witness to what was being done at the Machine, but for some reason, Inman wanted Agatha to discredit herself. I wanted to stop what was happening, but could see no clear way of getting her out of the hole Inman was digging.

His voice floated over the shouts and spoke directly to my heart.

Wisdom has left your people.

I looked up to see Ruach walking away through the trees.

"Silence!" Eliezer yelled out, "Silence!" He called the crowd to order again and again. Finally quieting them to a low hum, he spoke, "Agatha, you have lost your mind in that Machine. You speak the words of a heretic, of a traitor to our own people!"

"She should be judged for such words!" screamed a man.

"Agatha has lost her mind!" shouted more.

Inman raised a single hand of authority over the crowd. He spoke slowly, "We all know that we wait for the Door to open. We wait for what has not yet come, but is coming soon. We know the Simulacrum ways. We know the truth."

Words of agreement echoed through the crowd as Inman continued, "The Stairs of Ahaz, a long-forgotten whisper of something we have never seen nor understood. Is that the basis for your plan?" He turned to look around him, "to trust in the words of old women and fallen men?"

"These are the words of our Histories," said Agatha, attempting to straighten her broken frame, "I speak the truth. I have seen the Hidden Books. It is all in there."

Inman nodded several times and then raised his eyes to meet hers, "Please," he opened his palm, "If these are words written, let us all read them." His open hand hung as an accusation in the night air.

Agatha did not move nor defend with any words.

"What she is not telling you," he looked back to Eliezer again, "Is that these 'secret words' that she speaks of were written in 'Hidden Books' that we do not have. Books that some say exist, but that few have ever seen. And then, Agatha said herself, that some of the words are invisible. So even if we get these 'sacred' books, we can't read them!"

"I have seen them," Agatha retorted.

"You are one," Inman said shaking his head with concern, "but our ways require at least two to stand as a witness. Is there anyone else here who has read from the rumored, "Hidden Books?"

I looked to Deena. She kept her eyes on the ground.

"Deena?" I tried in vain to call her name, but she did not look up. Instead, she kept her eyes firmly focused on the dirt before her.

Agatha's shoulders fell in defeat.

Inman watched the two broken women, but his stare was a mask that I could not comprehend. Something about him stirred a memory in me. Something about him reminded me of something...of someone. Then it hit me; for some reason, he reminded me of the giant in the Tombs of the Forgotten. He spoke, moved, and acted like Uziel.

After a moment he said, "So what is the decision of the people? Will you use the help I offer? Will you use the help I have brought? Together, will you agree that we can build the wall around Red Oaks, the last remaining gate to the Terebinths?"

I remembered Ruach's words, 'Trust in the trees that were meant to protect, the watchers who were meant to guard, and the Eiani that was meant to redeem. Only in the ancient ways will you find what you seek.'

I shook my head. This was wrong! Wrong! Inman was wrong! I looked around; most everyone was being sucked in by Inman's smooth words and the promise of new technology.

"How long will they be here?" Eliezer eyed the group of Friguscor, "I want your word. How long, Inman?"

Inman spoke in the old language, the ancient words of our people as he said, "We will start now, and finish before first light. If you trust me, the wall can be completed this night. And in the morning, I promise you, you will find the safety you seek for our people."

"Speak English, Inman," Mattie commanded. "You do not need them to agree to your plan, just the Council. Speak English and don't scare the others any more than you already have."

Lightning popped in the air again.

Inman looked directly at Mattie, then faced the crowd and declared in the old language, "BaVil is coming! We must build! If we do not, we will all sleep in the Tombs of the Forgotten!"

Ausley 2:6

The mirror before me revealed the secret that no amount of fabric could hide. My limbs felt as foreign as though they were the rightful property of someone who lived far, far away from the broken vessel of the girl staring blankly into the mirror.

This cannot be my body. That cannot be my...

The very thought worked as a hypnotic on my fragile consciousness, closing my mind down into a low, dull hum of existence. I barely noticed the two women and one small man, or at least I thought he was a man, who worked diligently to dress me.

"Beautiful," soothed one of the women. Poured into a single form, this woman seemed to be made of all that was smoothed, perfected, and wanted in life, with skin glinting in hues that reminded me of the sunset in the desert. Black hair, like rich, flowing oil, hung freely to her waist pulling the eye toward the deeply-cut top that revealed everything but the center of her well-rounded breast. Colorful silk wrapped tightly around her small waist, revealing her stomach and accentuating her heavy but sensuous hips.

"Such a goodness to you..." she added, her lips puckering as though she aimed to kiss the very air around her.

Beautiful?

"What a strange illusion it is to believe that beauty is goodness," I whispered as they brought another silk gown forward.

Did ice form when I spoke or was it simply the coldness of my heart? Do they see it as well? The brokenness of my soul? Can they see it with such glowing eyes?

With the guiding touch of their hands, I moved my arms through the smooth material.

"Anna was beautiful as well, but in the end, it was her face that was spread across the train tracks," I murmured.

"What is that?" asked the man, but before I could tell him it was a quote from Tolstoy, he turned away from me. Clearly more interested in the ornate jewelry box before him, he opened the top and gasped, fluttering his hands before his mouth with excitement. Lifting several bracelets high so that he could marvel at their grandeur, his eyes bulged with deep desire as he whispered.

"Such," he paused to lick his lips, "beauty."

A distant sound of a woman crying floated through the air. No one seemed to notice.

He shackled the bracelets carefully around my wrist. Large, jeweled earrings were pierced through my ears with little care or ease, dripping a stark garnet against the blue and lavish gold on my gown. The picture before me was all wrong. I was dressed as though I were an Arabian princess from a long-forgotten story book. But my eyes were blue, and my hair blonde, and regardless of the image in the mirror, a terrible shadow lay just beneath my skin.

Veralee could have worn this dress. I shuddered and suddenly felt relief that she would never have to endure this nightmare. Wherever she was, at least she was far away from here. From him.

"Sundar," said the man with bright red fingernails that matched the sarong he wore. When he spoke, I immediately thought of a cat, even though his speech was accented by a heavy lisp. "Hmmm, Sundar!" he said again, but this time much slower. Our eyes met as he kept his hand on my collarbone for a moment too long.

His exclamation was followed by a breathy, "Jameela!" from the second woman. Where the other woman was small and slender, this one was curvy and round. Her face looked like it had been quilted together from the skin of several different women. Immediately I remembered my great-grandmother Vera's hand-quilted blankets from bits and pieces of leftover fabrics.

"Pieced by hand," said the woman. With sausage fingers that made my skin crawl in alarm, she positioned the gold and blue lace veil around my head. She put her hand over my tseeyen without asking permission.

"Alarm and warmth," she said in a guttural voice. Every time their hands brushed up against my skin, I grimaced with the urge to fight or flee. They were inhumanly cold, but it was the connection I found the most disturbing. Every encounter with their skin left me with something I could feel. Each brush, or stroke of their hands left the sensation that they were trying to penetrate my skin, as though I was receiving acupuncture from their minds.

"Do not be so," said the feline man. His face was covered in golden chains which hung from ear to ear across his nose, lips and forehead, making his dark eyes appear to be looking out from a mask of metal chains. Every time he spoke, the chains jingled together in a rhythmic sound.

"You are favored."

"Favored?" the word caused my chest to ache with pain. I did not want to be favored by anyone or anything here.

"Favored!" said the first woman. With great care she stretched out her hand and placed it on my belly, just below my naval and repeated, "Yes, favored."

My knees buckled. I would have fallen straight to the floor but for their arms wrapping around me.

"Please!" I shouted, "Don't!" My hands shook as much as my voice. "Don't touch me!"

"But your face!" said the slender woman, coming near me with wide eyes full of lustful want. "You have cut yourself. Let me help you, my dear."

I felt the side of my cheek. The earring had broken the skin. A small bit of blood on my fingertip testified that I had indeed been cut, but still I felt nothing. I feel nothing. I gathered the fabric of the dress against my body, needing to shield myself against the very air around me. But instantly I knew the truth.

There was not enough material, no where I could hide, no amount of numbness that would keep me from the memory of him. I buckled at the waist and gagged.

All three of them watched me with their gemlike eyes of mistrust. The man in the woman's sarong changed temperatures with the flick of his eyes as he raised a dismissive hand, revealing six long fingers as he exhaled.

"Fine!" His disdain was tangible as he added, "Have it your way."

With all the pomp of an offended child, he stomped away from where we were gathered in front of the deceptive looking glass.

Above me, the large chandelier took on all of the colors from the room. It was larger than any chandelier I had ever seen. The room seemed still. Too still. There was no movement anywhere, not even in the air. I noticed that the sun was coming through the large glass doors to the right of me which seemed to lead to a grand balcony, but there was no dust in the light. Nothing moved besides the voluntary action of the four of us.

"How did I get here?" I asked. The last thing I could remember was the Tombs of the Forgotten.

"We have told you," the slender woman cooed. "They brought you early this morning. These are your rooms now. We are here to serve you."

"Such fine things you have," said the other. "For one like yourself, it is remarkable actually."

"Why?" I caught her eye, "What do you mean?"

Her face morphed into the very picture of revulsion as her lips turned up.

"You are Simulacrum, and most of your kind will be dead within a few days, if they aren't already. You are disgusting. And what you carry in your womb should not be allowed to ... Eli baltuti ima idu mituti"

"Jaria," the slender woman pulled her hard. "Do not do this. He will hear of it, and you know that you will be finished."

"What did you say?" I screamed, fearing the words but needing to know. "What did you just say?"

"Phoebe, she is trash; worse than that, she is inferior to us, and yet he chooses her to carry his child?" Jaria spit back, frustration dripping from her entire body. They both ignored me as Jaria sneered, "It is unacceptable!"

"Stop it!" cried Phoebe, "Remember yourself."

Jaria added, "Phoebe, you know Adi La Base Alaku!"

Phoebe stepped closer to Jaria and placed a calming hand on her cheek as she intimately whispered, "Yes, you are right, it might all come to naught, but remember, dear sister, it is also said that Ana Simtim Alaku. It might just be her fate."

I heard them, but from far, far, away. For I had fallen down a deep hole where there was no escaping. My hand flew again to my belly. It was impossible, and yet I knew it was true. My breath began to labor. My stomach churned. My body refused to hear, to know, to listen.

No! I wanted to scream. But my lips were frozen. Could I breathe? Could a heart stop from pain?

"Look," the girl called Phoebe was pulling me to my feet. "Look at your rooms!"

My rooms? I looked around me. The rooms were larger than most people's houses. They were luxurious, decorated in claret silk pillows on deep gray couches, gold and silver tables adorned with jeweled items of various uses, large enameled vases filled with volumes of exotic flowers. Elaborately carved lanterns of bronze, gold, and silver hung on the walls, and gossamer curtains divided the large bed from the sitting area. The rooms were luxurious. But why?

And yet, he chooses her to carry his child.

Jaria's words taunted me. I studied the round coffee table in the center of the room. Inlaid patterns of gold and silver accentuated the crimson marble top.

To carry his child ...

"Come," said Phoebe. My heart raced forward.

Anywhere, I would go anywhere if it was away from here.

"Can you take me out of my own skin?" I asked, water filling my eyes.

Phoebe looked at me, and I found no compassion in her emerald green eyes. In contrast, her voice was cheerful.

"Don't be silly. You are favored!"

She smiled and placed her gloved hand on mine. Instinct caused me to jerk back.

"Now, my dear, you are still at the Machine, but you are no longer below ground. Now you are in the leaders' quarters. See, you have a wonderful view."

She ushered me toward the balcony. Large glass and iron doors were opened before me. I felt warm air blow into the room. Curiosity pulling me forward, I stepped out onto the large stone balcony. Phoebe walked out to the edge and leaned over the iron rail. The hot wind blew through the veil they had placed on my head, revealing my blonde hair. Outside, the grounds were beautiful. Green gardens, a large pond, a palace for a king or queen.

The rail was not high, it would be easy to ... I slid my foot forward.

Yes, it would be easy. Go now, Ausley!

I jerked forward but was suddenly pulled back. The man in the sarong stood just behind me, his long fingernails wound tightly around my forearm.

"Careful, favored one," he said with scornful emphasis. "We do not want you to slip. It was be a shame for you to end up like Anna."

The wind whipped around me as I turned back to see one last view of the balcony, the only way I would find freedom.

"Come," said the man, his grip strong and unrelenting. "We shall leave you to rest before the Anshargal arrives."

"The Anshargal?" I asked as he dragged me with little effort back into the room. Behind me I saw Phoebe lock the iron and glass door with an actual key, as though we were living a hundred years ago. Suddenly, I noticed everything in the room was old. There were no modern lights or screens on the walls as was the Friguscor way, but instead lanterns lit by actual candles. The chandelier above me was filled with candles, too.

"Why is the room like this?" I said quickly, the decor around me testifying that something was clearly not right.

"Because you are no longer where you started," said Jaria.

"You said we were still at the Machine."

"Technically you are," he sneered, turning away, leaving only his sharp shoulder angled toward me. He looked down his nose and whispered, "But you did not ask when."

"When?" I rose from the couch and worked my way toward him, the weight of the gown weighing heavily upon me. "What do you mean, when?"

The look on my face must have been amusing for they all three smiled. They obviously enjoyed my confusion. Their smiles turned from amusement to outright contempt.

I began to back up, away from the hatred I found in their eyes. Suddenly the question slipped from my mouth, "Where is Hegai?"

"Hegai?" Jaria looked at the other two and then back at me. "We have never met a Hegai."

"He's my guard, he's my ... he's always with me," I mumbled.

"Ahh," said the man, his chains clinking together. "The guard from back at the Machine? No, he is not here." The man stepped toward me, and I smelled the distinct odor of one who had continually been standing by burning trash. "We are to look after you now."

"But I had a room at the Machine," I ignored him, as I looked around again, "and you said this was the Machine." Fear began to tighten around my throat. At least at the Machine I had Jackson. I needed Jackson.

"You are at the Machine," said Phoebe, "We told you, you are just a few pages back from where you once stood. It is odd at first, we know. But soon living behind time feels natural."

"Behind time?" I looked at each one of their faces and noticed for the first time that they were very, very, old and yet still had the look of youth. The clear contradiction of their faces, the living evidence before me, sent fear up my spine.

"Are you alive?"

"Alive?" Jaria said, "We have not used those terms in so very long, I do not think they apply anymore. Alive is not a boundary we exist within."

"Who are you?" I shrunk back again.

The man took one small step forward.

"We are those who serve the Anshargal in the land of Shan'ar."

"The land of Shan'ar?"

Jaria bit the side of her lip, her eyes flashing something between pleasure and knowledge in them as she said, "The Land of the Watchers."

"The Watchers? You mean, the Archaon? We are in the land of the Archaon?"

Phoebe walked across the room, and I noticed how her sarong moved as though there were a breeze originating underneath her feet. It was slow, flapping in a breeze that did not exist. She stood beside a table which held several ornate bottles. Lifting a lid, she poured out a glass of deep, red wine. She sipped it before answering.

"This is where those who left the realm of mankind came. The ones, who as your stories tell, fell asleep when the Friguscor spread across the lands."

I remembered this story from childhood. Veralee had taken me to a giant oak tree where she read or told stories to me beneath its shade. For a brief moment, the memory was so real, that I felt I could reach out and touch Veralee's ten-year-old hand and hear her voice.

"Are you listening, Ausley? Do you understand what I'm telling you?"

I jerked my head to the right, expecting to see Veralee standing right before me, but instead it was the iron doors to the balcony. I closed my eyes, and I heard her again.

The Archaon who no longer wanted to stay with the Friguscor walked away from the land of men and fell into a deep sleep of silence.

"Veralee?" I said her name, feeling the hope in it. "Veralee, where am I?"

But it was Jaria who answered. "You are in the Land of the Watchers. The Land between yours and the Terebinths."

Phoebe brought the drink down slowly, her lips dyed red with wine. "What did you see just then?"

"See?" I shook my head trying to tether myself to some scrap of reality, feeling myself slipping with every second into a hole of insanity.

"Yes," Phoebe put down the crystal glass. "Here, you will find your memories will blend so much into reality that the two will soon become inseparable. The mind slowly slips into the dream, and from there it is only a matter of time before you forget entirely what was or will be. What is becomes all that exists. Hours become days, and days become all of the years you have."

"I want to leave this place." I said, as sure as I could be. "I want to go back to the Machine."

"But we have already told you," the voice came from the man, who had been so silent that I had forgotten his presence. He stood before a wall that had a large curtain drawn across it. Pulling on a golden chord that hung from the dark red curtain, he drew the curtain toward the left side, revealing a massive painting on the wall behind it.

It was so real that it looked more like a photograph than a painting. The scene was of a large assembly in a cavernous room. A procession of very large, physically-imposing soldiers marched toward a waiting army staged in front of a U-shaped, marble colonnade. Ten older children stood at the top of the stairs in the middle of the platform. Pots of fire cast eerie shadows on the walls.

"I've seen that place," I said remembering the room where Absalom had taken me just yesterday. "It's in the Machine."

The man nodded. "But here it is painted as it truly is. If your eyes could see past the reality, this is what you would see."

The paint lent such a sense of movement to the scene that I was sure I saw the army marching. The children seemed to be moving as well.

"Why does it move?"

Phoebe answered, "It is the paint of the Archaon. It is not of your world, but from this one. The paint creates a two-way window so that each side of the picture can see what is happening on the other side."

"Two-way window?" I repeated.

Suddenly I was standing in the hallway at Red Oaks. I looked down and saw that I was barefoot. My hands were much smaller than I ever remembered them to be.

"Mama?" I cried out.

"In here!" her voice rang out as though a bell calling me to her, "I'm in Veralee's room, Ausley!"

"Mama!" I cried out again as I opened the familiar wooden door. I ran to her. She was sitting in the vintage rocking chair that had always sat in the corner of Veralee's room. I saw nothing but her face as I fell into her arms. She wrapped me closely and pulled me into her lap, where I fit as easily as a five-year-old child could. How long had it been since I had sat there in her lap?

"Mommy," I whispered, "Mommy..." It was the only words that fell from my mouth.

Her arms tightened in alarm. "What is it, sweet girl? Why, you're shaking!"

She took my face into her hands and looked intently into my eyes. "Have you hurt yourself? What's wrong, baby?"

Tears fell down my cheeks, obscuring my vision.

"I miss you," I heard my childish voice shook as I said. "I miss you so much, Mommy."

Mother laughed, but it was not cruel nor dismissive, but warm and full of love as she hugged me to her breast. "I just saw you at breakfast. But the truth is, I miss you anytime I am away from you. It's because we love each other so much that it makes any time apart seem like an aching in our bones."

"Yes," I whispered and stretched up to put my hands on each side of her face, "I love you, Mama."

Mother caught something in my eye, or maybe it was in my voice, for she paused and watched me for a long second. "You seem so much older... I hadn't noticed how much you are growing up."

Suddenly I noticed the painting on the wall behind her. It was the painting of the two trees that had always been in Veralee's room.

I sat up slightly and asked, "Mother, who painted that?"

She shifted to look at the mural on the wall. "You know this story. Vera, my grandmother painted that during the Civil War. My mother always told me Vera finished it the night of the Battle here at Red Oaks when the Union soldiers finally broke through the Confederates line and overtook the house."

"Where did she get the paint?"

"The paint?" she shook her head. "I have no idea. It was in the middle of the Civil War. I can't imagine how she came up with sugar or flour, so how she got such expensive paints is beyond me."

Mother turned and called toward the closed bathroom door, "Veralee, will you come on out here. I want to see if the dress fits!"

Phoebe was standing right in front of my face.

"Have you seen something like this before maybe?"

I blinked, trying to stay standing. I had just been with my Mother. Veralee had been just behind the door. My mouth felt dry.

"A drink?" Phoebe handed me a glass of what looked to be red wine.

I put it down quickly.

"No, I need water."

Jaria turned and poured from a different pitcher. She held the glass of water before me, but with a barely outstretched hand. I had to lean in to take it from her. The water was cool. My head raced. The painting in Veralee's room. The mural was painted with the same paints. I was sure of it. And if that was true, then the painting in Veralee's room must be just like this one. It must be a window. This painting showed the altar back at the Machine, but Veralee's showed the horizon between the two trees.

"Have you remembered something?" Phoebe asked again, her lips twitching with excitement.

"Leave it alone, Phoeb," said the man. "You are not to feed off her memories."

Phoebe's eyes flashed with anger. "I know my place here." She turned away from me and addressed the unnamed man, "I'll not touch her, but he said nothing of her memories."

Her words triggered dread in my chest. I had remembered something, but it was not the memory of home that filled me with alarm, but Jaria's words from earlier.

Then, suddenly the wide doors to my left shuddered as someone banged three times hard from the outside.

Jaria, Phoebe, and the man jumped into action. Their nervous excitement was tangible as the women straightened their clothes, and the man ran like an obedient dog toward the iron doors.

He breathed in deeply and then with great pomp placed his hands on both of the large handles. With a great jerk, he opened the double doors.

A giant man with skin the color of the moon stood outside the right door. The right side of his body was tattooed with tribal markings from the top of the head down his face, neck, arm, chest, abdomen, legs, and to his feet. Long white hair grew only on the left side of his head, while tattoos covered his bald right side. His ears were covered in gold and silver loops that connected on both sides by chains that lay across his eyes, nose, and lips. His only clothing was a black leather pant that covered his left abdomen, crotch, and thigh; the pant tied with leather thongs around his body which extended down the right leg in a zig-zag pattern. His muscles looked like they were sculpted by Michelangelo and were ready to break through the leather ties with any movement. In his hands, he carried a heavy chain. I was sure it was a weapon of some sort, but I had never seen anything like it. He stepped through the door and positioned himself like a guard for the president.

The man in the orange and pink sarong pulled the left door open until it was fully extended, careful to give a great amount of space between him and the creature on the other side. Both bowed low, almost touching their noses to their knees. I felt the darkness enter the room first, a great heaviness that filled the room as black shadow. It stretched across every inch of the room, claiming all from the ceiling down to the ground. The dim light became as though it was simply a candle burning in the darkest part of a cave. The shadow came toward me, but it did not touch me. Instead, it made wide circles around my feet.

I held my breath and closed my eyes, wishing that the earth would open up beneath my feet and pull me down beneath the dirt and rocks. The darkness was so thick I was sure I would suffocate beneath its weight. I opened my eyes, afraid that the candles would go out, and we would be left in total darkness. They faltered, I could tell, barely able to stay lit at all. It was as though the very presence in the room made light of any form an impossibility.

He stepped through the door, and I heard the sound of rushing wind. The light was so dim that I could hardly see him, but I felt him. I felt him immediately.

Fear climbed over me, arresting my breath and stealing any hope that remained in my bones. I began to shake. My lips trembled, and my breath came in short, jerking gasps.

"I have come," he said. His voice scraping against the air like fingernails breaking against pressure. "I have come to you."

"No," I whispered, or at least I thought I did. My lips were frozen with fear. I could not move even the smallest of muscle in my body. I felt suddenly entombed alive before the darkness. Silver hair fell down to his waist. It was the brightest thing against the darkness of the room. It showed his crystal blue eyes but kept most of his face beneath a shroud of shadow. He, too, was the color of the moon and had a chiseled body like no human I had ever seen. His only clothing were black leather pants and a black cape fastened around his neck. It was Uziel.

"You have life inside your womb," he said stepping closer. His outstretched hand grasped my belly. I wanted to scream. I wanted to hit him, to fight him, to... but I did nothing. Deep shame filled every part of my body, even places that I knew I could never reach to remove it. Guilt layered over the shame so heavily that I no longer had the strength or the will to fight.

"No," I denied it, "It's impossible."

"And yet you know it is."

I hated him.

He pulled his hand away from me. Directing his commands elsewhere.

"Balaam!" The man in the orange and pink sarong came quickly forward, keeping his head obediently low.

"Sir," he said in a low, submissive tone.

"These are the last days. We are almost where we seek to go. She is to be kept until the child comes forth and then, take her to the Machine."

"Yes, Anshargal."

Uziel turned again and with the flick of his wrist he commanded, "Bring her."

The guard who looked like two men, one a tattooed circus freak and the other a giant warrior, bowed once and then dropped the chain he had been holding in his hand. He repositioned himself so that he was in a squatting position before he took the chain back into his clawed hands. With great strain he began to pull the chain, and I could hear something being dragged toward the room from outside the doors. Every muscle in his body bulged as he opened his mouth, revealing large, pointed teeth, and gasped in more air. He pulled the unseen weight on the other end of the chain forward hand-over-hand, as a pile of loose chain formed around his feet.

The giant roared with effort, and I saw the beginnings of a brilliant light inching forward. As it moved forward, and I saw more of it, I gasped. It was a wheel of gold within a wheel of gold just like the symbol at the Terebinths of Mamre!

When I saw it all, I realized it was in fact, three intersecting golden wheels, which circled each other over and over, in constant movement. Large, rusted chains were wrapped round and round the golden orb of light and yet they could not stop the movement beneath them. The orb could not fit inside the doors but filled the entire space outside so that nothing else could be seen but its presence.

What is this?

Uziel stepped forward, his black leather cape dragging the floor behind him. I watched as he reached beneath his leather armor and pulled a golden key of light from his chest where it hung around a golden chain.

I saw no place for a key, but Uziel forced the key inside the circling golden bands and found a lock previously unseen. Jaria, Phoebe, and Balaam shrank back several steps from the orb. They were trembling and pulled their veils tightly over their fearful faces.

As Uziel twisted the key, the golden bands opened, unfolding gently as petals on a budding flower. Something stirred within. Uziel stepped back in anticipation of whatever was coming next. The golden bands rejoined, clamping tightly together and morphing into one long, straight line. Uziel smiled with satisfaction as the golden band morphed and formed and reformed with great energy.

Heat radiated, and the gold became almost liquid and then took form again, shifting and sliding until the head of woman erupted out of the gold, flinging her hair as one coming out of the water. A golden hand reached awkwardly toward the sky and came down hard on the marble floor. Watching the figure struggle so intensely to come forth filled me with compassion and pity, but I watched until finally the form of a woman lay beneath the heavy chains. The woman began to scream, obviously in agony. I covered my ears, trying to drown out the sound of her torment, but she continued to shriek for what seemed to be an hour, or maybe days. I felt helpless, listening to her suffering.

Finally, she quietened and opened her eyes for the first time. She was still a golden color, but I had no idea what reality she composed. She was not gold. Not human. And though she stood before us, I was suddenly unsure if she had always been there, or if she was actually in front of us, or maybe she was about to be standing in front of us. The feeling was so odd, it felt like it was tearing the very fabric that held my reality together. The air, the walls, the space around us seemed to move like it was on the tip of a phonograph needle, jerking back and forth in one place.

She stood before Uziel, naked but unashamed. Chains dug into her skin, wrapped tightly around every part of her. They covered her head, her torso, her arms and her legs. It looked so very painful.

"Why, why, why?" she said as her voice jerked through the fragile thread of time around us, each word repeated in the air multiple times after they were spoken.

"Why do you wake me?"

"Wake you?" Uziel spoke with controlled contempt. "You have not been sleeping. Though under lock and key, it was you who turned back the sun on the stairs of Ahaz. It was you who coiled time upon itself when the Seventh Gate-Keeper's blood touched the earth."

She turned her head to face Uziel but not her body, which remained uncomfortably straight forward.

"There is no lock which can keep sealed doors which the Man of Words has opened."

The monstrous guard yanked heavily on the chain in his clawed hand, jerking the golden woman's entire body. She cried out in great pain, but her body neither bent nor gave in any way. It was as if her very body was the prison holding her in this constant state of pain, and Uziel knew it.

"It is hard to be confined in such a restrictive prison," Uziel hissed. He leaned closer but was careful not to touch the woman as he growled. "It is almost as though someone has cut the wings from your back, causing you to crawl as a snake across the ground, eating the dust of this damned world day in and day out for all of eternity."

Uziel smiled, and it was awful.

"But of course, if anyone can understand eternity, it would be you, Tera."

"My name," she said, and I felt fury radiate from her, "is Moed."

That name I knew from the Old Language. It meant time. Was she truly Time itself?

Moed turned and looked at me.

"Remember me as I was before the key was placed, and I was imprisoned into this body," she spoke, and her words echoed through the room. "One day, as it already has been, soon, yesterday, today, tomorrow, I will be as I truly am. I am placed here until the final beginning, to drag all of eternity toward a great and terrible end."

"No!" Uziel screamed, and darkness vibrated in the room. The few candles still lit dimmed even more, leaving only two shining in the room.

Uziel raised his hand as though to smite her, but she turned her eyes to face him with the clear invitation of a challenge. Moed spoke clearly.

"Touch me, Child of Darkness. Just once, stretch out your hand and let it fall upon my beauty."

"When we open the Eighth Gate," Uziel said, keeping his hand poised to strike, "I will call you whatever I please. For Moed will be no more, and I will bind you for eternity into this body. I will drive my sword through your heart and pin you to the ground. I will have servants fill your mouth with the dust of the earth day in and day out, and you will never escape my purpose!"

Uziel did not give her a chance to speak but turned to face the giant guard.

"Open a tera." He directed. The giant jerked all his weight on the chains as Uziel looked at me. "I want her ripened to her final month."

The giant strained, tightening the chains around Moed. I saw on her face the deep pain that hid just behind her eyes, though her body did not bend nor give in anyway. She raised her hands slowly and spread her fingers.

Uziel pulled a small vial from his pocket and opened the lid. He stepped nearer to me, and I shrunk back in fear, but he did not touch me. He stopped just before me, and with evil pouring off of his skin, he poured out a small splash of blood onto the ground. Instantly the scene before me turned into a swirl of water. A tera had opened before me, and I knew it was coming from Moed.

Uziel motioned with the jerk of his chin, and Jaria stepped close behind me.

"No," I cried, but she had shoved me, head forward into the River.

I woke on the floor of the same room. I was alone. The room was silent. It was night outside, and no lights were lit around me. I rolled to my right side. My hands flew to the roundness of my full belly.

"No" I whispered in the dark. "No, it can't be!"

Day 3 Boker

Separate seed according to their own kind.

Veralee 3:1

Slowly, I pulled my hands from my face and opened my eyes to the world behind the door. Atticus knelt beside me. "Are you well?" His calming tone matched the silence and stillness around us. The only sound was a distant babbling of water and the presence of trees.

"I think so," I answered honestly, breathing in the smell of his nearness. I fumbled over my words. "Your ... your blood opened the door. You have the key to the River in your blood. You never told me that you had the key to the River."

He looked away, purposely not answering me.

Beneath me was something like earth. It was dry, but foreign. It felt thinner than dirt, as though the surface of earth could simply peel away. We were in a forest, but the forest was dying. The colors had faded into a dull nothingness; the trees had no new growth. They were skeletons left naked against the elements. No fresh flowers or grass grew here. We were inside the tomb of the forest.

"Look," Atticus said gently, pointing above. What I saw made no sense. Large, dangling roots hung from somewhere high in the sky. They were as round as they were long, knotted tightly with age and weather. A heavy fog blanketed the world around us so I could not tell where the roots began, though a glimmer of golden copper pierced the cloud now and then.

"Where are we?" I looked at the vastness around us. It made me feel as though I were a mole crawling beneath the earth. Even the air felt different.

"Those are roots from the great Oaks above," it was Thenie who spoke, "I have seen this place in my dreams."

"You dream of roots?" I asked, carefully leaning over the edge of the cliff where we sat. Below was a massive river of what looked like melted silver.

Atticus grabbed my arm, cautioning me with a look of disapproval.

"Yes. What do you dream of Veralee?" Thenie asked.

I looked at Atticus and answered, "I dream of trees, the door we just walked through, and," my eyes stopped and held onto Atticus, "And I dream of him."

Atticus did not say a word but kept his eyes trained on me.

Thenie nodded, "You dream of what is, and I dream of what will remain."

"Roots?" I said, unable to hide the doubt in my voice, "You think that is all that will remain?"

"Of course. You know the Histories." She walked toward the edge of the cliff, "What is beneath something, the roots of it, is what is truly important. The things unseen are the things which will remain when all other things burn."

"Burn?" the word sent a chill down my spine, "What do you mean, burn?"

Thenie touched a dead twig and pulled it easily from the tree, "All that will remain is what can go through fire. Everything else, the surface things, like the top of the trees, the part you can see with your eyes, will be burned away. But the roots, the things below, the things unseen by man, those are the things that will remain forever."

Briefly I remembered a dream from long ago. I had dreamt of a ball at Red Oaks with Mother. A glass wall had grown up between us. Behind the separation, my dress had become the roots of a tree, wrapping round and round me. Nathan had walked by. I remembered the desperation in my voice as I called to him, "Help me!" I had screamed, "Nathan, go and get help!" as the roots began to wrap tightly around my neck and strangle me. He had walked past me, never stopping as he said, "You cannot change the roots of a tree, so why do you fight what is so deeply rooted in you?"

I stood quickly to get away from the uncomfortable memory. Atticus watched my face and slowly rose to his own feet. I wavered and fell sideways, but Atticus caught me and set me back upright.

"It is the absence of time, that makes you feel so unstable on your feet," he explained. "Here, time is only in the River below, for the Lady Moed is held prisoner still."

He watched me for a moment longer and then turned away, running his hand through his thick hair like he always did when he was secretly nervous. It made me smile to know that about him.

"The Lady Moed? Who's that?" I tested my legs. I was sure that I could fly to the top and touch the trees themselves if I so pleased. But instead I eased my hand forward and touched one of the great roots that hung from the sky.

"Lady Moed, Lady Tempus, Chronos, or what mere men call time." Atticus explained, scratching his forehead in thought as he surveyed the area around us.

"Time?" I said trying not to sound too snarky. "Time is a lady named Moed? And she's a prisoner?"

"Yes," Atticus said, missing my sarcasm. "Not a woman as you," he said quickly looking down, "More as Wisdom who guards the Gate to the Terebinths. Time also has a form, and she was meant to walk through these great woods, keeping order. Yet when the first woman, Chauvah, believed the Nachash and ate of the Tree of Shadows, Time was imprisoned into a tomb of flesh. There she waits until the flesh decays, and she is no longer bound by the days of men."

"A tomb of...of flesh?" Ernest shook his head, "Why would time be put into a tomb of flesh?"

Atticus turned slightly so that he could see Ernest when he said, "Because all flesh is bound to time. It is the promise that one day, this will all end. If it was not so, then the Friguscor would never end but would continue forever."

"So where is Moed? And who governs these woods if she is not here?" asked Thenie.

I pulled on the strong root from above, testing it slightly as Atticus answered, "Imperium in imperio."

"An empire within an empire?" I asked. "What do you mean?"

Atticus smiled, casting his eyes toward the ground as he answered, "The old ones told stories that she was imprisoned by the One Tree in order to contain the Nachash"

"The Nachash?" Ernest asked the question on my lips, "I have not, well, I am not sure, but I do not believe I have heard of one called 'Nachash'."

Atticus grew serious, "Nachash is the father of the dead ones, or so the stories say. As to these woods, well, they are like an empire within an empire. A world within a world. A wheel within a wheel." Atticus looked at me, "They are a wild place, governed only by the words written about the end of time. And time is running out, so this place is dying."

"But the River is here ..."

"And it is lower than I have ever seen it before," Attius said looking down, "Time is drying up."

Before us was a walkway that hung suspended above a great canyon. Moving from one root to another I walked across the thin bridge until I stood in between the two sides of the canyon walls, the mighty River rushing far beneath me.

The warm feeling of home pulsed through the roots and into me as I said, "These are the roots to the trees of Red Oaks." Closing my eyes I felt the truth, "We are below them, where the roots connect beneath the earth."

"Where the roots connect?" Ernest said, standing flat against the canyon wall, "What, um, what do you mean?"

Atticus was standing at the beginning of the small natural bridge, watching me with all the intensity of his usual nature. He answered Ernest, "All of the Terebinth trees are connected. See how the roots grow all the way down and rest in the River itself?" He motioned to the silver waters of the River that moved as molten lava, "All of the trees, through the roots, are all connected to the One Tree by the flow of the River."

"And they were born in the first days of time in order to bring about the end of time," I quoted from the Histories.

Atticus looked at me and nodded as I said, "Whatever it means, it's real. Every word of those books. They're real!" A smile of pure awe erupted across my face and spread down to my toes. I had waited to see this place, to know that the words of my youth, the promises in those books, the stories told from generation to generation, were all real. Every word of it was true!

"Atticus," I turned quickly to face him, "Is this where you met the Man of Words after Decimus changed you? Is this where you jumped into the River and began your journey as an Ayindalet?"

Atticus looked at the ground as he decided how to answer and then looked back at me. I realized he was uncomfortable.

"It is," he replied cautiously, keeping back what I knew he wanted to ask. The question was hidden right behind his steady gaze.

How do you know me?

His lips parted as though he would speak, but then he simply shook his head and remained in his silence.

"And who's likeness is that?" Ernest was pointing behind me. I turned around carefully balancing myself with a strong root in my hand.

A statue, cut from the stone canyon wall itself and large as the ones in the entrance to the Terebinths of Mamre stood towering over us.

"What has wings, but the likeness of a man?" asked Ernest again. Massive wings, which were raised in flight, made the statue look as though at any moment it might take flight. The movement of the clothes, and the position of the large sword in his right hand made his face seem hard and dangerous, and yet I knew him.

"It's Achiel," I said, and the air shimmered around me. I watched it as I continued, "He is the Archaon I met in the woods at Red Oaks. He is the one who, who saved me ..." I looked down at my leg and smiled, remembering the blue light, "on so many occasions."

"Yes," Atticus said, "I know him as well."

"When you met the Man of Words!" I cried. "I remember you saying you met him there."

Atticus flashed me a look of narrowed curiosity, reminding me again that here in this time he did not know me.

"Atticus," I began, but he held up a hand and said. "Please, Miss Veralee, do not tell me of tomorrow when I still have today to navigate."

"But tomorrow makes you happy, because you finally come home," I said.

"Home?" Atticus was cautious but I could see the very word spark light in his eyes, "Where would an Ayindalet call home?"

I turned my arm, revealing the burn marks from the bonding chord that that ran across my tseeyen into his, burning us together for all time.

"Here," I said, begging him to understand. "You find it here."

"Something is coming," Thenie said in an urgent whisper. My tseeyen burned, but it was not with danger.

Below us a large boat was coming smoothly down the River. We stood watching in wonder as it docked on a small, dilapidated, wooden platform. A hooded captain tied the magnificent boat to a sturdy tree. The boat, no larger than fifteen feet, was smoothed to the point of art. The womb of the boat was carved from a rich wood which flowed to a long, slender point at the front of the boat. And though it moved through the water with a fluid motion, the boat had no sails and no ores. The point, though still made of wood, resembled a ribbon that had just unfolded, hanging it's head backward, as though it wished to drink from the river.

"Who is that?" I said, keeping my eyes on the hooded man below.

Ernest said, "My companion. He is the one who will show us to the matching book."

The hooded man raised his long arm and with a simple command of "come," he beckoned us to join him at the River below. By way of a simple trail, we worked our way down the side of the canyon wall, one foot in front of the other. Careful not to slip, I held onto the side of the rock face. Ernest led our small party down, with Thenie just behind him. I followed Thenie, and Atticus walked at a close pace right behind me. The nearness of him made my throat constrict with waves of loss and want.

I turned slightly to face Atticus, keeping a watchful eye on the ledge that fell sharply down into a ravine, "Watch out, that rock is slippery. You don't want to fall down there."

Atticus raised his eyebrows, and I detected amusement in his voice as he answered, "Thank you. I will do my best to stay the course before me. As you should as well."

"Well," I said, reaching out to grab hold of the tree trunk before me and swinging around the dying trunk with a little too much flair before stepping back on the slender path. "I'm just saying..." but I couldn't finish what I was saying because my hand slipped, and I faltered toward the edge of the ravine.

His right hand wrapped itself over mine, gripping us both to the trunk of the tree, while his other one wrapped itself around my waist. We stood like that for less than a second, for he righted me back on the path before I could even take another breath.

"You are correct, Miss Veralee," Atticus said. But the closeness of his body to mine was louder than his words. He stood for a moment, and then he released me as he added, "The rock is wet, and we should watch our feet."

He smiled and gestured for me to continue down the path. He would never go ahead of me but would stay just behind me the entire way. That was his way. It had been from the day I met him.

"Are you laughing at me?" I said as I started back, moving dry branches out of the way, "Huh?"

"No, ma'am," Atticus said without a hint of laughter in his voice, "It is not laughter I feel when I look at you."

"Not laughter?" I said flippantly, "Then what?" I stopped and turned to face him.

His face surprised me. It was not as I expected. My smile faded.

"What do you see when you look at me?" I asked, holding my breath.

His green eyes fell on mine, and his look was stern as he wiped his palm across his hard jaw and shifted his weight from right to left foot. He considered me and then weighed his words, one on top of the other on his mental scale before answering.

"I see a girl who is too far from home."

"A girl?" I said as though the word was a slap in my face. Tears brimmed in my eyes as heat raised up my spine. "I'm more than just some girl," I spit out, "And you know it."

I turned back around and stomped angrily forward. After some time we reached the sandy bottom where the river ran with melted silver instead of water.

The hooded man stood before us. Pulling back the cowl that shaded his face, he revealed a man more beautiful than any I had ever seen. His eyes shone like the first morning sun. His skin was smooth, poured over his finely crafted features that showed not one sign of age. He had the look of one who had never been touched by minutes, hours, or days. Though he was clearly older, he was too perfect to be considered aged, and therefore I had no idea as to how to guess his age. Was he twenty or eighty?

We all gazed at the man. My tseeyen warmed with familiar comfort.

"Sir," Atticus spoke first, "We have come with Ernest, to find you."

"Lignum Vitae, Malachi Killer." The man from the boat smiled at Atticus. Atticus in turn looked uncharacteristically stunned.

"Malachi Killer," the words were familiar as I said them out loud. I looked to Atticus, "That is what the Boged called you."

"It is you. Your face has crossed my mind through these many years. I hoped that you had survived, and so I see now, you have." Atticus was filled with visible relief.

He had been branded a traitor by the Boged during the Dividing Wars. Wars fought between the Simulacrum and the Boged. The Boged believed Atticus had abandoned his post as a soldier in the midst of a battle for Jerusalem. Worse, they had also wrongly believed that he had killed a man who wore a golden mask, the one they called Jeremiah, the last of the Original Men.

A bone-deep warmth began at the base of my wrist, at my tseeyen and pulsed up my arm and into my chest.

"Jeremiah," Atticus said his name with absolute certainty, "The man beneath the golden mask, the son of Seth, the defender of the Malachi." Atticus paused and then added, "or so the storytellers claim."

"It is a goodness this day brings. To see you again, Atticus, Ayindalet, Chosen One of the One Tree." He moved his head with the grace of a king, reminding me of the stories of the legendary King Arthur as he asked, "Do you still follow the River as the Man of Words commanded you?"

Without waiting for a reply, he answered, "Ahh, you do."

His eyes shifted, and fell over me, but still he spoke to Atticus, "I see you carry the key. By your blood the way will open, bringing them to the One Door."

"The key?" Atticus looked startled. He shifted his weight and glanced toward me as though it was me he was trying to balance out. "You speak the promise of the Man of Words. The words he spoke to me the day he brought me to this River. How do you know these words that he spoke to me in secret?"

Jeremiah turned back to Atticus, "I have read them. Are not all his words written in the Sefer HaChaim?"

"The Books of Life?" Atticus shook his head. "I would not know. I have no knowledge of what is recorded inside such books."

"No," Jeremiah chuckled, "you are honest, and there is no lie within you. One day you, too, will read the Books written by the Man of Words. He has remembered everything from before the beginning to beyond the end, and all that is remembered by him, is written in the Sefer HaChaim."

"Look," Ernest said motioning toward me with wonder in his eyes, "You are glowing. You are golden, as though..." he shook his head, "as though you ate the sun."

"It is the key within her," Jeremiah said, "The Eighth key. She is the Malachi now."

Ernest was staring at me as he said, "She is the one for whom you have been searching?"

"She is," said Jeremiah as his hand flew up to his own chest.

Tears rushed to my eyes as an unforeseen emotion burned up from my tseeyen and through my heart. Forcing control from my lips I said with quivering words, "You are Jeremiah, you are the man Achiel showed me. The man from the battle, the night of the at Red Oaks. It was you who came for Vera, my... my mother. You are—"

"Your father," Jeremiah answered. We stood still. Everyone looking back and forth between the two of us.

Jeremiah bowed his head slightly, "I have had many names since my birth. But you, my daughter, are Veralee, the shelter of the truth within your veins, the Malachi, the Last of the Guardians of the Gates."

I put my hand over the spot where the golden key was glowing beneath my skin, and I felt every word in the depths of me.

"Achiel bought me back, he showed me the night I was born. He showed me Red Oaks the night—"

"The night you were born," Jeremiah finished.

"And, that night, you gave me the key," I answered.

"Yes," he said gently. "That is why I have come back for you."

"Back?" I shook my head. "But for you this hasn't even happened yet," I stumbled, wiping quickly at the rogue tears. "You won't even meet my mother until 1864 or something like that." The truth was I did not know when they would meet but knew only the year of the battle, the year I would be born.

"I have seen you in my dreams," he explained. "In my time, I have already met your mother. You are growing in her womb even now. She waits for me to return to her. I have been gone many months now, tracking the Hidden Books. And now, I have come to find you, to prepare you and to unite the Hidden Books. I have looked into the pools of the Archaon, and I know my final destination. I am on my way now, to place the key within you." His eyes were sad, and yet so full of life as he said, "For this is my last voyage on the River."

"What do you mean?" I asked. I know I needed to tell him about the book, but I had to know more about him.

"I love your mother," he said with great longing, "With all that I am. I will do what I can to protect you both from the Rephaim who search even now for the key within your heart."

"Why do they want it?" I asked suddenly, "What door does the key in my blood open?"

"What door?" he cocked his head slightly and said quickly, "Come with me."

Without knowing how we got there, suddenly we were all seated in the boat.

"Go," Jeremiah commanded and the boat began back the way it had come. He turned to the four of us and said, "Do not touch the silver waters."

"This is not made of Acacia wood," Atticus motioned to the boat.

"No," Jeremiah looked impressed with Atticus as he added, "Those trees went extinct the day the doors fell in Aria."

Atticus explained to me, "Shittah wood is the only wood that can withstand the power of the River. See," he pointed to the edge of the boat, "already the River is eating at the wood."

The River we were navigating began to widen quickly until suddenly we came through the roots of the Terebinths and a vast River of silver-like water flowed before us. The great energy of the River was causing massive erosion on each side, eating away at the earth. Flat terraces formed layers of earth and pools of water where dead plants floated. The silver water was sometimes opaque in the shadows but then luminous as the moon in other places. It moved with clear intelligence, with unnatural understanding and purpose.

We left the tributary and entered the main body of the river. The silver water changed slightly.

"The water is changing but still blends together," I said watching the movement of the River. "It's not all the same?"

Jeremiah nodded, "No." He pointed out toward the large body of water, "This is not a River of water, but it is filled with the very presence of Paraclete himself."

"What do you mean?" I asked, fascinated. Paraclete was the leader of the Archaon. I had met him only once, at the One Tree after I had traveled through the Cave. Though he had the shape and appearance of a man, he was no man. He was made of bronze and fire and his eyes; his eyes were beyond description. He had touched my hair, and it had turned a glowing white. My hair was the mark of having been in the presence of Paraclete.

"How is the presence of Paraclete in the River?" I asked.

"How do you describe a color you have never seen?" Jeremiah said, "It is not an easy thing to understand, but this River, the same River which controls the Lady Moed herself, derives its physical essence from Paraclete. There is nothing that is not controlled by this River.

I leaned slightly over the side of the boat, wanting to examine the River more closely. My eyes could not penetrate its depth, but I stared intently into its molten current. Suddenly, out of the corner of my eye, I saw a large, cloudy shadow glide beneath the boat. I jerked away from the edge of the boat. Fear surged through my tseeyen, warning me of great danger.

Atticus touched my arm and with concern he asked, "What do you see?"

"What is that?" I whispered hoarsely, my mind working quickly to determine the size of the boat verses the size of the creature below.

"Can you draw out the Leviathan with a fishhook?" Jeremiah began to speak in prose, "Or press down his tongue with a cord? Can you put a rope in his nose or pierce his jaw with a hook? Has he made many pleas to you? Will he speak to you in soft words? Will he make a covenant with you to take him for your servant forever? Will you play with him, as a bird in a cage?"

"A bird in a cage?" I began, and for a flash I was back on a dark ship. I heard the voice, remembered my recurring dreams of waking up on a sinister sailing vessel, named The Leviathan. It housed terrified birds in huge cages. When the birds saw me, they would beg me to free them. Sometimes in these horrific dreams, I would see Ausley in one of the cages, but before I could free her, a dark figure discovered me. The figure always said the same menacing words to me:

We see you.

The image of my dreams vanished. I blinked to reorient myself. I was back on the boat in the River, and Jeremiah was still speaking his riddle.

His voice like the sky above us, grew darker with every word he spoke.

"Who can open the door cast over his face? Around his teeth lie terrors unmatched. His back is made of rows of shields, his mouth is a flaming torch, his breath kindles coals and the folds of his flesh stick together firmly. The seal has been placed upon him, the door firmly locked until the latter days have come, and the Last of the Guardians has fallen."

Jeremiah and I were suddenly no longer on a boat at all, but standing in a familiar wood.

"How did we get here?" I asked.

"We are not really here," Jeremiah said, "We are at this very moment, sitting on a boat with your companions. Close your eyes, you will feel the slow and steady movement of the River beneath your feet."

He was right and yet all around us we were ...

"I've been here before," I whispered, my eyes wide open as I added, "This is the way through the Terebinths of Mamre, the way Atticus led us to the Meeting with the Archaon in the city of the Original Men."

"Yes," Jeremiah said softly. "Do you remember what happened to you here?"

A small bird flew down and landed on the leaves by my feet. The large trees were vibrant with life and the feeling of peace was so thick in the air that I was sure I could grasp it in my hands.

Jeremiah pointed to my right. I moved forward and stumbled slightly. My hand flew out, and I caught his arm. A shock of pain ran through my arm, causing me to jerk back.

He looked apologetic as he said, "I apologize, Veralee, but you must not touch me. We both have the key at this time, and if we touch for too long, it would be fatal to you."

"Oh," I said trying to understand.

I walked around the large tree trunk and stopped. Adair?

"Veralee?" she called out.

Before I could answer her, she began walking briskly through the trees. I turned to see where she was going, and that is when I saw myself. More than twenty feet in front of her, I was walking as though in a dream through the trees.

"That's me..." I suddenly felt as though I was inside a nightmare. Seeing myself filled me with panic.

"Do not be afraid. You cannot be harmed in your own memory. Follow Adair. I will stay with you." Jeremiah urged me forward. I swallowed and nodded as I walked toward Adair who was now calling out, "Veralee! Where are you going?"

Adair picked up the pace and walked briskly through the foliage. Suddenly she stopped in front of a well forgotten path that was covered with heavy vines and tree limbs. I saw myself standing with Adair, and she grabbed my arm. Strangely, I felt her hand on my arm as I stood there with Jeremiah.

"Look," I heard myself say to Adair as I watched myself raise my arm to point through the vines. Barely visible, I saw two tall rocks leaning on one another, creating a small opening in the middle.

"Something," I heard the hesitation in my voice as I continued, "something from the very beginning is down there. It waits for the end. But the way is closed, a fiery sword stops any from coming near, for the way is locked, closed until the appointed time." A fierce wind rushed around us. I stood back and watched as Adair grabbed hold of me to steady herself.

"Veralee?" Atticus called my name in my memory.

I watched as I answered, "Coming!" And then I disappeared with Adair down the path from which we had come.

I realized Jeremiah was standing beside me.

"What is that place?" I motioned toward the two rocks down the forgotten path, "I remember it was calling to me. I remembered hearing it call my name as though it was calling to me from the beginning of time. How is that possible?"

"It does not call you, but the key within you. This is the Eighth Gate of Bariyach. It stands in desire, in the time of the beginning, never moving forward, never seeing the next minute or hour, but waiting always for the key to appear, and the gate to finally be opened."

"The Eighth Gate?" I remembered the City beneath the earth where my father fell asleep, "Why are these gates here?"

"Not all are here in the Terebinths. The other seven are behind the Eighth Gate, farther from here, in the City of Bariyach which you have already seen. But the Eighth stands here," he raised his hands, motioning to the forest,

"Where time began and the Original Men were created and placed by the One Tree."

"Why would the gate be here? Isn't it evil?"

"No," Jeremiah shook his head. His eyes beamed with the light of knowledge, "The Eighth Gate is not evil. It is the Creation Gate. On one side is the Terebinths of Mamre, on the other, the City of Bariyach. It is this gate that was opened three days before time had even been born. When the One Tree made everything out of nothing. Behind this gate is the ability to create, to start again, to make a new earth for man to dwell as he did in the beginning."

My mind began to race to put pieces of a puzzle together, "You mean the Eighth Gate ... is The Door that the Simulacrum await?"

"No, and yes," Jeremiah paused and looked down the pathway then back at me, "The Simulacrum missed The Door of which you speak when they missed The Man of Words, whom they called Beged. He was and is and will be The Door, the first Door, which the Histories reveal. Every reference is to Him, for those with eyes to see. The Eighth Gate is the final beginning. The Door that was and is to come must open first, and then the Eighth Gate must follow."

"That was? You mean Beged," I looked back at the Eighth Gate, "And is to come, because the Door will open again for the Simulacrum."

Jeremiah smiled, obviously pleased, "Yes, my daughter. The Eiani has opened your mind to this understanding."

He motioned around him, "I stood here the day The Door opened the first time. Rarely did I ever allow myself to come into the Terebinths, for it is not safe for the Malachi who holds the key to come so close. But every three hundred years I allowed myself entry to eat from the Basar tree. That day," he stopped for a second, lost in the memory before continuing, "that day, something was different. I felt the change in the air and the movement of the trees. They were whispering, revealing secrets from ancient days to the birds. I listened to the chatter, trying to understand it, and heard something about opening the gate. So, I hurried to be sure the way to the gate was still closed.

I was trying to keep up. "There were stones in front of the gate?"

He nodded, "Great stones, massive stones, placed by the Archaon to block the gate after my mother, Chauvah, betrayed the One Tree. Those stones had blocked the way to the gate all of my life, and I had lived much longer than any other Image-bearer. But as I stood in front of the stones wondering about what I had heard, the ground began to shake, and the sun above me turned dark. A ripping sound broke through the sky, and I feared that the very fabric of the Terebinths was splitting from top to bottom. A fog billowed from the ground. I dropped to my knees and covered my head in fear and dread."

He shook his head and furrowed his brow in wonder, "But when the fog began to clear, I saw that the stones had been separated! The way to the gate had been revealed."

My pulse quickened as I looked out toward the large stones, "Did anything come through?"

Jeremiah smiled slightly and nodded, "Just a ram. A single ram. After the ram ran by me, I tried to enter through the stone pillars, but I could not. The stones were gone, the gate was revealed, but it was still closed. "

Lightning snapped through the sky, and Jeremiah looked knowingly upward.

"I don't understand," I said, feeling the wind pick up, "The Rephaim, the ones I saw beneath in the City of Bariyach. They want to get to this gate. They are seeking to open it?"

"Yes," said Jeremiah, "And they will stop at nothing in order to find the key, which is hidden within you."

Instinctively I placed my hand over my heart and felt the glow of the key.

"This key," I whispered, "opens the Eighth Gate, the Gate of Creation?!"

Jeremiah nodded.

"Why," I began to back up slightly, "Why, why, would you give that to me? Why?!"

"It is not about you, Veralee, or me, but mankind. The One Tree created mankind in his likeness, to be Image-bearers of the One Tree. The key that you carry is no ordinary key. Within it is the original plan for the first human ever created. It is the code, the message, that was breathed into the dirt vessel that brought man out of the earth."

"Why was this given to us?" I interrupted.

"It is the promise that the One Tree will always have an untainted remnant of his creation, no matter how far the Friguscor spreads across the earth, or how much the Nachash tries to distort the image in mankind, or how deep the days plunge into the night. That key," he pointed to my chest, "contains the promise made by the One Tree to all of creation at the beginning of time, the guarantee that mankind would one day return to live beneath the branches of the One Tree, and that all creation would be restored to its original beauty. The kingdoms of man may rage and Leviathan, the Nachash himself, may scheme, but ultimately, it will all come to naught. When the One Tree sends forth an utterance through the Man of Words, it abides forever, and that word will accomplish its purpose in the fullness of time."

I remembered when I first saw the Man of Words, and that when he spoke, the words planted into the ground and began growing trees. "Ahhh... that's what that meant!" I exclaimed, "but the shadow beneath the boat?" I trembled slightly, "That is the Nachash?"

"Yes," he sighed, "All you see is the shadow of the Leviathan. Once, he was the most beautiful and powerful of all creation, but in his beauty, he became filled with pride and arrogance. His honored position among creation was not enough for him; he desired to lift himself even above the One Tree. He enticed a third of the Archaon to join him, and he led an insurrection against the One Tree. When the Archaon who remained loyal to the One Tree put down the rebellion, the One Tree cursed the Nachash and took his beauty from him.

However, the Nachash remains crafty and powerful, and he hates the One Tree. The Nachash knows his fate is written in the Histories, but he has convinced himself that he can still change it. "

I was trying to absorb all of this, "So is the Nachash behind all of this... this evil?"

Jeremiah nodded solemnly, "Yes, and no. He has no form in our world. He exists in the shadows, the dark places of the earth, the deepest parts of the oceans, but he is ruler of the City of Bariyach. There he walks freely, but to accomplish his purposes in our world, he must have the cooperation of man. He sends his subjects to our world to influence humans, but the One Tree gave mankind free will; therefore, humans bear responsibility for their actions."

"Well, if he cannot overcome the One Tree," I reasoned, "why does he try? What does he want to accomplish?"

"Ah," Jeremiah answered. "Two things. Because he hates the One Tree, the Nachash wants to destroy anything the One Tree loves. That includes all creation and all humankind. But, he hates the Simulacrum most of all because they carry the image of the One Tree and because the One Tree still has a plan to use them to redeem the earth. So, he hopes to completely wipe the Simulacrum and even the memory of them from the earth.

I frowned at this and remembered how the Friguscor had killed so many of my people over our history. "Wait! Are you saying the Nachash is behind the Esurio?"

"Indirectly. He knows how to use the weakness of man. The Esurio is a combination of the Nachash's hatred and man's own greed. The Eursiro destroys the humanity of the Friguscor who is infected, and the infected Friguscor is then a killing machine. It is the physical representation of the Nachash's insatiable desire for death and destruction.

"So, what does that have to do with the key?" I asked.

"The Nachash wants more than anything, to get through that gate," Jeremiah pointed across the field, "And if he gets through, he believes he can start creation over again. What was will never have been, and what will be, well," Jeremiah sighed, "all will be rewritten, and all made in the image of the Leviathan."

"It's about us? All of this is about us?"

"No," Jeremiah said bravely, "It is all about the One Tree, Veralee. That you must learn. It is not about man, or the Leviathan. It is all about the One Tree."

He reached out his hand toward me, but did not touch me as he asked, "May I see?" with such tenderness that I immediately held out my arm to him so that he could see my tseeyen.

"A sparrow made of pieces of time," he nodded and said, "I have seen this bird fly over me many times in my dreams. It is always in flight, always moving toward the horizon," he mused, as he turned over his own arm.

"Your tseeyen," my eyes fell on the mark that covered his right wrist, "It's the dekeract," I added, "Just like the one on the Hidden Book I had! Why do you have the same mark?"

Jeremiah smiled revealing dimples on each side of his cheek, "Though it was not my mind, it was my hand that pinned those books with the ink of the Archaon and scrolls made from the very bark of the One Tree."

"Not your mind?"

"No," Jeremiah said thoughtfully, "I wrote what I heard in my dreams from the Eiani. I wrote what Paraclete wanted the Simulacrum to remember."

"Did you write the Histories as well as the Hidden Books?"

He nodded.

It all felt so right.

"Growing up, I would spend hours reading the Histories. They always felt like they were a part of me." I paused, not knowing how to say what I was feeling.

"Knowing that you were reading them brings me great comfort." He said, "If the world was different, if we were different, I would have loved to read them with you as you were growing up."

We stood together in the woods. A father and a daughter that had never known the other, but somehow, deep down, had always loved one another. I bit my lip and then forced the words, "I bet they would have made a lot more sense," I motioned toward him, "If you had been the one reading them to me."

A pang of guilt rose in my throat and I added, "But Daddy, I mean, my father Edwin, he did a great job reading them with me."

Admiration flashed in Jeremiah's eyes before he said, "Of course. The Archaon are wise and led by Paraclete. You were meant to be raised by Edwin and ..."

"Gail," I said Mother's name and felt the pain of it strike across my heart. I missed her so much.

"Yes, Gail." Jeremiah stood silent for a moment and I could not help but think of Atticus. Atticus had always told me that the mission of the Eiani would cost me everything. I stood looking at the father I had never known, and for the hundredth time I realized the truth of Atticus' words.

"Why the dekeract?" I asked quickly.

"It is the molecular shape of the Eiani. It is the very thing that connects all of creation through one point."

"One point? What is the one point?"

"The One Tree. Listen to me, Veralee," Jeremiah grew even more serious as he continued, "Ernest brought you here because you must secure the Hidden Books. The Simulacrum will need them, and the Rephaim will try to destroy them."

"Destroy them?" I felt sick. I only had one book, and Sarah had just given it to me...again. I had lost it twice. I had to tell him, but I could not bring myself to do it.

"When he has both, he will read from them, and then he will burn them," Jeremiah advised soberly.

"Read from them? To find out what will happen at the end?" I asked for clarification.

"No," Jeremiah said, "He knows what will happen at the end. The words of the books have the power to pull the key from your chest. He cannot touch the key, but he can use the power of the books to pull it from you. And then he will destroy the books to ensure that the Door will never open."

My hand flew up to my chest, instinctively protecting the key within me.

"And no one will be able to escape," I said.

"All of the Image-bearers will fall if he opens the Creation Gate. He will erase all made in the image of the One Tree and will start creation again in the image of the Nachash."

This time, at the mention of the name, I found myself standing in a beautiful garden of unsurpassed beauty.

"This is not from my memory," I whispered.

"No," Jeremiah confirmed, "This is mine."

A woman who shined as though she were made of pure light held a baby in her arms. He played with a key that hung round her neck. The light danced off of it making rainbows on the baby's face. She kissed the baby gently, letting her lips linger on his cheek. A smile spread across her face as she looked at the baby. The sky around them moved as though it were water, sparkling against the light of the woman and child.

But darkness was forming on the clouds, and everything suddenly changed. The woman still held the golden key around her neck, but she was running in sheer terror. Her bare feet were bloodied and caked with mud. A great roar in the distance shook the trees and caused the earth to tremble. Fire blazed from the sky as a great dragon came into view; it covered the light of the moon with its massive size. As the woman ran, the child, who was now a toddler, lay silently on her back. The dragon's wings hurled dust and earth into the wind which then pelted the back of the woman. Fire kindled again in the throat of the dreadful creature, his guttural roar echoing across the sky. The flames of fury ignited the trees and surrounded the woman. When she reached the edge of the River, she sat the child down.

"Listen to me, child of my womb," the woman says into the boy's ear, "The One Tree will open the door. They will destroy the Door, and in three days, he will rebuild it. In you I place the key. You are the Malachi. In your blood remains the key to the Eighth Gate, the Creation Gate. It is this gate which leads back to the beginning. That is what the Leviathan seeks. If he enters, then he will destroy everything. Do you understand? The Malachi is the message from the beginning, written by the One Tree, breathed into man when the first man was created."

"The image," said the little boy, "The Malachi is the message to man that we are created in the Image of the One Tree?"

"That the One Tree is the creator, and mankind is his creation. It is the message told at the beginning that must be brought to the end. The dragon above seeks the key to go back to the beginning, to erase the message of the One Tree."

"The Image within man?" said the boy.

"Yes, the dragon wants to erase the Image within man, but you will guard what is entrusted to you. You will carry the key until you find the Last Guardian and the final Door will open. Then and only then, may the key be placed within the Eighth Gate. The Key cannot enter the gate before the Final Door opens. Remember my words, remember!"

"I have to go into the River?" asked the little boy.

"Yes, the River will keep you safe."

"I've seen this before. You were that child. She put you in the River to protect the Malachi, the key to the Creation Gate!" I said quickly, excitement pulsing through my veins.

"Yes," Jeremiah said softly, "You have dreamt of this moment?"

"Yes," I said, "And your name is Seth?"

"Once, a long time ago."

"Your mother was Chauvah, the first woman?" I said, understanding on a level that I had not seen before, "So, the Nachash, the dragon, and the Leviathan are all the same creature. That makes sense, I guess."

Another thought hit me.

"Were you the brother who killed the other brother and brought the Friguscor into the world?" I said, remembering our history.

"No, those were my older brothers," Jeremiah answered. "The Friguscor was spread through my eldest brother and took over the world of man. I survived by being hidden through the centuries in the River. I would surface like an Ayindalet, every now and then, but I could never stay in one place long. The Rephaim were always looking for the Malachi."

"This key?" I touched my chest, feeling suddenly like I was drowning on dry land.

"Yes," he looked at the woman who was his mother who stood crying as the basket with the little boy floated out of sight, "I have brought you here for a purpose, Malachi. You will need to be able to navigate the River when the time comes."

"What is coming? What time?"

"When the enemy is biting at your heels," Jeremiah said, his eyes flashing fierce. "You must be ready. You must be able to come to reach your hands into the River."

"I can't navigate the River. I couldn't even get to River if I tried ..."

"No," Jeremiah smiled and suddenly we were back on the boat, floating down the River. He pointed to Atticus and said, "But he can."

Ausley 3:2

"There it is again," I rose from the small wooden bench where I sat, in the room that served as my prison. The far wall of the room was draped in a large medieval tapestry, depicting a massive battle at the front of a great city gate. Its ownership of the wall told me it had undoubtedly hung for hundreds of years in that very spot. The sound I continued to hear was coming from somewhere behind the wall.

"I hear a woman crying," I said.

Cautious of my steps, I moved toward the tapestry. The sound was faint but distinctly female. I couldn't tell, was it coming from behind the wall? Maybe it was coming from beneath the floor?

"I hear her," I repeated.

Phoebe cut her eyes over to Balaam who smiled at me with evident desire. He put down his glass and came to stand beside me. Leaning in, much too close for comfort, he caressed my arm.

"Do you fear?" he cooed. "Do you seek comfort?" His tongue clicked on the edge of his teeth as he dragged a single fingernail up my arm.

I jerked back from him. "No!"

"Muchas mujeres cry aqui," said Jaria, her hand working to soothe her slicked back hair. A broad, cruel, smile spread across her mouth as she added, "And many more find mukavuutta, in the arms of the Anshargal."

"He is so beautiful," Phoebe sighed, her hands touching her own neck longingly.

At the mention of him, I turned my head, coughed, and vomited bile directly on the floor. My stomach churned. The baby moved and pain shot up under my ribs. I was so sick here, I could not stomach much more than a small piece of bread much less the name of Uziel, whom they called Anshargal, an old word that Jaria has said meant "prince of the air."

Prince? His name was darkness to me. And here, in the world between worlds, I have learned for certain, there is no beauty in darkness. Only light can produce what is truly beautiful.

"We must hurry," Phoebe said as she stepped easily over the bile on the floor allowing her long train to wipe up the mess. "Now let us go."

"We, meli, take care," explained Jaria, her eyes full of excitement as she moved fuildly between languages, "She is still bashri, human; she is not like the others."

"This is why they should not come here while they still carry their flesh," said Phoebe disdainfully, though her tongue circled around the word flesh with intense desire. She sighed. "It has been too long since I have had the flesh of man wrapped around me."

"But the Anshargal," Balaam paused for a moment to make sure I was over my nausea. He handed me a glass of water and continued only after I had swallowed, "he has commanded her presence at his table this night."

Balaam took the glass of water and looked me over, like an artist searching for a last detail to complete his masterpiece. The three of them had worked most of the afternoon dressing me in luxurious silks and gems. I hated each second of it.

Balaam clucked and put the last flower in my hair. "There," he folded his hands together, pressed his lips against my cheek, and mouthed the words, "you look like something to eat."

I jerked away before his tongue could once again taste my face.

"Well, let us tarry no longer," he said, his eyes constantly watching mine. With a twirl of movement, he waltzed toward the door. He produced a single key from beneath his rope bracelets which were safely tucked beneath larger, gold bracelets indicating his enslavement.

The door was so heavy it required great effort from all three to open. Beneath their thin silk sarongs, I saw rippled muscles tense against the weight of the old door. It opened, but only far enough for the four of us to exist in single file. I stepped carefully in my silk shoes onto the marble floor outside of the room.

"Oh!" I exclaimed involuntarily when I stepped through the door. We stood on the second floor of a great hallway which wrapped in a square around an open atrium. Exotic orchids of lavender, yellow, and white hung on the walls and splashed color against glazed blue brick. Masses of dark pink and purple bouganvillas cascaded over the rails and dripped color toward the floor below. Roses and gardenias scented the air with a sweet, delicate fragrance. Climbing vines of fuchsia-colored bleeding hearts and white stephanotis curled around the red pillars which supported large arches, that opened to the atrium. The ceiling above was a lattice of tightly woven vines of yellow flowering jasmine through which bright silver stars twinkled in the dark night sky. The sound of a gently flowing waterfall echoed somewhere. I closed my eyes and for a brief moment dreamed of home and Mother's beautiful gardens.

Balaam interrupted my reverie, "Voste, you have been summoned, so we must go."

They ushered me toward the stairs, and as we walked, I noticed that the glazed brick walls were accented with gold relief in a Middle Eastern fashion across the top and bottom. The blue walls were imprinted with gold relief forms, the most prominent being the form of a man with outstretched wings between stylized striding lions. The brick looked ancient, but the forms looked familiar. Where had I seen these before?

"Down the stairs we go, down the stairs, but take care and stay on the rock, do not fall to the side, you must not fall to the sides," babbled Jaria as she slinked her hips down the first set of stairs we came upon, "Und denk daran, dass du immer noch fleisch an diesen knochen hast."

"Summoned?" I questioned, feeling my tseeyen vibrate with warning. Fear and bile were rising in my throat. I focused on counting the enameled blue and gold clay jars that overflowed with flowers, like water pouring over the edge of each step. It helped calm my trembling as I asked with dread, "For what exactly?"

"Do not wrinkle your face," said Phoebe, "it is not attractive. You must look perfect for him. Do not fear. He will not destroy you yet. You carry the flesh that is most valuable to him."

"Oh, yes," added Jaria, sucking deep breaths of air as she eyed my belly jealously.

"Tu llevas the child of the Anshargal, az aldott! Mimba ya thupi!"

Jaria's speech, I had quickly learned, was more often than not, schizophrenic nonsense, a constant barrage of sound. How many languages did she speak? She was a ping pong ball of conversation, her words a constant switch from one language to another, leaving most of her sentences a confusion of verbal tossed salad.

Instinctively, I wrapped a protective hand around the mystery growing within me as we came to stand in the large hanging gardens.

"Who is out there?" A voice called loudly from behind a door nearby. There were more doors than seemed possible around the square garden. Single doors, taller and slimmer than any doors I had ever seen, were lined up one after the other on the walls.

"Open the door!" cried another voice. With that, a great horde of voices began to call out from behind the doors. The sound confused me. My tseeyen began to burn. I felt as though I was suddenly spinning round and round with the voices pushing me into a deeper tailspin.

"If you can hear me, let me out! Please!"

"Is that you? I know you have the blood in you!"

"Let me out! Free us! Free us!"

Confusion flowed until I heard one distinct voice, "You are the child of Gail," I turned around and knew immediately which door the voice hid behind, "I feel my bloodline in your veins. Run from here! Return the way you came while you till have flesh on your bones. While your eyes are still open!"

"Who are you?" I called back, but suddenly I am not in the atrium with Balaam and the others.

I was somewhere in the past.

Thunder rolls in the near distance. The smell of rain is in the air. Lightning flashes, revealing a woman standing directly beside me on the long wooden dock. I jump back and scream, but the woman obviously does not hear me. She neither flinches nor looks my way. Instead she keeps her focused gazed on the boat slipping silently toward her through the clear waters. Tall, dilapidated buildings stand on either side of the river, which looks more like fluid silver than any water I have ever seen before. Made of smoothed wood, the boat is long and thin with the bow splitting at the very front into twin horns of a ram which curls backward, almost touching the gunwales on either side of the ship. The horns, however, are not made of wood, but in their previous life had been the actual ornament of a great beast.

Silence hangs like a dangling knife on the edge of the woman's fearful expectation. Her fingers twitch at her side. The facial veins in her neck pulse with tension, revealing sharp but beautiful collarbones that testify of the need for either flight or fight depending on whatever approaches.

The boat hits the dock softly, gliding to a perfect halt.

A woman in a scarlet robe, her face hidden in the cowl, stands at the helm of the boat. She speaks,"Vera, you have come. I am thankful."

"Vera?" I ask as I turn toward her.

"Had I a choice?" Vera's voice is strong and direct as she adds with great certainty, "I was given no choice."

"Choices are for the free, and we," the woman raises a hand bound with an iron bracelet, "are not free women."

Vera nods as she raises her chin just as Mother always does when she is determined not to be ruled by fear.

"I am not like you, Zulika. I have not lived a life bound to the will of men, as you well know."

"Zulika, is that you?" I ask aloud, but neither woman acknowledges me.

Zulika laughs beneath the shadow of her hood.

"Why, then, did you become Guardian of the Gate, even before your mother had left for the Alabaster City? Yes, I remember much about your life."

I see Vera's resolve weaken, and her hands tighten into nervous fists at her sides as Zulika continues to speak.

"I knew that Red Oaks was in trouble and that when Ernest fell ... May the One Tree protect him where he lies in the Tombs of the Forgotten until the day he is awakened by the blast of the final trumps, for he was the greatest bridge-builder of his time."

Her blessing complete, Zulika goes on.

"I knew that when he fell, Barthenia could no longer bear the weight of the key that had been given to her. So, you took in your hands the torch that your mother could not, in her grief, bear to hold up to the darkness."

Vera remains silent, so Zulika continues to speak.

"So, I know you are brave and I know you are not afraid to carry the weight of others, but I have come to ask you. Will you again protect those whom you love?"

Finally, Vera speaks.

"I am no longer the Guardian," she says. "What you seek from me, I cannot give. You ask because I am the daughter of Ernest who worked to bridge the world of the Simulacrum and the Boged, but you must know better than to ask for me to give what I no longer possess. I carry no key in my veins. This is my home now."

With those words, she lifts her hand, and I see behind her a beautiful city of white alabaster.

"Here, I am simply part of the great cloud of witnesses. We have finished our fight. We have run the race and have passed the torches to the next generations. From here, on this great hill of rest, we can see the dark clouds of the last days rolling in. And I know as you do, that it matters not what the darkness brings. The oaks will remain across the horizon between the two trees, until they meet their end at the great and final beginning."

Vera pauses so long that I think is finished speaking, but then she speaks again.

"My time is over, Zuilika. My journey has ended. Now leave me and call on me no more."

Vera's shoulders sink low. She begins to turn away, tears falling down her face. Zulika stands and stretches out her hand.

"If you do not return," she says, "the books will be lost and all that you did, all that your father did, will be for naught."

Vera speaks without turning back toward Zulika.

"I have told you. My part is finished. What I have done is done, and what they will do now is up to those who are still awake. Call on me no more for I have finished with the days of men. William is long gone, Zulika. You cannot use that against me any longer. The bond between us went with him to the Tombs of the Forgotten.

Vera begins walking away, but Zulika's words stop her.

"It is not a man that they are seeking, but a girl. There are rumors in the darkness ..."

Vera spins around, pinning Zulika into abrupt silence.

"Do not speak to me of the things you have learned from the darkness. I will hear no words from your forked tongue. It is treason against your own to listen to those voices. I told you when you opened that tera to close it and never open it again. You are deceived, Zulika! You are a blind seer for your people because you look into the faces of the forbidden, and you listen to the voices of the damned!"

Zulika countered, "Any soldier would listen to the plans of the enemy if he had the choice. I am a soldier, Vera; I have been since my beginning, since the blood first transformed me."

"You deceive yourself. Those words are from the darkness below, that tera is connected to the City of Bariyach itself, and you will not come out unscathed, Zulika. They must know that a portal has been opened."

"You may question my methods, Vera, but you cannot question what I have heard whispered in the dark. They speak of a baby, a girl who was lost to the River and—"

"A baby?" Vera looks instantly terrified, as though her heart had suddenly turned from flesh to stone in the measure of a single breath or maybe a single word.

Zulika takes five quick steps toward the side of the boat and leans over one of the horns, "Yes," she says with great excitement, her head still hiding behind the hood, "They speak of a baby that was born to the Simulacrum. You know the words from the books, 'Taken from one, given to the other. A crown of snow above, and fire within. To gather what has been scattered, to join what has been divided, and to—"

Vera finishes the sentence for her, "keep what has been hidden."

Zulika continues, "They do not know the exact times, but they are looking for this child which has been hidden." Zulika tightened her hands around the horn. "They said she had a key, but Vera. I think they are talking about the Nikud, the Malachi. The messenger who will unite the Boged back to the Simulacrum. She could be the one, Vera! The one who will bring our people together as we were always meant to be!"

"No," Vera whispers, her mouth evidently dry.

"Yes," Zulika hisses, "And they spoke of more ... of an Ayindalet. Did you not tell me you had met one? What was his name, Vera? What was the name of the man you met?"

Vera's eyes narrow, "I never told you it was a man."

"I must know his name."

"No," Vera shakes her head again, "All of this is in the past. All of this is lost to me. I do not want to return to the memories. At least here the pain of it all no longer weighs me down when I walk. Here, all the pain seems suspended above me, as though it waits for full reconciliation at the end. Here, I can breathe. I will stay here, Zulika, where the pain is manageable and besides, soon Richard and Sarah will join me. I am waiting for them."

"Richard will not be joining you," Zulika interjects.

"Has he decided to stay away from the Alabaster City even longer? Surely, he is almost finished? Gail and Edwin must be almost ready to take their place as Guardians and GateKeepers at Red Oaks."

"Richard is not coming because he has fallen, Vera," Zulika clarifies.

"Fallen?"

"And even as we speak James Jackson is bringing Sarah to hide within the walls of the Boged," Zulika adds.

"James Jackson Westbrooke? What? Why?"

Zulika answered, "From what we hear, there was a secret meeting in the woods before the Council Meeting. Sarah was banished from your people."

"Banished?" Vera spits the word as though it is a curse, "Why would a Guardian be banished?"

"Vera, this is what I have been trying to tell you. She has been banished for something to do with the laws of Padha, just like Ernest," Zulika says emphatically.

"Ernest?" Vera narrows her eyes, "My father was not banished; he fell in the fields by the hand of the darkness."

"Yes, because he was finding the Boged in the Friguscor and giving them the blood of the Eiani." Zulika presses, "And now Sarah is coming to us for breaking your law of Padha. Do you not see it, Vera? Sarah has changed someone just like your father did. She must be the girl the voices from the tera are searching for! She is your only daughter, and she could be the one! The one who could unite our people! You must come with me. We have waited for this day!"

"I was a child when you filled me with those dreams, Zulika. It was different then. Sarah is not the girl they seek."

"How can you be so sure, Vera? I admit she does not seem to match all of the prophecies, but perhaps, we have misinterpreted the prophecies. William was certainly no Original Man, but there are no more Original Men. So maybe we misunderstood or maybe Ernest read it wrong. He said it would be a child of three threads, one from the Original men, one from the Simulacrum and one from the Boged, but that is impossible today. Think of it. Sarah is Simulacrum from you and Boged from William. And now she is Simulacrum, coming to find a safe haven in the shadow of the Boged wings, and she has changed a child with her own blood! That could have been the three threads all coming together in one person."

Vera is silent for a moment and then slowly her words come forth, "I came here because you said the one we had waited for had been found, but hear me, Zulika. Sarah is not the one my father spoke of from the Hidden Books. I am going now."

Zulika turns her face, revealing a small part of her chin, "The Hidden books, they are no longer hidden."

Vera retorts, "My father built that entire house to ensure that they would stay safely below in the River."

Zulika challenges, "I do not know how or when, but we have been told that Sarah comes with one of the two books in her hands."

"One? Where is the mate?" Vera asks, concerned.

"I do not know who has the other book or its location," Zulika answers. "Vera, you have to return with me."

Vera throws her hands up with frustration, "Even if what you say is true, even if this has all come to pass, you know I cannot help you! I have no key inside of me. I cannot go past the Gates."

She points far behind Zulika, "I cannot help you or anyone else!"

"There is one more thing," Zulika seems desperate, "The Tombs have been seized. All the Simulacrum that sleep in the Tombs of the Forgotten are now prisoners."

Vera lifts her head, "No," she breathes and clutches her right side protectively.

Zulika follows Vera's hand and says, "You brought it." Zulika nods eagerly, "I knew you brought it to the Alabaster City with you."

Zulika sneers derisively. "William should never have given it to you! I am the Seer! I should have had that book, not you!"

Vera clutches again at her side, "I will not give it to you. Your message said that the child had been found. But you lied, Zulika. I was a fool to bring it here, I am putting it back where it belongs. Never contact me again."

Vera turns sharply and begins to run. The edge of her cloak flies behind her in the wind.

Zulika draws a long bow from beneath her cloak.

I try to scream out, to warn Vera of the coming danger, but she cannot hear me.

The arrow strikes her in the back, and I see her eyes close before she even hits the wooden dock.

The deed done, Zulika pulls the hood from her face, revealing the distortion that lay beneath. Her eyes are slanted like a snake, and her tongue is forked.

Quickly, she jumps from the boat and rushes toward Vera. Gathering Vera in her arms Zulika reaches inside of Vera's cloak and pulls out a small, palm-sized golden box. She examines it was bright eyes.

"The Mashak!" she says, her lips trembling with pleasure, but she does not open the box.

She bends over Vera's ear and whispers: "I wanted you to come willingly, but now you will go as a slave. Remember that I love you, Vera, and for the love I have always had for you and your father, I will place your body by my son William in the Tombs of the Forgotten. There you can sleep for eternity." She gently places the box back into Vera's pocket adding, "You can keep The Mashak for a little longer; it will be safe for where you are going, only your dreams will be heard."

The cutting of her nails on my arm brought me back to the gardens in the palace. Phoebe was pulling me, "Come or you will be lost to the dreams of sleepers. You must keep moving or they will take you under, and you will never surface again."

I looked toward the door once more. The copper door with an artistic maze on the front stood silent. While in the room upstairs, I was losing my mind to the memories of my childhood; that much was true, but what had I just seen? That was not my memory, but the memory of someone I had never met before, my great-grandmother, Vera. It was her voice that I had heard a moment before the memory swept me far away from here. And it was her sobs I heard each night from my room.

We moved as through a dream from one hallway to the next, which all held the architectural signature of a palace until we stopped at the end of a large hallway. The only light came from parallel Egyptian obelisks topped by large, bronze bowls of fire placed about every three feet down the hallway.

Between each obelisk were large statues of men, with great beards and the wings of eagles. Their wings stretched out across the hall, touching their tips together, forming a canopy of wings above my head. They wore what appeared to be leather battle skirts like Roman soldiers and greaves on their lower legs. Their faces were gaunt, and their mouths hung open. Each statue held a shield in one hand and an Egyptian sickle in the other. Swords hung from sheaths fastened to their belts and knives were belted to the greaves on their lower legs. Each part of the body was made of a distinctly different metal. The horrific heads appeared to be of gold, their bare chests of silver, their thighs of bronze, while the legs were iron. The toes, visible in their sandals were odd, appearing to be a mixture of some kind of clay and a metal, perhaps iron.

"They are glorious are they not?" Balaam asked as we came to the end of the long hallway, stopping before massive bronze doors.

Jaria said, "They are Rephaim, the Kings of old!"

"I've seen them before," I said looking back at the statues, "They look like the symbol for BaVil."

"Of course," said Balaam, "As she said, they are the Kings of Old!"

"Why?" I pointed to the toes, "Why are they made of iron and clay?"

All three of them smiled, and something about it made my stomach churn. Balaam turned and wrapped a hard fist on the doors. It echoed through the hallway. Phoebe turned and prepared herself. Only Jaria still looked at me. She floated one step toward me and touched my bulging belly.

"Iron and clay, my dear, iron and clay!" she whispered.

I jerked back from her, but she pressed forward.

"You are the clay, and he is the iron. And within you grows the new man. The one that will be both of his seed, and the seed of woman."

"No," I shook my head, "I will not be a part of this."

Balaam shrugged and cast his hand toward the statue. "You already are. Look at the history here." His hand pointed to each section of the statue, "It was written before you took your first breath. The Kingdom of the Rephaim will be established. Already the landscape of your world is being transformed. Mankind will no longer be as they were yesterday, but they are being changed, transformed into new men. They will be like gods! Half Rephaim, half man! The days of legends have come to life!"

"And in you," Phoebe whispered, "is the next heir to the throne of men, after his father, of course. Uziel was born of Rahab, the daughter of the Nachash and the seed of Absalom. Your child will be a child of iron and clay as well, but this time, it is different! This child will be born of a Daughter of the Blood! Mixed with the seed from the Prince! It is a perfect way to end such a long, long, battle!"

"Battle?" I said, my body suddenly feeling like a traitor to my own soul, "Between the Simulacrum and the Friguscor?"

They all three laughed as Jaria answered, "No! The Battle between the One Tree and the Nachash!"

"All that is left now, all that is needed is to kill the Eighth," Phoebe began to salivate with excitement, "And then the blood of the new child can open the Creation Gate! A new day will dawn, and the light of men will be no more!"

"The Eighth?" I asked, trying to sound totally ignorant. I had realized that they could not stop themselves from talking when they felt they were showing their superiority over me. For some reason, I knew I needed this information, "What do you mean?"

Excited words spilled from Phoebe's mouth before Balaam could stop her, "Why, your sister, Veralee! She has the—"

"My sister?" I grabbed her by the throat and the front of her dress, "What do you mean? What does he want with my sister?"

"She's the Sapru, the Nikud, the Malachi!" Phoebe said quickly, dropping words like glass on the tile floor. "She is the one that has the Eighth Key in her veins to open the Creation Gate in the Terebinths of Mamre. Once they find her, the world you live in will be all but a memory."

I pulled back, both hands covering my gasping chest.

"He will kill her..." I began to tremble.

"Of course," Balaam said with smooth, cooing tones again, "But do not worry, child. You will be dead long before that happens."

"Dead?" I said.

"Yes," Balaam said, running a long finger over my head as if he were a mother comforting a child. "You will not survive the birth of such a child, for how could a mere mortal survive the birth of a King?"

Adair 3:3

Stand by the roads, and watch. Ask for the ancient paths, the sacred ways where good was found and rest was never hidden.

Hidden. Never Hidden.

Hidden Books.

The weight of the book in my hand steadied me as I walked. My leg was almost completely healed. I walked with ease toward the giant wall that stretched out at the end of the alleyway of trees. There was a tranquility in the air that was as clever as Inman, but the peace of the morning could not lie to me with the wall looming outside. A wall I did not build. A wall I did not want. A wall that made me a prisoner inside my own land.

The wind blew through my hair, and I felt him before I saw him.

"Ruach?" I asked in my mind as I turned toward the treeline to the left of the Big House, "Is that you?"

"Yes, we are still here," he answered in his lovely sing-song cadence. It was easy to talk to him, for we could speak inside my mind, though I was still unable to speak.

"Why don't you come and walk with me?" I asked inside my head.

"We will stay with the trees," he answered. "The ones that remain."

"I'm sorry," I said looking at the outline of his giant shape among the foliage. "I'm sorry for what we are doing, for what we have become."

"We have seen this before," he answered. "Our memory is tied to the roots of the trees."

"Before?" I asked, our entire conversation occurring within my mind.

"At the beginning, with the Original men. It is as the cycle of the moon for mankind. Men trust too much in the ability of their own hands. This we have seen time and again."

My cheeks colored, and I looked to the ground to hide my shame. Dust swirled around my feet. With limited hours of daylight, and barely any rain, the whole country was turning into a large dustbowl. It was as though the very landscape of the land was reminding us of the futile state of man. From dust we once came, and to dust we would all return. These were the words of the Histories.

Because of the drought, food was becoming more and more scarce. A woman told me yesterday that people were paying over eighty dollars for bread in Samson. I raised my head back to the giant in the woods.

"What will you do this time? Will you stay with man? Will you stay with me?" I asked.

The great giant came out from the trees just enough so that I could see his bright, explosive eyes. He watched me, and I wondered if he was weighing the content of my character on the scales of the Archaon. His fierce eyes left my face, and I followed his steady gaze down to the book in my hand.

"Tell me," I said, stepping toward him, "Does Agatha speak the truth? Are there other books? Books that we have never read?"

Ruach stood silent.

"I met another giant," I began to babble, slightly nervous with anticipation, "His name was Uziel," I paused as the wind blew again. "In the Tombs of the Forgotten, I was in a tomb. An empty tomb that he said belonged once to Boged."

Ruach stood silent before me, but suddenly I found myself telling the entire story that I had never fully told anyone, not even Phineas.

"He said that a long time ago, there were wars. Wars between the Boged and the Simulacrum. But when I asked how something this important could be forgotten, he told me that these were recorded in books that had been lost long ago. He called them the Hidden Books. When I asked if we needed to find these Hidden Books, he said, 'or a key'. He spoke in smooth riddles that I still cannot fully understand.

"And he spoke about a boy. A boy from the Original Men who had cursed a girl that refused to die. What did he mean, Ruach? What does it all mean? Are there really Hidden Books? Does Agatha tell the truth?"

Ruach still watched me, and still he said nothing. I knew I was almost babbling, even inside my head, but I had to tell him, because I knew he would tell me the truth about it all.

"And now Agatha is telling me that my grandfather, and his father, that they were all killed for the sake of these books. Is it true? Why would our Gate-Keepers fall for books? But it has to be connected to the keys as well. Mother put the key of the Guardian into Mattie. But who was the boy Uziel spoke of? The Original Men have all been gone for ages. There are no Original Men left, right? So how can an Original Man have a girl who refuses to die? And who was Boged really? Ruach, you showed me the scene in the library, didn't you? It was you who allowed me to see Mother talking about finding Veralee in the Big House, with Richard and Sarah, and it was you who showed me the death of my grandfather, Richard. I saw Sarah with him. He said I would avenge him. It was you who showed me those things, wasn't it?"

"From our memories," he finally said.

"Your memories?" I said breathing in deeply. "So you have been watching for years. But from the shadows, because we never knew y'all were here. So that means you know a lot more than you tell us."

I stopped and looked at my hands, half expecting them to be covered in blood, though I had no idea why.

I looked back at Ruach and knew the question I had to ask, "Why have the Archaon not told us all this?"

"Why have the Simulacrum never asked?" he answered my question with this question.

He nodded once and opened his mouth wide. The wind around me began to blow. I heard Phineas in the distance yelling, "Friguscor are coming!"

But the wind was ripping around me, pulling me closer to Ruach as I heard another voice scream in alarm.

"They have the Esurio!"

Then suddenly, everything was different.

"Ruach?" I called, but no one answered. The wall, that was before me only a moment ago, was now gone. The Big House was as it once was, with no evidence of the fire. The fields were green, and the sun was warm but not scolding. I heard the rustle of the wind in the trees and smelled the peanuts in the fields. Tractors plowed lazily in the distance, churning up the dust that danced through the sunbeams on the tip of the air. I was back home. The home of my youth.

"Adair," Mother stuck her head out the kitchen door, wiping her hands on the edge of her apron. "Adair!"

My feet rushed forward, and without thinking I began running toward her as she called me.

"Adair, come on in now!"

"Mother!" I screamed, running with all my might to get to her, to touch her again, to have her arms wrap me in the safety of her smell.

But before I could reach her, a small, blonde child came running out from beneath a large Oak calling behind her, "Veelee! Mother's calling us! Come on, Veelee!"

Two girls, one tall, slender and tow-headed, the other with hair the color of chestnut and eyes like the moon, climbed the stairs and went inside, leaving me alone, staring at where they had just been.

"Mother," I breathed out her name. And though I wanted to go inside more than anything, I felt a pull that was undeniable coming from the treeline where Ruach had just been standing only moments ago.

I turned back to the Big House. Mother was singing.

"And if that mocking bird won't sing ..."

Wind wrapped around me, forcing me toward the pull of the treeline. Ruach was pulling me back, and I had no choice but to obey. It was his memory that I stood within, not my own. I lifted my foot, but it landed not on the dirt road in the alley of trees, but instead I was instantly transported deep into the forest of Red Oaks. The stairs to the gate stood before me.

"You are but a boy; turn back and let the heat cool from your head. Then we will talk."

I spotted the two men talking as they came to stand in front of the stairs to nowhere. The stairs that, if taken, would lead to the hidden Gate of Red Oaks. Richard, my grandfather, stood in deep dialogue with my Uncle Austin. Austin was young, younger than I had ever remembered him to be.

They neither saw me nor knew that I was near them, so I stepped closer until I was standing in an uneven triangle with the two men. Richard looked like he had been working in the fields for most of the day. He was covered in dust, with a button-down shirt and mud-covered cowboy boots. He took a white handkerchief from his pocket and wiped his brow before stuffing it into his back pocket again.

"Listen, Austin," he said with an air of repetition as though he was tired of repeating himself, "You are a good kid. But you need to realize that not everyone is on the right side."

"Yeah, I know about the Esurio—" he began, but Richard cut in.

"That is what you are too young to understand. The Esurio is a real threat, but it has been from the beginning, and it will be until the end. It is an ever-present darkness, always lurking in the distance, waiting for its moment to conquer. But that is not what I am speaking of."

Austin knit his eyebrows together with confusion.

"When you have lived as many years as I have, you cannot help but learn a little." Richard put a hand on Austin's shoulder and looked into his eyes, "And what I have learned in my years on this earth, is that the real danger is not the danger from outside your house, but within. We always fear the sound of the wolves in the distance, when it is the wolf that we have invited inside that will ravage us all."

Austin took a step back, dropping Richard's hold on his shoulder.

"I don't know what you are talking about."

"Yes," Richard sighed, nodding. "Yes, you do. Why have you come here today. Austin?"

Richard looked at the trees around him, waiting for Austin's answer.

"I told you," Austin said, kicking the dirt with his shoe. "To see Edwin. He's my brother, you know."

"Hmm," Richard said. "Yes, you have said as much, but that is not the only reason, is it?"

Austin's face was all too easy to read. He smiled and looked at the ground.

"No, I guess not."

Richard waited silently.

"I came to see Edwin and the girls. But, I was also ..."

"Sent?" Richard said.

Austin's eyes flew up, and he looked surprised. "How did you know?"

"You have been in the library every night after we go to bed."

"I didn't think I was bothering anyone. Everyone was asleep," Austin replied truculently.

"And yet, you were not. You have been looking through the Histories. You know you can read them freely; they belong to all Simulacrum. You need not read in the dark at night."

"I know," Austin retorted.

"And yet, you have not felt the freedom to read during the day. Why is that, Austin? I have known you for many years, and I have never known you to be interested in our Histories before."

"I need to look through the books."

"For?" Richard pressed.

"Well, it doesn't matter. I couldn't find it. The book is not here," Austin's voice sounded defeated.

Richard's face changed as he asked, "What book do you seek? Tell me, and perhaps I can help you."

Austin seemed to become younger as he spoke, "The book I need has some kind of symbol on the front. Some kind of pointed thing with a bunch of lines connecting it."

"So, he knows it is here," Richard said to himself, but I heard him. When he spoke again, I realized he was not speaking out loud at all, but that I was hearing his thoughts.

"Absalom knows that the books are here."

Before I could breathe again, I was standing in Daddy's library with Richard. He was dressed in a nice suit I had seen before in a photo from the day he married my grandmother, Sarah. Looking intently at the books that lined the walls he whispered, "What are you trying to tell me, old man?" Richard scanned the books and added to no one but himself. "You've pulled me in here, so what now?"

Looking over several, he decided and pulled an old dusty book from a high shelf.

"Is this the book that fell from the sky in my dream last night?" he was speaking as though someone else was in the room but, besides me, he was alone.

"Where is the letter that became a bird and flew away from my hands?" Richard flipped through the heavy pages one by one, as though he was looking for something specific.

Then he stopped. He held his finger on something. I moved forward and found he was reading a note which had been placed in the book.

It began: The last time we spoke ...

I glanced quickly at the bottom of the note. With great care, looping the capital E in an extravagant manner of old, it was signed, Ernest.

The letter was lengthy. Richard fell back into the leather chair that my father had sat in all of my life. His face grew pale and tight. His muscles tensed, and it appeared he was having a hard time breathing. He placed the paper down on the desk again and then, buried his face in his hands over the letter.

"No," he whispered with a painful groan, "what have I done?"

While he was bent over in grief, I leaned over and read the hand-written letter dated 1863. I noticed the calendar on the edge of the desk, showing me what day Richard found the letter. The letter had been written more than fifty years before.

Richard,

The last time we spoke, I told you that I would tell you everything when it was time. You begged me to explain, and I refused. I knew of the decision that hung around your neck, though you did not express it. I knew the pressure of the Council. I also knew the risk I was taking and still, I chose to do what I had been called to do, regardless of the consequences.

I do not hold your choices against you and I ask that from this point forward, you do not hold mine against me. During the War of 1814, I bonded myself to Barthenia, the daughter of the GateKeeper, Chief Liam, and the Guardian of the Gate, Sehoy. I am sure you remember them well. For you, Chaim Arukim, have seen many days and have many more ahead of you.

I do not write this letter, a ghost of my memory, for the sake of my legacy; I know if I have fallen, then I have fallen well. Many things were revealed to me in my youth when I went beyond the door and saw the River. Inside a pool of water there, I saw that my eyes would be closed by the hand of one I knew well, though I did not see when this would occur. The One Tree has predicted it, and it will be, so I do not count it a thing worthy of dread or worry. Since I am alive and well as I write this, I tell you so that you can release yourself from the guilt of my death.

That was not the most extraordinary thing that happened there. I met a man who lived in the Original City as a boy. In his blood runs the last of the Original Men. I fear I will never again see the face of the one who turned me from Friguscor to Simulacrum.

He charged me with a sacred duty. And to the one who gave me life, I owed a life back, so I accepted. Here I have built a house for my beloved and my daughter. She is almost grown now. She has been to the Terebinths herself now, and I see that she will be a strong Guardian just as her mother is today. Part of why I write is for her sake. Protect my daughter, Richard. She is the Guardian of the Gate, and she must be preserved. There is a darkness that seeks to bring down the gates, and I am afraid you still do not understand. The ways of the Simulacrum are not the only ways in the world. The Law was written to protect us, but as I have found in my lifetime, it has become a noose around our necks, blinding our people, and causing us to become mute and dumb.

I have broken the Law and for that I am willing to take the consequence that I saw so long ago, in the pool of water beside the River. I knew then what I know still today, that finding the Boged and changing them into Simulacrum would cost me my life. I do not write to argue this point, but instead to tell you the true reason I will fall. Right now, perhaps this very moment, you are making the decision with the Council, that I must fall because I refuse to acquiesce to the demand of the Law. But this is not the true reason behind the plan to end my days.

The location of this house is not a coincidence but has been placed exactly where it is so that it stands as the "X" on the treasure map. The trees I have planted, I have planted by perfect design. They are the alleyway into the River. You must start at the end of the trees and walk all the way through into the house and stand in the library. In the floor you will find a hatch. Below is a pathway that leads out to one of the servant's quarters. This is all by design. For what you see in the physical is a pathway, but if you have the key, then it can open the doorway to the River.

Richard, below you, far, far, below, where the roots of the Great Oaks hang in the sky, I have left the Hidden Book. For when the time comes, when the people are ready to know about the Boged, you must read it to them. They must know what the Council has been hiding all of these years. As the Judge, you have heard, and you know of the Hidden Books of which I speak.

I should have told you long ago. But you were not ready, and my sacred oath to protect what is hidden beneath the Big House of Red Oaks would not have been in safe hands. The secret is now yours to keep. I have seen you in my dreams. You are standing at the bonding tree with a girl who I do not know, but in her chest, she has the glow of the Guardian Key of Red Oaks. If in the days to come, you will become the GateKeeper of Red Oaks through bonding to the Guardian of the Gate, know that he will come for your blood one day as well. For I am the third GateKeeper whose blood will fall on this land.

Protect the shore of the River that lies beneath the house. Protect the secret of the Hidden Books, for the darkness seeks them even now, and protect the baby when she comes through the River. Name her Veralee, for she is the Malachi. Tell no one what you have heard here. You will only endanger anyone who knows. For the one who has stolen your trust will be looking for the child who holds the key for the end. From this time forward, you will be held accountable for every word you speak.

Remember the true danger is not so much the enemy without, but the wolf who wears sheep's clothing within the house.

Someone among you seeks the death of the GateKeepers, the discovery of the Hidden Books, and the location of the door to the River beneath the house.

-Ernest

As soon as I read the last word, the letter began to burn from all four sides. Richard looked up and cried, "No!" He reached to put out the fire but was unable. The letter was consumed before he could even grab it.

"Why didn't you tell me?" Richard said, grief-stricken. He stood, "I have to see Sarah."

And then he was gone, and I was standing back in the woods with Richard and Austin.

"Did you tell Mother what name to give Veralee?" I asked out loud, forgetting that he could not hear me, "That's how you knew what to name her when Mother found her in the tunnel beneath the house? From Ernest's letter!"

Neither one of them acknowledged me.

"I just need a book," Austin said. "If you give it to me, I can leave."

"That is not all you want, is it, Austin?" Richard said, but before he could finish his sentence I was gone from the forest and was now standing in the library again. The room was silent and dark. The clock on the wall showed it was two o'clock. The entire house must have been sleeping. The sound of someone entering the library startled me. It was Richard. He was moving through the house by the light of a small flashlight.

He paused before the old Persian rug, bending down and flipping it over to reveal the tunnel door in the floor. With great effort to remain as silent as possible, he eased himself down onto his knees and hoisted the door open. Quietly he propped the door back and shown his light inside the tunnel.

"You have to be here," he said, mumbling to himself like an aged man. He reached far into the tunnel but came up empty handed. Then, he dangled his feet into the dark hole until his body disappeared within. I got to my knees and peered into the tunnel. By the light of his flashlight I saw Richard locate a clear box with golden trim lying next to wall of the tunnel. He tried to open the box, but then found his hand just went through the top. He withdrew his hand, holding one leather-bound book. He retrieved a second book in the similar manner. Then as though I was standing right before him, he looked up and made eye contact with me.

"I have waited almost eighty years for these Books," he said. "This very evening Gail found the girl child, and now the Hidden Books are back in the hands of the Simulacrum. I admit I did not until this very moment believe they existed." He looked down at the leather-bound books.

"And yet, here they are."

"What do they say?" I asked, but I was back in the woods again with Austin and Richard.

My head felt as though I was on a train moving much too fast. Scenes were switching back and forth so quickly. Ruach was remembering too fast for me to keep up. The memories were blurring together.

"Do you have the book?" Austin said. I was standing in the woods again. The scenes were flipping so quickly it was making my head spin.

"I don't even know what they are," Austin said "or why they are important. But, he told me to come and fetch them for him. He said if you didn't know that you could ask someone named Ernest where they were?"

Richard's jaw tightened and then released several times before he answered, "Did Absalom send you here to find a book?"

A flash of concern crossed over Austin's face.

"I ... I'm not suppose to ..."

"He told you that I should ask Ernest?" Richard said, looking down at his hands as though they were soiled. "Absalom is the one seeking the books? Absalom was the one behind the decision to fall Ernest."

Austin was becoming increasingly nervous. He began looking back and forth between the trees.

"Listen, Richard. I have to have this book. Please, just give it to me and I will be on my way."

"No," answered Richard with pure disgust. He turned away from Austin. "Get off this land. You are no longer welcome. You were always a weak child, and you have grown to become an even weaker man."

"Watch out!" I cried, but Richard could not hear me.

Austin drove a knife into Richard's back. Richard jerked and fell to his knees, bringing Austin down with him.

"Tell me where the book is, and I won't finish you off completely," Austin said, his voice much too young to sound so dark.

"No!" Richard said, putting his hands flat on the ground. "You will ..." he struggled to breathe, "... still shed my blood into the ground ... with or without the books."

Austin pulled the knife out with a rough, jerking motion, then he drove the knife into Richard's back again.

"You stupid old man," Austin said, his teeth crushed tightly together. "I'll get Sarah to tell me. When she finds your body here, she will be much more ready to talk than you are."

Austin pulled the knife out of Richard's back. Richard fell on his back, hands splayed out on the grass as he gasped for air. His blood was pooling behind his right side, spreading all the way down to his knee.

"Grandfather," I said and fell beside him.

"I didn't want to hurt you." Austin said in a child-like voice. "I'm so sorry it had to come to this. I just, I ... I needed to get the book, and I have to get back to California. I have a girl there. Her name is Caraway. You understand, don't you?" He stood there, waiting for Richard to respond.

I looked at Austin in horror, my mouth open in disbelief.

"Just, remember, I didn't want to hurt you. And I'm really sorry, but you are the Sixth GateKeeper."

"Edwin will ..." Richard coughed and gasped, "be the Seventh." He said it like he was questioning Austin.

My father, Edwin would be the Seventh, and Austin would be as responsible for his brother's death as he was for Richard's.

I stood up and with all my power slammed both hands into Austin's chest. He faltered and took two steps backward to steady himself as the knife dropped to the ground.

"I will kill you for this!" I screamed, and my voice echoed through the air as though we were inside a tunnel.

Kill you. Kill you. Kill you.

Before I could give another blow, Richard reached up from the ground where he lay, grabbed my hand and said, "Adair, avenge my blood."

Gasping for air, I sat up in the middle of the dirt road between the alley of trees. The wall stood towering before me. I looked to find Ruach, but he was gone. In great leaps, I saw him running toward the wall. A string of tension was held in the air, as though the scissors were poised to cut at any time. Something was wrong, terribly wrong.

Everything was silent. The hot, humid air did not move. The wind was still, and the trees motionless. All life, animal, tree ,and man, was holding it's breath. I stood and turned my head toward the wall.

An untamed sound cut through the air. It started low and grew as a wave washing over the land. Louder and louder, faster and faster. The sound of voices. Men calling, whooping, and screaming from the other side of the wall. It was so loud that it seemed to thunder from every direction. Bodies in motion. Hordes of men. Running. Screaming. Calling. Then, a pounding sound began so light that at first, I thought it was my own heartbeat before I realized it was the sound of the alarms that Eliezer had set up.

For a second, I was paralyzed by fear. I could not move. A single shot of a gun. One more. Then another, and another until the sounds were too quick and loud to distinguish. From the wall, Simulacrum warriors were shooting as fast as they could.

I turned and began to run toward the torrent of sound.

Women were running in the opposite direction, herding children back toward the safety of the Big House. Screams ricocheted off the wall and across the fields. The wall! I stopped for a moment, my eyes working to comprehend what I was seeing. Hordes of Friguscor were streaming into Red Oaks through the unfinished section of the wall. Like water through a broken dam, they poured in, piling one on top of another, with no care or regard for the bodies suffocating beneath the weight of the masses. All they wanted was inside. All they desired was our blood.

Inman and Eliezer stood in the field, screaming orders at men and women who were trying to fight, run or hide. I watched as Inman pushed forward, his lean muscles tensing as he pulled the trigger to his gun over and over again.

My heart pounded, my body ached with fear, and my mind screamed at me to run! A woman on my right fell in the dirt. A teenage boy, no more than eighteen pounced on her back, pressing her into the ground as he sank his teeth into her right shoulder. His skin was grey and white, flaking off in large places, revealing raw flesh beneath. His movements were volatile, but with the fluid motion of a predatory animal.

Dust swirled in the air. The sound of terror filled my ears and clogged my lungs.

Men, women, and children came running through the gap in the wall like tarantulas, grasping with arms, and legs that seemed to multiply by the second. They poured in, being led by madness and propelled by the Esurio.

"Adair!" I heard my name, and it called me to action.

Bodies were colliding with a violent impact. Their heads hit the baked, hard ground and split open. A little girl screamed in panic, a boy protected his face with both fists. A young woman, in a dress was beating a man in a business suit with a rock; she pounded the rock into his skull again and again as she screamed a survivor's cry.

Ruach was fighting with great swings of his sword. Like ants on a mountain, they piled on top of the giant, trying to bring him to his knees. Eliezer's men were battling on top of the freshly cut wall but the Friguscor were climbing up, scaling the wall like spiders and the unfinished parts were crumbling beneath the weight of them.

"Adair!" he screamed out my name. Something flew past my face. A rock, or was it a piece of the wall? No, it was a foot. A human foot fell in the dirt not two steps from where I stood.

"Phineas?"

I turned around and then back again, a twisting dance of confusion until I found him. Phineas!

At full speed, he was running toward me. In one hand he held a shovel, in the other he pointed out past me, with one of Daddy's rifles. I turned, following his gesture and saw her.

Mattie!

My feet flew at a pace I had never known.

"Mattie!" I screamed again and again inside of my head, as I ran toward her. With both hands extended before her, she was backing into the tree line as three men encircled her. I screamed as I ran. "Don't touch her!"

Her hair was blowing as gold, moving in the wind at an unnatural pace. The men stopped. With gaping mouths, they watched her as though momentarily hypnotized. Inman ran toward her, moving with impressive speed. He cut down several men with a rain of bullets, but he was not fast enough. A large, man, with the wing span of a bird, reached out and grabbed Inman's bald head. He did not bite him, or begin to ravish his skin, but took Inman in his hands and smashed him like an egg against a large rock in the earth. Inman laid lifeless, his blood draining out on the ground, but none of the Friguscor seemed to even smell it. They stayed trained on Mattie.

I was still twenty feet from her when one of the three men, turned and smelled the air. He pulled his gaze from Mattie and in a feral posture, set his shoulders toward me. I tried to slow myself, but it was too late. He ran after me, and the impact of our speed together brought us down, one on top of the other, in a hard crash. Daddy's double-barrel shotgun rang out, announcing its arrival by placing a bullet in the man's back.

The man rolled slightly to the right into the dirt. Blood oozed from his wound, mixing into the dirt and yet he did not stop. He dug his fingers into the earth and tried to pull himself toward me as he growled like an animal.

I kicked at him, both feet working quickly to get me upright again. Behind me more and more men and women were pouring through the gaping hole in the wall. Sweat poured down my face and soaked my dress. Numbers began running through my head as I counted the Friguscor coming through the wall, until I could no longer keep up. Too many to count. Too many.

"Mattie!" I whispered.

I moved with urgency to get to my daughter. She stood by the trees. One hand behind her on the trunk of a great oak, and the other stretched out before her. Her body was tensed. An unnatural bend in her fingers arched her wrist forward as she held them out. She jerked slightly as though she was struggling to keep control.

More men had huddled together to stand before her. Their eyes were fixed upon her flesh, and they moved in slow swaying movement like dogs waiting to attack. My attention moved from the men to Mattie's hair. It swirled and floated as though time itself was moving slowly round and round it. I noticed the color was getting brighter, shining more and more golden as the moment stretched on before me.

Screams and gunshots sounded all around me like fireworks. We were surrounded by our enemy, pinned within the wall, but here, watching Mattie, everything seemed to slow. The sounds became muffled as though they had moved beneath water. Everything around Mattie swayed and floated. She turned her head and looked directly at me.

Run!

I heard her speak though she had not moved her mouth

Run!

I defied this madness. I would not leave her.

"No! Mattie!" I tried to scream.

Together, as though they shared one mind or one thought, the men turned to face me. Their eyes grew wide with hunger as they bent their backs and began to rush towards me. I turned, feeling my hair slapping at my cheeks as I heard Mattie scream.

"Mother!"

Yes, was my only thought as I began to run. Follow me!

The dirt beneath my feet was sodden with blood. It stuck to my shoes and splashed onto my legs as I ran. I passed an old man lying dead on the ground, eyes wide open, staring into the nothingness.

Suddenly, three of the large combine tractors from the cotton fields came bursting through the front of the yard like Patton's tanks arriving at the Battle of the Bulge. The large tires turned, running over Friguscor men and women, chewing them up beneath the combines. Slowly, a path of safety surfaced through the chaos. The wheels churned up ground and flesh together as it moved across the Friguscor like they were cotton ready to be harvested. Simulacrum warriors, poised on top of the tractors, were shooting down every Friguscor that the combine missed. The land was strewn with bodies and yet the tractors forced themselves forward. The three tractors weaved in and out of the Friguscor which ran at the them without fear or rational thought.

I ran toward the tractor. A rock sliced across of my face. I heard glass crash from the house. And then, I heard the broken crumple of the men pursing me being hit and ground beneath the combine. Immediately I turned back around. One of the men on the tractor screamed at me, "Are you alright?" He seemed familiar, but I could not think. The Friguscor were too many. How can we stop so many?

"Adair, Adair?" he knew my name. The man jumped down from the tractor and ran towards me.

I couldn't answer. I shook my head and opened my mouth, but nothing came out. Only my ragged breathing could be heard.

"Are you hurt?"

I still had no voice. I stood looking at the carnage around me. Several men jumped off the combine and ran toward the Big House, shooting everything that moved in front of them. A woman came running toward me, her hands outstretched to grab hold of me. But before she could reach me, the man beside me shot her down. She fell into the dirt as though she was nothing more than an animal.

"Mattie?"

My daughter's name was the only word that escaped from my mouth when my tongue finally engaged. My voice came back suddenly, with surprising strength and volume as I yelled again, "Mattox!"

The combine rolled forward. I ran behind it, working myself back to the place where I had left my daughter. She was still there. The Friguscor were growing in number around her. A large group were frozen in front of her. She was still standing as she had been. One hand on the trunk of the oak and the other outstretched, holding the Friguscor prisoners in some way.

Phineas was behind her, shooting as fast as he could.

One, two, three, four. I counted every shot and every thud of a body hitting the ground.

Suddenly someone came from behind me. He was faster than me and overtook me quickly.

"Phineas, I am on your right!" called a voice.

Phineas turned and yelled back, "I will take the left side!"

The man ran to the right side of the gathered Friguscor and began cutting them down with two blades, one in each hand. The horde of Friguscor was so dense and the move of their swords so methodical, that I found myself thinking of harvesting season. The swing of the blade, from right to left, left to right, cutting down men and women before it.

"Phineas!" I screamed as I came up behind him.

One. Two, three, four, five, six. They fell to the ground, but still there were more. They were still pouring through the hole in the crumbled wall.

The ground shook. I fell to my hands and knees. Behind me, I saw Ruach moving toward the wall, with Friguscor biting and clawing at him. He stopped before the wall as the Friguscor began to cover him like a swarm of scorpions.

"Ruach!" I began to call, but the sound stopped me. Everything shook as the sound of a great wind, a torrent of air flowed from where the pile of Friguscor lay biting and devouring the giant.

Ruach has opened his mouth, I thought, remembering the power he held in his lungs. Clouds suddenly formed where there had been no clouds. The wind rushed from the trees and pulled the dirt up from the ground. It filled the air around us. And I could not see my own hand in front of my face. Dirt, and blood, and sticks whirled around as though we were suddenly in the midst of a sand storm in the desert. A clash of metal and screams of men muffled the wind. I heard the giant scream, and then all went silent. The wind stopped, and the air grew still once again. I opened my eyes and saw what I had most feared in life. Red Oaks had been ravaged.

"Mattie!" I tried to get up, falling several times and began to run toward her. Mattie lowered her arms, dropping her hands by her side. The man with the blades ran to her. Phineas and I followed. As she fell to the ground ,the man cradled her gently in his lap.

I fell down beside them desperately searching her body for injury.

The man spoke softly, with a calm that I could not understand.

"She is just sleeping, Adair. Just sleeping."

"Atticus!" Phineas said his name before I could. I kissed Mattie's cheek and knew that Atticus was telling the truth. I felt for her breath on my hand as I had done a million times when she was a baby sleeping beside me at night.

"Atticus?" I looked at him, but he pointed behind us with his one free hand and said, "The Archaon."

Ruach was walking away from us, his blade dragging behind him, pulling up the earth as he went.

"Ruach," I called out in anguish. "Where are you going?"

"This was just the beginning," he called back over his shoulder. "From the depths of the forest the dead ones are calling, and we shall answer them with the edge of our blades."

Day 3 Erev

Ausley 3:4

Rising carefully, I crossed the dark room to pull helplessly on the doors. The handle betrayed me, staying defiantly locked. Still, I pulled again and again. The sound could wake the sleeping trio on the couches in my room, but I didn't care. I had eaten my last meal with the monster, Uziel. I could not bear it anymore.

"Who's there?"

I spun round, expecting to see Jaria or Phoebe, but saw instead, that they were still in a restless sleep. Their arms twitched, and their bodies convulsed. They seemed to find no peace in their dreams either.

"Is that you, Ausley?"

I stepped toward his voice, "Daddy?" I whispered in the dark room.

Suddenly memory took hold of reality, and I was lost to it again. Back at Red Oaks, I pushed open the library doors. Daddy stood over his desk with a magnifying glass, inspecting a large paper on his desk.

"Ausley, you can't be in here right now. Run on and see what Veralee is doing. I'm sure she has something fun up her sleeves."

"Veralee isn't here, I haven't seen her in so long. I can't remember the last time I saw Veralee," I answered, my voice sounding like a faded dress, worn out and long forgotten. Smells of home wrapped around me as I moved through the familiar room. Old-world leather, peanut dust in the air, well-worn books, and Daddy filled my lungs with comfort and longing.

"Ausley," he said as I approached the desk, "This is for work. I'm sorry, but it's very important that you run along and play."

His hand was covering a large architectural blue-print which was scrolled ever so carefully across his desk. On the top was a name that I could see clearly, "The Leee...vi...a..than?" I read aloud.

"Ausley," Daddy reprimanded absently, "Skedaddle."

The memory was so strong that it felt as though I was truly ten years old again. Ten years old and home at Red Oaks. Had I ever truly left?

"Yes, sir," I answered, "But, Daddy?"

He did not look up. Instead he continued tracing a long line from one part of the blue-print to another as I pressed, "Are those drawings? I love drawings!"

Daddy stood upright and shook his head. I realized his frustration was not directed at me, but at the picture before him, "No," he said distracted by his own thoughts, "That won't work."

"Let me help you!" I said excited as I ran back over to him, "I am very good at drawing! Just let me ..." He grabbed my hand with his strong grip as it hovered just over the top of the blueprint.

"No, Ausley! Do not touch these. Your prints cannot be anywhere on these. These are very important papers from my work. You cannot touch them, do you hear me, Ausley?" His grip was too tight, and it hurt, but he did not release my hand. He held it firmly in what I suddenly realized was his own gloved hand. Tears sprang up in my eyes, and before I could even allow one to drip down my cheek, he fell back into his chair and gathered me protectively into his arms.

"Your picture is all underground," I said meekly, peaking at the blueprint. "It's a machine?" I said reading the small printed letters on one side that said, The Machine. I craned my head to see more. "What's the machine going to be?"

Daddy shook his head as he looked at the small printed words. The Machine.

"I don't know," he sighed, "I have no idea what I'm looking at or what to do about it." He seemed very far away, and I longed to bring him back and help him.

"It's like an underground world, isn't it? I see the top of the ground there," I pointed, "And it's all underground like the secret tunnel over there." I motioned to the floor by the fireplace.

"Tunnel?" Daddy pulled me to one side so that he could see my face. "I forgot you had found the tunnel in here."

"Remember, Veralee found it." I said, suddenly nervous, "but I didn't go in it. Veralee and Jackson did. Well, no I didn't go in the first time. But the second, I went in. I did."

Daddy's eyes fell on the small trap door that we both knew was hidden just beneath the round Persian rug that had been there since before the Civil War. Daddy sat up with a jolt of renewed energy.

"A tunnel would work," he gently put me down, standing to inspect the blue-print before him as though he had just discovered the key to an important puzzle. The clock on the wall began to ring out. Bong, bong. Two o'clock. He regarded the old clock as though it was something altogether cruel. A reminder of seconds lost, and minutes building one on top of the other until time was gone.

"Yes, the work tunnels. They could be left open for ventilation. And the train-tracks ..." Daddy ran his magnifying glass carefully over to the right, with his left hand, he pulled out a ruler, "If they are never filled in ..."

"Daddy," I began, but he turned toward me.

"No more, Ausley," he said authoritatively. "I have to leave in an hour to get this back. I need you to go now."

"Yes, sir," I said, biting my lip to avoid the tears that were inevitable. I walked slowly to the door, expecting him to call back to me, but as I turned to close the door, it was only sweat forming on his brow from fervent concentration that told me goodbye.

The edge of the coffee table ramming into my knee brought me back quickly. The dreams, the memories, were coming faster and faster, and I was struggling to know when I was awake and when I was asleep or lost in a memory. I had forgotten about that day. Daddy had been looking at blue-prints from work. Blue-prints with the words, "The Machine," printed on one side and a title name of "The Leviathan" on the top. That must be the name of the underground facility, or it was years ago. In that memory, I had been only ten years old. The Leviathan I thought to myself, was the true name of the Machine.

With my hands beneath my belly supporting the aching bulge, I moved quickly to the far wall which was covered in the heavy hand-woven tapestry. The depiction, woven in silk and wool was fought in hues of blue, gold and red, and revealed life-like soldiers in the midst of a great battle over a city that looked much like the walls of Jerusalem. It both fascinated and scared me to look at it for too long for the soldiers looked much too familiar. I thought they looked like Simulacrum on both sides, at war with themselves. My fingers traced the face of a soldier high up on the wall.

"Atticus?" I breathed out his name as a question as my fingers touched the tapestry. "Could it really be?"

Trying to be as quiet as possible, I walked to the edge of the tapestry and peeked behind it. Careful not to wake my lifeless prison guards, I moved between the tapestry and the wall hoping to find another exit out of the room. Instead, I found a surprisingly life-like painting of the underground facility on the wooden wall.

I hate that place.

I put my hand up but thought better of touching my skin to the canvas. It had breath in the brush-stokes, living movement in its two-dimensional world. The painting was of the large structure inside the large open room inside the cave within the underground facility.

The Leviathan. Absalom had taken me to this room just before...before...I fought the urge to vomit again. I put my head in my hands to clear my head; I refused to think of that again. I looked at the painting; looking at that was better than remembering Uziel.

The painting was definitely of the room I had been in. The structure was the same, the U-shaped marble colonnade with stairs filling the middle of the U. The same large, stone table was positioned at the top of the platform, firepots burning on the platform and around the room.

And though so much was similar, there was something decidedly different. I kept staring at it, like one of those puzzles where you had to spot the subtle variances between two pictures of the same thing. I inspected the Greek-inspired frescos of giants fighting mere men, the ornate pillars which were carved in symmetric patterns, and the structure itself. Somehow, I had the unnerving and yet distinct impression that though I had just been in that very room with that very structure, I had never truly seen it before. But now, through this painting I was seeing the structure for what it really was instead of what it appeared to be. I leaned in close, smelling the hues of fresh paint. It was clearly more Greek than American, more ancient than modern, and darker than light.

I suddenly saw myself in the painting, or what looked to be me. Daddy was there as well. He fell to his knees, and I ran toward him. Rahab, the woman whom Absalom had introduced to me in the room, intercepted me and I watched as she stabbed me in the stomach with a large blade.

"No!" I said grabbing my stomach which was now full of life. The baby kicked hard inside of me.

Don't be afraid. I closed my eyes and felt the baby moving inside of me. I will protect you. She will not harm you. No one will harm you. But I could not stop the fear rising within me, and I heard the question I had asked myself over and again.

What is inside of me? Is it from Jackson or the monster? What am I carrying within my womb? Was Jaria right?

The painting began to shift again.

"This is the Leviathan," I whispered to myself, shaking from fear. "It has to be."

"No!"

The voice made me jump. And I fell forward slightly, both of my hands landing flatly on the painting. My hands fell slightly into the painting. I jerked them back, blinking from confusion.

The voice spoke again: "This window gazes into the world of the sons of men. Here, you are looking upon the Seat of Pergamum which is housed underneath what you call the Machine. The structure is ancient for your world, but in truth, it is from the beginning. It sails beneath the earth on a vessel that houses both this and The Machine. The vessel's true name is the Leviathan."

A giant man in a dark hood was standing close enough to touch his elbow to my shoulder. I would have screamed had I had a voice. My throat constricted, and I felt myself losing conscious thought.

The large man grabbed my arm and steadied me with a voice of a thousand.

"Do not fear ..."

With those words, hope flooded into me, tucking me inside the safety of his presence.

"... Daughter of the Blood."

"You are..." For a moment the word was lost and then I remembered Veralee, and I knew who he was. "You are the, the, you are the Archaon?" I said, beginning to cry. "You are!"

The creature turned his face, revealing inhuman eyes. They danced like lightning bugs in a mason jar on a dark summer night. Just like when I was a child. The thought triggered a memory and pulled me back to Red Oaks again.

Adair runs with an open jar in one hand, the lid in the other, expecting a catch. Golden lightning bugs float all around me. Veralee is beside me.

"You can do it, Ausley," she says, offering me an empty jar. Her hair is wild, blowing with ease in the summer breeze. Her eyes are bright silver, matching the moon above. Between the great oak trees and the twilight, she looks like a nymph which belonged neither to this world or another.

"Veralee," I spoke her name and it lingered on my lips as I reached to touch her in vain. "I can't." I whispered as my finger fell lifeless by my side.

She laughs, and it seems lighter than I ever remember it being, "Fine. I'll do it for you. I'll catch them all and give them to you so that you can set them free."

Daddy watches us from the gardens behind the Big House. Mother sits on the bench beside him, her hand in his. The moon is rising, full and bright above us. All the stars are waking, their light twinkling across the sky, as if they are responding to the fireflies below. I turn my face to the sky and held my hands out wide.

Let me stay here, let me stay forever, I think, but when I open my eyes, they are gone. I turn to search for them. Mama and Daddy are gone. Veralee and Adair are gone as well. I turn around again. The only reminder that they were here is a single jar of lightening bugs sitting on an exposed root of one of the oaks. I did not move but stared at the jar of twinkling light that had been left in the dark. Something moves. I search among the trees and make out the giant form of a man standing beneath the Oak tree. Shining from underneath his hood are catlike eyes of every color. He is watching me.

The memory blurred, and I was standing in the clinic back in Samson.

"Ausley," Amy, the head nurse who had three kids and an alcoholic husband.

I had not seen her in so long ...

"Ausley," she repeats, "Who was that man?"

"Man?" I ask, trying to focus. I am wearing my volunteer nursing uniform again. It smells like Mother's washing powder.

"Yeah," Amy says, snapping her fingers in front of me. "He just saved your rear. You have to be more careful. This virus is out of control and it is very contagious! That patient was running for you; he intended to bite you. If that man hadn't grabbed him, you could have been seriously hurt."

I turn to look for the man.

"I don't know," I say, "He was just ... there! The guy came at me and suddenly, the man, whoever he was, was there pulling the patient away from me. Isn't he a janitor or something?"

Amy shakes her head. "Janitor? Not that I know of. I've never seen him before, and I've been here for ten years."

Suddenly the memory was gone, and I was again standing before the painting and beside the giant man.

"Do not be afraid," the giant said. "We are Mikahel. We have been with you since the first day you breathed life into your lungs." And somehow I knew it was true. "We have been sent to stand beside you now."

He looked down at the undeniable truth which stood between us. Shame filled me, and I wished for a hood of my own to cover my face from his knowing eyes.

"Do not be afraid, Daughter of the Blood," he said gently, not mentioning my bulging belly. "We were to be here earlier, but we were delayed by the Prince of Persia."

His face was stern, fierce and warlike, but in his eyes, I saw true kindness.

"We have been sent to stand with you and your people against these days of distress."

His eyes saddened. "These are days like no other in the history of your people, and many will fall. But there will arise a remnant, and they shall grieve over the stone that was rejected. He has returned to his place, but he will return when they remember the covenant of old and call upon the One Tree. Everyone whose name is found in the Books of the Man of Words shall be delivered. They shall come forth with singing and everlasting joy shall be upon their head. Let that which was sealed, now be opened."

Tears flowed freely down my face at the promise in his words. I staggered to the left, but he caught me and set me securely on my feet.

"I'm sorry," I said, feeling so overwhelmed that I was sure I would pass out. "I ... I ..."

I stopped speaking and tried to disentangle my thoughts from my feelings as I started again, "I don't deserve any help. I ..." I gestured to my belly and felt the war within me again.

I could feel this baby. He or she was a part of me. But then, as it had since that night, the memory of Uziel would flood over me, and the thought would come like a hammer, slamming over me. The familiar words rolled over me again.

Should I destroy us both? Would it be better for everyone if I ended my days?

Tears fell harder down my face. I knew I had to remain as quiet as possible, but I wanted to convulse in sobs. My chin fell to my chest. I did not want to see his eyes anymore. It reminded me of everything I was not and everything I now was.

Maybe that was why he had come. I remembered the painting. Rahab had stabbed me in my belly. I was sure of it, and though I could not place when it had happened, I knew that it had happened. And now, I could not help but think maybe that would have been better. Maybe that would have been more humane than whatever was growing within me. The union of Simulacrum blood and the Rephaim. Maybe it would just be better if ...

"If?" Mikahel asked inside my head, using no audible words. "You wonder if death should replace life?"

I looked up and slowly nodded.

"Yes," I whispered. Shame covered me. I felt the hand of it crushing me.

"Have you learned so little?" he spoke patiently into my mind, and yet with full conviction. "Have you forgotten your name? Has Essie replaced everything within you? Has Ausley fallen asleep here inside the Tombs of the Forgotten? Did the blade of Rahab kill her as well?"

I stood silent, unable to answer him, but then I asked, "Inside the Tombs of the Forgotten?" I looked around. "We are inside the tombs?"

"Of course," he tilted his head. "This is the home of Uziel. He thrives off the death of the Simulacrum. His power is strengthened by their dreams. So, he rules over the rooms where they sleep until they are freed from this prison."

"Their dreams?" I said, "While they sleep they dream?"

"Do you not dream while you sleep, Daughter of the Blood? Why would they not dream as they sleep? The dreams of the fallen ones are very powerful. They speak of things from long ago and things that are yet to come. Have you not found yourself consumed in your own dreams here?"

"Yes."

"And why are you here, Daughter of the Blood?" he asked without using any words, just like the Archaon did at the meeting in the Terebinths.

"Uziel placed me here," I began but felt him stop me mentally. Then he asked again, and I saw myself at Red Oaks with Uncle Austin the day I left. How could I have been so naive? Then I saw myself at the Tower of BaVil, lying in a hospital bed, giving large amounts of my blood away for research. Dr. Gerhard was standing beside me holding an AR screen in his hands as he checked my progress.

"I know," I said feeling hopeless again, my voice breaking. "I know I chose to come. I thought that I could help, that giving my blood would change them all."

"True change only comes through the mystery of the Eiani, not the labors of man. Your kind always believes it is possible for man to change himself, but you do not see as we do. The physical response is simply a reaction to the transformation that the Eiani produces within. Only when the Eiani generates change is man truly a new creation. The old passes away, and behold, the new is come. You tried as so many before you have done. But man cannot produce what only the Eiani can create."

My breathing came in ragged gulps.

"I know that now. I made my bed, so I deserve to lie in it. But did I deserve this? Is that what you are telling me?"

I was not angry, there was no anger left in me. I was really asking. There was little of Ausley from Red Oaks left in me at all. I wanted to think that I had just been idealistic and naïve, and that was mostly true. But, I had known when I left that I was defying the wishes and the wisdom of my parents, and I would be hurting all who loved me. Still, I had gone willingly with Austin, thinking I knew better than all of them. Through my rebellion and arrogance, I had started the events which had eventually brought me to the place where I was now. Absalom had been all too happy to point that out to me back at BaVil. He had been right, and I had had to acknowledge it. In many ways, I had brought this upon myself, so maybe I did deserve this. Suddenly I was sure of it.

Mikahel put his hand out and placed it gently on my belly. His large hand covered almost my entire womb. The baby began to kick with vigor as the giant spoke inside my head.

"You left home out of ignorant rebellion. And your consequences have been great. But know this ..."

The memory resurfaced. I saw Hegai leading me down the hallways, sitting outside of my room, watching me as I walked with Absalom and Austin, turning every corner with me. I relived the moment when he pulled his mask off, revealing himself as Jackson, and kissed me.

I heard Mikahel's voice inside my head, "You were never alone. Though you ran from the safety of the branches of the Oaks, you were never allowed to go too far from the covering. The Eiani in your veins tethers you to the One Tree. We have been with you, covering Jackson in a shadow of camouflage and pulling you forward."

His hand, still resting on my belly, began to glow with a blue light that pulsed through my womb. He spoke to the baby, "Blessed are you, Child of the Blood. May you possess the strength of your father and the compassion of your mother. May you be a lion among your people, leading them in the truth until the Day."

He looked at me, "The gift of life is never a punishment. Life is always a gift. Here, within you, is the possibility for a new beginning. The child within you is not from the violence of Uziel," the blue light emanating from his hand was bright and warm. "Death cannot birth life."

"Jackson!" I began to cry with such emotion that I could no longer stand. The gentle creature wrapped me close to him and held me as I cried. "I am so afraid. Where is he? Where is Jackson? I have lost everything," I cried into his chest, "I have lost everyone..."

"But you will not lose this child. Even now, he is filled with the light of the One Tree," he said, speaking words of promise without even moving his lips, "But you must now walk in full obedience. You must stay the path and see him home. For he will be for you a light that guides you forward even through the darkness."

"How?" I pulled back and looked up. "How can I protect him? I can't even protect myself! I'm losing my mind inside this place. The memories, they are pulling me under, trying to drown me."

Mikahel nodded his great head, and for a minute I felt nervous again against his massive size.

"We have come to see you through," he said, and I followed his gaze toward the picture. "It is a window into to your dimension. You are not meant to be in this place with those who wish to suck your life and possess your body."

I knew he spoke of the Jaria, Phoebe and Balaam.

"How to enter," he said looking directly into my eyes. "is always easier to find than how to leave." Then he spoke into my mind and I understood that he was speaking of so much more when he said, "That is the mystery that most will never understand. But you, Daughter of the Blood, we have come to lead home."

Hope pulsed through me. I looked down. I raised my wrist slowly, barely believing what I saw. My tseeyen was glowing with blue light.

"You will return to your home; he will weave all things together for your good, for you are called to his purpose," Mikahel promised before turning toward the painting on the wall. "You will have to move quickly, for the moment I open the window, they will know as well."

"They?" the very thought of Uziel caused my breath to quicken in panic.

"Do not fear," he said again, and I didn't, "When you enter your world, find your bondmate. You must remember what you have been shown and shear the grapes from the vine."

I backed up into the stiff curtain behind my back.

"Grapes?" I asked.

Mikahel did not answer but pulled a brilliant sphere of light from his breastplate. Inside I saw what appeared to be four great birds flying round each other. These, however, were no normal birds but had bodies of lions with wings of eagles.

"Wrap this around them, their wings will cover your people," he commanded.

"Wait," I said, holding the sphere of light in my hand. "What do you want me to do?"

"You have seen the plans of men who built the Leviathan, the Machine which imprisons the people of the blood. Use what you were shown that day to bring your people to freedom. Remember what we have shown you. "

"The plans of men?" I began to panic. "Wait! You want me to free the people in the Machine? I ..." fear began to choke me, "I can't ... I don't know how to do anything about the Machine!"

Mikahel turned to me and placed his steady hand on my shoulder. His eyes were ready for battle.

"You do, and you will, for it is already written, Daughter of the Blood."

He lifted his hand and placed it over my heart. Warmth spread over my body with a soft blue light. He spoke softly, with great compassion.

"If you remain here in the castle of the Prince, you will be as your people on the Leviathan, drained until you are no more than hollow bones. If you keep silent, if you do not act now, then you and your father's house will perish just like them. You have been born for such a time as this; this is the call of the Eiani in your veins."

I felt a peace, a confidence that I had been missing for most of my life, if not all of it.

"The Nikud has come and will show you the way. Be strong and courageous, favored one. Do not shrink back from the task before you! The Eiani within you is greater than all other; trust in it."

"The Nikud?" I said quickly, but then froze, "Mikahel!" my throat constricted, "I cannot leave yet. My great-grandmother is here. Vera is in a room right beneath mine."

"Vera? The Guardian?" Mikahel cocked his head to the side, and then his eyes filled with knowledge. "Yes, we hear her voice."

"We must bring her with us. I can't leave her here, I whispered. "I can't."

Mikahel thought for a moment and then said, "If we begin to move through the halls, the darkness will know we are here."

"I can't leave her here. I must get her before we go!" My hands covered my stomach, willing courage to flow between us. "I won't leave her ,Mikahel."

"You, Daughter of the Blood, cannot free her from a door that has been closed. For what is closed shall remain closed until Moed opens her fist and releases those who have fallen asleep in the Tombs of the Forgotten."

"Moed," I said quickly, "The woman of ... time? She is a prisoner here as well! She can't do anything to help!"

I remembered how I was but days ago only a few days pregnant and now ...

"Trust me, she is as much a slave as Balaam."

"No," Mikahel shook his great head, moving his long dreadlock like hair cross his shoulders, "Moed is no prisoner to the darkness; she serves in chains to bring creation to completion for the One Tree. Vera and all the others will be freed when Moed opens her fists. Then, the prison doors shall be opened, and the sleeping ones will awake. For it has already been written, so it shall be. Moed will act in the fullness of time."

"That seems like a riddle to me," Desperation laced my words. "I can't leave her. Please help me get her out of here."

Mikahel took a strong step toward me and placed his large powerful hand on my head. He spoke to me like a child.

"We know it is hard to understand the things of the One Tree, for you are bound to Moed, and she is bound to you. Moed is time. She was never fashioned to be bound to linear chains, but in order to bring about the final beginning, she must be pulled between the two trees until the end. Then, and only then, shall all things come to pass."

He dipped his head down. His eyes flashed as he spoke the words.

"It is the end that begins it all, but take heart Daughter, for the words have already been spoken."

"Words?"

His eyes sparked like a fire, and once more he placed his hand over my heart and filled me with the blue light of the Archaon, "The oaks will remain in the horizon between the two trees until the final beginning."

Peace. Calm. Confidence. Certainty. These words began to write purpose on my heart.

"Girl?" Balaam's scratchy voice broke the silence. "What are you doing?"

"Remember what you have been told," Mikahel said inside my mind. He held up his palms as though he were holding an imaginary ball. Slowly a dim blue light began to pulse round and round between his fingers. As the ball of light spun, it began to grow, and heat radiated from him. It felt like we were standing beside an open fire. The sound and energy grew louder.

"Girl?" I heard Jaria call.

Then someone was jerking on the side of the curtain.

"Now go," Mikahel spread out his hand and covered the painting in a thin film of blue light and energy, "You fight the battle on your side of the window, and we shall battle here. Now go!"

Just as the curtain pulled back, I stepped into the unknown of the blue light. I felt fingers for a brief moment clawing at my back and Balaam holding on to me screeching, "I will go with you! Do not leave me in this waterless place!"

"No!" I screamed, "Let go of me!"

Mikahel spoke, and his voice felt as though it was calling down a long hall.

"You cannot inhabit her body. She is a Daughter of the Blood. Now get behind her, Balaam!"

Suddenly I passed through the blue film and everything was completely silent; not even the sound of my own heart beat was audible. I stumbled, my body moved forward. And with my hands wrapped around my baby, I found myself for the first time in months, on solid ground.

Veralee 3:5

"They fled away at twilight, abandoning their tents and horses for the Rapha were close behind. On the edge of the realm they approached, entering the greatest tent first, but they found no blood there," Wisdom says.

She walks before me, gesturing with her hand for me to follow. Eastern tents flap carelessly in the wind. The night is hot and damp, nervous anticipation braided into the heat.

The voice of Achiel bellows out, "The cities have become a byword, cursed from the wars of men. The Dividing Wars are threatening to destroy them all."

A golden woman that shines like the sun stands with him, "While they war with one another, the ones that belong to the night grow stronger. They will arrive on this very night."

No one is here. The camp is empty. Cooking pots, stools, and animals go without use. All have been abandoned. Only silence sleeps in the once-occupied beds.

"Once again, it will be civil war," A man speaks with a pipe balanced on the corner of his mouth. Without seeing his face, I know him. My chest begins to burn with fire and the golden key, just beneath my skin, shines brightly.

"Father," I whisper. His head raises toward me for a moment, but he does not hear me, not really.

Wisdom, who stands beside me, speaks to me alone. I know I am dreaming when she says, "During the days of the Dividing Wars, many moved out to the wilderness, and lived like the Primogenes once again. Wanderers in the wilderness. But the Rephaim, the Rapha, the Dead Ones, began to hunt them in the night, following the scent of their blood. Though they could not see them, Achiel and the loyal ones stayed with the Simulacrum. This is why I have brought you here...for you to see."

Cool air from the desert night blows across my face, a welcomed relief from the heat.

Wisdom turns. A trail of energy moves slowly around her face, "The others are the ones who followed the Nachash in the rebellion."

"When they turned against the One Tree?"

"The Dividing Wars did not begin with the Simulacrum and the Boged, or even with the Simulacrum and the Friguscor. The Dividing War began long before man arrived. It began when the Nachash divided the Archaon, the army of Paraclete, from the One Tree. Those who followed Nachash into the rebellion were cursed to survive outside of the realm of the One Tree. They fell upon the Daughters of Earth and created the Rephaim, the Dead Ones. Neither Archaon nor Children of Men, the Rephaim sought a place for themselves, and they desired the dominion of man. Those that stayed loyal to the One Tree, the Archaon led by Paraclete, imprisoned the rebels in the City of Bariyach below while the Dividing Wars tore sons and fathers apart above."

I stop and look over to see a great walled city in the distance. Fire burns every five feet around the wall. Everything is quiet, but nothing is at peace. An electric unrest has the night alive with fear.

Wisdom points back to the tents, as Jeremiah says "The GateKeepers have stayed behind. They wait to war against the Rephaim."

"Yes," Achiel nods his head. "We are watching with them."

The golden woman says, "Tonight, the Dividing Wars will erupt within the wall of the city, but you," she spoke to Achiel, "must stay by the River, to fight the ancient war. It is here that the GateKeepers will prove their valor."

Jeremiah speaks roughly to the woman, "You should not have come here."

She faces him, "And yet, you are here as well. We all have our part to play, Malachi."

"They will be looking for you," Jeremiah speaks as though someone in the night could be listening, "They will know you are here as soon as they arrive."

"And you as well," she answers Jeremiah and then turns to Achiel, "I have brought the keys for the Keepers. You must give them on this night."

All three of them stop and share a moment that I cannot fully understand. Her words are weights, let down one at a time. Achiel says nothing but opens his hand.

For a moment I see a flash of light and Achiel standing proudly over men on bended knees. Then I hear the waters. The camp is beside a river. Above, the moon does not shine. The golden woman is walking on top of the water with a sword in her hand.

"Who is that?" I ask Wisdom.

"The Lady Moed," she answers.

My chest burns like fire, red-hot and heavy. Jeremiah begins to walk toward me.

"Father?" He does not answer but walks past me. He takes hold of a horse and mounts with ease.

"Remember the will of the Man of Words," Achiel comes out of the tent before Jeremiah can leave, "Remember what we fight for, Defender of the Malachi."

"I will keep the Watcher safe," Jeremiah responds.

A large black cloud moves over the city.

Achiel speaks, "He is already there."

With a hard jerk to the right and a kick to the sides, Jeremiah's horse bolts into the night.

"Where is he going?" I ask Wisdom.

She answers, "To the city."

"Why? You said the real battle would happen here in the camp! So why would Jeremiah go to the city if it doesn't matter? Why would he not help the GateKeepers fight the Rephaim?"

"That is not his purpose," she answers as we watch him ride away. "He is the defender of the Malachi."

I looked at Wisdom, "But he is the Malachi, the key is within his chest during this time. Why would he come anywhere near this place? Why would he risk losing the Malachi to the dead ones? Why would he come here? Why now?" His outline slowly disappears as the darkness envelopes him.

"He is the defender of the Malachi," Wisdom says, "On this night, two wars will be fought, and two battles lost. The Dividing War will rage from above, and the Dividing War will continue below."

Suddenly I am no longer me. I am a bird, made of clock parts, flying high above, watching rows and rows of uniformed soldiers marching toward the walled city. Their spears are raised high into the sky, which is growing black from great clouds that cover the moonlight.

Wisdom speaks to me as I fly. "Here, on this land, men will fight for territory while at the River, the dead ones will fight for the dominion of men."

"The dominion of men?" I am back from the sky. Below me, I stand on the water of the River. Lady Moed walks further down the River. Something moves beneath my feet.

I scream as I see a woman beating on the water beneath my feet as though it is a wall of ice. I feel the water, it moves freely beneath my feet, and yet I see the woman screaming beneath it. I reach for Wisdom, but my hand falls through her and I fall onto the surface of the water.

Wisdom looks at me. She does not help me up. Her eyes hurt my mind.

"He could not take it from the man, so instead he took that which the man loved."

Loved? The word fills my heart with one name.

"Wait," I spin around. I look first at the river and then at the walled city in the distance. I remember this story, "What night is this? What part of the Dividing Wars have you brought me to see?"

Atticus. His name slips from my mind into the night.

"Is he in there now?" I stand to my feet, "Is he in the city?"

"He wears chains in the dungeon even as we speak."

Beneath the belly of the great oaks, there was no moon, and yet, there was light. The sky, ablaze with a thousand spotlights, but not the light of stars, was bright blue. Beautiful blue light shone from the roots that twisted and turned in beautiful patterns, creating a canvas of color which stretched across the darkness. In various hues and shades, the blue light was the same as that of the Archaon. Here, below the masterpiece of color, the connection was undeniable. Their light was connected to this light, and this light was connected to the River, and the River connected all of us to time. Time, in turn, was controlled by Paraclete, Paraclete led the Archaon, who followed the Man of Words, who brought it all back to the One Tree.

My tseeyen beamed with the same light because I was also connected to the One Tree by the Eiani in my veins. I stared at the River. If I could travel far down the River, farther than any eye could see, past the dead trees, and the sandy banks of different eras and ages, I would eventually come to the One Tree. There it hovered above the crystal sea of glass. A new thought came to me; the River was a circle. It began with the One Tree, and it ran to the One Tree. Wherever it went, the River's origin and its completion was in the One Tree. So, it was with time.

Something in me longed to go, to return to the One Tree, to abide in the perfect peace and indescribable joy its canopy offered. I lowered my eyes. The One Tree was too far away, and I knew that for now, I was called to stay.

"Hear the drums of the Archaon," a voice floated on the air. "Hear the call to battle pulsing in your veins."

I knew that voice. I stood quickly, planting my feet firmly upright.

"Is that you?" I spoke to the empty wood around me. Jeremiah, Thenie, Ernest, and Atticus were all asleep. I stood and looked around. The night was silent. The air still. A trembling passed over the withered leaves and flowed across the ground. Small rocks from around my feet began to quiver. From the river bank came a quick and thick mist which spread across the ground, blanketing everything in a white fog. Lightning popped in the sky where it could not possibly rain. Everything felt tighter, closer, more compact, as though the connection between all things was suddenly called to attention.

"Veralee, you are the Last of the Guardians."

I dropped to my knees, the power of the voice stripping my ability to stand. A pale light moved around me with the fluttering of a butterfly's wings.

"Yes," I answered obediently, and then the words that I had dared not even admit in the secret parts of myself came out of my mouth, "I am the Malachi."

The fog formed and shifted until the shape of a man was both clearly visible and yet somehow amorphous, a thing not willing to be contained even by the eyes of men. He came near.

"Do you know who I am?"

I swallowed. My lips trembled.

"You—are the Man of Words."

"I am."

A gust of power drove me facedown to the ground. The taste of dirt filled my mouth. I wiped it off with the back of my hand as I rose to my knees.

"From the dust of the earth you have come and to dust you shall return. You have been fashioned to carry the key forward, to the end. Do not fear those who can kill the body, for why fear one who may stir the earth, but cannot grasp eternity?"

I looked at the smeared dirt on the back of my hand. Fear rose in my throat, and I could not catch my breath.

"Why me? It's just that, I ... why would you chose me to do this? Jeremiah told me that if the Leviathan gets the key, the beast will kill everyone, and I'm not sure I can do what you are asking me to do. First it was the Boged. Paraclete told me to find them. And changing them...that cost me everything. My family, my entire life ... and now the key? What will this cost me?"

"It is a wise King who counts the cost of the building before he begins. But, how can you count what you do not own. How can you speak of cost when you have nothing of your own? Was it you who put breath into your lungs? Or brought life to your form?"

I lifted my hands up, panic rising in my chest. But as suddenly as it began, it stopped. Slowly I lifted my head up toward his face.

"I'm just afraid that I can't do it, that I will fail."

"You will not fail. I will see you through to the end. Follow your father, do as he instructs. You are the Malachi, protected by the plan of the One Tree which was spoken before the foundation of the world was poured. Gather what has been scattered, and fear not the darkness that comes against you."

"I will," I said. "I will follow."

The Man of Words then blew on me and a misty fog arose, "Receive the strength and the power to do as you have been asked."

I felt confidence and strength rising in me as I breathed in his breath.

The fog began to move away from me, and I stood up. The Man of Words was leaving.

"Wait!" I begged. "Did I ever have a choice?"

"Did you ever want one?"

I thought of my life at Red Oaks, of going to the community college in town, of my friend Emmalie who died at the train station in Montgomery, the man from Congo in the dressing room, the boy killed by the train on the tracks right in front of my eyes, of Tessa, and finally the look of death on Nathan's face as his head bled out on the concrete sidewalk that day in Montgomery. Mother's words echoed in my heart so loudly that I thought for just a moment, she was near.

Sometimes you are most free when you have no choice, Veralee.

She was right. He was right. "But why..."

He stopped and turned back to me and before I could ask the question, he answered.

"Jeremiah is the last of the Original Men who were placed in the gardens and walked beside the One Tree in the cool of the day. You are right to believe your blood is not as strong as his, and your mind not as pure. But you are wrong to value your blood any less. A cord of three strands cannot easily be broken. In your veins pulse all three bloodlines of mankind. Through your father, you are Original Man. By your mother, you are both Boged and Simulacrum. That is why you are the Last of the Guardians. In you is the promise of the beginning to the remnant of mankind which the One Tree will see to the end."

"Then why take me away from them?"

"By the command of the One Tree, the Word of my mouth and the hand of Paraclete, the Archaon moved the Malachi down the River. At the foot of the gate, the key was hidden in plain view for all to see and none to understand. You see, the foolishness of the One Tree is wiser than the greatest understanding of the darkness and men."

"You hid the key."

"At the proper time, you were planted to grow beneath the protection of the Oaks until you were ready to shoulder the burden you were born to bear. You were to gather what had been scattered by bringing the Boged back to the Simulacrum. The two women you have seen in your dreams, the bride split in half, the message of the Malachi, and the prophecies of the star of the Nikud, they are one and the same. The Simulacrum and the Boged are destined to merge once again into a single tree. As one people they will come to Final Door."

"Where is the Final Door?"

The Man of Words seemed to smile, and I sensed kindness in his answer.

"Ask the Aiyendalet. He has been given wisdom for the end of days. He will protect the key and lead the people to the Door. Listen to him, for he will guide and protect you."

"Why," I said quickly, needing to know this last thing before he left, "Why did I never see you as a child? Why have you always seemed so far away, like a dream instead of reality?"

"I came as an open Door to your people and they turned away, rejecting what they could not understand. Ah, how I would have gathered them beneath my wings as a hen protects her chicks, but they would not."

"And that's why the Simulacrum never speak of you?"

"Your people were sent as messengers for the One Tree, to teach others truth. They were given the Histories to read and wise men and women to interpret them. They were called to know the appointed times and seasons. Yet, when the prophesied signs appeared in the skies and among the kingdoms of man, they did not see. They had lost their ability to read and understand, becoming blind to the truth by their own interpretations and traditions. When the Door opened, they would not believe. They missed the time of their visitation, and so they were scattered to the four winds of the earth, banished from the Original Cities of the Original Men. The houses that they did not build became desolate lands where the hedgehog and the deer lay down to give birth, their vineyards became dry wastelands where the lizard and the sparrow built their homes. For their rejection, they have been as aliens in a foreign land, existing in the world of the Friguscor until they enter through the Final Door, the Eighth Gate."

"They left the cities because they missed the Door?"

I shook my head, remembering the Original City of the Original Men where we had met with the Archaon after the Council Meeting in the Terebinths of Mamre.

"I don't understand. I thought the cities had been long abandoned because of the war between the Friguscor and the Original Men. After that, there were four hundred years when only Friguscor existed on the earth, before the Primogenes were led to the blood of the Eiani. That is when the Simulacrum were born, so how could the they abandon cities that were long forgotten before the Simulacrum came to be?"

"Come!"

Immediately I was standing on the thin bridge I had walked upon earlier. The same roots were hanging all around me. I grabbed hold of two, one in each hand, to steady the tremors running up and down my legs.

"Jump, and I will show you."

I looked over the edge. It seemed double the distance it had earlier. In fact, it must have been triple the distance and below, the once-tame River now looked like the bottom of Niagara Falls. I hated heights; I always had. My heart pounded against my chest, warning me to go back to the safety of the solid ground, but my tseeyen was warm with safety.

My mind screamed at me to stop.

"Jump," I said aloud to myself. "Just jump."

I forced my disobedient body forward, but I still stood frozen to the small bridge, holding onto the hanging roots.

"You gonna jump, or am I gonna have to push you?" said a voice.

"Ahh!" I screamed in fear and surprise.

"Mr. Frost, you scared me. Where did you come ..." I smelled the foulness of his Friguscor skin, stopped and stared at the old man before me. He was dressed in a Confederate officer's uniform with a leather sword belt and an Alabama buckle that matched the double rows of gold buttons on his frock coat.

"Mr. Frost? Is that you? How?"

I had last seen Mr. Frost dressed for the last reenactment of the Battle of Red Oaks in October, the month my whole life had changed. Mr Frost had shared his life story with me, and I had been terribly moved by his loneliness and pain. He had made me wish that there was some way I could have helped him, some way I could have introduced him to our Simulacrum way. So much had happened that day. It was the same day I had first met Atticus, and the day he had revealed to my parents that he was Aiyendalet. It had set in motion all the events that had led me here. How long ago was that? Six months, a year, two years? I couldn't really remember. Time had lost its meaning.

Wait, I had also seen Mr Frost in Montgomery too, when Atticus and I arrived there after the meeting with the Archaon. The city had been in chaos then, just after a meteor strike and the arrival of the Aluid.

I turned toward Mr. Frost, careful not to let go of the roots and asked, "How are you here?"

"Here?" he looked around, lifting his chubby chin and giving me a wink. "Here seems as good a place as any. Right, Miss Vera?"

Miss Vera. I remembered he had enjoyed pretending that I was Vera Weekes instead of Veralee Harper.

"But you are Friguscor," I said quickly. "How are you...here?" I emphasized the world around us, using the large root in my hand as a pointer.

"Now you are about as mean as a junkyard dog," he laughed, causing his lungs to rumble with phlegm. He coughed and wiped his mouth with the back of his hand, and I saw a smear of dirt had come from his mouth. Then all the laughter left his face as he looked at me.

"You asked me a question, and so I want to give you an answer."

"A question?" I became unsteady on my feet and shuffled to hold on tighter to the root. A small clump of dirt fell over the edge and I followed it down until it dropped in the River.

"You mean how you came to be here—" I began, but when I turned to face Mr. Frost, I found a woman standing beside me instead.

She was bone thin, the size of a young girl rather than a woman. Her hair was as thin and dirty as her clothes, and as it fell to her shoulders, it barely covered the sharp, angled bones beneath. On her hip she balanced a chubby, crying toddler. Her face was marred and pitted with acne scars, and there was an emptiness in her eyes that I recognized as Friguscor. Again, the smell of rot filled the air, clenching my stomach into knots. Suddenly I remembered her. She was the woman Ausley and I had met at the gas station the day we were delivering costumes for Mother, the day I had changed Nathan.

"We took you to the clinic in town." I whispered in awe, remembering the whole day. "You said your grandmother had told you about magical creatures that—"

She finished my sentence, "—that live here like regular folks. They kinda look like ever'body else, but they ain't the same, really. They's different somehow."

I stared at her and then I remembered her name.

"Sandy?"

She moved the baby to the other side.

"Ausley asked you if you were going to tell her the truth about the Simulacrum when you went back to the car. And you said 'No,' but that was not entirely true. You wanted to tell her, didn't you?"

"Yes," I said. "I wanted to stop her—your pain," I corrected. "I wanted to give you the blood..."

"You asked me a question." said Sandy. "You asked, why you never saw me. Why I seemed so far away."

The fog rolled up and around Sandy and when it lifted, the Man of Words was again before me.

"You see, I have always been guiding you even when you did not recognize me."

"It was you? You were Mr. Frost and Sandy? But they are Friguscor..."

"And without the blood of the Eiani in your veins, so are you."

I had no answer, my mouth hung as open as my mind suddenly felt.

"Let go of the roots you hold so dear and come with me."

He raised his hand and covered my clenched fist. Without another word he began gently working my hand free of the root. With his help, my fingers loosened. Together we fell down into the River.

Someone was shaking me, "You must wake!"

"Mattie," I sighed and rolled over. "Can't you ask Ausley to put on your cartoons? I want to sleep."

Another shake, followed by a more forceful one.

"No, girl, you need to wake up! You cannot sleep on the streets."

My eyes opened, and I realized I was lying in a filthy mixture of dirt and grime. I sat up quickly, making my head spin. A familiar weight came hammering down on my chest, and for a moment I was sure I would suffocate.

As I grabbed for my chest and throat with frantic gestures, the young man's brown eyes grew wide with horror.

"Can you breathe?" He spoke as though his words were formed deep in his throat, his accent cutting his words one by one behind his tongue. "Can you breathe?"

But just as suddenly as it began, the feeling abated and left me with a low, but constant heaviness in my chest.

"I must have gone back again. But further this time," my hand rose to meet my chest as I forced air into my lungs, "much, much further."

The young man who could not be more than eighteen years at most leaned closer to me, his one knee on the ground, his other bent where his arm rested comfortably supporting his weight, "Back? Back where? Where are you from?"

I took in the man. He wore a red wool tunic that stopped just before his knees. His head was covered with a white hood that laid across his shoulders and fell down his back. Tall leather boots matched his leather vest, but it was his belt I found the most fascinating.

"You wear the symbol of the Terebinths," I pointed to the crest on this belt. "A wheel within a wheel."

"Come, I will take you to the city," he said. "You must not be out here sleeping on the streets. It is dangerous, and besides, you know the law."

"The law," I blinked several times, clearing the haziness from my eyes. As he helped me to my feet as I added bleakly, "Oh, I know the law."

"Then why," he paused, and I realized quickly that it was my dress that had stolen his words. He looked at me, but I had no answer for him. Atticus would know how to do this, I thought.

The young man nodded once, then twice.

"Stay here until I return."

Without a moment's hesitation, he turned and disappeared into the busy street. I made my way slowly toward the open street, hugging the side of the building to my right. As I got closer, I heard more and more of the noise from the city. Donkeys pulling carts trotted up and down the street. Vendors with rolling carts hawked spices, clothing, and almost anything one might need. A mother and child passed by but did not see me. The mother held the child's hand in one hadn and a basket in the other. The child was focused on the lines he was creating in the sand with the stick he dragged in his other hand. To the right was a pebbled road lined with buildings of stone and wood. To the left the road converged on a great set of stairs that were wide and steep, yet surprisingly simple in design. Rising more than ten flights in the air, the staircase was comprised of flights which themselves contained at least twenty steps that had to be seventy feet wide. At the top there was a wall, above which bronze domes, sand-colored flat tops, and terracotta tiled roofs painted the skyline in an earth-toned palette against the afternoon sun.

The man who had awakened me came quickly toward me, gesturing for me to get back into the safety of the alley. I squinted, trying to see what was at the top of the stairs, but the light from the afternoon sun was hovering just above it, blocking my view.

"Here," said the man, "put this on quickly."

I looked down at the dark burgundy material and then back at him, "Here?"

He did not answer but turned around, leaving only his back as my answer.

"Okay," I said as I tried desperately to work the buttons on the back of my dress.

Why did Barthenia put me in a dress with so many buttons?

"Ugh," I dropped my hands in defeat. "If you want this done quickly, you're gonna have to help me out here."

The man did not turn around but answered.

"Help you?"

"Yes," I said to his back. "Help me get the buttons. I can't get them."

"Buttons?" He asked as though he had no idea what I was talking about, but he stayed still.

"I'll just wear this dress. I don't really need to change." I moved to begin walking, but he held out a single hand of objection. Slowly he turned around, his face unable to hide his embarrassment as he pulled a small dagger from his belt.

"Are you going to use that to undo these buttons?" I asked unable to hide my shock. I knew he was Simulacrum by the color of his eyes, skin and hair but still ...

"Lignum Vitae," I said testing the waters.

He nodded as though he understood before answering, "Et sanguis est essential."

"Okay," I answered again and turned around, biting the side of my lip to stay still.

With little hesitation and a steady hand the man ripped easily through the buttons. Without a word he stepped away from me and turned back toward the street. I let the dress fall to the ground and worked quickly to put on the... I tried the thing on one way and then the other.

What was this? I almost gave up entirely before I figured out the neck opening was not an arm hole. Quickly I adjusted the gold and burgundy gown. It had long sleeves which widened toward the wrist so that the arms could move freely. I fastened the gold belt around my waist. It was surprisingly comfortable.

"I'm ready," I said hoping that was true. Without turning he said, "Follow me. We are losing light, and you know what comes with the dark."

I stopped, and he turned back to face me.

"No," I said. "I don't know what comes with the dark."

"Then let us hope you do not, on this night, find out."

He grabbed my hand and with great haste, I was thrust out into the busy street of a busy city.

"What city is this?" I asked, noticing that there were no cars or even carriages, only people on foot or horses moving through the streets.

He looked back at me and narrowed his eyes. "Ariel, or as the Friguscor say, Jerusalem."

We began making our way up the massive set of stairs.

"How long does it take to get to the top?" I asked, doubting my ability to keep up with his determined speed. My lungs struggled to find air, my legs grew heavier with each step and I began to slow.

"As long as it takes you," he answered pulling at my hand. "But at this rate we will not make it inside before the sun sets. You must make great haste."

Huffing I said, "I can't!" I waved my hand at him to stop. "I'm not from here," I began to explain in between great gasps of air. "I've been sent back down the River. Do you understand what I'm telling you? Do you know about the River?"

His brown eyes flashed with knowledge, "Of course I understand the River, but one cannot move back or forward in the River. We are simply in the River."

I caught my breath, but instead of answering him, I used the moment to think.

But before he could ask me another question, the position of the sun caught his attention.

He pulled on my arm and pointed.

"See that next level?"

I nodded.

"If we can make it there," he said with his thick accent, "you are halfway. If I must, I will carry you the rest. But if we are caught out in the city after dark, if we do not make it through the doors, then it will be the end of us both."

"What happens?" I began, but he thrust us both forward, taking more than two steps at a time.

I tripped and fell, cutting my forearm open on the stone steps. Several people passing by us turned as though I had called their names.

"No," said the man when he saw the blood. He reached inside his tunic and produced a strip of fabric, "Wrap the arm. Quickly!"

With amazing strength, he lifted me to my feet. Then, as though I was a sack of potatoes he hoisted me sideways over his shoulders. He began to run up the stairs. Men, women, and even children stopped and turned as though a switch had been turned on in their heads. All were Friguscor. As we ascended they seemed to come closer and closer. They began licking their lips, and their eyes dilated into large empty pools, devoid of life. As the edge of dark threatened on the horizon the city seemed to go still, and it was the noise of silence that filled my ears now.

"The Esurio?" I asked the man who carried the weight of me on his shoulders. "Is the Esurio here?"

The Friguscor around us did not run after us or chase us down, but just stood, like statues of death as we passed by. Finally, with great effort on the man's behalf, we reached the top.

"There," he leaned down putting his hands on his knees as he gasped for breath, "Go there," he added again pointing to a double set of green copper doors.

"I'll help you," I said offering my hand.

"No," he shook his head, "I will be on in a moment. Go ahead." I looked at the door and then back to him. The light was almost gone, and the oddness of the city seemed even more striking. But I remembered Napoleon and Albert. I could not let one more person offer their own life in place of mine.

"I will not go without you," I said just as he stood to his full height and began moving quickly toward the door. A large clock down in the center of the city began to ring out. The man beside me began to pick up his pace. Without being told, I followed suit, until we were both running toward the door. As the last sliver of sunlight slipped away from the city, we both passed through the door into some kind of great hall.

But where I thought we would find solace, the man only began to run more quickly, "Come, we must make it to the doors."

"The doors?" I said, fear creeping up my spine and threatening the stability of my stomach. "What doors?"

But he did not answer. In front of us, maybe four hundred feet forward was a row of doors. All made of bronze. All with different symbols and pictures on the front. He reached them first. Just then a long, screeching scream erupted in the air, followed by another and then another. The first set of doors through which we had just entered began to rattle. Someone or something was trying to get inside.

"What's that?" I looked at the man who had led me here. Fear pulsing up and down my tseeyen.

He looked down, "You have light coming from your tseeyen?"

"Yes," I said, putting a single hand over the light as he said, "As it is with him."

"Him? Who?"

"You will see," he turned and opened the door, flinging it wide open before saying, "Go in and you will be safe."

I looked at the open door.

"It's the Terebinths?" I asked.

He took no time to respond but pulled me through the door, slamming it shut, silencing the screams of the creatures on the other side.

Once inside, or outside, I was not so sure which, I felt the full weight of time fall from my shoulders. I breathed in once, twice, three times and until every muscle, bone and part of my body filled to the brim with relief.

"Oh," I sighed, stretching my arms and legs. The blood pulsed through my veins, and I felt strength returning.

"Welcome," said the man. It was then that I noticed for the first time that we had just passed through the entrance to a massive city.

"We are in the Original City!" I exclaimed, the familiarity of the Simulacrum washing over me. My tseeyen warmed with comfort. "Aren't we?" I turned to face him.

"Of course," he answered looking somewhat confused, "You've never been here, have you?"

"Yes, I have, but it was a long time ago."

"You do not look old enough to have 'a long time ago' in your past..." he answered with more than an edge of doubt in his voice. "And why may I ask, were you out sleeping on the streets when you know it is not allowed."

"Not allowed?" I shook my head. "Why would it not be allowed to sleep on a street? Don't get me wrong, I think it's a terrible idea, but it's definitely not against any Simulacrum law."

"You are Simulacrum. How is it," he asked suddenly with a tense edge to his voice, "that you do not know our ways."

I looked at the man and considered answering him but then asked, "Are you a soldier for Rome?"

"No," he answered warily, obviously aware that I had changed the subject and avoided his question.

"Then why dress as one?"

"I am the last patrol before the night. I dress like this to move easily through the streets in order to be able to search without attracting attention," he explained, narrowing his eyes.

"Search for what?"

"For you, and others like you," he continued.

His words seemed to be a veil that hid something underneath.

"Like me?"

"Yes," I thought he would say more, but my lack of knowledge about this seemed to add to his concern. Instead of explaining himself, he adjusted his weight from one foot to the other and added nonchalantly. "Those who stay too long in the outside world and do not return by curfew to the Original City."

"Curfew? You have a curfew to get into the Original City? And what time is that? At six and half years everyone has to be through those doors?" I laughed at my own joke but found I was the only one in the conversation who found it remotely humorous.

"Six and a half years?" the man narrowed his eyes again and tightened the muscles in his jaw. "Try by high noon. They may go out in the morning if they need, but they must be back by high noon. We cannot risk someone being left behind after the sun is gone. We cannot risk the spread of the Esurio."

"Wait," I held up my hand. "You come into the city every night. You live here?"

"Yes," he said, "but you do not, do you?"

"No," I said honestly, "I am not from the here."

"If you are not from Jerusalem, then where are you from?"

Honestly is always the best possibility, and the most plausible, I thought.

"I told you. I am from far down the River."

"But you are Simulacrum," he asked and waited for me to answer.

"Yes," I said with great caution.

"But you can move against the tide of the River?" he said. "But none can move forward or backward in the River. This River is simply the River. I do not understand."

I started to explain but he grabbed my arm tightly.

"I will take you to the Council. They will know what to do with you."

The Council. The words brought a familiar dread to my mind. I did not have much luck with Councils, Simulacrum, or Boged, for that matter. We started toward the great city which was built in concentric layers around the base of several massive trees. Instead of working against nature, the city incorporated it. It gave the city a unique look of being both urban and pastoral at the same time.

We passed large statues of the Archaon and of the Original Men standing like guardians around the city. Grandiose archways and elaborate stonework mixed with copper doors and bronze rooftops. Hanging vines of vibrant greens and royal purples draped over rooftops and archways, splashing the stone and baked brick walls with color. In the center of the city was a large metalwork of gold that extended up the base of the central oak, connecting several layers of the multilevel city with such an opulent staircase of imposing size, that the one back in Jerusalem seemed suddenly...obsolete.

"This is the not the Original City," I said as I was ushered forward, past two very simple stone pillars that served as the entrance gate. "This is the not same city I saw before."

As I spoke my foot caught and I fell hard onto the stone walkway. A shock of heat burned my foot, and I saw that the shoe I was wearing had a hole in the heel.

"See, look here," the man said leaning down and pointing to a barely visible line that ran through the ground. "It is the gate that protects the city. You have to be careful to step over it for to touch it is fatal."

Our eyes met, and he said, "But you did not know that either, did you?" It had been a test. And I had failed. Or maybe passed? I was not sure.

"Why would you need a gate to protect the city?" I said as we made our way past several Simulacrum men and woman. "We are inside the Terebinths. Why would you need protection in here?"

The man shrugged his shoulders.

"We do not know. From what we can tell it was the Original Men who placed the gate in front of the city. It could have been during the Friguscor wars. Maybe they created it when their numbers dwindled and the Archaon left, but to be honest, we do not truly understand it. It does seem pointless to have such a weapon of protection inside the Terebinths. This is the safest place for us, and we will live here forever."

"Live here?" I stopped at the base of the golden staircase and looked up into the clouds where the staircase ended. "But you can't live here, you can only enter every seven years. That's when the gates open."

"The ceremonial gates?" He laughed as he began to work his way up the stairs, "Though they are wondrous to behold on high days, they are not our primary way of entering the safety of the Terebinths of Mamre. We come through the doors."

"The doors we came through?" I asked as I followed him up the stairs. Several women nodded politely at me as we passed. One offered me a piece of Basar fruit, and I suddenly realized that I was starving.

"Thank you!" I said, as I stuffed my face with the fruit of the Terebinths. "Where did those doors come from?" I asked, between large bites.

"From the Garden of the One Tree."

"The Garden? Of the One Tree?"

"Yes, the Primogenes were each given a door to enter into the Terebinths. We use the doors every day to avoid the night in the world of the Friguscor, as I have already told you."

"Why do you ever leave? Why don't you just stay here?"

He shook his head, "Time does not move forward here. There is no aging, no maturing, no marriage, no birth nor falling asleep. We must still go outside the Terebinths to continue life."

"Right," I said remembering that from Mother's teachings. "I remember that. So everyone goes out each morning. And the city outside does not notice?"

"The city outside is cursed. They have the hunger that comes with the absence of light."

"The Esurio is controlled by the absence of light? You mean during the day they do not attack? I've never heard of this before. The Esurio doesn't care about light; it is always ready to attack."

"May it never be as you have spoken," he said with dismay in his voice. "For how would we ever fight such a disease? At least now we have the daylight hours to protect us and this city at night." He walked on, leading me up three more flights of steps as I thought about what he had said.

Here, the Esurio was controlled by daylight, the Terebinths were accessible daily instead of every seven years, and the Simulacrum lived inside the Original City of the Original Men. The Man of Words was showing this to me for a reason, but what? What was I supposed to learn from this? That we didn't understand our history? That everything we thought was somehow twisted, somehow far removed from what had really, truly been?

Suddenly I remembered Atticus telling me the story of him in Jerusalem with Zulika.

"Beged was Boged," he had said. "They changed his name."

Even that had been taught to me incorrectly, but most of all—the Door. We, my people, had missed the Door. How? How could we miss something so blatantly obvious? How could we miss what we had been searching for, waiting for since the original Primogenes drank of the Eiani?

"Do you need to be carried again?" said the man with clear humor. He turned toward me adding. "I was not offering, I was merely—."

I held up my hand.

"No, I just realized I have never asked your name. I've been following you all of this time, and yet, I do not know your name."

He smiled, and I saw the warmth in it.

"Decimus," he said with a small bow. "I am Decimus of Rome."

Adair 3:6

"Deena has fallen, along with two hundred and eighty-six others," Eliezer said, his face heavy with sorrow as he threw down a hammer. It landed with the head buried in the dirt as he added. "I counted everyone."

"Others ..." I felt the plurality of the word in a way I had never done so before. The sound of building echoed in the air. It was all around us. Hammering, sawing, machines running. It was suffocating. I wanted to scream, to demand it all to stop. I wanted the world to stop spinning, for the clouds to be pulled down from the skies, and above all, I wanted unconsciousness to take us all beneath the earth.

Bury me deep where none can find me.

"We've buried most all those who fell; we will finish tomorrow," Phineas affirmed. "They sleep now, together in the earth."

"They should have gone into the Tombs of the Forgotten," lamented Agatha. "Meridee should have been placed in the Tombs, not beneath the earth!"

Issachar had arrived with Meridee last night by way of a tera, but today he looked suddenly old. It was a shocking thing to witness. Age, it seemed, had been sped up with time at an alarming rate. He stood with his pipe in his hands, turning it round and round but never lighting it.

"Agatha, we attempted to bring the girl below, but it is like many things that are no longer."

"By the law of the Simulacrum, they must be buried the same day if they cannot be taken to the Tombs of the Forgotten," I spoke, reminding everyone of the law.

"Attempted?" Agatha said watching her old friend closely. Issachar was speaking of the teras.

"The ways beneath the earth are closed," he said. "and I suspect it is as it always should have been. The teras, I fear, should never have been our way. We learned the way of them from dark shadows and yet in our stubbornness, we used them, though we knew they were not the way of the One Tree. So many things have come from that road. But now the teras are no more. Though we poured the blood of the Guardian," he looked at Mattie and nodded with respect, "and the GateKeeper, the earth will not open."

Mattie said, "It is time we left many of the old ways behind, TimeKeeper."

Agatha stood in agreement by her side and added, "The Guardian is right."

They exchanged glances, and I wondered if Agatha had told Issachar everything that had happened while he was gone.

Issachar nodded his head, his beard moving up and down.

"If what you have spoken is true, it is time we let go of a great many of the old ways."

Eliezer was fuming.

"If I know anything, it is that war is not the time for philosophers, but for the force of soldiers." He turned to face his warriors so that they could look into his face.

"I suspect there is a time for everything," Issachar said slowly moving his pipe. "Soldiers will do what is required of them, as they have for centuries. And philosophers, in due time, will deliberate and then weigh on the scales of justice what was done. And laws will be written to ensure a safer tomorrow. But it is our people who will bear the burden, for they will have to endure it all."

Our people. Every time I blinked, I saw their faces. The faces of the fallen. We had lain them all out of the grass. One body after the next. Mattie and several other women had washed away the blood from their wounds as a gesture of normality. The memory made my hands began to tremble again. I shoved them hard into my pockets, refusing to let the tremors out. I must bury them down, deep inside where they can never come out.

A face flashed before my eyes. Inman. Only an hour ago, Phineas and I had carried his body to lie with the others awaiting burial. His head was laid open, his brain exposed and half gone. It was sickening to see. This land was collecting so much blood. What was meant to be the land of the living was quickly becoming a tomb for the dead.

The smell of the smoldering wood, smoke and death drifted on the twilight air, and a few random oil fires still burned beyond the barn. I could not tell if it was sunset or fire that colored the sky in red and orange hues. The forest was silent. The fires had done their work.

"Only four barrels remain," a young man said to Phineas, who nodded before asking, "And how did they get all the way down there?"

Phineas was shaking his head, his hand still dirty from hours of digging. His beard was full, covering most of his face. The oddest thought crossed my mind. Hadn't he shaven just this morning? I had never seen him with a full beard.

Before speaking, Phineas wiped several drops of rain from his forehead.

"We hid those supplies. They were covered. I can't believe they were able to get to them so quickly. The good news is that we still have the crops in the west fields." He looked toward the fires, "Or we should, if the fires didn't get to them. They are ready, and we need to get all available hands over to bring in the crops first thing tomorrow morning."

"What? Those crops have at least three more months until they can be harvested," said Miss Rosa.

Phineas shrugged his shoulders, and I saw how very tired he was.

"I don't know," he said. "I can't pretend to understand what is happening to the days and months now. All I can tell you is what should have taken months has taken days. The harvest is here."

A young woman who had come last week from North Carolina with her two siblings spoke up.

"I was outside by the barn when I heard the screaming. I ran inside and barred the doors, but they came so fast. Lorene and I went out the back, through the hayloft. They cut her down before she could even get back on her feet. I fell and rolled into the wall. I hid behind a pile of old wood. They didn't see me. But Lorene, they drained her body. I watched them. I watched it all. Then the barn was on fire and I..." she stopped speaking mid-sentence as though her words were much too hard to continue.

Mattie stepped from the crowd and put her comforting hand on the woman's shoulder. We stood outside, for the fire had left us with no building large enough to gather such a great group of Simulacrum. We were together by the north side of the wall with the Big House behind us. The closeness of the others made my tseeyen calm to a low buzz for the first time since before the attack began. Most were busy moving lumber and helping along the last part of the wall. On the front porch of the Big House, Miss Rosa worked to help those who had been injured. Even from here, I could see the spark of Ruach's blue light. He was healing all that were injured.

"What do you have left?" It was Atticus who asked the question on everyone's lips. He stood leaning against a portion of the wall. I looked back at the fields and the surrounding woods. Most of the fire had burned out, but still, the hours of the day had been most damaging. What was only this morning fresh and green was now ash and black. The horizon showed the dull, low burn of the fires that had still not been extinguished.

Though no one knew how, the fire had started at the barn, consuming most of our resources stored there. In addition, it had kindled the drums of oil Eliezer's men had managed to procure, and the resulting explosion had spread the liquid fire over the grounds and into the woods. Red Oaks was ablaze within minutes and had burned for the better part of the day. The quickness of the fire, its far-reaching destruction had been mind-boggling to watch and heart-wrenching to endure. With everyone available battling the overwhelming onslaught of the Friguscor, we could do little to stop it. We simply were left to watch it burn.

Then, around four in the afternoon, when the heat seemed to blaze the highest, rain fell from the sky. No thunderclouds announced its arrival; the sky did not even churn with wind or clouds, it simply began to rain. Without warning, the rain came as unexpectedly as the fire, but we welcomed its relief. It had snuffed out most of the fires, but some of the spilled oil still burned.

"It is time to regroup," Atticus took one of his knives from his belt and began to whittle at the wood in his hand. I noticed the smile that touched the edge of his mouth as he said, "To gather what has been scattered," he looked up at me, "for I tell you, the Door is soon to open."

"People have been saying that all of my life," said an old man, "and yet, here we are."

"What are we going to do about the Esurio?" said a young man. "They will kill every last one of us. And they know where we are! That was just the beginning."

"We must finish this wall," said another. "It's our only way. We have to finish it tonight."

Silence spread across us. Anger, fear, and dread grew between us. A few raindrops still fell on our faces. The sound of falling trees and cracking wood spoke from the horizon. The burial dirt beneath my broken fingernails taunted me.

Mattie kept her arm wrapped around the girl from North Carolina as she spoke, her eyes trained on Atticus.

"Ruach has told us that we are in the final days. He has said that time itself is speeding up. And, I above all people believe him, as I believe you, Ayindalet."

Atticus looked at Mattie and asked, "Do I know you?"

"Yes," Mattie smiled, "I am Adair's daughter, Mattox."

Atticus looked around and found me.

"How many years have I come forward? You said that I had not lost much time. Veralee is not here, and yet Mattie was a child the last I was here. Now she is a woman grown. What have you not told me?"

"She is telling you the truth, Atticus," Mattie answered, and in turn addressed all of the others around her. "I was a child only days ago. At the same time as the Vanishing, the painting in Veralee's old bedroom poured time over me like paint from a jar. The Man of Words gave me years for the purpose of the end. I am a promise."

"A promise?" Eliezer asked, "of what?"

"I am the Guardian of the Gate for Red Oaks," Mattie asserted, her hair stirring around her head though there was no wind. She looked at me ,and I nodded, giving her my full blessing to continue.

"In me is the key to the gate. The Man of Words gave me years as a promise to you, to our people. He will restore the years the locusts have consumed. Our years will be given back to us, we will make it to the Door, and we will be fully restored. Look," she pointed her long delicate hand toward Atticus, "Even now, the One Tree has sent us an Ayindalet for the remaining days. I have seen it! The Door will open to us a second time."

"A second time! So, you understand!" Atticus threw down the piece of wood and marched into the midst of us, every step taken as though it had been preplanned. He let all of the eyes fall upon him, knowing what it meant to our people to have him with us, "I am Ayindalet. The watcher for the Door. And I tell you that the birds are circling, that the time of the end is here, and that the final Door is loosening from its lock. We need to prepare..."

"Prepare?"

We all turned toward the voice. Inman came through the crowd, which parted like water on either side of him. Semira, walked beside him with their steps perfectly in sync. He had a bandage wrapped around his head, covering his right eye and his right arm was in a sling.

"Even now we are finishing the breach in the wall. That is preparing, Ayindalet."

The crowd gasped at the sight of Inman and began murmuring loudly.

"Inman?" I managed to get out, "How? I saw you fall! You were—"

"Unconscious," Inman finished for me. "I lay there for hours."

"No," Phineas looked at me and then back in disbelief at Inman. "No, man, you were ... we were ready to bury you. Your head ... you had ...you had ..."

Phineascouldn't finish, but merely pointed toward Inman's head. Semira glared at Phineas in silent, but clear denial.

"A bad gash on my head," Inman said, "but it is healing even now." He patted the bandage tenderly. "I don't know, though, if I will regain my sight in this eye or the use of my arm."

Atticus narrowed his eyes and studied Inman. He shook his head slowly but didn't say anything. Phineas and I just stared in confusion.

"These are not ordinary times," Inman began smoothly. "Mattox has just shared how the Man of Words worked what seems impossible to the rational mind for the purpose of the end of days. Yet, you do not doubt her. Do you believe that the One Tree holds the power of life and death? Do you believe that anything is too hard for the One Tree? You say that I fell, but here I am. I do not pretend to know what has happened to me, but I do know if we are to survive, we must also be prepared to anticipate the unexpected, to look beyond the norms of yesterday, to take our lives into our own hands. The very survival of our children, our people, our way of life depends on it! Look around you! How has the wisdom of the past served you thus far?"

Inman turned and grasped Semira's hand, and she spoke for the first time.

"Perhaps Inman is the one chosen for a time such as this to save our people from certain destruction. You must trust what you see. Inman has been saved by the One Tree for great purpose! To save our people!"

As Inman spoke, I watched our people nod in agreement. Eliezer and his warriors, in particular, were rallying at his side.

Atticus turned toward Inman, the slow trickle of rain making his face seem even harder.

"You speak with words that are well-oiled with the wisdom of man but yours is not the plan of the One Tree. That wall," Atticus pointed to the monstrosity, "Will not save the Simulacrum from what is coming. I have been below to the Gates of Bariyach."

"But it might help," I said.

Inman spoke, "I see you have finally found your voice, LawGiver. I am glad to see it has healed stronger and wiser than it was before the beast took it from you."

Phineas ignored him and turned to face me. His eyes filled with confusion.

"Adair? What are you saying?"

Mattie looked at me and whispered, "Mother?"

"Maybe Inman is right. I've never seen anything like what happened today. I, I thought Inman was dead," I looked at Inman. "I'm sorry, Inman, I mean no offense, but I saw the Friguscor bash your head with that rock. It was ... horrible, but there were so many. I could not help you," I said, forcing my voice out.

I looked at Atticus and then Phineas. I could still only whisper. "I've never buried a fallen one before either, but if more Friguscor are coming ... and Inman has said they are, then we need this wall. We need everything we can get."

Phineas tossed the shovel to the ground that he had been holding.

"Just wait one second, Adair, Deena said that ..."

"Deena is dead, Phineas!" my voice trembled, and I felt the crack beginning at my feet and making its way up my spine. "How many others are left? Are there more left outside Inman, or are we it? You are the only one who has been outside this wall. Tell me, are we the last of the Simulacrum?"

Inman shook his head. "I have seen no others outside. Those whom I have found, I have brought here, and the rest are inside the Machine."

Atticus looked at Inman as I imagined a mountain lion looked at a mouse just before he ate him. He did not hide his disdain as he swept a long, uncomfortable look over Inman.

"And who are you exactly?" he said.

Inman seemed almost amused by Atticus's display of testosterone. "I am Inman, son of Absalom, and this is my bondmate, Semira."

Their faces looked as though they were locked in an inner war that none but they could decipher. I felt it in my bones. I was in a constant state of chaos inside. No longer did I know what was up or down. Should we build a wall or not build? Should we trust Inman or not trust him? I looked around at the broken lot of us and felt the wave of uncertainty washing over all of us. How do you know who to fight when you do not even know what to fight?

"I have been below the earth. To the City of Bariyach." Atticus said again, "and I saw the Seventh GateKeeper fall."

Suddenly I remembered Tessa, one of the Boged whom Veralee had changed, speaking of these gates below the earth. I looked at Phineas. He was the acting GateKeeper now. Tessa had said the Man of Words had appeared to her and shown her many things. He had also sent her with a message to Phineas: someone was coming who would try to kill him, for he was a luminary light.

At that time, I had thought Tessa was a threat, that she and all the other Boged that Veralee had changed and sent here to Red Oaks were proof Veralee was a law breaker. I was furious with Veralee and horrified that Boged were stepping onto our property and expecting us to take them in as Simulacrum. Mother, of course, had welcomed them with open arms. Phineas and I had had a huge argument over it, and he had accused me of being so concerned with the law that I had no mercy. He had told me that without mercy, there was no justice.

I remembered part of the conversation Mother and I had had with Tessa. The Man of Words had shown Tessa a vision of the City below. She had seen the Eight Gates, and then she had seen eight luminaries. When one luminary went out, a gate opened. In Tessa's vision, the Seventh luminary was flickering and dimming, but the Eighth was still burning brightly. As the Seventh luminary dimmer, the Seventh Gate bulged.

Mother had revealed that the last six GateKeepers had fallen on this land, and that my father was the Seventh GateKeeper. She feared he was faltering. Everything Tessa had told us, everything Ruach and Wisdom had shown us, I now knew to be true. Daddy had fallen, and my mother, too. The gates below were opening, and the horror of today proved the black days of night were upon us. My heart yeared to protect Phineas. Please, I whispered, don't take him from me.

Joab and Agatha surfaced in the crowd. Their shared horror seemed to tie them together with an invisible chord of single purpose.

Agatha spoke first, "I have read of the City of Bariyach in the Hidden Book. What he speaks is true. The fathers of the Rephaim, the dead ones, were locked away beneath the earth for their crimes against the One Tree. Each GateKeeper held in his blood the key to one of eight gates below the earth, while the Guardians held the keys to the gates above the earth. That which is seen and that which is unseen. Keys to both sides of the Gates. Above and Below."

Agatha worked her way feebly forward.

"And now the Seventh has fallen," she said. "The Dark One will be looking to open the Eighth Gate. The final gate."

"What happens if the Eighth Gate is opened?" asked a girl named Nancy who was holding on to every word Agatha spoke. "What happens then?"

Agatha turned to face Atticus, "Let the Ayindalet tell us."

Atticus looked past Agatha to Nancy. He held her gaze, steadying her with his own presence as he said, "The dark kings of old, the sons of the fallen watchers plan, through the power of the Nachash, to restart creation. To wipe out any trace of the Simulacrum or the Boged from the bloodlines of men. To make mankind in their image instead of the image of the creator, the One Tree. They plan to destroy us all and to reshape the DNA of man. Once the Eighth Gate falls, they will have what they seek."

"These are nothing but old wives tales," Semira said quickly.

"What is behind the Eighth Gate," Phineas asked, "that could be so powerful?"

Powerful! The memory of the creature attacking just two nights ago burned fear into my veins.

Agatha answered, "The book said that behind that gate..."

"... is the beginning," Mattie finished her sentence with a smile.

"The beginning?" Phineas asked, "What does that mean?"

"I don't know," she said honestly.

"You don't know ..." Phineas repeated.

I wanted to scream. I looked to Atticus and then Inman, "Does anyone know? Does anyone really know what it means? What any of this means?"

Atticus said, "Who are we to know the plans from before we existed?"

"Spoken well for an Ayindalet," Inman said, his face drawn tight into a serious frown. "But what about the here and now? For those of us who cannot escape the present terror by escaping into the River of time. What is to be done for right now? For the protection of our people?"

With Semira by his side, he turned to address the people, "I tell you, the wisdom of the past has failed. Hasn't Wisdom herself abandoned you? Has not most of your Council been decimated? I say that in itself is the judgment of the One Tree! You must use the intellect that you have been given, you can no longer rely on failed tradition. To ensure that we survive, we must finish this wall! We need to fortify the areas that were damaged in the attack. You do not have the luxury of time to overthink this. The mindless Friguscor of today are nothing compared to what is on the horizon. As we sit here doing nothing, a well-equipped, well-trained, professional army is marching toward us, and it will be here soon!"

Semira added, "Do we want to repeat the devastation of today? Think, people!! Remember what you saw when they came through the wall!"

"An army?" challenged Atticus, "What Army? Why would an army be coming to Red Oaks?"

"Seems you have been gone swimming longer than you think," started Semria, "They will be here in two days' time."

"What do they seek?" asked Atticus, his green eyes blazing.

"The fall of Red Oaks, the demise of its people," Inman said, his face serious, "And the gate. They march on Red Oaks for the control of the gate."

"But Wisdom is gone..." Mattox stated, "The gate will not open without Wisdom."

"They will not need Wisdom to enter anymore. The gate you knew will fall shortly, if it has not already now that Wisdom has abandoned her post. They seek another way, and they will take the land to find it," Inman explained.

A collective gasp of horror could be heard across the crowd. Inman turned toward those gathered close, "Hear me. I do not mean to frighten you more that you are now, but I am telling you the truth. I make a vow to you on this day. To the best of my ability. We shall finish this wall!"

He pointed out toward the damaged wall, "Look! Even now the ones I brought are working tirelessly to repair the damage and build the rest of the wall. The wall is a symbol that stands as a promise."

Inman looked pointedly at Mattie, "Not as a promise that stands far off, but one that is here. Right now!"

Inman retrieved the hammer from the ground where Eliezer had carelessly thrown it, and lifted it high for all to see.

"Because of this wall and the unity of purpose that we now embrace, you shall not perish by the sword, nor shall you wither from famine. Even now there is a miraculous harvest, ready in the fields. In it, we reap the fruit of our own labor; see that as the promise of the future! The woods," he pointed toward the scorched forest, "the sacred trees which you have trusted for protection have burned. They are the symbol of the past, and we taste the ash upon our lips even now. But, from the ruins of yesterday, we can build a new tomorrow, but only if we are of one mind and heart. I assure you, let us work together to finish this wall tonight, and I will give you peace!"

As his words blanketed the people, something happened. A stirring in the crowd, a sliver of hope and a will to survive came rushing to the surface.

"Inman for the Judge!" Semira said, lifting his arm up for all to see, "He who has been saved should lead us!"

"Inman for Judge," someone from the back yelled. It caught on as fast as the fire had spread. Moving from lips to lips, "Inman as our Judge! Inman! Inman!"

"No wall can promise this," Atticus tried to interject, raising his voice as a banner of reason above the sea of people, "It is but wood against an army of iron! You must trust in the plan of the One Tree!"

"Wood from the Oaks that have remained here since the beginning," Inman said, matching Atticus' tone, "And we have bound them with these," Inman reached in his pocket and brought out two smooth oblong objects that had a metallic phlange on each end.

"What are those?" Atticus inspected. "I have never seen such work."

"It is the work of the Aluid," explained Inman, "We will use their own technology against them."

"Against them?"

"It is their army that comes from the east to take down Red Oaks. With these we will ensure our survival. These bind molecules with identical resonance through a wave of sound. No need for traditional nails or screws. So much faster! Just tack one of these between two boards, and it creates a solid bond that cannot be broken by any traditional means. I brought some through the tera when I came last. "

"Inman!" men shouted, "Inman! We are saved!!" they raised their hammers, their shovels and whatever tool was in their hand. "Inman!"

Inman looked to Eliezer who had a flash of uncertainty run across his face as he looked to me. The roar of the crowd made it impossible to speak or hear myself think. I looked to Mattox and Phineas. They were frowning as they watched the people. Atticus was obviously disgusted.

"Inman!" they shouted over and over. "We choose Inman as the Judge for our Council! Deena has fallen, Inman shall rise to her seat!"

"Do not lose your hand from the inheritance the Eiani has promised in your blood," Agatha tried to say. Her frail voice was lost, drowned beneath the waves that were pushing forth with desperation and madness on its crest. She tried again, "Cursed are those who put our trust in a man when we are called to believe in the Eiani within!"

Hearing Agatha snapped courage back into me. She was right. I had been momentarily swayed by the horror of the day, but Ruach had shown me the history of this place. Absalom had killed Ernest, my great-great grandfather and through Austin, my grandfather Richard. He was a part of this madness, I was sure, and Inman worked with Absalom.

I remembered the vision the Man of Words had given me of all my family together once again. Nathan, Mattie, Veralee, Ausley, Mother and Daddy, all of us. He had assured me that many would fall, but in the end, we would prevail. It was tempting to trust Inman and his smooth words, but I determined to trust the Man of Words, the Archaon, and the Eiani. We were Simulacrum, and we were never alone.

"Inman!" I screamed out and turned to face Inman, "You are right. My voice is stronger and wiser now that it has been broken and healed again. I am

Adair, the daughter of Gail, mother to the Guardian of Red Oaks and LawGiver for the Simulacrum."

Inman's eyes flashed with surprise as I continued.

"We must remember the One Tree. We must remember that we are Simulacurm and we are never alone! Do not let fear rob you of reason!! Inman cannot sit as the Judge. He is not of the bloodline of the Judges. He cannot possibly take the seat. We must follow the true ways of the One Tree. The ways that Ruach and Achiel have tried to explain." The loss of my voice had given me so much. The past two days I had been listening and watching instead of talking and doing. Suddenly I understood, suddenly it seemed so clear, "I am the Law-Giver, and I am here to uphold the Law. Not the Law that we created out of fear and anger, but the true law, the Law of the One Tree! If we stay the course and find the Hidden Books, we will know what the One Tree is asking of us! We will know how to make it to the Door!"

"Change the law!" screamed the masses, "We seek a new law for a new day!"

"Your sister didn't follow the Law!" screamed another voice, "The Law must be changed!"

"We will write a new law!"

"No law, no law!"

"Inman! Inman!"

No one would listen. They were chanting Inman's name over and over.

One of Eliezer's warriors stepped forward.

"Inman gave his right eye in the battle for Red Oaks," he said, "a great heroic feat to help save as many as possible! He has proven himself to our people, and it is he who is providing the means to build the wall for our protection! It should be him that sits as Judge over us. Issachar said it himself, we have to let go of the old ways. And we renounce the old tribal way of deciding, and we choose for ourselves our leader! We choose Inman as our Judge and leader!"

Inman bowed his head respectfully as the throngs of men calling for him to take the position echoed in the night. Semira raised her voice and began to chant Inman's name with the masses, passion dripping from her lips as she spoke over and over again.

But Agatha spoke louder.

"I speak of the old ways that covered up the truth of our people. Listen to our LawGiver! She speaks truth! We have missed the Door! We rejected the Man of Words when he came to us because he broke our laws! Laws that we made to protect us because we feared the night. Do not make the same mistake again! Do not elect one out of fear that is not called to the position! I see clearly now! He is the son of the Blind Seer, Absalom, who sent our people into the Machine! Look at me and heed my words!"

But as Agatha spoke, the warriors were surrounding Inman. I saw them moving like a wall to protect their leader. It because apparent to me that this was not as spontaneous as Inman wanted it to look. Alliances had already been made. Secrets had been spoken and deals cut in the dark of night. As far as the crowd was concerned, Inman was now in control.

Joab made his way through the crowd. Unlike Agatha, Joab had taken the healing of Ruach. He looked like the mighty warrior he had been before he had followed Absalom from the Scared Oaths and into the Machine. Agatha still refused to be healed.

Joab stood beside Agatha.

"She speaks the truth," he shouted. "Hear our witness! See hers! We have been inside the Machine, and Agatha has read the Hidden Books. This wall will not save us from what is coming! The only way we can be saved from the destruction that is coming, the only way our people can survive this darkness, is to listen to the Ayindalet and find the way to the Door. We must leave this place if we want to survive."

Semira shook her head.

"No! Do not listen to this drivel."

"Joab, you were once a mighty warrior," Inman continued, "and we appreciate what you have done for us in the past. But that is the past! There is no second Door! Your ordeal in the city not only drained your blood, but your reason."

"No?" Joab looked at him. "You are not our Judge, Inman. We will never recognize you." Agatha stood straighter by Joab's side. "I know you say Absalom let me out of the Machine, but I see in you his true plan. You are the son of the Blind Seer, and all you will bring upon us is destruction!"

Inman looked perplexed and raised his head.

"These are fickle times indeed," he said. "Was it not you, Joab. who spoke at the meeting with Archaon about a line that would need to be drawn?"

"I spoke out of ignorance," Joab retorted.

"You said that a line had to be drawn between those who are willing to sacrifice for the protection of our people and those who are not...willing, that is, to sacrifice for the sake of our people."

Inman looked as though he were truly asking a question and not pushing Joab against a wall before he continued.

"And was it not you, in your very own words that day that said we needed a leader who could 'take charge and keep our people together.' I am that leader that you spoke of Joab. The people have chosen me to keep them together."

"I was wrong," Joab stated without an ounce of pride left in his humble body. "I was wrong to believe the nonsense of your father, Absalom, and it cost me dearly! But I will not stand by and watch him take over what is left of the Simulacrum. You cannot be the Judge."

He looked at Agatha and at me.

"The LawGiver has spoken against you, and so do I. We will never allow you to take the seat as the head of the Council of the Simulacrum. Never!"

From behind Inman a spear came hurtling through the air. Atticus lunged from where he stood, trying to stop the weapon from hitting its intended target, but he fell short into the hard earth.

Joab flew back as the long spear pierced his chest and pinned his body to the wall. He fell limp and hung lifeless, suspended above the ground.

Someone screamed, and I realized it was me.

I sucked in my breath, but before I could scream again, a second spear struck Agatha, pinning her to the wooden wall where she had stood. Her face hung slack, and blood dripped down her body onto the ground. Her knees were bent up beneath her at odd angles. She said nothing.

A third spear imbedded itself beside Agatha.

Issachar, who had been standing right next to Agatha, was on the ground, but Atticus had saved him.

"They wanted to stand as witnesses," said Semira who stood beside Inman. "Let them stand here, on the wall, as witness to those that oppose Inman as the Judge of the Simulacrum."

"You!" I shouted. I could barely breath, the words were lost. I moved forward with outstretched hands to grab the neck of the monster. "You have taken their lives! Just like your father! Joab was right, you are the son of perdition!"

His warriors immediately covered him, and Phineas grabbed me from behind, pulling me back. Atticus came forward, and stood between us, a blade in each hand.

"You are a murderer!" I screamed and kicked against Phineas who was lifting me and dragging me back. "You will never be the Judge! I am the Law-Giver! You will never get what you want!"

"Take her," Inman said, and then looked at Atticus. "Take all of them who are going to divide the people. We must walk in unity now. We must be a unified front. If they change their minds, let them out. We want them to be with us, but we cannot allow them to stand against us. Not now. The stakes are too high."

Atticus swung his dagger out, catching the ear of the soldier. The soldier screamed and dropped his weapon as two more advanced.

Phineas tried to protect me, but there were too many. They dragged us across the fresh dirt of the graves and pulled me up the steps to my own house.

Miss Rosa, who had gone into the house before the fracas asked, "Just what do you think you are..."

"Run, Rosa!" Phineas screamed. "Take Mattie with you!" Too stunned to answer, she did as Phineas told her.

Ruach was not on the porch. He was nowhere to be seen. They forced us up the stairs and threw us in Veralee's old bedroom.

The large windows had been boarded up. Even the doors to the balcony had been nailed shut with heavy beams.

I fell on the ground beside the bed. Phineas was tossed into the corner.

"You can come out when you are with us," said the warrior, "We need you to stand with us, not against us."

The second soldier, whose name was Leon, added, "It's about time your family was dethroned."

Before I could say anything three more guards came in, holding the limp body of the Ayindalet in between them. They tossed his bloodied face onto Veralee's bed and turned without a word, closing and locking the door behind them.

"Atticus," Phineas got to him before I did. He rolled the man over. Blood was coming from his arm, his face and his stomach. He had been stabbed in the lungs and was struggling to breath.

"We need Ruach," I said as his blood leaked onto my dress, "The Eiani cannot heal this in time. He will bleed out before ..."

But Atticus opened his eyes. He gasped and wheezed. His lungs sounded as though they were filling with fluid. He rolled to his left side and then moaned, gasping for air.

I looked to Phineas, "What can we do?"

Phineas grabbed the pillow and pulled the casing off, then applied pressure to the gash in Atticus's right lung. Atticus gasped over and again for air and the sound of it made me want to scream.

Phineas sat with Atticus and tried to stop him from flailing so violently. Then Atticus went still. His breathing became shallow. A wrasping wheeze hissed from his lungs. His eyes were closed tight, and I could tell that he was working to control the pain. We sat in silence for more than an hour, listening to the sound of a man who was slowly drowning before us. The house below us grew eerily quiet. We could not see outside the windows to know what was happening. So, the three of us sat together in the dark. I moved to touch Phineas, and he gripped my hand tightly.

"Mattie is safe." Phineas assured me. "From what I saw yesterday, she is equipped to take care of herself."

"Yes," I breathed out in the dark, "Phineas, what is happening to our people? We have an army of Friguscor coming against us, we are killing each other, and we are locked in here. Someone prepared this. Who boarded up the windows in this room?"

"From the looks of it," Phineas said. "Someone was in here preparing to board up this room entirely. I don't think they planned to let anyone in this room."

"When would they have done this? Who would have done this? We are always here at the house."

"They must have done it today We were gone for the whole day. Someone was trying to board this room up, but they didn't quite finish the job." He pointed to the pile of wood on the floor, "I don't think it was meant as a prison. The door to the bathroom is boarded up as well."

Atticus stirred and then rolled over again onto his back.

Phineas leaned in close to Atticus to see if he was breathing.

"I do not wish to be kissed by you, Phineas," Atticus said and I immediately leaned over to look at him too.

"Nor by you, Adair, though you are much more beautiful than the GateKeeper."

Atticus sat up slowly.

"You are healing!" I said.

"Ahhh, I hate that part." Atticus groaned.

"How are you already healed?" Phineas asked.

"I am Ayindalet," Atticus said with evident pain in his voice, "but that does not mean it does not hurt."

Before I could ask anything else, Atticus said, "Adair, you told me that Veralee was not here, but you still have not told me where she is. I must go to her."

My lips quivered. I did not want to speak it aloud. If I said it, it would make it true.

"She is in something called the Machine at an underground facility owned by BaVil. At least, that is what Inman and Joab told us," Phineas answered for me.

I heard more pain in his voice and I wondered what his face looked like as he said, "When did this happen?"

"Months ago?" I said shaking my head. "We don't know really. Three days ago, my mother fell. The Boged all disappeared, and Ruach says it is because my father fell."

"Three days ago the Guardian of Red Oaks fell? It has been only three days?" Atticus asked.

"Yes," I said, remembering her face as she fell. "It's hard to keep time straight, but I know that it was three days ago. It was just before Deena arrived with news of Joab and the Machine."

"The last thing I remember, is being in the city of Bariyach with Veralee. We were both thrust into the River by Achiel and were separated."

"Because of the stairs of Ahaz?" I asked.

"Stairs?" Atticus said. "What stairs?"

I explained as best I could what I had learned about time going back three days.

"Three days from the moment your father fell?" Atticus said working it out. "So that would be three days before we were in the City of Bariyach."

"No," Phineas said. "Well, I don't know. Time did go back three days, but Gail was still gone."

"Yes," Atticus said, "She fell with the GateKeeper, who you said was the trigger for the Stairs of Ahaz."

"The trigger?" I asked.

"You said that it was the death of your father, the spilling of the blood of the Seventh, that enacted the Stairs of Ahaz, the turning back of time for three days. So it can't bring back the one who is the trigger. And if Gail was somehow connected, then she would not come back either, though everything else would turn back."

"I don't know that I understand," I began, but Atticus stood up, holding his side.

"So three days back would put Veralee with the Boged," Atticus said aloud but I felt he was speaking more to himself. "But you say the Boged are all gone."

I watched him as best as I could in the dark.

"You won't stay, will you?" I asked him.

"No," he said without a breath of hesitation. "I am going to find Veralee."

"But you are Ayindalet. You are supposed to watch for the Door and lead the people to it. You said yourself that the Door is going to open soon. How can you leave us now?"

"I will return in three days," he said as a promise, "And I will bring Veralee back with me."

Atticus put a hand on Phineas's shoulder.

"On the third day, have all who are willing to go through the gate ready. Until then, you must protect the Guardian. Do not allow anyone to use Mattox to open any door."

"I don't know where Mattox is...and what gate?" I said, "Why would we go to the gate? It can't be opened for another six years."

"The birds are circling, Adair," he said as though it were completely obvious. "The gate will open when the alignment is right."

"How?" said Phineas, "We can't open any teras."

"That is what Issachar told me, maybe it has something to do with the wall..." Atticus seemed to stop mid-thought and continued. "Still, I do not speak of a tera. I speak of the gate. It will open for us."

"It won't. You know as much as I do. Mattie could try again and again, and the gate will only open on the set dates at the appointed times. It has been like that since ..."

"Since your people rejected the first Door, and all the Doors fell flat, closing off the Terebinths except for every seven years." Atticus stated.

"What?" I shook my head.

"To be honest, I was not there during that time, but an old friend told me about it." He answered and then added, "But trust me. This gate will open."

"How?" I said again becoming annoyed.

"Because I have the key," he said and leaned toward me. "I am Ayindalet, Adair. I have one purpose. In my blood is the key to open the Eighth Gate, when the alignment comes in order and the time for the Door comes to pass. The Man of Words put the key to open the gate inside my blood for the appointed time, but I can only open it once, and Veralee must be with me."

"Veralee? Because she has the key to the Eighth Gate in her blood?"

"Yes," color returned to his face as he spoke of her, "She is the Malachi. The key to the Eighth Gate. We must open the gate together."

"But why?" I said aloud, "Why would the One Tree put such keys into mere humans?"

Atticus shook his head, "In the beginning, the war began with a woman and a man. When they ate of the fruit, they gave the keys to this world to the Nachash. The Man of Words has won his battle with the Nachash. He has won the right for us to ask the One Tree to give back what was stolen."

"The dominion of the world..." I said slowly, "The keys to the new world."

"Wait!" I said confused, "where is this gate?"

Atticus nodded and then began to stand, "In the Terebinths, Adair. Be ready. In three days' time, I will return. Make sure Mattie is with you. We will need her blood as well."

"Wisdom is gone," I said. "The Gate at Red Oaks is no more. We cannot enter the Terebinths that way."

Atticus smiles, "There's always another way, Adair. The Eiani will provide."

Phineas nodded his head, "Okay, in three days. We must be ready on the sixth day of the final week."

"The final week," I repeated. "That is what Ruach said."

"Yes," Atticus said, "it was he who taught me."

Then he stood up on the bed.

"You said this painting did something to Mattie?"

"What?" I could not keep up with him. "Yes, it...it poured out of the wall like water, but wait ... Did you know you had this key in you or ..."

"I was here the night Vera finished it; she painted it for Veralee. She was born that night." Atticus said. "I watched Vera finish the last details. It was the night of the battle. But it has changed since I last saw it in the Civil War. It shows Veralee now," he said pointing to the woman with white hair in the middle of the trees.

He looked down at his arm. He had double bonding marks, which had begun to glow. I looked down at my own bond mark to confirm what I was seeing. I had one distinct line that wrapped around my arm, joining me to Phineas. Atticus, I was sure, had two interweaving lines that were glowing as the sun on his arm.

Atticus put his right arm out and touched the painting.

"The bond can take me to her," he said.

"Take you to her? Veralee was born that night? What are you talking about? Veralee wasn't born in the Civil War," But I remembered Agatha's words. She said she believed Vera was Veralee's mother...

"You have lost a lot of blood, Atticus. The painting can't ..." but I stopped short.

Atticus was putting his hand through the wall. Paint began spreading up his arm and over his chest. He turned back just before he went in.

"Three days...Remember the Door."

And then, just like that, Atticus was gone. I stared at the painting and shook my head to clear it. Too much was happening!

For a moment I heard Veralee's cheerful voice, teasing me, "Watch out! She labels!" Well, I couldn't label this and for the life of me, I could not explain or make any of the events of the last few months line up in neat rows.

Outside the boarded-up windows, I heard muffled voices. Phineas heard the same thing. He moved to the window, and with our hands touching in the middle, we learned in to listen. I recognized Inman's voice. He was speaking beneath the balcony at the front of the house.

"Our time is ticking, Comrades!" he asserted.

"Comrades?" I said, but Phineas hushed me.

"We must begin now. We must fell as many trees as we can tonight. Those that are already fallen in the woods are to be moved to the sawmill and cut into boards. The final parts of the wall must be done tonight! Everyone must work! This is a new day. A new revolution for our people. The key to every new era is always power. Who holds the power? I say we recognize the power of the blood within our veins and renounce the old ways of having Judges, Seers, Discerners, and any other place of authority. These just rob the common man of the power and authority that is rightfully his and keeps it locked into the privileged few. No more bourgeois ideals that allow certain people to be chosen to do certain jobs like the LawGiver and the GateKeeper. All of us are now equal. All are called sacred! And the Guardian of the Gate ..."

"Mattie!" I whispered her name.

"... Will work just as hard as the soldier," Inman continued," and the soldier will work just as hard as the laborer! Our people have been oppressed for too long under the weight of the old ways, the broken Law, and the Judgment of the Council. So, from now on, see me as your equal, not as a Judge who stands above you, but a friend who sits among you! Soon, the days will come when new laws, new ways, and new standards will be written for our people. Great orators will pronounce grand speeches and philosophers will debate among themselves, but tonight is not that night! I stand as your leader, only until the days are full of light again, and then, of course, I will return the power to the people! The new Law will reflect the will of the people! Until then, I must lead you, and you must give me the authority I need to accomplish the task at hand. But I promise you this. The rule of the Council is over. Tomorrow you will see the LawGiver and the GateKeeper work side by side with you as the Guardian of the Gate carries buckets of water to quench your thirst!"

Day 4 Boker

Separate light from light…to rule the day and night

Ausley 4:1

The sound of water dripping and the dull smell of fire roused me to awareness that I had not felt in years. The cold, stone table beneath my back told me I was no longer in the room with Jari and the others. My fingers felt the loose, tiny pebbles of aged rock that had slipped from the stone over time. Instinctively, my hands flew to my belly, and I breathed a sigh of sincere relief as I wrapped both arms securely around my baby.

"You're safe," I whispered to him. "I'm here with you."

My tseeyen hummed a low burning of comfort. The room was empty; we were alone. Slowly, I raised myself to a sitting position. I was not on the altar of what Austin had called, "The Cathedral of Lights," down in the depths of the Machine, as I had expected. Instead, I was back in the Tombs of the Forgotten. The painting on the wall, back in the land of dreams, was of the room where a large staircase that led to the altar-like structure where Daddy was killed, but I had not come to that room. I was back in the empty tomb. This was the place where Uziel had ... I closed my eyes and let the nausea roll over my body. Bile rose in my throat, and I turned to vomit but stopped short as I saw the painting before me on the wall. A golden child stood staring at me with such intensely blue eyes that I thought he could see through to my bones.

I heard Uziel's voice.

The one with the key, refused to die.

Somehow, I knew it was simply a memory of Uziel's voice. A memory the tomb held. I looked at the boy and slowly moved toward the painting.

With a tentative hand, I reached to touch his small, round face.

"He wanted you dead, and you refused to die ..."

My baby kicked. I looked down and spoke a promise or maybe a hope over my baby.

"You will be the same. Just like the golden boy, you will defy Uziel."

I heard voices, like those I had heard back at the land of Shan'ar. Speaking names.

The wall was decorated with gold filigree. The vine-like design was made up of names interlaced with branches of a giant oak tree. On one wall was a picture of a tree made of fire and twelve men standing before it.

"Those are the Primogenes," I said, suddenly aware of the room. "And those are the lineage of names from the Primogenes ... or maybe?"

I turned and looked at the table. The table where my worst nightmare had occurred. I fought back the urge to recoil and stepped forward, hearing a memory of voice whispering in the room,

It is an empty bed, the bed of one who once slept, but has awakened before his time.

"An empty bed?" I looked at the stone table harder, willing it to tell me it's secrets.

Who? The only Primogene who fell outside the Terebinths, Boged, the traitor who broke the Law.

It was Adair speaking! She had been in this tomb! My heart rapidly accelerated, and though I knew she was not there I still called her name.

"Adair!"

But it was the memory of Uziel's voice who answered.

The pages of a lost book have been hidden, and yet, your family lies sleeping in the Tombs. More will join them soon, for the war is far from over.

His voice echoed against the walls of the tomb, but they did not touch my heart. I stood bravely before the stone table. So, this is where the bones of Boged were laid so many years ago. But Uziel believed he had already left this empty tomb, that he, unlike all the rest of my family in the tombs, was already awake. Before the appointed time for those in the tombs to arise.

"So, this is why you brought me back here," I laughed, and tears rolled down my face as I spoke to Mikahel who I knew was not far away. "So that I could see why he ... why he brought me to this tomb to ..."

I still could not say it. Uziel, the Prince of the Air, had brought me to the tomb of Boged, his greatest enemy and defiled me. I looked at the golden child on the wall.

"If you are his enemy, then you are my friend. And if you are awake, please, wake my family in this tomb so they can be free from the prison of Uziel."

Mikahel had given me a choice by sending me back to the place where Uziel had defiled me, and I knew which way I would go. The baby inside of me was a piece of Jackson, and I would find him. Together, we could set our people free.

With all my effort, I turned away from the stone table, and as I crossed the threshold I made the decision to shut the door behind me. What was done to me, I would leave in that room. Maybe, one day, Boged himself, the one who could share his blood and change a Friguscor heart to life, could heal my heart too. But for now, I would leave it on the stone table where the bones of Boged had once lain.

"Are you ready to return?"

His voice shocked me as much as his size. Mikahel stood so large in the hallway, that he filled most of the space around us.

"Yes, I am ready."

"Remember, what will not open to you will open with these words."

He said words in the old language softly into my ear, and I listened carefully to remember every syllable. Then he gave me direction.

"Wait until the light fails, and then go inside," he said. "It is the only way to enter the control room of the Machine. Once there, turn it off and follow the plans that your Father gave you."

"Yes," I remembered the plans in perfect detail that had once, a very long time ago, laid on Daddy's desk in the office. "I have seen the tunnels that he left open. Those are the way out?"

"Get them to the tunnels," Mikahel said. "We will hold back the Shadow Kings and give time for the Sons and Daughters of the blood to move toward freedom."

Suddenly a blue circle of beautiful light opened before me and I knew I was to go through it.

"Why can't you just go with me?" I asked, hesitating to step through the circle. "Why do I have to go alone?"

Mikahel smiled.

"There is much more to do than what you can see," he said. "We will be there, just as we always are. We are simply on the other side."

"Like the other side of the painting." I said. It gave me hope. The Archaon were with us, even when we could not see them.

"Listen to the Eiani in your veins, the One Tree will lead you. Now go."

His breath pushed me forward, and I walked two steps. One, still in the Tomb. Two, into the underground facility of BaVil. It was as though I had just walked through a door I could not see. I turned to see him, but as I suspected, Mikahel was already gone.

I touched my belly and leaned against the concrete wall, my knees weak for a moment. I was back, inside the facility, on one of the hallways that looked identical to every other hallway. Where should I go? How would I find Jackson?

The halls had cameras everywhere. Soldiers would be here in seconds if anyone was paying attention. I had to move and move now. Forcing myself off the wall, I started forward down the hall and then, deciding against it, turned and hurried the opposite way. Suddenly my tseeyen began to glow a warm, blue and white light.

Listen to the Eiani in your veins, the One Tree will lead you.

Remembering Mikahel's words, I began to quicken my pace forward. I had to find Jackson first. The lights above me flickered on and off and then on again. I felt the walls tremble, as well as the floor beneath my feet.

I ran forward my breath coming hard and fast with the weight of the baby on my back and hips. Suddenly, the lights went out entirely. I stood still for one moment, looking down at the light of my tseeyen. It still burned bright.

I forced myself to move quickly using the light from my tseeyen to light the path for my feet. The lights flickered back on, and I froze. Soldiers came running down the hall. I flattened myself against the wall as they rushed past me without turning a head or speaking a word in my direction. It was as though they didn't see me, but I knew they did. The floor shook again and plaster from the walls fell in chunks. More soldiers ran down the hallway.

"Hurry!" shouted a man from the other side. "We need all hands! The Caldron! It's going to blow at any minute, and we will go up in flames if it does!"

I remembered something that Jackson had told me, maybe it was from a dream... that the Caldron had ten thousand magnets with a gravitational pull a hundred thousand times greater than Earth. The ground shook. This was the work of Mikahel, it had to be.

Go! To the end of the hall!

I heard his voice command me forward in my mind. Out of breath and scared, I obeyed, as quickly as my swollen feet could go. Which door? I stood at the end of the hallway with doors on either side of me. I breathed in and waited for my tseeyen to direct me, but it was the sound of his heartbeat that clicked in my ears.

"Jackson!" I whispered. He was behind the door to my right. The bond between us was so strong I could feel his heart beating inside his chest. The doors had no handle and no apparent way inside. I scrambled, looking up and down the door frame but found nothing. I slammed my hand on the white plaster, and a small holographic box appeared on the surface of the wall. A key pad. My heart sank. A key pad? But as I stared at the numbers, I remembered Jackson telling me, the first night I arrived here, when he had come into my cell that all prison rooms had the same entrance codes.

22845... I guess it's because no one escapes from here.

Quickly, I punched the number into the wall and the door, slid obediently open. The room smelled of vomit, but the lights were on. Jackson lay huddled in a corner, pale and weak.

"Jackson!"

I crossed the room quickly to reach him. He raised his head

"Ausley?" he said, weakly.

"Jackson, get up! We have to go. We don't have much time, the Archaon are here. They are helping us to get out, but we must get to the control center for the Machine. We must get there before the lights ..."

He stood slowly, and I noticed how he swayed.

"Ausley, is that really you? Are you really here?"

"What did they do to you?" I touched his face and saw the deep bruises all over his arms and neck.

"They gave me the vaccine, Absalom knew. He knew what it would do to me, and now ..." He tilted his head back to rest against the wall which trembled again with a fissure of energy from the Caldron. "My body, it can't take it. Go without me, Ausley. This is as far as I can go."

He slid down the wall and made it almost to the floor, but I leaned down and put my full weight against him to stop him.

"No!" I said directly into his face. His eyes fluttered and then opened. "Feel this," I grabbed his hand and placed it on our baby. His little feet pushed back, touching the edge of his daddy's hand. "This is our baby, Jackson. You and me together. I will not leave you here, and I will not let our baby die at the hands of these monsters. So get up and start walking!"

I stepped back, shocked by my own words. Nervous energy made me second guess myself, but I saw that Jackson was smiling, though he was weak.

"Our baby?" his eyes widened as much as they could. They were almost swollen shut and his skin was oozing with sores. "Alright, Little Harper," he smiled, calling his childhood nickname for me, "I'll go with you."

Placing his right arm around my shoulder, I helped him to his feet. We went out the door and began to make our way back down the hall.

"Do you know the way to the Machine?" I asked, trembling under the weight of his body.

"It's right here." He stopped and turned toward the door beside us. "That was where I was going if the vaccine didn't kill me first."

The entire building shook violently, throwing us both off balance. I caught myself against the wall, and Jackson fell weakly to his knees.

"Can you open the door?" I asked.

"No," he breathed. "It is retina coded." A dull, but sure sound began building in the hallways. I could not see anything, but I could hear screams of people coming from all directions. I looked at Jackson, the blood draining from my face. Those were the screams of the diseased.

"The doors must all be unlocked," He said with trembling words. "The Esurio has been released from their cells."

Gunshots rang out in the halls.

"Try the door, Ausley," Jackson demanded as he dragged himself up the wall to an upright position. I hit the keypad with my fist, not knowing anything else to do, and the door slid open.

"Go inside quickly now," Jackson whispered. "We have very little time before one of those animals finds us. If this door was open, they are all open."

I slipped through the door, out into the hallway, tugging Jackson behind me. A woman came running just as we were nearly in, but the door closed behind us before she could come through. It severed two of her fingers, which fell to the floor inside the room. Outside she screamed.

“Now where?” Jackson said, his voice barely audible. He mumbled feverishly. “We have to get in there, right? Into the control center? Is that it? Is that what you told me?”

I looked at the next door. Heavy and closed.

“The control center to the Machine is behind that door,” Jackson said. “I've seen them go in there.”

He stepped to a panel in the wall and pushed against the lower right corner of the panel. It opened, revealing a black gun. I was suddenly even more thankful he had been a guard in this facility.

"He said to wait until the light failed," I said, my voice shaking despite the heat within the small room, "and then we go inside."

I stood unblinking watching the large metal doors to the control room, afraid to appear uncertain. Jackson's turned around, his back touching my back, to face the door we came in. We heard a hard thudding on the door to the hallway. It was the woman. She was still out there, banging again and again on the door.

“Is the door locked again?” I questioned with hope.

“No,” Jackson said. “She just hasn't figured out how to open it yet.”

"Ausley, they already know we are here. The soldiers are watching us. We have maybe fifteen seconds before we are surrounded."

"It doesn't matter," I said trembling, absently placing my palm flat on my belly. "It will work. Mikahel said it would."

I heard his voice again, deep within my bones as though he was standing here speaking to me once more.

I am he who stands guard over your people. I am he who has been sent. I come with the sword of the Man of Words who keeps all whose names are written upon his bones.

Suddenly the lights flickered above us.

"Yes!" I said out loud, getting into a ready position, sweat pouring down my brow. "As soon as the power shuts down, we run for the doors. We must get inside to turn the Machine off."

"They will have a back-up power grid."

"Not if the Caldron explodes," I added quickly.

Suddenly Jackson became rigid.

"They're here."

In one fluid motion, he flung the gun around in front of him facing the coming tide, as the hallway filled with soldiers running at record speeds. Their eyes blazing blue with hatred.

Jackson wasted no time, but began to fire, over and over, still it made no difference. They did not fall nor stumble.

"They are the Trestrengets," he said just as the hallway went black.

He pushed me forward with one hand while the other kept the gun trained forward in a repetitive onslaught of worthless bullets. Though we both knew the bullets were pointless, he kept shooting. When death is coming for you, pointless seems better than nothing, so he fired again and again as we ran straight toward the metal doors.

"How can we open them?" Jackson words were rushed with panic. "What did say Mikahel about doors that weigh more than an elephant?"

Without answering I did just as Mikahel had said to do. I stepped forward and closed my eyes as I placed my lips on the crack where the two doors merged tightly together. Slowly, I repeated the words Mikahel had given me.

"Noten laYaef Koch ul'eyn oniym atz'mah yarbeh."

The steel doors did not move. They did not blow up or inch slowly open. They simply disappeared as though they had never been there. I fell forward, catching myself with my hands as my knees hit the cold tile floor.

Before the questions could form in my mind, before I could doubt what was happening right in front of my eyes, fear drove me back to my feet.

"Go!" Jackson yelled, strength returning to his voice.

He turned his flashlight forward, illuminating the scene before us. The light showed us what we had not expected. Instead of an ordered system of controls, we found a pile of mechanical chaos. Wires, lights, and knobs had disintegrated into a smear of melted metal and plastic. The entire room had been sliced away as though a sword had cut it down.

"Something tore it all apart," Jackson said in awe.

The stomping sound of boots were almost upon us.

"That means the Machine is off!" I screamed. "Are they waking up?"

I looked through the observation window but saw only darkness in the room. I knew what lay on the other side of this window and it made me sick to think of it.

"Take that door," Jackson motioned forward with his light. "It leads down a set of stairs to the ground floor of the—"

Before he could finish a man slammed a heavy fist into Jackson's already swollen face, just as emergency lights flickered to life around us. Suddenly a large bang that shook the entire room sounded over the voices of the slower soldiers who roared toward us.

"The doors are working!" I cried out, but Jackson was covered by the soldier's giant body. I looked around the room for a weapon and found a small AR screen. I crashed it over the soldier's head, shattering the glass, but it didn't slow his assault on Jackson.

"Get off of him!" I cried several times. The young soldier looked up briefly at me, and I saw his blue eyes. Empty, inhuman blue eyes. Fear ran down me, and I remembered Jackson's words.

"You can't fell them. They will not die!"

Jackson took full advantage of the soldier's momentary distraction, flipping his gun and firing at the soldier point blank three times in the face. The power of the bullet's pushed the man backward and he fell sideways enough that Jackson freed his legs.

"Down the stairs, Ausley." Jackson worked quickly to rid his face of the blood of the soldier which he wiped onto his shirt sleeves.

As my feet hit the stairs I heard from behind us, the deep groaning of the soldier. Instinctively, I placed one hand under the roundness of my belly while the other one held tight to the railing. Sounds of mayhem spread through the massive bay of the Machine. Waves of nausea passed over me as the memory of that forsaken Machine surfaced like acid burning away at my bravery. Bodies, Simulacrum bodies, hanging like grapes on the vine, like cattle in a slaughter house, on a giant machine with black, arms that stretched out like branches of a massive, metal tree. The Machine kept my people alive, but only enough to drain them daily of their blood as they slept in a comatose state.

By the emergency lights, we could see that the arms of the metal tree from which the Simulacrum had hung in clusters as though they were grapes had lowered and were now heaped onto the ground. Suddenly, an explosion burst out from the far-right side of the crumpled machine. We heard screams as the fire spread through the large bay.

"They are burning!" Jackson screamed, but he didn't have to say it. Several men and women were still connected to the machine through the tubes that ran in their veins, and they were now on fire.

Heat was building throughout the facility. Naked bodies hung and stacked in heaps all around us, coming slowly awake.

"There's no way to get all of these people out!" I felt the room closing in around me as cries and screams became louder.

"Ausley!" Jackson shouted, getting right in my face and shaking me. "Get them unhooked. One at a time. Get them unhooked!"

"Why is it catching fire?" I shook as another explosion went off in the room. Smoke and cinders began to fill my lungs, drowning me in fire and the sounds of dying men.

"Ausley!" Jackson pulled me close to him and this time he spoke directly into my ear. "You have to move. Remember you carry our baby inside of you. Get as many people out as you can. Unhook them."

My hands flew to my belly as my mind grasped the scene around me. There right in front of me, was a woman, tangled up in tubes and wires, her breast being beaten by the metal she kept slamming herself into as she franticly worked to be free.

Without another word, Jackson released me, and I ran to her. I worked to free her mouth from the black contraption that had been shoved down her throat. Pulling quickly but gently as I could, I worked to pull the tube from her esophagus.

When it came out, she began to scream.

The metal hooks that had encircled her waist, chest, neck and head were open. Once she was freed from the contraption in her mouth, she ripped forward, pulling out the tubes from her veins.

She had no hair and was grotesquely thin, but her eyes were open, hyperaware, like an animal who had just been freed from the slaughter house.

"We have to get the others. Pull this out," I said to her, holding up the contraption which only seconds ago was down her throat. "Pull it out, and then they can get themselves free."

We began working, side by side. She was naked and bald, a living skeleton, but her hands worked as fast as my heart was beating.

I worked down the line, freeing peope and giving them the same instructions I had given to the first woman. They all worked with the similar rabid fierceness of an animal scratching free from an iron cage.

Then a man, ablaze with fire came running behind me, his screams cutting through my heart as I turned to face him. He fell just before he reached me, and the rancid smell of his burning flesh made me vomit onto the floor. Wiping my mouth with my sleeve I stared at the body.

I forced myself to turn back to a boy still hanging on the Machine behind me. He was no larger than four feet and was jerking frantically at the tube in his mouth.

"Here," I said. "Let me help!"

My hands matched his fervent pace as I pulled the mouth piece out. The boy gulped in air, blowing out a mucus from his nose. I realized their nostrils were probably all plugged. The thing in their mouths was breathing for them. With the machine off, they would suffocate if we didn't get to them. I turned around, seeing flailing bodies, hung by metal hooks. Arms worked to free themselves, legs kicked as though to get above water. How many could we get out before they all suffocated? How many?

The heat was becoming unbearable.

"You must help the others," I said to the boy who nodded back to me.

"I will," he said and took two steps before staggering and falling by the charred body of the burned man. I ran to the boy and lifted him.

"You have to be strong now," I said just as a familiar sound of horror ripped through the smoky air.

"No!" I whispered.

"What?" said the boy. But there was no time to explain.

"It's coming!" I screamed, pulling the boy to his feet. Tearing the ground with it's clawed feet I saw the shadow of the beast burst forth from the flames with a roar of teeth and claws. The rolling sound of its feral purr ripping from the back of its jaws. I pulled the boy close to me. We could not fight this thing nor outrun it. I remembered running from it in the basement of BaVil.

It is a hunter. And we are its prey.

As it came toward us screaming, I hoped that it would be quick in its purpose. It's head flew forward, exposing rows and rows of fangs, arching it's thick jaws toward us. I closed my eyes and breathed my last just as the beast flung it's teeth into the charred body at our feet. It began tearing flesh, picking up the body over and over and slamming it to the ground as it worked to consume the man. With its clawed foot he stepped on the man's skull, crushing it, revealing a liquid mass of tissue that spilled out onto the ground.

Ash, blood, and flesh filled the air as I turned the boy around and broke into a full out run, pulling him after me. Crowds of survivors collected in the center of the room, close to the Machine. We were being surrounded by the beasts. They were circling, picking weak ones off, one by one. Still we worked to free our people. Our mothers, our fathers, our sisters, brothers and children. They hung naked and exposed all around us.

To my right I watched as a woman covered herself just before a beast smashed her to the ground, pulling skin from her bare back as he took the life from her body. The sounds of mortal agony began to chime in my ears over and over as they were announcing the death of us all.

"How do we get out?" asked a man, thin as a walking skeleton. He grabbed my shirt as though he could pull the answer from me.

"Get out?" I said. "Yes, we have to get out."

I remembered the plan. I remembered the way.

"Follow me. We must work toward the north side of the bay, there is a way that leads out."

"We will be eaten alive before we make it" cried another skeletal man. The fire was also spreading with each passing second, surrounding us as a hedge of heat.

Quickly I held out my tseeyen, and I saw four shining spheres lying as flat as a tattoo around my mark.

Their wings will cover your people.

"Give me your hand," I commanded, and the man held it out.

From my arm a silver sphere materialized and rolled from my palm into his.

"There are four," I said quickly, moving to the woman next to him and then on to the next man. "You four must go to the four corners of this group of people. To the north, south, east and west. As long as you do that, these will protect us."

"How?" asked a woman who had been badly burned on one side of her face. "How will they protect us?"

"I don't know," I said, "But you must stay on the outside of the group like the four points of the compass."

The sound of running animals made our eyes grow wide. We were being encircled.

"Now!" I said, as Jackson approached us. "Put the children to the inside." I ran to the front of the group, standing with the man who held the first silver sphere. "Hold it out as we go."

We began forward, through the smoke and heat, grabbing the Simulacrum who were awake and pushing them to the center of our group as we passed. The silver spheres, somehow given to me by Mikahel, opened into a wide sphere of blue energy. The light of the sphere spread out before us, stretching until it reached the light of the next sphere, until we were enclosed in the hedge of silver-blue light, radiating from the four points of the compass.

"It's a wall of light," I said, as we ran, grabbing children and pulling them forward.

When one stumbled and fell, another would pull them back up. We moved together. Bones of people who once were Simulacrum men and woman.

Working together, we moved through the large bay. And though we were a great crowd, all that I could see was the faces of those we could not reach. Mothers, fathers, aunts, uncles, grandmothers, grandfathers, daughters, sons, and lovers hung lifeless, with nothing to cover their nakedness all around the room. We, the living, were inside a large tomb.

From the left came one of the giant beasts that had chased me so long ago in the basement of BaVil. A collective gasp came from our herd as the beast gained speed and slammed into the blue light and disintegrated. It happened almost too fast to fully see. Over and over again, beasts ran toward us, exploding into a mass of tissue, claws and skin on impact with the light.

"Keep moving!" It was Jackson, from the back of the crowd who urged us forward. I focused myself and led them forward toward the north side of the bay where large metal doors stood open before us.

I wondered who opened the doors just as we passed through, but only seconds passed before the answer appeared before us all. A single woman stood there. Red emergency lights cast an ill shadow across the blue of her eyes, turning them magenta in the dark.

"You cannot leave," said the woman.

"There is no way out for your kind," said a second voice, just as a man appeared. He had not been present before he spoke but as his voice came forth, so did he. Both he and the woman were dressed in long flowing black robes. But where their feet should have been, a black, oozing smoke came billowing across the floor, spreading toward us as though they were tentacles seeking flesh. Many in the group began dry heaving.

Jackson, who now stood slightly in front of me, spun the gun around and fired, but only a single bullet left the chamber. As the bullet went through the air the man held up his hand and stopped it midair just before he threw it to the ground with the flick of his palm.

"Oh, winnowed and threshed ones, have you not understood the day in which you live? The sun has set upon your kind, and the dawn of the long night has finally come," said the woman, her voice stretching out and strangling the hope from our hearts.

"We will drink from your veins. Every last one of you shall be drained to give us life."

The man let his hood fall back, revealing not a man but a young teenage boy.

"We have filled these vessels, and now you will give us the lifeblood to raise them up."

"Raise them?" whispered a young girl behind me. "Are they dead things?"

The woman jerked her head toward the sound of the girl's voice.

"The fear is intoxicating," she said and let her head fall back as her mouth errupted into a horrid smile that stretched across her face. She trembled with pleasure before us, and her words dripped from her greedy lips. "Let me taste of the richness of the fear in your blood. It will hurt, but it always does." She slunk toward us.

Fear threatened to disable me. We all felt it gripping us, as deer caught in the headlights of a car. I wanted to move but found I could not move. As she moved toward us, another figure appeared. Then another, and then another, and still more appeared out of thin air until ten black-robed men and woman stood before us.

"Let us drink the blood of the Simulacrum," said the teenage boy.

Screams of fear broke the silence in the hallway. I turned, and saw the open doors shutting behind us, the bay that held so many more of my people, now ablaze with fire. Before us another set of doors stood firmly shut. We were locked in. We had been driven into this area as cattle to the slaughterhouse.

The woman was behind me before I even felt her pass. As though she were but a shadow, she slipped behind me. The girl who had been behind me screamed as the black robe fell across her, taking her to the ground. The smell of blood filled the room and the ten shadows screeched with pleasure as they each brandished a cup from which to drink.

Jackson grabbed my arm, pulling me forward.

"Open those doors!" he demanded as he pulled me forward away from the midst of shadow. My mind was just as clouded as the air around us.

"Use the words, Ausley," he said again. But he felt so very far away.

Was this even happening? Suddenly I felt as though I was simply in a dream. In a horrible, nightmare of a dream.

He took his hand and pushed me toward the door.

"Say the words, Ausley! Remember?"

But I didn't. I didn't remember at all. A shadow filled my mind. And all I could see was darkness.

"What were those words?" Jackson said as more screaming sounded in the hallway, "Noten ..." Jackson faltered. "Ahhh!" he hit the door again. "Ausley!" What were the words? You must wake up!"

I placed my hot forehead on the cool of the door and the words poured into my mind and out of my lips.

"Noten laYaef Koch ul'eyn oniym atz'mah yarbeh." I fell to my knees as my mind came free of the strangled fear.

"Run!" Jackson commanded to the group who was pushing their way around the shadowed ones. "Run!"

Adair 4:2

The sound of war drums is so loud that all my other senses fail to react. Only the smell of smoke and fire calls me to attention. The trees are all on fire. I stand in a forest of burning trees. I have been here before.

Red Oaks is on fire.

People are standing beneath the falling limbs, they are falling to their knees as they try to breathe through the smoke. Cinders fall and burn their clothes and hair.

"Get away from the trees," I scream to those nearest to me, "We must stay together. We must work together if we are to survive!"

I run forward, trying to move the people toward the riverbank. They are confused, scared, and too overwhelmed to understand me. Their cheeks are hollow, and they look as though at any moment they will fall down from exhaustion and hunger.

The fire bursts into heavier flames as a tree comes down.

We scatter and run.

"Come," I call, "Follow me! Do not stand and let the fires burn you! Run to the River!"

At the edge of the water a little girl grabs my hand. Tears stream down her eyes as she cries.

"I can't swim, I can't. I will drown!"

I lean down and pull her into my arms as I wade in deeper.

"It doesn't matter little one," I say.

Behind us, the fire is taking Red Oaks under it's powerful flames. I kiss her forehead just before we go under.

"The true evil is not the drowning, the true evil is getting out of the water."

"Here, drink some water."

Miss Rosa held the bucket up, offering me the ladle.

"It sure is hot out here. And that smell ..."

Though it had to be nearly noon, the sun was just now rising over the east side of the wall. The smell of smoke still burned through the air from the fires in the fields. And in the distance, I could see the strings of lights that marked where the wall was still being built.

"Drink up!" Miss Rosa insisted with guarded eyes. She turned to a young soldier who was watching us. "You look about as worthless as nipples on a boar hog standing there watching me give out water; don't you have something productive to do? Or are you just supposed to sitting on your hind side and watching the grass grow?" The young man turned red with shame.

Good.

Early this morning or maybe late last night, we had been forced from the Big House to work on the wall, just as Inman had promised. Several soldiers had apologized to Phineas, and he had taken it all in stride. Even though I knew Phineas was in survival mode, I could not even feign humor.

I was sick to my stomach that we had been locked inside all night. Locked up in my own home, by my own people. Now we had been dragged out like prisoners. I found myself struggling with a nagging truth that had always been at the core of me. Mother might have considered it unkind, and Ausley would have considered it cruel, but maybe Daddy would have understood. I loved our people, our laws, and our way of life as a whole, but sometimes the individuals drove me absolutely crazy. How could they follow a man like Inman? How?

Phineas reached for the ladle and drank. He looked at me, an unspoken apology in his eyes. He squeezed my hand and as we parted, and I couldn't help but notice how calloused his hand was against my own. I took another drink and took the moment to search around us, for I still had not seen Mattie this morning.

"Hey, give us a hand over here," Phineas called to the man to help lift another tree trunk onto the tractor that would drag it down to the sawmill. The soldier tossed his gun across his back and ran to give assistance.

Rosa took full advantage of the moment.

"Inman met with everyone last night while y'all were locked away like prisoners in Veralee's bedroom," she whispered to me. "Dirty scoundrel. He gave a dramatic speech about the Council and how it had been oppressing the people. Then he told us that the vaccine was too late in many parts of the world, and that authorities are estimating that three billion people have already died."

"Three billion?" I whispered in wonder.

"The cities are devastated, and the people are desperate for food and resources," she continued. "There has been a lot of rioting and mob violence. Most cities have set curfews, and many of the sick are being shot where they stand. Martial law has been declared. The president himself has died."

"What?"

"Martial law has been declared, not just here, but everywhere. And now, the nine nations have decided to resurrect the United Nations under some kind of Security Council to help distribute food. With the decreased daylight, crops are failing all over the world. People, entire cities are starving to death. On top of that, soldiers from the army are moving through the cities killing those who are diseased and capturing anyone who is not, and—

"You need to stay hydrated out here." Rosa straightened up, speaking to me in a louder voice, as a woman named Stephanie passed by.

Then tears crested from Rosa's eyes and slid down both cheeks. She grabbed my hand, and I felt desperation in her tseeyen. Instinctively I twisted my arm and placed her tseeyen on my own. The connection was instant.

"Lignum Vitae," she said.

I did not answer.

My mother's best friend moved closer to me.

"Adair," she said with iron in her raspy voice, "I said, 'Lignum Vitae'!"

The girl named Stephanie came back to us, smiled, and leaned in.

"Lignum Vitae," she said to us.

My grandmother had always said that inside of words was the power of death and life. Words can kill, or they can birth life, and in that moment, I felt life spark in the womb of my spirit. Not everyone was with Inman. Not all believed his lies. There was a remnant still!

"Et Sanguis est essentia!" I answered.

The blood is the essence. The blood is the essence!

As Stephanie walked away I had the keen feeling that I had another sister.

Rosa felt our time slipping away.

"The National Department of Health says every citizen not infected with the virus must take the vaccine," she said hurriedly. "You can't do anything if you haven't had it. They are so paranoid about the infection that they've decreed that you cannot even buy a loaf of bread without it!"

“How do they know who has taken—” then I remembered Inman in the library.

“Their eyes, Adair, and then there's the fingers,” she said. “Once they have had the vaccine they have the oddest colored eyes and six fingers on each hand. BaVil is head of the program. Some states have even closed their borders to keep people out from other states! California, New York, and Texas were the first. Even Alabama and Georgia are expected to follow suit. Can you imagine? Closed borders between our own United States?" Her face showed the stress in her voice. "The whole world is on fire, Adair. And I still don't know where my son has gone!"

"Listen to me," I grabbed her hand, my belly suddenly full of hope. "The blood is the essence, Miss Rosa! Jackson will come home!" I realized that I could be wrong, but right now we both needed to believe. "But we have to take care of Red Oaks right now.”

“If you do anything he might kill you,” Rosa said, her eyes full of fear.

“Maybe Inman has given me more freedom than I realized.”

“What?”

“Have you seen Mattie?" I had no time to explain.

"She is with Semira,” Rosa said. “I ran into them walking around the land not twenty minutes ago, but don't worry. She is not afraid. And she knows what it means to be the Guardian."

"Why is everyone listening to him, Miss Rosa?" I asked, realizing we had little time.

"They're scared, Adair," she said, propping the water bucket on her hip, "and fear is a fierce motivator."

"Adair," his voice startled us both.

It was Eliezer. His sleeves were rolled up, and with the rising sun, I could see the sweat and dirt that lined the fine wrinkles on his face.

"The LRADs are going to work. In a few days we will be on the other side of this battle and then—"

"Then what, Eliezer?" I said shaking my head. "Our entire way of life is being rewritten."

"I know, Adair," he said. "I have lived many years and experienced too many wars. But after the wars, well, what was uprooted will be replanted. Take heart, LawGiver, you and I both know the truth. No matter what Inman says, we need only to outlast the Friguscor and the Aluid, and then get our people to the door. All of this will soon be forgotten."

He took two steps closer as though he was pleading with me to understand.

"You see, the enemy is crouching at the door, Adair, waiting to devour us all. We must keep our perspective; the little decisions we make right now don't matter, all that matters is where we are going. We must survive, all we can do now is survive. And that is what I am going to help our people do."

"Eliezer, do you honestly not see?" I countered.

He leaned back, doubt filling every open space between us, and folded his arms.

"The enemy is no longer outside the door," I said, pointing back to the wall. "The enemy is within! We have become our own enemy. We have allowed the Friguscor inside our walls, we have cut down our trees and we have slept in the bed with—"

"I have not slept in anyone's bed!" he said, his face suddenly flushed with visible anger.

"No," that's not what I had meant, "I—"

But he was gone before I could finish.

Issachar was standing nearby with a shovel in his hand. His white hair stood on end. Dirt, leaves, and other debris were intertwined in his curled locks. For the first time in my remembrance he looked tired. He was the caterpillar, forever wise and never tiring of his days, but as I looked into his eyes, I saw a cocoon of weariness wrapping around him.

"LawGiver," he bowed his head with the genteel respect of manners long forgotten.

"Issachar," I said. "Agatha and Joab—they still hang on the wall. They have been left to ..." I felt a wave of nausea roll over my body. "They will not take them down."

"Ah," he nodded as he bent to lift another log and toss it in the wagon. He patted at his vest, in search of something in his pocket. The smell of smoke rose from his clothes.

"Did you work in the smoke from the fields?" I said with genuine concern, wiping a tear from my cheek.

"No," he sighed. "They put those fires out yesterday. They are burning the bodies of the Friguscor now."

"Oh," suddenly the smell of the air felt like a betrayal. Red Oaks, my home, smelled like the death of the Friguscor.

"Dear child," he said, "you were made the LawGiver for days just like these. Do not forget that the Eiani in you is stronger than the evil in him."

My eyes rose to meet him. His face was stern but kind.

"You and your daughter have a duty still. Do not forget who you are. You are the granddaughter of Richard, the daughter of Gail and the sister of Veralee. You were born with a battle cry in your bones; do not let fear drown it out."

"What can I do? Look around, Issachar. We have lost everything," I felt the tears dripping down my face. "My own people have become my enemies."

Issachar rested his weight on the shovel.

"That seems to me only a matter of perspective. The only thing that is ever truly lost is that which can burn away," he smiled. "So, why fear what can kill the body when it is only that which cannot burn that matters in the end."

Veralee 4:3

From the base of a stone staircase, I watched the waking of the morning sun. A single ray floated down and touched my cheek, and I felt the promise within it. I breathed in the taste of morning fog on my tongue. Ten marble statues, five on each side, lined the stone steps. Marble shrouds covered their faded faces as women in mourning for the dead. Frozen in a state of permanent duty, their arms were outstretched, holding lanterns for the weary travelers below.

"The Lantern Maidens," I said in wonder. "I have been here before. But look, they all have fire in their lanterns." The first time I saw them, when we traveled to meet the Archaon at the Orginal City, only one lantern still burned. Ausley and I had fallen into the water while looking at them...

"The fire burns to light the way," Decimus said, moving forward. "Take care to watch your step. These are last of the voices of the Original Men. Forgotten words from a forgotten time."

"Voices?" I shook my head ready to question him but as we made it past the first two statues. A myriad of voices all speaking at the same time began to whisper all around me. The voices were not in sync but were more like cross-winds of words and thoughts.

"The hour of midnight," said one.

"There will not be enough,"said another, as the light within the lanterns flickered.

"Not enough for both you and me, the hour of midnight," another and another voice spoke until all were in chorus.

"There will not be enough for both me and you--the hour of midnight--there will not be enough..."

I stopped and looked into the face of the shrouded woman above me. She seemed to be crying cold, stone tears. My fingers felt her cold, lifeless bare feet.

"She mourns all that has been lost," I said. Suddenly I felt I understood the stone woman. "She mourns not only for the past, but for the future yet to come. She wears the shroud for the death of the world she knows."

Below her feet was an inscription roughly carved into the stone in the old language.

Though night and darkness cover all, an oath of light each will bear.

'Til man's account on earth is cast, a shroud of mourning will they wear.

If the gleaming light they lose, upon their hands be placed the blood.

For from this day they bear the charge, their light to shine through fire or flood.

Decimus put a hand on my shoulder, and I screamed.

"Peace," he said. "They are but empty voices now. See, the light grows weak with each passing day."

"Why are they losing the light?"

"The firstborn, the Primogenes, tell us that the light was bright when they first arrived, but slowly, each one is dimming. Who has understanding for such things? Now, please, we must tarry no longer."

Once we reached the top we came to a large courtyard which we crossed at great speed. I found myself half running to keep the grueling pace of Decimus. I remembered that Atticus spoke of Decimus as the greatest soldier he had ever known. We paused before large, double wooden doors, framed in intertwined patterns of stone and wood. The doors themselves were decorated by the simplicity of the natural color and movement of the wood. In the flow of the bark I could read the history of the tree itself. In those rings and lines, I saw stories of days long passed but never forgotten. Decimus opened them easily, and we passed through.

The doors led to a hall of unsurpassed height and great width. To my great delight and surprise, there was a crystal-clear River running through it.

Boats, made of the same wood as the doors, waited patiently for riders at the edge of the great marble entrance. The symbol of the wheel within the wheel was etched into the marble in gold and crimson red.

"This is just like the floor of the Sacred Oaks, where the Council sits at the stone table," I said to Decimus. "Is this the same River that runs through the Sacred Oaks of the Terebinths of Mamre?"

"Yes, this is the place of the Sacred Oaks," he said, helping me into the boat. "Here is where the council meets."

"This is the place? The Sacred Oaks?"

I glanced at the floor and realized this was the very floor on which I had stood when I had been banished. When we came through the doors, we must have come into the Terebinths. We must be somewhere down the River from where Jeremiah, Atticus, Thenie, and Ernest were at this very moment, just at a different point in time. This must be the city where Atticus and I walked with Mother and Adair to meet the Archaon—the abandoned city of the Original Men. And years from now—I had no idea when—this floor would be moved to become the meeting of the Council for the Simulacrum where the stone table of judgement sat.

A large flock of white birds flew through the openings in the buttressed ceiling. The braces were made of gold, bronze and copper. They connected to large tree trunks which served as the pillars on the right and left side of the walls, creating a perfect balance between nature and the architecture. Beautiful birds of all colors and types swooped down, landing on the crystal water. Gold lights floated high in the air, though I couldn't tell how they were suspended. I also could not tell what the windows were. They were perfectly clear but projected every color of the rainbow as the light poured through them. The air was crisp and full of comfort and serenity. My body relaxed, my mind slipped into a moment of complete awe that I had not felt since the first time I stepped through the gate and entered the beauty of the Terebinths. Or was this the first time?

Decimus stood, and using a long pole, piloted us through the water. Several boats carrying people passed by our right and left. The people smiled and waved, filling the open void that had been opened in my heart the day I had left Red Oaks.

"This feels like home," I sighed as I sat down lower in the boat. All thoughts and worries slipped from my mind. My shields came down, and my eyes grew heavy. I fell asleep and dreamt of ... nothing. I simply slept as I had not slept in my entire life.

When I awoke, Decimus was carrying me in his arms like a small child.

"You are awake," he said and respectfully set me down. We stood before yet another closed door as he added, "I trust you slept with peace."

I was at a loss for words. My body felt as though it had been massaged by a month of sleep. It was so refreshing that I did not even care to be embarrassed that I had fallen asleep and Decimus had to carry me.

"Yes. Thank you."

"We are here," he motioned to the door, "but I brought this for you." He reached in his pocket and pulled out a fruit I knew well.

I marveled at the fruit once again. Basar trees existed only within the Terebinths. This fruit had the power to replenish bones, heal worn muscles, and sooth aching joints.

"I fill my stomach with them while I am inside. It minimizes the amount of food I need on the outside," Decimus noted as I ate.

As I tucked the fruit into my pocket, the thought hit me. For these past months, Atticus and I had needed only small amounts of food.

"You mean this fruit keeps us fed outside of the Terebinths?"

"Of course," he said, smiling. "When you eat of the fruit of the Basar tree, here in the Terebinths, it is the food of the eternal. Not as the food in the temporal world which feeds only for the moment, the Basar Tree feeds outside of time. Whenever I'm outside and they offer me food, I smile and simply tell them, 'I have food you know nothing about.'"

I realized suddenly that I had been famished. But just as Decimus said, as I ate the last bit of the deep richness of the basar, I was completely satisfied.

We stood in a wide hallway. To my right was a stone wall. To my left, and as far as I could see around the curved hall, were open archways to the forest outside. Each archway was supported by large oaks trees that grew across the gold and silver ceiling.

"Shall we?" Decimus asked, and I nodded my consent.

I took a deep breath and made my back as straight as Mother's. If I was to meet the Council, I would meet them with the dignity she would have required.

Decimus swung the oak door open.

The enchantment of the room surrounded me. The floor of large, rectangle stones of amazonite marble cast a bluish haze across the room, like the early morning mist on the fields of Red Oaks. Before me, instead of a wall, the room was open to the outdoors. Starting inside the room, in parallel lines, was a row of trees so deep that I could not see where they ended. White foliage created a dense canopy, forming a backdrop for lanterns of all shapes and sizes. They cast a magical spell of bright, beautiful light in every direction. Tables of all shapes and sizes were scattered around the room on which sat various bowls of different materials and colors. The bowls were filled with seeds of every shape, size and color which gave them the appearance of precious stones. It was like being inside a jeweler's workshop.

A man came walking toward me from between the trees. On his right side, he held the hand of a young boy.

"Where is the Council?" I asked Decimus. "and why are there so many bowls of seeds?"

"I was not instructed to bring you to the Council but to the one who owns the seeds," He motioned to the man who was coming closer. Decimus guided me forward with a gentle hand.

"But you said you were bringing me to the Council," I half whispered. Decimus seemed cautious, so I followed suit.

"There are many ears in the city. I have brought you to the one who brought me to the city not long ago."

Decimus gave a small bow that I felt inclined to follow but was not quick enough to carry out. So, all I gave the man and his son was an awkward nod as they stopped just before the forest ended and the room began.

"Welcome, Daughter of the Blood," said the man pleasantly. He was of average height, dark, with a neatly kept beard and shortly trimmed hair. His clothes matched the ease of his face. He, like his tunic and pants, were simple, with nothing remarkable in texture or design. He dipped his head in greeting.

"I am Olam."

"I am Veralee Harper of Red Oaks."

"Yes," Olam nodded, "we know. You have come far, to see and find tabun, understanding. We see Decimus has brought you safely. He is a gifted darash, a seeker. Chosen for his ability to search and find what he seeks."

"A darash? That is your job?"

"I was brought to the city for that purpose," he assented.

"Brought? But you said you were from—"

"I am from Rome, but I have lived in Jerusalem since my father, the Precept, took office under the orders of Emperor Tiberius. And though my family does not know it, at the last full moon," Decimus held his hand out to the man and the young boy, "Olam found me and gave me his blood."

"You are Boged!"

"Beged? No, I am not Beged," Decimus shook his head quickly. With reverent loyalty, he gestured to the young boy. "This, Veralee of Red Oaks, is Beged."

My eyes most have shown the shock which lay just beneath my skin, for the boy watched my face with the patience of a much older man.

"You, you are Beged?" I asked carefully. "But you are a child."

I thought of Nathan, who was about his same age.

"I am," said the boy.

I looked from Olam to Beged.

"Olam, are you the one who gave the blood to Decimus?"

"No," he said, confirming, "it is Beged who came to share his blood with the Friguscor."

"But, I thought, Olam, that you were one of the Primogenes."

"I am one of the twelve," said Olam, "and Beged, my son, is the child of my bondmate, Mara, who also drank of the Eiani. Sometime after the blood, while we were still in the wilderness, Mara discovered that she was with child. Though I call him my son, Beged is the child of the blood."

A great sound blew through the air, and the lanterns seemed to grow even brighter. One long sound followed by ten shorter ones.

"Come," said Olam, "The Council has gathered." He looked to Decimus. "The hour draws nigh."

Beged turned and began walking north, as though he alone knew the way.

I followed obediently behind him until he said, "Veralee Harper of Red Oaks?"

"Yes," I answered. The boy dropped back to join me as Olam and Decimus walked in front.

"Did you hear the voices of the Maidens as you entered the city?" he asked curiously.

"Yes," I said in wonder. "They spoke in riddles."

"And had no fire," Beged added.

"In my own time, yes, that is true...but why? Why will they lose the fire?"

"They have run out of oil," Beged explained, his voice young and pure. "Without oil, the fire cannot continue. They will need fresh oil."

Beged stopped walking and faced me.

"You are called to gather what is scattered."

My mouth fell open and my eyes grew wide.

"How do you know that?"

"You are the Malachi," he said, putting his hand on mine. "When the Doors fall, and dust returns to dust, you must gather what is scattered so that there will be oil to light the fire in the end."

Beged smiled at me pleasantly and walked on ahead. When the row of trees ended, I recognized where we were. The Maqom. This is where the Archaon and the Original Men had long ago, in a time forgotten, gathered in honor of the One Tree. It was here that I had climbed with Atticus, Mother, and Adair to meet with the Archaon. It was just after the Council meeting where I had been banished from my family and my people for sharing the blood with Nathan. The steps were just as I remembered, cut deep into the mountain on which the giant trees grew at the top.

I caught up with Olam and Decimus.

"Olam," I said carefully, "How old is Beged?"

"Outside the Terebinths, he is the firstborn of children of the Primogenes but inside the Terebinths he has no age. It is as if he is the first and last of all men."

I must have slowed, for Olam walked on ahead of me.

Decimus put a hand on my shoulder, encouraging me forward.

"Trust me," he laughed, "those are the answers I seem to get as well. It is as if he is telling you the truth, plain and simple. And yet, though I try, I cannot understand a word of what he says."

At the top was a palisade of trees, surrounding the great, open space with the single tree growing in the center. Led by Beged, we all followed him through the entrance into the Maqom.

Arrow-straight white oaks formed the inner structure of the large, thick copse. Their many branches circled, scrolled, and laced into daedal patterns that gave the appearance of finely crafted stain-glassed windows and doors. Overhead, the branches shaped an intricate ceiling of sky, stars, and wood. Leaves of gold and white stirred gently with the night breeze, and between them, the stars twinkled like candles at a bonding feast table. At the center of the canopy, the branches framed a near-perfect circle around the brightest star in the sky, which bathed everything below in an ethereal tourmaline hue. But as I looked out, I saw on the horizon between, the hint of the first signs of the new morning which was quickly approaching.

The floor was made of rich copper-colored soil of the earth and as the fingers of the sun stretched out across the sky, it brought out the sweet-smelling vines of white hydrangea, purple wisteria, and yellow jasmine. Statues of the Original Men and the Archaon stood in unity around the circle, greeting the sun with faces of stone as we came to join the Simulacrum who had gathered together. In the center, by the single tree, stood ten men, each wearing a cloak of stunning red.

"Welcome, Olam," said a woman with eyes like the sea in turmoil. She was beautiful, there was no doubting that. Untamed power simmered just beneath her surface. Her skin was the color of the desert sands, and her black hair flowed free about her head and shoulders. I imagined it was akin to the spirit within her. Immediately I wanted to speak with her, to know her name, but there was no time. Olam was speaking.

"We have come at the Council's request."

The Council members did not seat themselves around a table as they would in my own time, but instead stood in a circle facing the sacred tree in the middle, as though it alone were their council and their judge. The mass of gatherers came as close as they dared, careful not to venture into the inner circle. I still wore the burgundy and gold dress of Rome, but suddenly I became self-conscious of my hair, which was surely a rat's nest on top of my head. I worked to smoothe it down, as I caught the eyes of several others around me.

"They do not know you," whispered Decimus. "It is a small community, and you are not known."

I made my neck stand taller, refusing to hide away from the curious gaze of the crowd. I repeated an inner dialogue of comfort

I am Veralee Harper of Red Oaks. I am loved by Atticus and Mother and Daddy. I am loved by Atticus...

Atticus.

Suddenly the thought occurred to me. More forceful than I meant to, I pulled hard on Decimus's sleeve to grab his attention.

"Olam said that you are a darash. He said that you have a gift from the Eiani to find what you seek."

"Yes," he whispered.

"I need you to find something, or someone, actually. Like you found me. I need you to find—"

"Shh," he held up his hand and motioned toward the twelve in the inner circle. They had been speaking in quiet collectiveness but suddenly the man in the center, a short, rugged man, turned to face the crowd. Then, as though it were rehearsed, three more turned out to face the surrounding crowd, leaving eight still facing the tree while four, the north, south, east and west of the circle, faced the crowd.

"We have come to discuss the Esurio that is spreading in the darkness," said the first man.

"Why are we meeting in the night?" asked a beautiful woman, "Why have we been called under the light of fire to such a meeting of secrets?"

"Yes," added another. "Why call us from our beds?"

"We have come to seek wisdom and understanding for the sacred path ahead," said a familiar voice. I searched for the speaker as he said, "To see into tomorrow, for what today will require."

I would know that voice anywhere.

"Absalom," I whispered his name.

He was standing on the other side of me. As I said his name, I was sure he cocked his head to the right as though he had heard something.

"No," Decimus whispered, "he is Avshalom, the Seer. He is gifted by the Eiani with the ability to see into tomorrow and beyond."

Sweat began to bead on my forehead. Could I never get away from this man?

Beged, I noticed stood outside the circle, watching patiently as though he expected them to convene at any moment. I was amazed that a boy of so few years could have such a presence of authority and peace. Though I was no Seer, I knew his future and it hurt just to think of it. One day, far from now, when he would grow to be a man, this Council would offer him up to the Friguscor for the crime of sharing his blood.

Decimus adjusted his weight from one foot to the other. Beged had already changed Decimus. How many others had he changed? How many more would he change before they would condemn him? Before he would fall asleep on the streets of Ariel? I closed my eyes and tried not to think of the stories Atticus had told me.

Atticus. Where was he now? Was he a young boy back in Rome living with his mother and father? For a moment I imagined going to meet him.

I could change him.

"We have gathered on this night because there is a traitor in our midst," announced a man of great age. "There is one among us who has broken the Law of the Simulacrum."

"Broken the Law?" said another woman in shocked surprise. "Who has broken the Law?"

"The Law is our way of life!" cried a man from the crowd of outsiders. "It is our only way to preserve our lives and our only protection in the Friguscor world!"

"It must be honored above all else," sang out a woman, "for my children and my children's children!"

"Who is the traitor?" several others questioned. "Speak the name!"

"Hold your voices," said the woman, and everyone obeyed. "We have no traitor in our midst."

Absalom turned quickly, his long cloak floating eerily in the air.

"Mara, what lies you speak with a double-edged sword. Like the lies you told from the beginning."

"I have spoken no lie!" said Mara with all the fierceness of a woman readying for battle. "From the beginning I have said only the words told to me in my dreams by the Eiani. The words of the One Tree."

"Dreams from the One Tree?" said one of the other twelve. "Why would the One Tree speak to a woman when no man in our group has claimed such an honor as this?"

Mara stood her ground, her passion driving her words as she said, "I did not decide my gender any more than I decided the time of my arrival on this earth. You, Reuven, should know more than most, that it is the will of the Eiani that decides. Was it not you who led us through the desert grounds until we found the blood beneath the One Tree? When we had almost died beneath the beating of the sun above, was it not you that led us on toward the call of the blood? Then, when we could find no entrance, was it not my dream which we followed to find the door? The door in the wilderness that let us into the dimension of world between, where the Tree of Shadows and the One Tree still dwell to this day? It was you who followed the dreams spoken by the Archaon then, so who are you to question them now?"

"The Archaon?" said Reuven derisively. "We have not heard of them since the journey. We have grown old waiting for their promise to once again walk with men to come to fruition. We have called out to them, sought them to the edges of the earth, and yet they remain silent, far away from the daily workings of men.

“No," Reuven shook his head. "We will wait no longer for the help of those who promise what they can never deliver. We must make our own way now. We must secure our borders and protect by way of the Law the life we know to be true."

The resounding voices of agreement concurred around the Maqom.

"And so, we ask once more," Reuven pressed toward Mara. "Who is the father of the boy? Is it your bondmate, Olam?"

Olam stood facing the oak in the center of the circle. He did not bend his head, nor look toward Mara. but stood a statue of confined control. Mara took no glance toward Olam either, but said with great authority, "He is as I have always said, the child of the blood, the child of the Eiani."

"Come, Mara," said Absalom. "Has time not softened your heart? Can you not give Olam the honor he is due? Name him the father and give him the honor of owning true manhood. To father a son is the ultimate achievement. Why steal what you know is his glory and shame him publicly for your own honor?"

"I shame no man by speaking what is pure. Olam knows this to be so. For he has spoken of it before you many times. But it is in secret meetings that you come to accuse my honor, and my child. You doubt the work of the Eiani, because you fear what it means for the control of men."

Another man, standing to the right of Absalom spoke up.

"Is this not the story she has told since the beginning? Why question her now? And why do so publicly?" He raised his hands to the massive crowd around them, "Why shame Mara? She has been with us since the beginning. I say let it go. Why bring this up now, and in such a reprehensible fashion...and in the middle of the night?"

"It is because," Absalom said in a low voice. "The bastard child is the reason the Esurio has appeared."

"What?" the man who had just defended Mara turned quickly to look upon Beged. "What could you mean? He is just a child! How could he possibly be responsible for what is occurring outside?"

"How?" Absalom asked raising his pointed finger at Beged. "Ask him yourself! Let him speak, and let his words defend his actions."

All turned to face the young boy. I wanted to stand beside him, to cover him from their accusations, but he spoke first, his voice calm and smooth.

"Who do you say I am?"

Reuven spoke, "The child of Olam, just like all of the children born after the Wandering Time. You are the son of Olam and Mara."

Beged shook his head once, but I saw his eye hesitate on Mara's face. Mara looked as I felt. Her turmoil was evident though her strength uncompromising. She was afraid, but that did not make her weak, only wise. The tension in the assembly felt like a sword suspended in air. None could know what was coming, but all could feel that no matter the direction this conversation took, it would come through the cutting of the blade.

"And what do you say I have done?" Beged said as though he was speaking of the past, of days long ago and not the controversy still at hand.

It was a new voice that laid the accusation down for all to see as he said.

"He has broken the Law. We know why we have gathered together. As the sun rises to the west, so it rises on the crimes done in the dark."

"Crimes?" Beged turned his face towards his accuser. "What I have done, I have done in the light. Nothing I have done was in the dark, but all that I have done, was done in the light for all to see. I have freely spoken as I do now."

"We cannot even live in the city now," said a voice from the crowds. "The ground beneath you is cursed! The stain of your actions will destroy us all!"

"Speak," Beged said, not raising his voice, nor his countenance, but staying calm as he began. "Speak what you hold against me. Let it be known clearly for all to hear."

The crowd stood suddenly silent, as though they had not the authority to bring the guilty of the accusation forward. It was Absalom who finally spoke. He spoke not in heat or anger, but in a cool contemplative voice that hinted of great patience and wisdom.

"Beged, you have been brought here to stand before the Council and the Simulacrum to speak your defense."

"I cannot give a defense for no charge has been laid before my feet," Beged answered.

Absalom sighed as though it pained him to speak the thing against the boy and yet somehow, he found it in himself to continue. I watched the boy as Absalom spoke the words that seemed to hang in the air, and float around us all.

"Beged," said Absalom, his voice low and groaning, "you have broken the Law. The Sacred Law of the Simulacrum. You have given your blood to the Friguscor, placing our way of life and all of our people in grave danger."

Beged raised his head and looked into Absalom's face as though he was searching for something there.

"When were you ever promised safety?" Beged asked the crowd but kept his gaze on Absalom.

None answered. All stood silent.

Mara was breathing hard and swallowing back tears that were gathering on her eyes.

"Are you guilty?" Absalom demanded. "Have you broken the Sacred Law?"

Beged said nothing.

"Speak man!" Reuven cried. "and tell us, let us all hear what you have done! Have you broken the Sacred Law of the Eiani?"

Beged spoke, "I have broken no law."

Reuven became irate.

"You deny these accusations? You deny that you have been giving your blood to the Friguscor? You deny this? What then is that?"

He pointed to Decimus, and all turned to stare at the man who stood beside me. I felt the heat roll off of Decimus's body. His breathe became elevated.

"Is that not the Precept's only son?" Reuven said the word Precept as if it were poison. "Are you not the son of the Precept, the son of Rome?"

Decimus looked at Beged who stood silent before his accusers.

"I am," Decimus answered.

Reuven began to shake his head with grand condemnation as he said the words slowly for all to hear.

"And were you not born of the Friguscor blood?"

Decimus looked to Beged again before answering.

"I was."

The crowd around us gasped, but the silent tension remained, electrifying the air and pounding through my veins.

"And was it him," Reuven pointed at Beged as a butcher pointing to the chosen heifer,"Was it him who gave you the blood that changed you?"

Decimus was completely perplexed. His lips moved, but no words came out. His shoulders fell as his eyes closed.

"Was it him?" cried Reuven again. "Speak now!"

The groaning pain was that of a heart torn in two.

"Will you have me speak the condemning words against the one who gave me life?" Decimus asked. "Shall I be forced to speak the words that sentence to death the one who gave me life?"

"Was it him?" cried Reuven, now hysterical with rage.

"Speak!" cried the men of the crowd.

Mara cried out, "Do not do this. Reuven, please!"

The sound of the shouting crowd became overwhelming, the anger built into a kingdom of men who had no king but madness. And Absalom stood silent, watching the mayhem as one shrouded in a protective shadow.

I slipped my hand in Decimus's hand. He looked down at our intertwined hands, and then back at Beged. Beged raised his eyes and nodded at Decimus.

Decimus shook his head.

"No," he whispered, but Beged kept a steady gaze and nodded once more.

Decimus looked at the crowds of men and women, at Mara and then Olam. Olam stood silent, hands folded before him with great sorrow in his eyes. Mara was weeping, her hand over her mouth as though she was stopping herself from crying out.

"Yes," Decimus said, and immediately rage took the crowd. They took hold of the boy, of Beged with rugged hands.

"What are you doing?" screamed Mara. "Let him go!"

But it was chaos, the chaos of men, and there is no thinking, no reason that can break through the chaos of men.

Reuven said, "You have betrayed your own people. You have broken the Sacred Law. So, we will give you to the Precept who is demanding a sacrifice for peace to be made for the disease in the city. They will do what they want with you to appease the disease. And then, with you gone, the disease will again retreat into the shadows. No more will you be spreading the blood into Ariel."

Absalom held up his hands.

"Is this the will of the Council?" he asked.

The Council turned back to the tree.

"Is it the will of the Council that Beged is given over to the Precept of Ariel in order to appease their anger for the disease?" he asked.

"Yes," the word was spoken once, twice, then again, again, again, and again.

"Yes," they agreed.

Mara shook her head, her hands shaking. She ran to her child and fell at his feet as the men pulled the boy back from her. She stood and touched his face. The tears ran down her cheeks freely and she did not try to wipe them away but let them fall on her child as though they were the only thing she had left to give him.

"Beged," she cried, "You are the child of my womb; you are mine."

She touched his face again and again, but he said nothing as she turned back to the Council.

"Do not do this! Please, you have known him all of his life. You have watched him grow into a man. You know him! Please, please, please..."

She did not attempt to stand but turned to find Olam standing with the Council.

"Olam!" she cried out. "Speak! Do not let them do this!"

Olam stepped forward and looked at Beged for a long moment. His sorrow was harder to see than Mara's for it was a torment of a father watching the death of his son. He came near the boy. The men tightened their grip on the boy's arms but there was no need. For Olam did not fight but leaned down and kissed the boy on the head.

"Though you are not the son of my loins, you have been my son from the very beginning," he said to the boy.

Then he turned out to the crowd.

"This is my son, and on this day as in all days, I am well pleased with him."

Then Olam stepped back from the boy and crouched down beside Mara. He grabbed her head gently. There at the feet of their son, he whispered words that none but her could hear. She cried out a long, moaning sound like a woman giving birth. Then he took her and wrapped her in his arms as she shook and convulsed. Beged watched them both, and I saw a single tear roll down his cheek.

Absalom stepped forward from the Council and raised his hands.

"From this day forward, let it be known for the generations to come that your name is wiped from history as Beged, the one who covers. It will now and forever more be Boged, the traitor to the Simulacrum."

"Noooo!" cried Mara.

My face was wet with tears. Decimus grabbed my hand.

"Come," he pulled me toward the moving crowd. "We must stay with him."

My feet were numb, my body did not remember the way down the stairs, nor the walk through the city of the Original men, or how we got back to the row of doors. But suddenly we were there, and the crowd was pulling and pushing the boy through. Only a few hands went through the door with the boy. Most stayed behind in a triumphant crowd of madness.

"I don't want to go," I said as I paused before the door. Knowledge of what was coming caused panic to seize me.

Decimus looked at me.

"I will not leave him."

I nodded. The truth was...I was afraid.

"I don't want to see this. Bring me back!" I cried out. I looked up into the sky but nothing happened. "Let me come back. Please, don't make me watch this."

But as I spoke, the door before me, opened up wider, and I knew that I had to go through.

"Girl," a woman about my size grabbed hold of my shoulder. "Do not go through that Door! You are too young to have blood on your hands. Stay here where it is safe."

"Safe ..." I whispered feeling the bitter word as a bite from a deceiving snake. That word could kill me. It was the answer I had been wanting for so long and now, suddenly, I saw it all so very clearly. Safety is the enemy of my calling. Safety is a lie that promises help while it wraps the noose around my neck.

"When were we ever promised safety?" I stepped through the door into the world of the Friguscor.

When I came through, I was alone. The weight of time pounded down on me like the chains of a prisoner. I took no time to breathe. Instead I ran as fast as I could. Everything around me seemed to blend together into colors, shapes, and places of loss. All that mattered was that I got to him, that I was there to see Beged give his life to the Friguscor. Down the stairs I moved as fast as I could, falling but caring little. Again, and again I got back up and ran until I saw the crowd of people gathered at the bottom of the stairs. Reuven and several others passed me as they ran at full pace back up the stairs. When he saw me, he stopped and pointed upward.

Behind me was a large crowd of Simulacrum, watching from the top of the steps. I turned, and from my vantage point, I saw a man standing in the midst of a hungry crowd. He was bound but he raised his hands up and turned his head toward the sky. A man began whipping him, over and over again, pulling the clothing from his back, leaving his skin exposed as his blood poured down into the street.

"Who is that?" I screamed. "Who is that man?"

I turned and saw Olam standing on the stairs.

"Olam!" I made my way to him, pushing past people. "Who is that man?"

Olam turned and looked at me. "That is Beged."

"Beged?" I shook my head and looked down on the man who was being whipped. "No, Beged was just a child ..."

"No, he was always a man, even at his birth," he said. "You simply saw him as I do. You saw a child, through the eyes of a Father, but they see him as he is. Beged is a man."

"Won't anyone help him?" I pulled on Olam's sleeve. "Why won't you help him?"

Olam raised his hand. "What he does, he does on his own. No man takes his life. He alone gives it."

Olam's lips trembled slightly and then he said, "In his blood is the cure to the Friguscor. Like the doors that bring us to the Terebinths, he is made of the One Tree. He is the Door that our Histories prophesy, and yet, none of us recognized what was right in front of us. Though seeing, we became blind."

"He is the cure?" I looked back at Beged.

He was naked, stripped of his clothing and dignity. I could barely recognize his face. He had been hit by the bite of the whip too many times. The disease. The death of mankind, the hunger that drives the Friguscor to the blood. The one my people called Boged? The one they blamed for spreading the Eusrio throughout the world. The one they called, Boged, the Traitor, for his crimes against us ... He was the cure?

The traitor was the cure.

I heard a man cry out, and it was Beged.

Then as if it were a dance of death, orchestrated before time, Decimus ran toward him, a flight of passion and sunk his teeth into Beged's shoulder.

My heart stopped. What was he doing?

Why, Decimus?

A woman ran behind him and bit him on the back. Then another came to bite his leg. Decimus had started a frenzy. Others came running, craze in their eyes. I closed my eyes, unable to watch or move. I knew the diseased crowd would devour Beged alive.

It was the scream of a voice I knew that caused me to look again on the scene of horror. Decimus raised up from the people and drove a dagger into the heart of Beged, but it was too late. Beged had already fallen.

Blood and water flowed from the wound.

The earth shook momentarily in an earthquake, and the sky was darkened as the sun hid behind storm clouds in the sky. Some of the buildings in the city toppled, but the blood-crazed crowd of people did not stop their advance.

I regained my balance as the shaking stopped and then I, too, ran screaming toward the crowd of people who were charging toward the body of Beged. Several people hit me with elbows and arms, but I pushed through the madness. Children also joined the melee, their eyes crazed for blood.

"Decimus!" I screamed as I ran. "Decimus, they will kill you!"

Somehow, I found him. He was standing at the edge of the crowd, staring at the blade in his hand. Blood covered his body.

When I rushed to him, he held the blade out to me.

"It was all I could do for him," he said. "I could not watch him suffer anymore, Veralee. I could not let him suffer ..."

"We must go, Decimus," I screamed, as the world moved in slow motion around us. "We must get back to the doors.

"Look," I said as I pointed up the stairs. "They are all running to the doors."

"My sister is here," Decimus said, "Zulika. She fell in the blood. I saw her and our slave, Julia. I saw them both. They were already gathered when we arrived. It had all been decided already. They were simply waiting for Reuven to deliver Beged."

Black clouds gathered in the sky. A great wind ripped through the city. A man ran up to me and tried to bite my arm. Decimus swung before he could touch me, and the man fell dead on the ground.

"This is the opening of the Door, Decimus," I screamed, "Beged gave his blood in order to open the Door wide to all of the Boged."

Decimus shook his head.

"The Door?" The word brought Decimus back to reality and he blurted, "I must take you back through to the Terebinths. They will destroy us all if we stay!"

The ground began to shake as more and more Friguscor ran out of their houses and joined the piles of bodies, where at the bottom lay the bones of Beged, the Man of Words, the One Tree. We made it to the stop of the stairs, but as we entered the great hall where the wall of doors stood, we stopped. All of the Simulacrum stood in stunned silence. All of the doors lay flat on the ground.

"The doors," said a woman, "as soon as Beged cried out, they fell flat on the ground."

"We picked them up," said another, "But they are turning to dust and blowing away. "

"The way to the city is shut," screamed another.

"What does it mean?"

"How will we get back?"

"We must get to the ceremonial gates!"

"Run! Run!"

Decimus heard the Friguscor outside and grabbed my hand.

"We must run as well."

But suddenly I felt dizzy and I knew my time was growing short.

"Wait!" I crouched down, resting on my knees and hands.

"I need more time," I whispered.

Decimus called my name. "Veralee, we must run. Now!"

Dust began to swarm around me, slowly and I saw that each particle, each molecule seemed to be connected like strings drawn between the dust. It swooshed and swirled and then I saw a perfectly formed dekeract.

"He told me to gather what was scattered to the wind," I reached down and with each hand, I gathered a single handful of dust and shoved it deep into my pocket, "Olam said these doors were made from the One Tree himself.

"Gather what is scattered."

Decimus pulled me up to my feet.

"Now, Veralee!"

"Decimus," I grabbed his hand, "you will survive this. Your sister Zulika will be changed, and I know what you are supposed to do next."

"Let me help you," Decimus said, trying to pull me, but I was slipping away and his grip on me fell short.

He looked at me, his eyes wide.

"Listen quickly. You are a darash, a seeker. You said it yourself. It is your gift from the Eiani. Go to the army in Rome. Find a man named Atticus. He's a soldier, or he will be. He is called by the Man of Words to be an Ayindalet. A Watcher for the Door. The Simulacrum, they have missed the first door, and it will take years to bring them back, but you must find the Ayindalet. You must find him, and you must give him your blood. He will lead the people to the second Door at the end of this age."

"My blood?" Decimus shook his head. "How?"

"Let him drink your blood as Beged did for you. The Man of Words will find him, and he will help lead the Simulacrum people back to the Door at the end of time."

I was almost gone.

"You must find him, Decimus! You must find Atticus!"

"Atticus? Beged ... he told me this name, but who is he? Who is Atticus?"

I thought of Atticus and felt for the seeds in my pocket that Beged had given me. Suddenly I saw Atticus jumping off the cliff, the Man of Words standing above, watching him fall down into the River.

Without understanding, but knowing the truth, I screamed, "He's the key to me. He is the Ayindalet, the watcher for The Door!" just as I faded beneath the waves of the mighty River.

It begins at the end, for it is the end that begins it all.

Coming Soon...
the Final Beginning,
the end of the Simulacrum Saga

GUARDIANS OF RED OAKS

GATEKEEPER — GUARDIAN OF THE GATE

CHIEF OPOTHLE — EYOTA

GK — GG

LIAM — SEHOY

GG — GK

THENIE — ERNEST

GG — GK

__________ — VERA — WILLIAM

GK — GG

RICHARD — SARAH

GG — GK

GAIL — EDWIN

ADAIR, VERALEE, AUSLEY

Glossary

Simulacrum: (sim-yə-'la-krəm): The people who have the blood of the Eiani inside their veins, making them image-bearers to the One Tree. Latin. Image or representation of something; Image-bearer.

Friguscor: People who have death in their veins. 95% of the world. Latin. Cold-heart.

Boged: Hebrew for traitor; Friguscor people who have Simulacrum hidden in their veins and can be changed into Simulacrum if they receive the blood of the Eiani. The people discovered by Veralee.

Absalom: The Seer for the Simulacrum Council. Hebrew. First meaning my father is peace, grew to mean usurper. Third son of King David.

Abram: Boged freedman of Ernest and Thenie; Helped Vera during the Civil War; father to Moses.

Achiel: Leader of the Archaon for Paraclete; Hebrew. My brother.

Alabaster City: City within the Terebinths were those who have lived past 110 years on earth go to retire until the opening of the final door.

Agatha: Once sat as the Discerner for the Simulacrum Council. Owner of the bookstore in Montgomery.

Albert: Follows Veralee and Atticus through the streets and helps them escape the beast in the bookstore. Grandson of Apex in the Boged.

Anshargal: Name used for Uziel in the Land of Shinar. Akkadian; Prince of the Air

Apex: Grandfather of Jackson, Father to Rosa Westbrooke. Boged councilman.

Aluid: Mysterious creatures which arrive in the Friguscor world; Latin for Others.

Archaon: Ancient Ones. Good and bad Archaon exists in the world of the

Simulacrum. Achiel, Ruach, and Mikahel are all Archaon who work for the good of Paraclete.

Arrow Paradox: Used at the end of the Horizon Between. Zeno's (the philosopher) paradox of the arrow; philosophy; motion is nothing but an illusion.

Ayindalet: Atticus is Ayidalent; Watcher for the Door; Hebrew for the years 5774 or 2014. Ayin meaning eye; to see, and by extension to understand and obey. Dalet meaning hanging tent door, also can mean the movement of one coming in or going out of a tent door.

Barthenia: Guardian of the Gate at Red Oaks; Daughter of Sehoy and Chief Liam; Mother to Vera.

Basar tree: Fruit in the Terebinths of Mamre which is eaten by the Simulacrum every seven years for rejuvenation. Hebrew; body or flesh.

BaVil: Resarch Company/Medical Facility where Ausley is held in Atlanta. Hebrew; babel. Genesis 11:9, "Therefore its name was called Babel, because there the Lord confused the language of all the earth. And from there the Lord dispersed them over the face of all the earth."

Beged: True name of Boged, the man. Hebrew; garment, covering. Concept derived from Genesis 3:21.

Boker: Morning in Hebrew; First used in Genesis chapter one.

Callie: Elder for the Boged. (Zulika, Apex and Callie meet Veralee in the Caves of the Boged)

Cephas: Leader of the Boged; Bonded to Zulika.

Chaim Arukim: Hebrew. Simulacrum who are chosen to live past the agreed upon 110 years before returning to the Terebinths of Mamre.

Chauvah: First created woman of mankind. Hebrew name for Eve; life.

Darash: Decimus, the Seeker. Hebrew word meaning, to seek out, to find.

Decimus: Friend of Atticus in Rome; Brother of Zulika.Latin for Tenth.

Dekeract: Ten-pointed star shape representing the ten dimensions of space and time. On the cover of the two Hidden Books. Latin.

Demara: Meets Ausley in the hospital. Hebrew meaning, she knows.

Deena: Judge of the Simulacrum Council for the Simulacrum people.

Dr. Gerhard: Eugenicist who works for BaVil in Book 2 and 3. (Taken from Dr. Mengele's, the Angel of Death of Auschwitz, the pseudonym he used in

South America)

EcoCities: Cities of the Friguscor.

Elektos: The Boged ceremony of choosing. Greek; laid out, chosen or choice.

Erev: Night in Hebrew; First used in Genesis chapter one.

Ernest Weekes: Originally from England. Changed by Jeremiah. Bonded to Barthenia (Thenie); Father to Vera; Grandfather to Veralee; Murdered during the Civil War.

Essie: Ausley's nickname given by Austin at BaVil. English version of the name Esther

Esurio: The physical reaction that starts in the veins of the Friguscor when they drink the blood of the Simulacrum.

Gates: 12 Gates around the world, which grant entrance into the Terebinths of Mamre. All connected by the roots of the original Terebinth tree, born in the first days of time. *Red Oaks is one of the gates.*

GateKeepers: Sworn to protect, guard and watch over the Guardian of the Gates. Holds the mirrored key to the Guardian of the Gate, which unlocks a gate in the City of Bariyach beneath the earth.

Guardian of the Gate: Born to protect, guard and watch over the key to the Gate which allows entrance into the Terebinths of Mamre. Holds a mirrored key to the GateKeeper, which unlocks the Gate to the Terebinths of Mamre.

Gates of Bariyach: Gates in the city beneath the earth that hold the spirits of the fallen; Hebrew; city of gates, of tribulation, a fortress, of the earth as a prison. (Taken from the Book of Job)

Gemina: First wife of Issachar; Killed by the Esurio during the Spanish Inquisition.

Gen: Origin.

Hadley: Harper family dog at Red Oaks.

Hall of Teras: Boged hallway beneath the caves; Described by Napoleon as a long hallway with doors that lead to different teras which remain open at all times.

Harper Family Tree:

-Liam (GateKeeper at Red Oaks; Father to Barthenia)/Sehoy (Guardian of the Gate; Mother to Barthenia)

-Ernest (GateKeeper at Red Oaks; Grandfather to Veralee)/Barthenia (Guardian at Red Oaks; Grandmother to Veralee)

-Vera (Guardian of the Gate; Mother to Veralee)/Jeremiah (Original Man and Father to Veralee)/William (2nd Bondmate to Vera; Father of Sarah)

-Richard (Judge for the Simulacrum Council; GateKeeper; Chaim Arukim; Father to Gail)/Sarah (Guardian of the Gate; Mother to Gail)

-Edwin (GateKeeper/Father to Ausley and Adair)/Gail (Guardian of the Gate/Mother to Ausley and Adair)

-Adair (LawGiver/Mother to Mattox)/Phineas (GateKeeper/Father to Mattox)

-Veralee (The 8th/Malachi)/Atticus (Ayindalet)

-Ausley/Jackson

Hegai: Eunuch placed in charge of the harem in the Book of Esther who helped Esther win the favor of the King.

Inman: Mediator between Absalom and Red Oaks; part of the Novus Council

Issachar: Holds the position of TimeKeeper on the Simulacrum Council. Nicknamed "The Catapillar"; Hebrew; one of the 12 tribes of Israel; one who understood time and what Israel ought to do in Chronicles.

Jackson Westbrooke: Childhood friend of Veralee, Ausley and Adair; Brought up at Veritas Hills; descendant of Moses.

James Westbrooke: Father to Jackson; Husband to Rosa. Served as a caretaker at Red Oaks and owner of Veritas Hills.

Jeremiah: Original Man; son of the first woman, Chuavah. Father to Veralee. Carried the 8th Key until given to Veralee on the night of the Battle at Red Oaks during the Civil War. Bonded to Vera.

Joab: One of the two warriors on the original Council of the Simulacrum. Defects with Absalom.

Jothunheim: Homeland of the giants in Norse Mythology.

Judas Gate: small door within a larger door.

Kaph: Tradition of walking the land to ensure safety and peace, performed by the Guardian of the Gate at Red Oaks.

Lantern Maidens: statues seen by Veralee in the Terebinths of Mamre. Matthew 25: 1-13.

Land of Shinar: Akkadian for Land of the two rivers; Hebrew Scriptures used 8x to refer to an early name of Babylon; Land of the Watchers where Ausley is taken.

Law of Padha: Law of the Simulacrum that allows an innocent life to pay for a crime of a guilty life. (Gail attempts to invoke Padha for Veralee at the Council Meeting in Book 1)

Leviathan: Book of Job; Hebrew for Sea Monster; The ship from Veralee's dreams that represents the evil creature she sees in the waters of the River.

Lignum Vitae...Et Sanguis est essentia: Greeting of the Simulacrum; Latin; The blood is the essence. And the Tree is life.

Macrobians: meaning long-lived; part of the legendary tribe of Aethiopia detailed by Herodotus. Referred to by Dr. Gerhard in chapter 4: of the Horizon Between.

Malachi: Prophecy from the Simulacrum for the one who holds the 8th key to the Creation Gate; See Nikud; Hebrew; Messenger.

Man Without a Country: Book by Edward Everett Hale; 1863.

Maqom: Hebrew. Place, Gathering or Assembly. First used in Genesis 1:9. From the root word, "to stand."

Mattox (Mattie): Ausley and Phineas daughter. Guardian of the Gate.

Mara: Mother of Beged; Primogene; Hebrew for bitter.

Meridee: Discerner of the Simulacrum Council.

Mikahel: Archaon who is sent to rescue Ausley.

Olam: Hebrew for Time in Perpetuity, Forever or Eternal; Primogene; Bonded to Mara; Adopted father to Beged.

Nachash: First Archaon who fell in the garden of the One Tree.

Nakusa: Lowest class in the Friguscor society. Used in the Horizon Between; Secretly the Boged in the Friguscor world; Indian name for unwanted girls.

Naphtali: Hebrew; my struggle; One of the 12 tribes of Israel in Genesis. Holds the position of wisdom on the Council of the Simulacrum.

Napoleon: Twin brother to Rhen; Boged; Real name Eustace; Travels with Veralee to 1814.

Nathan: Friguscor child changed by Veralee. Lives at Red Oaks. Hebrew; To Give.

Nikud: Star; Prophecy from the Boged for the one who can unite the Simulacrum and the Boged as one people. See Malachi.

Novus Council: New Council created by the Simulacrum who rebelled with Absalom.

Paraclete: Part of the One Tree. Veralee meets Paraclete in the land of the One Tree after travailing through the cave. Leader of the Archaon. Latin; advocate or helper.

Phineas: Bonded to Adair, the eldest of the Harper sisters. Nickname: PH

Primogenes: Latin; first-borns.

Rafa: The Lawless Ones; imprisoned under the earth; Genesis 14:5; parents of the Rephaim.

Rephaim: The Dead Ones, children of the Rafa. Genesis 14:5, Deuteronomy 2:11 and 3:13; Descendants of Nephilim in Genesis 6:4.

Ruach: Hebrew; breathe, spirit, air, wind.

Sapru: Akkadian; Spoken by the Rephaim. One who carries the message.

Sehoy: Guardian of the Gate; Wife of Chief Liam; Mother to Barthenia.

Simulacrum Council: Compiled of 12 Simulacrum leaders each chosen from one of the 12 tribes within the Simulacrum people. *(the Judge: Deena; Wisdom of the Council: Naphtali, the TimeKeeper: Issachar, Discernmen: Meridee, the Historian: Larius, the LawGiver: Sonith, the Warriors (2 seats Eliezer and Joab), the Healer: Hayden, the Seer:Absalom, Guardians of the Gate (12 Gates are given 2 voices on the Council to fulfill the last two seats).*

Sefer HaChaim: Hebrew: Book of Life

Semira: Woman who arrives at Red Oaks with Inman.

Sonith: Native American Name meaning Lawful; LawGiver for the Simulacrum Council before Adair.

Stairs of Ahaz: Prophecy that turns back time 3 days when the 7th GateKeeper is killed.

> **Hizkiah:** Prince that prays for the Stairs of Ahaz (Based on Hezekiah in 2 Kings 20 who prays to receive more time on earth)
>
> **Prince Sennache:** Enemy of Hizkiah in the story told by Ruach at the campfire meeting; (Based on Sennacherib of 2 Kings 18)

Sworn Oath in Chapter 2:1: Hebrew; Abstract from the Shema, a Jewish prayer, which refers to Deuteronomy 6.

V'hayu had'varim ha'eileh asher anokhi m'tzav'kha hayom al l'vavekha.

And these words that I command you today shall be in your heart.

V'shinan'tam l'vanekha v'dibar'ta bam

And you shall teach them diligently to your children, and you shall speak of them

b'shiv't'kha b'veitekha uv'lekh't'kha vaderekh uv'shakh'b'kha uv'kumekha

when you sit at home, and when you walk along the way, and when you lie down and when you rise up.

L'ma'an yirbu y'maychem vi-y'may v'naychem al ha-adamah asher nishba Adonai la-avotaychem latayt lahem ki-y'may ha-shamayim al ha-aretz

In order to prolong your days and the days of your children on the land that the Lord promised your fathers that he would give them, as long as the days that the heavens are over the earth.

Talitha Cumi: Spoken to Mattie by the Man of Words; Spoken to Veralee by the Man of Words. Aramaic; Mark 5:41; Little girl, arise.

Tera: Wormholes used to move through space and time by the Simulacrum and the Boged; Aramaic; a gate or door. Used in the Book of Daniel.

Terebinths of Mamre: World in the next dimension where the Simulacrum meet for the Council Meeting; Home of the Original Men; Hebrew. Genesis 18:1, where God appeared for the first time to Abraham.

Tessa: (Boged) Friguscor girl changed by Veralee in the street. Travels to Red Oaks.

The Histories: Collective stories/histories of the Simulacrum people.

The Three Servants: Jaria, Phoebe, Balaam; Servants to Uziel in the Land of Shinar, the Land of the Watchers.

The Mashac: Hebrew for anointed; Golden Box taken from Vera by Zulika.

The Machine: Nickname for the underground research facility built and operated by BaVil where Ausley sees her people being drained of blood.

The River: Represents sovereignty. Holds Time.

The Vanishing: Term used for the disappearance of the Boged from the earth.

Tseeyen: Hebrew. Marked or noted. Represents the gift the blood of the Eiani gives each Simulacrum.

Trestrenget: In the Two Trees these are the created beings, soldiers, by Dr. Gerhard that have a three-stranded DNA code of the Aliud, the Friguscor and the Simulacrum. Ausley sees them in the Machine. Akkadian word for a three-ply cord, from the epic story of Gilgamesh.

Uziel: Hebrew; name of fallen angel in Enoch.

Woman of Wisdom: The woman without form who stands at the Gates to allow passage in and out of the Terebinths. Wisdom; Proverbs 7.

Zulika: Sister of Decimus, wife of Cephas and the Oracle for the Boged who sold herself to the Dead Ones. Arabic: traditional name of Potiphar's wife in Genesis 39.

Made in the USA
Lexington, KY
30 November 2019